TURBULENT

By F.E. Ferguson

Dedication

To my wife, Pamela. Thanks for all the love and support.

I'm lucky to have married my best friend. You make me better.

Authors Note

This is a work of fiction. All events and characters in this story are solely the product of the author's imagination; any similarities between any characters and situations presented in this book to any individuals living or dead or actual places and situations are purely coincidental.

Table of Contents

CHAPTER 1 – RETURN

The violent shuddering of the plane awakes me from a sound sleep. This is the fourth time I've been awoken since we took flight but I'm relieved because I've been plagued by constant nightmares. These dreams consist of me either drowning, being shot, or both. Again, the plane struggles to regain a smooth path and to my relief, it finally stabilizes. I've tried to fall asleep several times but it seems that I won't get any rest on this flight. We are currently fourteen hours in on a sixteen-hour flight from West Africa to Houston, Texas. I remember leaving home from the same airport that I'm returning to. I haven't been home amongst family and friends since then; being away helped me to appreciate them more. Now the plan wasn't for me to visit home this soon, Sting-Ray insists that going home will hinder my progress. Once a year Sting-Ray and I, return to United States territory to keep our citizenship but we've made that trip this year. Sting-Ray preaches that he will accompany me on these trips but I guess he had other plans but that's not like him. He must be finally starting to trust me. Well, it's about time he starts trusting me! I don't understand why I can't recall what his plans are; he never plans without informing me of it. My pestering him to visit home must have finally worked; I've been home sick since my second month away. I'm excited to see my family, even though I know they will not let me get any rest. The sheer thought of them is making me nervous; I hope a drink can subdue my nerves.

"Excuse me, flight attendant."

"Hi Sir," she replies, "What can I help you with?"

"I would like a rum and coke."

The flight attendant smiles with approval. She briskly walks down the aisle before vanishing behind the blue curtain. The darkness of the plane quickly swallows the light that slipped in before the curtain fully closed. The coldness of the plane forces me to cross my arms and rub the goosebumps that are rising from my skin. The only visible light now. comes from the third row; it seems that a guy has fallen asleep while reading a book. Everyone else is reclined in their seats and snuggling with their blankets; the turbulence must have rocked them into a deep slumber. If not for a few air pockets, one could not tell that we were flying through the sky at around thirty-six thousand feet.

"Here is your drink Sir," says the flight attendant.

"Thank You."

"Can I assist you with anything else?" She asks.

"No! One drink usually does it for me."

She stands there for a second scanning the plane, looking to help anyone else before walking back down the aisle. She stops on the third row and turns the light off before vanishing again. The rum is smooth to the taste. It's pleasant, except for the lingering taste left by the soda. I should have asked the flight attendant if they had a zero-calorie drink. I really don't like to mix sugar and hard liquor together. Too many sugary drinks can leave you dealing with the consequences in the morning. I already have a nagging headache that I don't quite remember how I got or what caused it. Its best that I limit myself before it happens again. Suddenly, the lights turn on within the passengers' cabin of the plane. Flight Attendants appear on each aisle. The start waking the sleeping passengers; handing out towels, toothbrushes, toothpaste, and cups of water. I wash my face and brush my teeth. I hand over my supplies just in time to hear the captain begin his announcement over the speaker system.

"Attention ladies and gentlemen, as we start our descent, please make sure your seats and tray tables are in their upright position. Make sure your seat belt is fastened and all carry-on luggage is stowed in the overhead bins. Thank you and we hope you enjoyed your flight."

As we descend, I open the window blind and immediately, the warm rays of the sun begin to bake my arm. Clouds as white as cotton give me brief shade before the plane forces them to drift upwards, causing them to break apart. The ground becomes visible when the plane makes its exit through the bottom of the clouds. I feel like a volcano on the verge of eruption, building up pressure until it can no longer be contained. But instead of lava and molten rocks, pure joy and excitement overwhelms me. It has been a year since I've been home and I feel like running through the aisle of this plane with my hands held high, screaming hallelujah. But that's not an option with the Federal Air Marshall on board. Plus, I don't want to make national news. I can see the Headlines now, "Crazy Black man is killed trying to Hijack International Flight." The more we descend the more visible the ground is becoming. I have never been so happy to see green grass and the green tops of trees. We fly over more trees and more fields until I see a yellow house; who nearest neighbor must be at least a mile away. More houses pass my view, each with nice spacious yards. Next, we fly over a cluster of houses with smaller yards. That one has a pool. Wow, I can see a dog house. What highway is that? There are cars and buses traveling along it. I can't believe it, they're driving on the right side of the road. From up here the city looks like a miniature toy model. I want to just reach out and touch it. I feel like a kid traveling in the backseat of a car, who just saw his favorite store. Now looking through the store window seeing all his favorite toys, but not being able to touch any of them. Unable to withstand the immense sun light any longer, I close the window blind. If not for the melanin in my skin, I would have been burnt. Again, the captain makes an announcement.

"Attention ladies and gentlemen," he says. "We have just been cleared to land at International Airport in Houston, Texas. Please make sure your seat belt is securely fastened. Once we land, everyone is to remain seated until the fasten seatbelt sign is no longer on. The flight attendants are currently passing around the cabin to make a final cabin check. Once again thank you for flying with us."

The captain's announcement makes me anxious. I sit back into my seat and double check my seatbelt. I close my eyes and begin to meditate. I Concentrate on the flow of my breathing. With each breath, I inhale deeply and exhale slowly. This breathing technique was part of my training. It was hard for me to sit still and only breathe when there is so much that I need to get accomplish. Patience is not one of my strongest attributes but with training, anything is possible. Momentum pushes me forward as the tires of the plane contacts the runway. It feels like the runway briefly rejects the idea of the plane landing, causing the tires to bounce a few times before becoming steady. I continue my meditation, while the plane comes to a complete stop. I open my eyes as the final announcement ends. I'm right in time to see the fasten seatbelt sign turn off. Quickly, I unfasten mine. Suddenly, an uncontrollable wave of yawning and stretching travels throughout the airplane. I become grateful that the flight attendants awoke everyone to brush their teeth, when the breaths of the passengers behind me invades my breathing air. I stand up to retrieve my luggage from the overhead compartment, just as the aisles begin to overflow with people eager to get onto solid ground. These impatient people are deliberately disobeying the flight attendant's instructions. I notice her becoming visibly frustrated and I can't blame her because she had a good system going. One row at a time would stand and proceed to exit the plane, starting from the front moving to back. All was going well until the flight attendant had to help an elderly woman who was apparently stiff from the long flight. As soon as she turned her back, people started pouring into the aisles causing this congestion that is before us. I wait patiently until most of the passengers are off the plane before exiting. As I step out of the plane, warm sun rays and a gentle cool breeze embraces me. My breathing increases and water forms at the edges of my lower eye lids. An enormous rush of emotion quickly overwhelms me. I step out of line to my right and walk a few feet away from the other passengers. Suddenly it feels as if someone lands a swift kick to my backside because my legs give out. My knees hit the hot pavement; followed by my hands and a steady stream of tears. The force of gravity helps my head follow the same path as the rest of my body. I gently kiss the hot pavement, twice. The feeling of finally being back home is overwhelming.

"Are you okay Sir?" Asks a flight attendant.

"Yes! I am."

"Are you sure? Do I need to get you medical attention?" She asks.

"No, I will be fine. It just feels good to finally be back home."

"But your crying," she says.

"No, I think I'm suffering from allergies."

I wipe my face and rise from the ground. I rush to catch up with the rest of the passengers. We enter the airport to find ourselves standing in a long line. Slowly the lines move, making everyone resemble zombies dragging along. We zombies move from one line for security checks, another line for personal check, and then finally another line for luggage claim. After getting through the last security check, I realize that my wait is not over because I don't remember telling anyone that I was coming home. Now, I guess I need a rental car. I hope those lines aren't long like the lines I just went through. I don't like the long lines but my wait has been entertaining. The lady walking in front of me has walked the entire way with her high heel shoes on. I thought she would take them off and walk barefoot, after she nearly twist her ankle. Instead she acts as if nothing happened but something has happened; she has broken a heel. Now I'm walking behind her as she imitates a Tyrannosaurus Rex. Each time she picks up that foot, she nearly falls over as her luggage inches closer to falling. Suddenly, I stop as her luggage drops to the ground before my feet. The clinking of her heel draws my attention away from her bags. Surprisingly she runs through the airport like a track star. Her shoes fly from her feet as she hurls herself into the arms of an awaiting gentleman. The gentleman is more than happy to catch her in midair. He swings her around a few times, then they embrace and kiss. I can't believe she ran so well without breaking the other heel. I look for a sign that can guide me towards the car rental area. I follow a few signs that leads me towards the exit.

As I exit the airport, a strong hefty voice says, "Look at my boy. He is one bad motor scooter."

A smile instantly crosses my face. There is only one person in the world, who calls me a bad motor scooter. I spin around towards the direction that the voice came from. Standing there, as if he hasn't aged a day, is my Paw-Paw; smiling a timeless smile.

"Boy you're a sight for sore eyes," he says. "Come over here a give your Paw-Paw a hug."

My feet begin to move on their own and like the lady before me, I find myself running. We embrace and for the first time in my life, I can't believe I can wrap my arms around him. I give him a big hug and a few kisses. As a kid, I remember Paw-Paw being a gigantic figure towering over his family. He instilled respect, honor, and dignity into the people that he loved. He also tried to instill those same traits into everyone else that he encountered. He taught us by example and was not scared to discipline us when we deviated from a respectful path. Everyone knew one thing to be true and that's if Paw-Paw put his hands on you for whatever the reason, then you deserved the punishment. He always was fair and sometimes really fun. He would tell me to grab a hold of his bicep then lift me high into the air. Upon lift off, I would instantly burst into laughter. It was fun dangling from his arm. I remember thinking that he was the strongest man in the world. I would not worry about harm nor danger because I knew that I was in safe hands. Paw-Paw always gathered his grandchildren together in hope to create a bond that couldn't be severed. He would tell us to eat all our food and to drink plenty of water and milk, so we could grow as big and strong as him. Any time I spent the night at his house, he would awake me before the roosters began crowing. I would jump up and run to the bathroom to relieve myself. Being on time and doing what you say you will do, is one of Paw-Paw's pet peeves. I knew that if I dragged along, he would leave me behind because most of his work would be accomplished before most people wake up. But before he got going, he had to have his morning cup of coffee. The coffees aroma would radiate throughout the house and meet me in the hallway. Paw-Paw would have two cups of coffee waiting on the table for me and him. We would sit together, talk about our tasks and drink coffee. He would take out a few slices of bread, one for him and one for me. We would dunk the bread into our coffee. Once they were nice and saturated we would eat and drink to our hearts delight. I felt special because he would fit time into his busy schedule just to put a smile on my face.

"Paw-Paw, how in the world did you know that I would arrive today?"

"Well my boy," he says. "Lady De'LaReaux gave us a call a few days ago. She told us that you would arrive today around this time and you needed a ride."

"Huh, but I didn't tell her that I was coming. I don't remember telling anyone that I was coming home."

"Well my boy," he says. "I don't know what to tell you but I'm happy that I'm here to pick you up. I'm happy that your home. It has been ten years since I've last seen you, so I really don't care how she knew that you were coming home. Lady De'LaReaux is a very unique woman."

"What do you mean Paw-Paw? It hasn't been ten years."

"Boy, time must fly when you're having fun," he says.

This is confusing to me. It could not have been ten years since I've been home. It's only been a year. If he says it's been ten years, then how have I lost the last nine years of my life?

Paw-Paw looks at me with a helpless look on his face.

"Are you okay, my boy?" He asks.

"I'll be alright. I'm extremely happy to see you and I'm glad you came to get me. So how long have you been waiting for me? Why didn't anyone ride along with you Paw-Paw?"

"Well my boy, you sure have a lot of questions. But I guess that's typical for a man who can't remember how long he's been away," he says. "Just put your bags in the truck and let's start our journey. We will have enough time to talk about anything you want. Besides, I really would like to get out of the city before traffic begins. No matter how many lanes the city builds for these people, they still find a way to create traffic jams. Our two-hour trip will turn into four hours if we get caught in rush hour traffic."

"Wow! I didn't imagine that you would still have this old truck. I still remember the day you brought it home."

"Well my boy, you have to work too hard these days just to purchase the things you need," he says. "Being able to afford your wants is becoming nearly impossible in today's economy. So, you should always buy exactly what you want and maintain your investment. Too many people settle for less and find themselves paying for something they really didn't want. You see my boy, I wanted this truck and I did not dog it out nor did I let anyone else help wear it down.

"It sure runs better than some folks' newer model trucks."

"Well my boy, they sure don't make vehicles like they did before," he says.

I smile and nod in agreement, even though I would rather a newer model truck. As far back as I can remember, Paw-Paw has always been mechanically inclined. He is good with his hands and he don't believe that anything is junk. He believes things are just missing something necessary for it to function. He is the most reliable man that I know. So, if he has confidence in this old truck then I will too. He has never had me stuck on the side of the road; so, there isn't a need to start doubting him now. I climb into this truck and he takes off before my door is full close. His engine roars as he speeds out of the airport and quickly enters the highway. As we travel down the highway I feel as if I'm in an unfamiliar place. I thought the city would be a little different from what I remember, but a lot has changed since I last traveled to the airport. Apparently ten years ago and not last year; but what should I expect from one of the largest cities in the United States. Paw-Paw's expression changes from looking happy to a look of worry. I notice he is really pushing the speed limit but I remain silent because no one likes a backseat driver.

"Are you worried about something?"

"Well my boy, I'm worried about my Edna," he says. "I've been with that woman for over fifty years and I hope she is doing alright without me. Were my emotions that visible?"

"Yes Sir, they were. She always says that it's hard for us to hide our emotions."

"Yeah, my Edna has been telling me that since we met," he replies. "That was many, many, moons ago."

Paw-Paw is the only person that I know who can call her Edna. Everyone else who knows her and loves her calls her Big Mama. She is strong and unbending; probably as strong as Paw-Paw is. On second thought, she may be twice as strong as him, not physically but with everything else. She had the strength to hold together our family and community during a difficult time. It would have been easy for kids to dislike Big Mama because she applied law and order when Paw-Paw was busy working. She has always been sweet but strict. Sometimes so strict, that as a child we would get in trouble if we interrupted grown-ups while they were talking. Kids were not allowed to sit on her furniture; even though she covered everything with protective plastic. All kids had to be out doors playing while the sun was up, with one exception. No one could leave the yard. Being outdoors allowed all her grandchildren to burn away all our energy. We would play, argue and sometimes fight. Sometimes we got lost in our imagination. But mostly, we all would huddle up and plot on how to destroy the switch tree. The switch tree is a special tree that grows in Big Mamas' front yard. The switch tree is a beautiful tree, that stands about six to seven foot tall. The flowers that grow on it, has a naturally wonderful fragrance but we all were aware of its ugly truths. Anytime anyone broke a rule, that person would have to remove a small branch from the tree. Big Mama did not have favorites. She treated everyone the same no matter who their parents were and no one was exempt from their consequences. We would try to fool Big Mama by choosing smaller, weaker sticks from other trees but that only made things worse. Big Mama would hold the front of her gown off the ground and march straight for the switch tree. She would be seen choosing the biggest mini branch she could wield. She would remove the leaves and thorns on her way back to the Big House. What made the whippings worse was that she would explain exactly what you did wrong and why you were being punished. Now many people consider that child abuse but it made us understand the difference between right and wrong. She held us accountable for our actions and taught us that all actions have consequences; some good and some bad. Now, I can't wait to see her lovely face. I need to thank her for all she has done for me.

"What are you thinking about my boy?" Asks Paw-Paw.

"You got me thinking about Big Mama. Why didn't she come along for the ride? I know how much she loves to be by your side. You two are inseparable. Unless something has happened. You were worried about her earlier, has something happened?"

"No worries my boy," he replies. "As much as she loves to ride with me, she loves cooking even more. Before I left she said, 'Manc, I know our boy hasn't eaten a good meal since he went on his journey. You be a good dear and run down the road to get him. I will call the girls and we will cook a good meal for him.' So, you are in for a real treat my boy."

My Big Mama is the only person that calls Paw-Paw, Manc. Manc is his nickname, his real name is Emancipation James. He is named after his grandfather and he makes sure that all his family knows the significance of his name. My great, great grandfather was born on June 19, 1865 on a small plantation outside of the city limits of Galveston, Texas. On that day, a small band of soldiers were dispatched from the Union Army which had just arrived in Galveston. Something was happening that was mandatory for all the slaves to attend. The soldiers announced that the President of the United States of America had issued an Executive Order. The

Executive Order stated that on January 1, 1863, all slaves held within the rebellious states are now and forever considered "free". It also stated that the former slaves and former slave masters are now considered employee and employer. The shock of this life altering news gave my great, great grandmother labor pains. She went into labor at that very moment. While she was giving birth, she heard that the Executive Order was called the Emancipation Proclamation. Instantly, she decided that her new child would be named Emancipation. The slaves did not fully understand everything about the Emancipation Proclamation, but they knew that they would never be free if they stayed and worked on the plantation. They decided that freedom only exists away from their former slave owners. Not knowing what dangers that await them, they still decided to leave and explore the unknown. Some went on to explore the great western frontier but our family settled nicely in East Texas. Now every year my family get together to celebrate Juneteenth.

"Big Mama is absolutely correct. I don't remember the last time I had anything that would compare slightly to the gourmet masterpieces that she can create. Just thinking about her cooking has created a hunger bubble inside of my belly. With my memory being slightly off, the last good meal I remember was not even a planned meal. That day, after successfully defending a neighboring village from a greedy cooperation who wanted their land and natural resources, our group began heading back to the village I was training in. We were forced off course first by a savage pack of hyenas. We narrowly escape the hyenas but found ourselves looking at a river that was overpopulated with crocodiles and hippos. This forced us to travel many miles off our course. These detours left us wary and hungry. Luckily, we stumbled onto a small village, just as my feet became too heavy to lift. A flock of goat caught our attention as they tried to warn the villagers of our arrival. The plan was to grab one goat and then hurry to the rendezvous point where we would roast it over an open fire. The winds were in our favor that night. This should have been the easiest grab and go ever but the simplest plans can turn disastrous quickly, especially when you have bad intentions. Everyone took their positions and waited for the signal to begin the plan. Instead of the signal, we heard someone yell of excruciating pain. Quickly, I ran towards where the screams were coming from. I've heard people scream before, so I could tell that whatever was happening was painful. Only once in my life have I made a similar sound and that was because my hand was slammed in the hinge side of a car door. We all arrived at our screaming comrade to find out that he was bitten several times by snakes. Now we all know that Africa is home to the deadliest animals on the planet, so we looked around furiously but we could not find any snakes. Instead we found ourselves surrounded by many villagers. The villagers did not carry any weapons with them nor were they hostile. One villager walked up to us and grabbed our bitten comrades' hand. After a brief examination, she spoke to the villagers in her native tongue. She then pulled our comrade towards the village. We cautiously followed as the rest of the villagers lead us into their village. Our comrade was taken into a hut that was decorated by two totem statues guarding the door. The hut was solidly constructed and its location indicated that it was important to the villagers. All the huts were off the ground but this one was a little higher off the ground than the others. A foreign smell grew stronger as we passed the huts. The closer we moved towards the smell the louder my stomach began to growl. I notice that the village was designed in the shape of a circle and in the middle of that circle blazed a great fire. A slab of meat was being roasted above that fire. Looking at the way the fire would react every time the meat was turned, I could tell that it was juicy. But at that point, it really did not matter. I gratefully accepted the plate that was handed to me. The plate was completely made from tree bark. I don't eat from just anyone, so I was extremely cautious but my hunger made me get over that fast. After the very first bite, all my caution melted away. The meat was flavorful and tender, I could taste the salt and other seasoning that were used. The wood that burned in the campfire gave the meat a rich smoky flavor that was surprisingly delightful. Every bite was better than the previous bite and before long I found myself licking the plate clean. I notice the plate had a very intriguing pattern engraved into it. We enjoyed the villagers' hospitality so much that we stayed there helping anyway we could until our comrade recovered. To this day, I still do not know what kind of meat we ate that night, but I can tell you this Paw-Paw; it sure was good."

"Well my boy, you are in for a true treat," he says. "My Edna has been watching a show on television that has her glued to it. All day long, the only topic for discussion on that show is cooking. Sometimes she cooks along with them. So, I remodeled the kitchen to give her as much space as she needed. Now she has a television in the kitchen that helps her follow along without any interruptions. Do you remember how she used to watch her stories after she was done with lunch?"

"Yeah, they would come on one after the other. They would last for two to three hours."

"Well my boy, that cooking show has changed all of that," he says. "She doesn't follow any of those stories anymore. You know the best thing that came from it all is that I'm her sampler. I get to taste every single dish that she creates. Got my mouth running water just thinking about it."

Paw-Paw reaches into his pocket and pulls out a handkerchief. As he wipes his mouth, I take the opportunity to thoroughly look him over.

"Excuse me Paw-Paw, if you're doing all of this sampling; how are you staying so healthy?"

A smile crosses his lips and he begin to blush. "Well my boy," he says. "You see, every morning Edna and I start our day with a healthy breakfast. Of course, I have my coffee, while reading the newspaper. If the weather permits, we take a nice morning walk that starts out early. I like to get going before the sun has a chance to bless us with its beauty. We walk between three to four miles down to the park on the lake. Edna likes to stop for a moment to feed the ducks leftover bread or biscuits. Early in the morning a gentle breeze crosses the lake, skimming the surface of the water creating small waves. If you are in touch with nature, you can predict what the weather will be like for the day. If I smell rain approaching, we avoid lingering to long. On days when the weather is pleasant, we may sit on a bench and enjoy the many natural blessing that are taken for granted. We like to watch as the fish jump out of the water, flipping once then splashing back into the water and out of sight. I joke to Edna that the fish are training for the Olympics. We laugh and joke as we observe how the sun signals that the day has started, to all animals. Birds begin soaring through the sky, singing their morning praises. Squirrels begin gathering their food while investigating our presence. We really like to enjoy the early morning, before the world gets too busy. At that moment sitting on the bench holding Edna tight, the world is perfect. We are constantly reminded to enjoy those precious moments and we try to create new memories every chance we get. We fear that we will get old and helpless since we are now retired. We try to keep active because we don't want to have to depend on anyone to help us to do our daily activities. Most of the elderly that retire these days do not last much longer in this world because they stop being active. So, we keep our minds sharp and our bodies active. I promise you my boy we will not let inactivity take us out."

CHAPTER 2 – JAMES FAMILY

Talking to Paw-Paw, two hours passed before I knew it; I really enjoy sharing stories with him. He makes a turn onto a paved road that I'm not familiar with but who am I kidding, I'm not familiar with anything that I've seen so far. A few feet ahead, cars line the road leading straight to the Big House. At the sight of the Big House I now realize exactly where I am. Paw-Paw has finally paved James Lane. When I left home James Lane was just a dirt road. Big Mama stands on the porch waring one of her infamous Mumu's. I've never seen her in anything else but those Mumu's, except for when she dresses up for Sunday services. A couple of adolescent age kids, that I've never met, run from the front porch and to the backyard. As we drive into the driveway, Big Mama begin descending the steps towards us. Before I can fully step out of the car, she stands before me with tears in her eyes.

"Brody James, don't you ever stay away from me that long again," she says. "You had me worrying like crazy about you. Now come here and give your Big Mama a hug."

Paw-Paw takes my bags into the house as Big Mama and I exchange hugs and kisses. Voices are heard echoing my name, coming from the backyard.

"I can't make any promises Big Mama but I'll try my best not to be away from home that long again. The least I can do is come visit you."

"You better not be away that long again," she says. "You know that I'm getting older and I can check out from this world at any time. Now get your butt out back, everyone is here waiting on you."

Big Mama grabs a hold of my hand and leads me through the garage and out into the backyard. To my surprise, four generations of the James family gather in the backyard. We are swarmed by a mob upon entering the backyard. Everyone seem eager to greet me in their own way but Big Mama quickly takes control of the situation before everyone can rush us.

"You all will get a chance to talk to Brody," says Big Mama. "He is home and he will not be leaving us like that again. Now, Brody has had a long trip. I would like him to eat first. Before you all make him forget that he is hungry."

A welcome home Brody sign hangs between two trees, the switch tree and the tree that we planted for Bridgette. Balloons decorate chairs and a fun jump was set up for the children to play in. Under a shade tree, two tables were set-up; one to play dominos and the other to play spades. Groups of tables were arranged for eating. The largest collection of tables formed the letter "J", this table is designated for the grown-ups to eat. A collection of tables sat away from the larger group, designated for the children to eat at. Looking at the food spread reminds me how hungry I am. There is fried chicken, chicken fried chicken with white gravy, pot roast, deer sausage, mashed potatoes, corn, mustard greens, black eye-peas, yams, hot-water corn bread, red beans and rice, and chicken and dumplings. On the dessert table there is tea cakes, better than sex cake, seven-up cake, pecan pie, sweet potato pie, fruits and cheesecake. With no seating arrangement, couples sit together and everyone else fills the gaps. I sit at the head of the table between Big Mama and Paw-Paw. Besides Paw-Paw sits his younger brother, Pastor James.

Pastor James clears his throat then says, "Everyone, please bow your heads. Lord we gracefully and mercifully come before you to celebrate the return of our Brody James. We thank you for keeping him safe and healthy, while he traveled your beautiful world. Thank you for our many blessings which we take for granted every day. Thank you for the food that was prepared for us today and thank you for blessing the hands that came together to make this bountiful feast. Amen, Amen, Amen."

I reach for my fork but is stopped in my tracks as Big Mama rises from her seat. She looks around the tables and smiles.

She says, "Thank you all for coming out to join us on this joyous occasion. This family has suffered some grave wounds but now we stand together, reunited. STRONGER, than ever before! We cannot change the events of the past but we can learn from them and be present in times of need. I'm so proud to see much of our family here today. I love you all. Now please eat to your hearts delight."

I pause until Big Mama takes her seat before proceeding to eat. Paw-Paw begins to pass plates from my left side and Big Mama does the same from my right. I accept everything that comes my way. They continue to pass plate after plate until I am completely stuffed. If I try to force one more piece of food down, I'm sure to explode. Like always, the kids are the first ones to finish their food or to leave their plates. For a few minutes, I sit and watch them play. They run around playing without a care in the world. Their innocence is untouched by the worlds hidden dangers. I watch as groups begin to form, as others finish eating. My memories of the past ten years are foggy, but I do remember that I am training to stick to the shadows. I am learning to see without being seen. But that does not work at a James Family gathering. In certain situations, being the center of attention gives me an uneasy feeling. So, I would rather not be the center of attention, but this family of mine is tenacious.

"If you're finish Brody James, you should go speak to your family," says Big Mama. "Everyone is here just for you. Now get going!"

The first group I approach, seating on lawn chairs are three of my four Aunts. I approach them unnoticed as they watch the children run through the field. A curly hair woman with long eyelashes and long fingernails turns in my direction. She looks me over twice, then rolls her eyes.

She says, "don't come over here. I'm mad at you Brody James."

"Why is that Aunt Charlotte?"

"Because you don't care about anyone else feelings," she says. "You almost killed me Brody James. You had me sick worrying about you; now my nerves are all bad and I have to take hypertension medication because of it."

A natural hair woman with blond highlights interrupts, "don't listen to her Brody. She has been a drama queen since she began talking. If anyone caused you to have high blood pressure and anxiety, it's that sneaky eyed fool you married."

I love my Aunt Wendy. She is the type of person who does not hold her tongue for anyone and she does not care whose feeling gets hurt in the process.

"Boy, ignore them heifers," says Aunt Dorothy Fae. "They been arguing their entire lives and neither one of them can fight. Come over here and give your good auntie a hug."

Aunt Dorothy Fae is Big Mama's oldest child by one minute. Her twin sister name is Aunt Shirley Mae, who's at the table with Big Mama but looking this way. I wait patiently as Aunt Shirley Mae wobbles from the eating tables to where her other three sisters are gathered.

"Boy, aren't you a sight for sore eyes," she yells. "I don't know what they are lying about but I was the only one who came here to help Mama cook that delicious meal."

"No one isn't even talking about that," screams Aunt Wendy. "If you can take your mind off food for a while, then maybe you can lose a few pounds. I'm tired of you knocking kids out cold; while everyone else must dive out of the way when you pass by. Your butt should come with a wide load escort."

"As a matter of fact, my man loves it and yours be staring," replies Aunt Shirley Mae.

"Everyone stares at you Shirley, whether they want to or not," says Aunt Wendy.

All four of the ladies erupt into laughter. They really enjoy picking with each other, but they genuinely have unconditional love for one another. If someone else would try that with them, that person would have to run for the hills. As these southern bells shift their attention from me to one another, I quietly begin making my way towards the domino table. As usually the men are loud and rambunctious. They fuse and argue back and forth while drinking some cold ones. They talk the kind of smack that would be considered fighting words, in some places but just like the ladies they don't mean anyone any harm.

"Well if it isn't Brody James. Why don't you come sit down and give me a little challenge?" says Uncle Robert Wayne.

"Fool, you better check the score. We are kicking your butts," says Uncle Willie Mac. "As a matter of fact, give me a dime and that's domino. Now put your hands together so we can see what we get."

"All we need is twenty points," says a sneaky eye man.

"Well that's game," says Uncle Willie Mac.

"You see that's why I don't like playing with you two. You been pencil whipping!" exclaims Uncle Robert Wayne. "That's why I like keeping score with chips. You can't pencil whip me while playing with chips."

"I don't have to cheat," says Uncle Willie Mac. "Go get the chips then."

"You're Brody, right?" Asks the sneaky eyed man. "We haven't had the pleasure to meet yet. I am your Uncle Clarence. I am married to your Aunt Charlotte. We have been married for six years now, going on seven."

"Well, it's nice to meet you Uncle Clarence."

"Can you reach in that cooler and pass out a round of cold ones?" He asks.

"You really don't want to play with these cheating fools," says Uncle Earl. "Franklin and the twins went out back. I think you should go and talk to them instead of these old fools. They have something going on with their lives unlike some people I know. My boy Franklin has been promoted to State Detective and the twins started their own Private investigation firm. Well, I guess they are all Detectives."

"Jody! You better get away from them women," shouts Uncle Willie Mac.

"I don't trust no man named Jody," says Uncle Clarence.

"Me neither," agrees Uncle Earl.

"I don't know who invited that old pervert in the first place," says Uncle Robert Wayne.

"I got my eyes on him," says Uncle Clarence. "If he stays over there too long, I will drag him across this yard."

"Clarence, you couldn't burst a grape," says Uncle Earl. "Jody would drag you instead."

"Yeah Clarence, Jody been fighting since junior high," says Uncle Robert Wayne. "He has cheated with so many taken women that he had to learn how to fight. Now he loves to rumble."

"There isn't nothing worse than him sleeping with your woman, then beating you up," says Uncle Earl. "And you're in trouble. He been had eyes for Charlotte."

"I am not worried," says Uncle Clarence. "My big nephew right here has my light weight."

"Now, you trying to get us all killed," says Uncle Earl. "Mama would start shooting if someone touched Brody today."

"Yeah," agrees Uncle Robert Wayne. "You have to defend your own love."

"Now man up," says Uncle Earl.

"Ignore them fools," says Uncle Willie Mac. "They are trying to get you out your game. They can't beat us, so they want to play mind games. Besides Jody only messes with women whose husbands work offshore."

I pass out a round of beers and watch as they start another domino game. Seeing how this game has started, it looks like Uncle Earl and Uncle Robert Wayne's tactic has worked. Uncle Clarence cannot keep his eyes off Jody. I now see why Uncle Earl wants me to go out back; he doesn't want to have to give up his seat. I pass out another round then exit to where Franklin and the twins are. Towards the back of the property, I find my cousins. Everyone is gathered around the fire pit. From a distance the glare of the fire pit cast shadows across the ground, making them appear to dance to the music that is being played. Escaping to the fire pit was a habit that we adopted, to escape the long-winded stories told by the grown-ups. I don't mind a good story but after every meal the same stories were told over and over. Back then it wasn't a fire pit but instead we would light the burn barrel and just chill.

"Paw-Paw didn't tell me that he put a fire pit and some benches back here."

"Yeah, it's been back here for seven years now," says Franklin dryly.

Franklin stands strongly, with a good posture. I can tell that he has been in the gym because of his broad shoulders and ripped arms. His eyes display a look of confidence, experience, and awareness. I can tell that he is paying attention to everyone while holding a conversation. He is no longer the scrawny boy that once followed my lead, he now looks like a leader himself. The twins wear a look of questioning on their identical faces. They are a year younger than Franklin and I but they still hung with us. When we were kids they would follow us around everywhere.

"Your dad told me that you're now a Texas State Detective, Franklin."

"Yeah, the events from fourteen years ago help to motivate me to join Law Enforcement," says Franklin. Plus, I have the added bonus of having the twin's assistance whenever it is needed. We help each other from time to time. Things have gotten rough at times but we have each other back when no one else has it. We have been making a real difference in the community both locally and statewide."

"I can't believe it is really you," says a woman with reddish brown hair. "I should punch you in your face."

"Let me get him first," says a woman with solid black hair.

Both ladies stand taller than the average woman. The looks in their eyes tell me that they are serious. Saundra and Shondra are identical from head to toe and they are the toughest girls that I know. But they really did not have a choice in the matter. Neither Franklin nor I ever took it easy on either of them because of their tempers and smart mouths. Big Mama always said that Aunt Wendy cursed them girls with her mouth. So, because of their flip/tongued mouths, we had to teach them how to defend themselves from both boys and girls. The only thing that helps to tell the two apart is that Shondra loves to color her hair. Shondra hair can be any color she likes at the moment, while Saundra keeps her hair its natural color. They both wear their hair natural but every woman in the family does, Big Mama never believed in perming their hair. She says that if God wanted their hair to be straight then he would have made it that way. Now they all have beautiful natural hair.

"Have you forgotten about our pact?" Asks Saundra.

"No, I haven't forgotten about the pact. I just had to take a different route than you all but from what I can remember I have upheld our pact."

"That's good to know," says Franklin. "So, do you have our backs now?"

"Always."

After the events of fourteen years ago. The four of us made a pact, to never be weak and defenseless again, to always watch each other's back and to do our best to help improve the world.

"We will see," says Shondra.

"Don't be like that. You ladies are too radiant to be giving me all this shade. I've traveled the world and still I haven't seen anyone that could compare to your beauty. I will most definitely watch your back because I know there are some angels out there who are jealous of you."

"Brody, boy you haven't changed a bit," laughs Shondra. "You sure know what to say to make a woman feel good about herself."

"It's my job to uplift the sisters, if we don't do it then no one else will. Also, you know what I say ladies, if your weak your beat. You should be strong in three areas: mind, body, and soul. If you don't have a strong will, you may fall for the banana in the tail pipe."

"Speaking of banana in the tail pipe, we pulled one on a bail jumper" adds Saundra. "A few months ago, we were assisting a friend, who works as a bounty hunter in Louisiana. The bail jumper we were looking for had made bail for robbery. He missed his court date and left the state. We got the call and took on the job for them. It didn't take us long to track him down because this fool was shacked up with a white girl in the wrong East Texas town. So, he stood out like the color red at an all-white party. We stopped at a gas station to get directions and I could instantly tell that those folks thought differently than the civilized world. But we were there for a job and I refuse to let people with horrible morals stop me from doing my job. When we told the gas station attendant that we were looking for that particular man, he was more than happy to tell us exactly where we could find him. Apparently not everyone in that town has horrible morals because the store attendants' lead was accurate. We found our bail jumper getting drunk at a local bar."

"His information was accurate because we were spending money. People with horrible morals will put up with anyone, if money is involved. Besides, he wanted him out of town because our bail jumper stole his woman from him," interrupts Shondra.

"Anyway," continues Saundra. "With the help of local authority, who Franklin vouched for, we were able to locate his motorcycle. He parked his motorcycle on side of the building where he could easy escape if needed. Shondra and I stuffed his tail pipes with bananas before we tried to apprehend him. The bar was off the ground, it looked more like a house on stilts that someone turned into a bar. Local authorities surrounded the bar as Shondra and I proceeded to make the arrest. When he noticed us in the bar, he immediately ran to the side of the building where his motorcycle was parked and he hopped over the handrail without giving it a second thought. I was in awe watching this man scale down two stories before hopping along the tops of other vehicles to reach his motorcycle. This man was athletically gifted. I believe he would have escaped if it was not for our preventive actions."

"That fool loved that bike so much that he tried to start it repeatedly," adds Shondra. "Even after consecutive failed attempts. Smoke rose from the bike and began to engulf the entire parking lot but a steady breeze gave us a little visibility. He was determined not to leave without that bike and we were determined to leave with him. So, I ran through the smoke. I jumped in the air and tackled him to the ground. The spectators in the bar began cheering and yelling, Great tackle."

"He was so embarrassed when we pulled those bananas out but he was still alert. When everyone was busy laughing, and celebrating; he managed to get away from one of the police officers. He tried to make a run for the woods," laughs Saundra. "But at this point he was already in handcuffs. He didn't see that line that ran from the building to a pole and got himself clotheslined. We laughed at him all the way to Lake Charles, where we handed him over to the bounty hunters.

I stand there in shock, looking back and forth at both Saundra and Shondra. I knew that they were tough by I couldn't image them being this tough. I thought by now they would be married with children, or modeling, or acting.

"It's your turn now Brody," says Franklin. "Where have you been all this time?"

Peering into Franklin's eyes, I see pain. Before I left our bond was rock solid. He was my best friend. At one point, we did everything together. I know he missed me but I missed him also. I missed everyone. As I stare into each of their now ogling eyes, a sense of conviction overwhelms me. But how can I explain where I've been if I can't remember it myself?

"Enough procrastinating Brody," says Franklin firmly. "Just spit it out and we only want the truth. Remember I can tell if you're lying but if I can't figure you out, I do have a lie detector at my office."

"I've been doing a lot of traveling while I was gone. I've traveled to many parts of this world. Each place different from the next. I've been training my mind and body to be the best me possible. For a year, I studied at a University in Egypt. I've been learning different skills and arts. When I left, I also left the protection of this great country behind and once you leave these borders, you are no longer protected. You must learn to protect yourself quickly and you must be able to live in the shadows. If you bring attention to yourself, you are sure to draw the wrong type of attention. Many people outside of this county has been misinformed to believe that every American is rich. This thinking can lead to you being abducted if you're not careful. I learned to play the hand I was dealt and to roll with the punches. I left and I grew up."

"We all have grown-up," says Franklin. "Are you back to stay or are you just visiting?"

"I have no idea what tomorrow will bring but until someone tells me otherwise, I am home to stay."

"Well good," replies Franklin. "Every morning for the past year, we all have been working jointly to solve the same case. The twins and I share an office in Lufkin. If you're truly sticking around, you should come join us. Do you have any other plans for tomorrow?"

"Actually, I did not see my parents here. I was hoping to go visit them tomorrow. I was going to see if Paw-Paw would take me to them."

"I'm sorry to tell you this but your mother still has not recovered and your father is currently a resident at First Step Rehabilitation center. He has been there this time for three months," says Franklin."

"He just couldn't put the bottle down," adds Saundra.

"We tried interventions, consoling, and anything else you could think of," says Shondra. "The family came together and decided to have him admitted. It was our only possible option to save him."

"So, nothing has really changed for them. I hoped that things had gotten better."

"It's still not too late Brody," replies Franklin. "They just might need to see you again."

"Okay, I will be ready to go in the morning. I will help you as best I can. After that can you bring me to whomever is closer?"

"No problem," replies Franklin. "First-Step Rehabilitation is the closest."

"Well, I'm getting tired you all. I've had a wonderful day catching up with everyone but I think I have reached my limit for the night."

"Hey Brody! Welcome to the team," says Franklin with a huge smile on his face.

I follow a cobble stone path back to the rear of the Big House. I slip by everyone who is still enjoying the night, without being noticed. Before I enter the back door, I remember to remove my shoes. Growing up I learned the hard way that Big Mama did not play when it comes to her floors. One of the worst mistakes one can make is tracking up her floors. Now to prevent any confusion, I make sure to remove my shoes before entering. I ascend the stairs not fully sure if I still have a room up here or if they turned it into something else. My room was always the second room to the right. As I open the door it feels as if I have entered a time capsule. A decade has passed but everything still looks the same as before I left. I notice Paw-Paw has placed my bags at the foot of the bed. I walk over to the bed, kicking off my shoes and undressing in the process and I collapse onto it. I really need to take a shower. I'll just deal with it all in the morning, it's been a long day. My eye lids grow heavier and heavier and I drift away into what I hope is a peaceful slumber.

46

CHAPTER 3 – DETECTIVE FRANKLIN

Zero six hundred hours arrives fast. It feels as if I only slept for an hour, but still I better hurry to my feet. If Franklin hasn't changed too much, he will be here for zero seven hundred hours; on the dot. Sluggishly, I drag myself to the bathroom and turn on the shower. I need to take a shower and grab something quick to eat before he arrives. My initial plan was to jump in and out of the shower as quickly as possible but the hot water caused me to puddle duck for a while. Having hot water readily available is one of those blessing that is taken for granted, along with having soap and shampoo that actually has a smell. With the water spraying down onto my head it feels like I am in heaven. I've met people who believe taking a bath or shower is a nuisance. They would jump in the shower and two minutes later, they are out and dressed. If you would go in the bathroom behind them you would swear that no one had been in there. Unlike them, I'm in the shower for a minimum of fifteen minutes. I touch everything at least two or three times. I love the feeling of being clean. Whoever came up with the saying "Cleanliness is next to godliness" must have felt the same as me. After getting dressed I notice that the clock on the wall indicating that it I have thirty minutes left before it's zero seven hundred. Upon opening the bathroom door, the smell of breakfast slaps me in the nose. The smell continues to engulf the house as I walk back to my room. Quickly, I put a way my dirty clothing because the smell is now calling me to its source. I'm forced to follow my nose down the stairs, through the wash room, through the formal dining room, and into the kitchen. Surprisingly the kitchen is empty. I notice a note on the kitchen counter that reads, "We are off for our morning walk. Eat as much as you would like and bring the rest with you for the others. The food is in the dining room, on the dining room table. There is: pancakes, eggs, bacon, sausage, biscuits, gravy, hash browns, and grits. Please lock the door behind you when you leave." If I would have been eating like this for the past 10 years, I would have been as plump as a pigeon. This is a lot of food but I'm about to go in. Franklin drives into the driveway just as I finish packing breakfast. I shake off a sense of excitement as I lock the front door. Unlike me, the look on Franklins face is serious; he displays no sign of emotion as I enter his vehicle.

"Man, your ten minutes early."

"I couldn't sleep. I was up thinking about the possibilities today may bring. How did you sleep?" asks Franklin.

"I slept like a baby being cradled tightly in his mother arms, while she gracefully rocks back and forth in her wooden rocking chair."

"Oh, that good?" He asks.

"Yes sir, we tend to take basic things like a bed for granted sometimes because it has been present in our life since birth. But sleeping on the cold dirty ground or in trees has helped me to appreciate the simple things, like a mattress. I haven't felt this energized in forever; plus, it was the first night in while that my sleep was peaceful. So, what is today all about? I've been gone for quite some time. I really don't see how I will be of any real assistance?"

"All of your questions will be answered in due time," replies Franklin. "This case is also for the twins as well. If I tell you all the details now, that would be a slap in their face."

"I understand. Well tell me how you became a Detective for the state of Texas."

"It was all luck," he says.

"No, it wasn't. Please don't diminish your accomplishments. I am sure you worked hard and jumped over numerous unnecessary hurdles just to be considered."

"You're right, it's been hard and nearly impossible at times but I never quit. It has been a long road to get where I am. I started as a local police officer but I felt like I wasn't making a difference. The politics inside of the department I was working for made it impossible for me to advance. So, I worked hard and did everything that I was required to do without question. As soon as I met the eligibility to apply to the state police I did just that. I earned my chance to become a State Detective when I was stationed just outside of Dallas, I was working as a state trooper at the time. The mayor of Dallas was a man named Mayor Robert Richman. I would work part-time on his security team until we grew closer. After that he convinced my superiors to let me work on his security team full time. A larger trooper detail was needed because Mayor Richman had just begun his campaign for a Senate seat. All was going well until right before election time, when the daughter of the Mayor of Forth Worth was kidnapped while leaving school. He was the key opponent to Mayor Richman's Senate run but they were also close friends. Mayor Richman decided to stop his campaign to find his friends daughter, who was also his god-daughter. All the top State Detectives and Agents from different agencies arrived in the Dallas-Fort Worth area to help expedite the search for the missing girl. Because of my close relationship with Mayor Richman, I joined the case as ground support. Night and Day, we searched the entire Dallas-Fort Worth area and the adjourning counties. After two days of continuous searching, the investigation was going nowhere and fast. I found what I thought was a clue but no one would listen to a word I said. After that I decided to take matters in my own hands and without permission, I launched my own investigation. It felt like we were chasing our own tails. Things just weren't adding up to me, so I went back to ground zero. At the high school, I talked to students and teacher but still I wasn't having any luck. My break came from the janitor, a short Asian man who spoke horrible English. He kept repeating the word 'West.' When he noticed that I didn't understand what he was talking about. He led me to the parking lot and pointed towards the East. I didn't make sense of it at first because the Detectives were convinced that the getaway vehicle was a car. Tire makers found at the scene of the crime, along with expert analysis helped them to come to that conclusion. Twelve hours after I launched my own investigation I nearly get run off the road by a speeding van. One of the decals on the van said 'Quest.' At that moment, I realized that the janitor was not pointing to the East, he was pointing to a van that was parked in the parking lot. The whole time he wasn't saying 'West' rather he was saying 'Quest.' I began to follow the van deep into the countryside, where it drove straight to a house whose nearest neighbor was miles away. With my headlights turned off, I trailed them at a distance. I parked off the road behind a cluster of trees, then I ran to their fence line and began surveillance of the property. Two guys stood outside arguing while two others unloaded the van. Their voices could be clearly heard from my vantage point. As soon as the two who were unloading the van vanished into the house, a fight broke out. They fought for a solid minute until the two guys who were unloading the truck emerge from the house to break them apart.

The guy who was driving the van said, 'Hey man, I told you don't put your hands on me. I don't work for you and I haven't done nothing wrong.'

The guy he was talking too appeared to be their leader. He said, 'You imbecile. Who told you that you could leave this house? Your actions could have jeopardized our mission.'

The driver responded, 'Man you were gone and 'm not staying out here that long without a drink. Stop tripping, there wasn't even one car on the road. I got in and out just like a thief in the night.'

'You better be right,' said the leader.

'Man, just relax and drink with me,' said the driver. 'There isn't another person around for miles. We now have all this alcohol and very soon we will have a whole lot of cash.'

'Shut your pie hole and get in the house,' said the leader. 'After you two are finished getting that liquor out of that van. I need one of you to drive it around back and the other to start perimeter checks."

"Did you go in alone? What did you do next?"

"That was all I needed to hear," continues Franklin. "I made my way back to my car and I headed back to the city. On my way, I saw Sheriff Deputies investigating a robbery. Someone did a smash and grab on a local liquor store. I hurried to headquarters to present my findings to the leaders. I asked for a tactical team and full support to investigate my findings but I was denied because I was not a Detective. The people in charge told me that 'my investigation was way off base and I needed to follow the real Detectives lead.' I was threatened with termination but they didn't pull that trigger only because Mayor Richman intervened. Without any support from them, I turned to the only people that I knew I could trust; I called up the twins. Back then they were still trying to get establish but they had worked a case or two in the Dallas area. They were more than happy to assist me with the investigation. They also knew a couple of local officers that owed them a favor, who agreed to join our team.

Two days later, our team drove back to the house I surveyed. The guys inside of the house must have been real comfortable because no one was on lookout. We surveyed the property then we decided to split into two groups. The entry team consisted of myself, Shondra, and Saundra. The containment team consisted of the two uniformed officers. The officers positioned themselves along the backyard where they could cover the rear exit and sides of the house. Without hesitation, the twins and I stormed the house. First, we kicked down the front door, where two suspects were in the living room. They didn't notice our intrusion because they were in the middle of a fierce video game battle. They were subdued rather quickly. The twins proceeded to clear the first floor while I went upstairs to investigate a noise that I heard. Before I reached the top of the stairs, two shots passed right above my head, hitting the wall behind me. I ducked and returned fire. I broke the light that shined on the stairwell then I threw a smoke grenade up the stairs where the shots came from. Fierce coughing ensued before the sound of a window being broken was heard. I prepared myself to charge upstairs but was stopped in my tracks when a suspect came charging at me. The impact of our collision sent us both tumbling down the stairs, painfully hitting the floor below. When I finally regained my senses, I noticed that the suspect was the first to get to his feet. Things began to move in slow motion as he bent to pick up his weapon. He smiled wickedly as he pointed his weapon in my direction. He winked then prepared to shoot but like an angel descending from Heaven, Shondra appeared. She hit the suspect right on the temple with a running knee, causing him to drop the gun and stumble backwards. Saundra followed behind her, to finish him off with a haymaker to the jaw. The fourth suspect was apprehended by the two officers after he broke his leg trying to jump from the second-floor window. We found the daughter of the Mayor of Fort Worth in the closet beneath the stairs. Even though we saved that girl, my job was still threatened because I didn't follow protocol. Luckily, I had the twins there to take responsibility for the operation and because they are Private Investigators protocol went out of the window. The Mayor of Fort Worth was grateful and when he heard what all the fuss was about he made it his top priority to celebrate our accomplishment. We were rewarded the keys to both the city of Dallas and the city of Fort Worth. But because of the stress of his daughter being kidnapped, the Mayor of Fort Worth dropped out of the Senate race. Mayor Richman won the election for Senator unopposed. For our heroic actions, I was promoted to State Detective. With the reward money and the publicity that came with this high-profile case, the twins' Private Investigation Firm became extremely popular."

"That's impressive Franklin. I am very proud of you all, especially the way you didn't let an obstacle stop you. You followed your instincts and won. It looks like Mayor Richman also was a big winner."

"Yes, he was," says Franklin. "Mayor Richman became Senator the following month. You will see him on television soon. He announced that he would be running for the Presidency. Senator Richman is good people Brody, I will introduce you to him one of these days. He will be a good President. Who knows we may be able to get on his secret service detail."

"I don't know about that Franklin."

"It's only a possibility," he says. "Now as a State Detective, I have been placed on the missing person's cases. I have more access to files and I now have the freedom to work anywhere in the State of Texas. Like I said earlier, the twins and I are now working on a joint case. We believe that a serial killer has been preying on women throughout the great state of Texas and we need your help. I really believe that you can assist us with this case, Brody."

"Well I'll do my best."

"That's all that I need," replies Franklin. "I don't know what you have been doing while you were gone but just having you here, motivates me to do more."

"Why are you stuck on cold cases?"

"Some people didn't like the way I became a State Detective," he says. "Because I was part of such a high-profile case, some people turned their noses. They also didn't like the fact that a Mayor and a Senator vouched for my promotion. I was forced to work undercover for a few years but I didn't let that stop me either."

"Wow, you worked undercover?"

"Yeah but that's a topic for another day," he replies. "As for why I'm on cold cases, I really can't answer that. Every undercover assignment I went on was a success but I was still forced into working cold cases. It doesn't matter because I am right where I needed to be."

"What do you mean by that?"

"You will see soon," he says. "We're here."

CHAPTER 4 – BRIDGETTE

It didn't take us long to arrive in Lufkin. Franklin drives into a parking lot that is adjacent to a white house. There aren't any signs indicating whether the house is someone's home or a business but the landscape is well maintained. This area is also quiet. Plus, there isn't any traffic on the street and the parking lot is empty; except for a jacked-up truck and a boat that's sitting underneath a tarp. Franklin eagerly puts his car into park and quickly exits the vehicle. He walks towards the house but he stops when he notices that I'm still in the car.

"Come on Brody," he roars.

"What are you in such a rush for? We are the only ones here; besides I can't forget this food."

"No, we aren't the only ones here," he replies. "That's one of the twin's trucks right there. Now hurry up."

"I'm coming man, hold your horses."

"Well put some pep in your step," he says as he opens the front door. "Welcome to our office."

Their office is much more spacious then it seems from the outside. Some of the walls were removed, which created more space. Awards and Newspaper articles cover the walls. The stories he told me were very much accurate but there isn't anything about his undercover work.   Before I can read more articles, Shondra and Saundra emerge from the back.

"Good morning ladies, Big Mama sent breakfast for you all."

Shondra smiles as she takes the breakfast. She replies, "Good Morning Brody."

"This way Brody," says Saundra as she walks back into the room she emerged from.

Franklin disappears into the same room Saundra went into, while Shondra prepare to eat breakfast. Unlike the previous room, the walls of this room are covered by many posters labeled "Missing." I walk along the wall reading the posters for each missing girl.

The first poster reads: Melanie Gonzalez, missing since February 28, 2017, born December 16, 2003, currently 13 years old, Hispanic female, black hair, brown eyes, height 5'1", weigh 110 pounds, last seen in Corpus Christi, Texas.

The Second poster reads: Kirsten Smith, missing since December 23, 2016, born October 14, 2004, currently 12 years old, Black female, black hair, green eyes, height 5'5", slim build, last seen in Houston, Texas

The Third poster reads: Emily Stewart, missing since August 24, 2016, born February 21, 2004, currently 12 years old, Caucasian female, sandy hair, brown eyes, height 4'10", slim build, last seen in Austin, Texas.

The Fourth poster reads: Bethany Perez, missing since January 1, 2016, born June 8, 2002, currently 14 years old, Hispanic female, black hair, black eyes, height 4'8", weight 101 pounds, last seen in San Antonio, Texas.

The Fifth poster reads: Elizabeth Simpson, missing since July 4, 2015, born November 22, 2000, currently 16 years old, Black female, blonde hair, hazel eyes, height 5'4", medium build, last seen in Dallas, Texas.

The Sixth poster reads: Stacie King, missing since October 30, 2014, born May 9, 1999, currently 18 years old, African-American female, black hair, green eyes, height 5'5", weight 101 pounds, last seen in Beaumont, Texas.

The Seventh poster reads: Amy Perry, missing since January 12, 2009, born June 21, 1996, currently 20 years old, Caucasian female, blonde hair, brown eyes, height 5'2", slim build, last seen in Lubbock, Texas.

The Eight poster reads: Carol Anderson, missing since August 11, 2005, born September 4, 1988, currently 29 years old, Black female, blonde hair, grey eyes, height 5'8", slim build, last seen in Fort Worth, Texas.

I am unable to take another step, I feel frozen in place. I stare at the final poster. While looking at her face, my left eye begins to violently twitch. Anxiety overwhelmingly speeds up my respirations; while my heart uses my ribcage as a drum set.

The Ninth poster reads: Bridgette James, missing since Saturday, September 14, 2002, born September 13, 1986, currently 30 years old, Black female, black hair with grey streaks, grey eyes, height 5'9", medium build, last seen near Lufkin, Texas.

A firm hand clasps my right shoulder causing me to turn slightly in that direction. I turn my head slightly to not lose sight of the photo, I notice that the hand belongs to Franklin. The room is silent as my vision returns solely on my sister's photograph. My body feels as if an earthquake is occurring inside of me, I want to scream. Another hand lands on top of my head and gently guides it until the side of my head firmly rests against Saundra's forehead. The words come as a whisper, soothing but firmly Saundra says, "We haven't forgotten and we will never quit searching."

"You'll need to try Big Mama biscuits," interrupts Shondra. As she continues to smack on her last pieces of a biscuit.

Slowly I turn towards Shondra, rolling my eyes in the process. "That sounds disgusting. Close your mouth when you are chewing food. I know Big Mama taught you better than that."

"No, I won't. Close your ears," she replies. "Don't you have something you should be doing instead of worrying about me?"

"Let's focus people," interjects Franklin. He taps on a chalk board like an elementary school teacher to get everyone's attention. "We need to bring Brody up to speed with our investigation. Also, Brody we need you to describe in detail everything you remember about the day your sister was abducted. I know the thought is painful but we are here to help you get through the pain. I linked these nine cases together because they follow a similar pattern. Whoever this person is, he or she is not leaving any evidence. There is never a witness, except for you Brody. You are the only possible witness to anyone of these nine abductions. These cases are now all cold cases. They have been forgotten because of lack of evidence, lack of witnesses, and lack of suspects. The only thing that is left behind are broken families. These families suffer every day; wishing and hoping for one more moment, just a little more time, or one last glimpse of their loved one alive. Their missing love ones forever haunts their every thought and memories. We know the feeling and we continue to live with the aftermath of this horrific event. I want to bring these families who are unfortunately linked together, some closure. It's not fair that someone out there knows what happened to these girls. We want to. NO, WE MUST bring this psycho to justice. But we need your help to do that."

"We believe that Bridgette was his first victim," adds Shondra. "We believe that her abduction went wrong somehow. Which may explain why it was nearly three years before the abductor struck again. Since then this psycho has gained confidence and is now kidnapping girls with more frequency. He has perfected his craft, traveling around unnoticed, while plotting and patiently waiting for his next opportunity."

"So, will you help us Brody?" Asks Saundra.

"I will help and you all are right; this person must be stopped. I will help you out as much as I can because as you all know; Bridgette meant the world to me. By taking Bridgette, this person has destroyed my family. Her being taken out of my life, forever left a void. It left an emptiness that can never be filled, not by any person nor any amount of money. It's a feeling like being on the edge of despair, contemplating whether to dive in."

"We feel the same," says Franklin.

"OKAY, I will help! Every time I think of that day, I also think of the day before. So, I will start there."

"Start where ever you would like," says Shondra.

"The day before was Friday, September 13, 2002, it was Bridgette's sixteenth birthday. That day we attend school as normal but I remember being excited the entire day. Bridgette was expecting to get a car for her birthday and she promised me that she would take me on the first ride. I remember rushing home after school so I wouldn't miss out on the occasion. I just knew my mom would have already baked a cake but when I walked into the house, instead of a joyous occasion it was more like walking into a funeral. The entire aura of the house was depressing. Bridgette was heartbroken standing there in tears, while mom was fussing at dad. Apparently, our dad lost Bridgette's car money gambling, the night before. I must have walked in on the end of the conversation because mom ensured Bridgette that she would have her car by next week. She then took dad's keys and tossed them over to Bridgette. She told her that until that day comes, she'll have full access to his vehicle. Dad agreed with what mom had said and all was good. Bridgette ran out of the house and drove off before anyone could change their mind. That night the high school had its homecoming football game. Bridgette was just a sophomore at the time but she was still co-captain of the cheerleading squad. I remember going to the game that night with Uncle Earl and Franklin. Do you remember that Franklin? We had a blast that night. The Panthers won by a seventeen-point advantage and Bridgette stole the show with her performance that night. After the game, Bridgette made an announcement that her sweet sixteen Barn-Fire Birthday Bash would take place after the game at the Barn. Now the game was fun but that Barn-Fire was the best party I have ever been to. It felt like everyone in town was at that party. I could tell that Bridgette really enjoyed herself that night. She told me to take pictures until I run out of film. I really enjoyed that, I wanted to grow up and become a photographer. I would capture her with some of the biggest smiles on her face. I don't know exactly how long the party lasted that night because mom and dad forced me home around midnight.

I awoke the next day around ten hundred hours. I was still drained from Bridgette's fantastic Barn-Fire Birthday Bash. That day was Saturday, September 14, 2002. The sun was up and the birds were chirping. A cool breeze entered through my window and found its way underneath my sheets. The breeze left me shivering as it seemly passed through my body. My shivers did not last long due to the sound of a slamming screen door. I soon heard my mother yelling. Next a car speed away, kicking up rocks in the process. I hurried to the kitchen. Bridgette was already in there and Mom was just reentering the house. That was the first time I ever heard my mom use a cuss word. Her attention immediately shifted to me and Bridgette. She was angry but she calmly told us to go get cleaned up. I could tell that something was wrong with her because her eyes were red. I didn't have the courage to ask her what was wrong; instead Bridgette and I turned on our heels and made our way to our rooms. I slowly washed my face, brushed my teeth, and I put on some clothing. As I was lacing my shoes I heard mom calling for us. I walked into the kitchen to see my mom handing Bridgette a slip of paper. She told me to walk with Bridgette to the store because she would need help carrying the groceries. I didn't have any objections because I loved being with my sister and she didn't mind having me around but I was concerned for my Mom because it was evident that she was crying.

Normally, we would have never been allowed to walk to the store but since The Jungle had been cleaned up, I thought things were changing. Between our house and the store there was a stretched that was called The Jungle. On this stretch the road curves wickedly then it straightens before it curves again. There were three abandon houses, followed by a hill, and then another abandoned house which sat by the creek just before the road curves again. There have been many terrifying tales of people being attacked on The Jungle stretch. The police were always in that area because of drug activity, but lately the streets were clean because of the community's commitment to safety. Once the community came together we started to notice less police activity in the area which ironically resulted in less drug activity.

Saturday, September 14, 2002 was a beautiful day. The sun shined brightly but it wasn't hot. The wind blew constantly but it wasn't cold either. It was the perfect fall day, it was a great day to take a walk and the grocery store was only four blocks away from our house. Our walk began quietly while I watch two neighboring dogs bark at each other through the wooden fence that separated them. My distraction caused me to fall back. I had to run a little just to catch back up to Bridgette. Bridgette still wasn't talking and I could tell that something was on her mind. I grabbed her hand and began swinging it as we walked. She looked down and smiled. I remember squinting my eyes a little because the sun was in them but her smile was still radiant. She asked me what I wanted. I told her that I wanted to know what all the fuss was about. At first, she was tentative but she began to explain to me how our dad had a gambling problem. She explained that he had always gambled but he was currently in the worst six month slump he had ever face. What made matters worse was his new found drinking habit. With his up and down ways, mom still found a way to save enough money to get

Bridgette the car she wanted. Somehow, she budgeted and saved money despite his reckless behavior. The night before Bridgette's party, dad decided that he would double-up the money but his plan backfired horribly as he not only lost his entire paycheck but he also lost the money they saved to purchase Bridgette's car. Mom tried her best to keep it together but she no longer could stomach the disappointment. Bridgette stopped me on the street and told me that no matter what happens with our parents, she will always be by my side. She said things will get rough, so we will have to grow strong. She kissed me on my forehead and pointed out that we had made it through The Jungle to the grocery store. There were only two vehicles in the parking lot, one was a black SUV and the other was a silver mini-van. We laughed and joked about buying things that were not on the list but ultimately, we knew better. Checkout went swiftly because there were only four people in the store, besides the employees. When we exit the store, the same vehicles were outside but the main street was busy. We began to follow the same route back home. Halfway home one of my bags burst. Unfortunately, the bagger had put a damp item into a paper bag and groceries fell to the street. They rolled around and some items nearly went into the creek. Bridgette told me to hurry up as she continued to walk because she noticed I only had four items left on the ground. I quickly put them into other bags so I could catch up to her. As I bent to pick up the bags, I heard a car engine accelerate. When I turned to see where the car was, I heard Bridgette scream. I really don't remember what happened after that. The next thing I remember is when I awoke lying on my back in a hospital bed. A nurse was talking to me but I couldn't understand what she was saying at first. After the medicine wore off a little, I finally could understand her. She was telling me that I was restrained because I had tubes coming from my mouth, nose, and penis. I felt like I just came off an assembly line. That was six months after the accident. I needed another six months to learn how to walk and control my other motor functions. I didn't even know that Bridgette was missing. Everyone came to visit me but no one wanted to tell me what was going on or why my parents hadn't been there to visit me. I knew something was wrong even though everyone was trying to hide it from me. It wasn't on their faces but their aura was one of sadness. That's all that I remember."

Glancing at the others, I notice that Franklin isn't moving. His fist is clenched, and he is gazing downwards. Shondra's legs and arms are crossed as she sits back in her chair staring at me. Saundra is silent, but she is nervously tapping her right foot against the floor at a steady pace. This is the first time I have ever told them what I remember from that dreadful day. I never wanted to talk about it before, so everyone else respected my wishes. I felt that just talking about it over and over would do nothing for bringing Bridgette back. So, I choose not to talk about it at all. Yes, that was selfish but I was kid. In one day I lost my mother, father, and my sister. I was never taught how to deal with situations like that. So, I stuffed it all within me. On many occasions, I can honestly say that I was suicidal but fortunately for me my Big Mama and Paw-Paw never let me out of their sights. They took me in and loved me unconditionally. They talked to me daily until they were comfortable with my mentality and these three were in my face until I left on my journey.

CHAPTER 5 – FIRST STEP REHABILITATION

The past three hours were spent going over each case file. We would visit and revisit each crime scene in search of any missed clues or evidence. We notice that the kidnapper's target age group were girls between the ages of twelve to sixteen. We notice a decline in the kidnappers preferred age group. His current trend leans more towards twelve years old girls. The only thing the victims have in common besides their gender is that they all were popular in their school and liked by their communities. The popularity of the girls resulted in huge search and rescue parties each time, which would last for months. Unfortunately, the result always remained the same, nothing new is ever found.

"This dirty, slimy, rotten son of a sea cucumber is extremely clever," says Franklin as he grabs his keys from a table. "Where is your camera Brody?"

"What camera?"

"The one you had the night of Bridgette's Birthday party," he says. "If we can look through the pictures from that night, we may find something new. We can look for any unfamiliar face and check the backgrounds for anyone that was lingering. There is a strong possibility that the kidnapper was at the barn fire. If that is true, then he may be on one of your photos. Brody, please tell me that you know where that camera is? Well do you?"

"Let's see if I remember. After the party, my parents took me straight home. I was so tired that I went straight to bed. I haven't had it since, so it must be still in my old room. I took great care of my camera. I would have placed it somewhere safe no matter how tired I was. Everything in my room had its own space because I tend to be obsessive sometimes. I like things to be in its assigned place. The camera should still be in its place unless it was moved by someone else. From what you have told me, my Pops has been in a bad place of late. He may have moved it or he may have sold it."

"There is only one way to find out if it's still there. You did say you wanted to see your dad, right?" He asks.

"Yeah, he need to answer a few questions. Will we be able to see him today?"

"Well, I have a good relationship with the staff of First Step Rehabilitation Center," he says. "I send them a whole ton of business. We can grab a quick bite to eat before we head over there."

"Already, let's get moving. I haven't seen my pops in a long time."

"I probably will not be back today, says Franklin. "Please lockup when you'll leave?"

"We always do," replies Shondra.

"Bye Franklin. Let us know if you all find something," says Saundra.

Franklin drives with only his knees, as we devour our lunch. I can tell it isn't his first time driving this way because he never decreases his speed, but that still isn't enough to ease my nerves. My comfort level isn't as tolerable to his driving or lack of driving. I sit on the passenger side with my butt clinched tight, with a vice grip like hold on the seat. My eyes fill up with water, after he swerves rather closely in between two 18-wheelers. It nearly causes me to choke on my food but to prevent from choking, I quickly drink a sip of my beverage. Thankfully that helps to assist my food down my throat.

"How much longer do I have to endure your dreadful driving? You drive like you are in a constant competition with every other car on the highway. It's like you lose your mind if someone passes you by."

"Man get your panties out of a bunch. We are nearly there," replies Franklin. "Just up ahead we will turn right onto a private road. First Step Rehabilitation Center is located two miles deep in the heart of this forest. So, stop your whining because I don't have any pacifiers handy."

"You know you can stop the car, Franklin. There isn't nothing but air and opportunity out here! Neither any witness nor anyone to stop us."

71

"You aren't ready Brody!" he exclaims. "You're lucky I'm bringing you to visit your old man. If I wasn't, you would get the business. Besides you just got home and Big Mama would kill me if I messed you up."

"Yeah whatever. It's best for you to start crawfishing."

"Man, I can go for a couple pounds of them mud bugs right now," he says. "With some corn, potato, and sausage. You need to call your folks in Louisiana and tell them to send us some sacks. Now you got me wanting some boiled crawfish."

"Do you always think about food?"

"Nope," he replies. "I don't think about food, when I'm eating."

Franklin turns off the highway onto a narrow one-way road, that leads into a forest. The forest consists mostly of pine trees. Their long limbs which are filled with pine needles block our view at each turn. The sweet smell of pine sap grows thicker the more we proceed down this rocky path. For the amount of money one must pay to stay at a rehabilitation center, you would think that the road would be much smoother. The road first starts out paved for a few feet off the highway before it turns into a gravel road. That was okay for a while until the gravel stopped. Now it feels like a game of dodge the pothole. If my back isn't hurting after this ride, I am sure that my neck will be. I'm starting to have second thoughts about visiting the place at the end of this road. Branches of trees dangle dangerously low, nearly scraping the top of

Franklins truck. At the precise moment, I would think we were just about to hit a branch the road would make a hard drop. After enduring an unwanted roller coaster ride, I notice our first opening and seeing the path clear to this opening is a needed relief. The rocky road turns back into gravel, somewhat smoothing out. Just beyond the trees a gate that stands around fifteen feet high becomes visible; making it impossible to see what lays beyond it. Atop of the fence is a series of interlinking barbed wire. The forest seems to merge with the fence as vines grow onto areas of its surface. A huge iron gate stands between me and the discovery of what lays beyond this fence. A small building sits to the left of the gate a few feet off the road. A small air conditioning unit droops from one of the windows. Gravity would have forced it to the ground if it wasn't for the stick that props it up. Suddenly the door to the building swings open and a short stocky security guard emerges from the building holding a clip board. He inhales roughly through his nose then spits to the ground. With his head held high and chest protruding forward, he slowly walks over to the truck. Without saying a word, Franklin shows the security guard his badge. The security guard observes the badge, then looks Franklin squarely in the face. This guy clearly loves his job. He straightens himself, spits again, then walks away. Slowly he walks to the rear of the truck. I assume he went to the rear to write the license plate number onto his clip board. Slowly he walks back to the driver side door. He clears his throat and spits again.

"You know I could have been your partner Detective," says the security guard. "Yeah, the state police wanted me to join their force a few years back. They had heard about my success in the community. But, I said No! The life of a security guard is more dangerous and someone of my skills would help the community more by staying on the security force."

"Already," replies Franklin. "And the forest thanks you. The animals and trees have never felt safer. Keep up the good work."

The color slowly drains from the face of the security guard but he doesn't reply to Franklins statement. Instead, he turns around and stomps back to the small building. He slams the door causing his air conditioning unit to fall to the ground. Foul language is heard coming from the building as the gate begins to slowly open. A bright lush green becomes visible as the gate opens fully, revealing an embankment that rises equally as high as the fence does. The gravel road turns into pavement and makes a sharp right turn upon entering. Traveling between the fence and the embankment feels like being trapped in a maze. The road curves again but this time to the left, away from the fence. The embankment ends and at this point the pavement turns into cobble stone. Suddenly, a massive fountain appears into vision. It's shooting large streams of water into the air. The stream of water soars through the air ascending to unbelievable heights before reversing course to dive effortlessly into the water below. Beyond the fountain emerge a building whom closely resembles a massive five-star resort. Marble statues flank its entrance, welcoming new arrivals to First Step Rehabilitation Center. Franklin drives around the fountain, then parks in front of the entrance. Two polite young men open our doors for us to exit. The young man on the driver side of the car hands Franklin a ticket before getting into the car and driving away.

"It would be embarrassing if that guy just stole your truck, Detective James. Just to think, you handed him the keys."

"You better hope not," replies Franklin. "It's a long walk back to my office."

The sound of someone clearly their throat ends our bickering before we really get going. A sharply dressed slender guy, with what appears to be make-up around his eyes, on his cheeks, and covering his facial hair; pops his lips together before saying "Hey."

"Hey," repeats the sharply dressed slender guy. "My name is Zan Quan, but you can call me Quan. Welcome to First Step Rehabilitation Center. I will be assisting you today on your visit. Please follow me."

Franklin gets my attention when his elbow strikes against my ribcage. I ignore the fact that I should case trauma back to his ribs because he starts pointing rather excitedly towards our guide.

"Don't let that rooster-fruit get you Brody," he whispers.

"Rooster-fruit? Where? What is a rooster-fruit? I don't see a rooster, nor do I see any fruits."

"Where have you been all this time?" he inquires. "Just look at the way he is walking. Do you see that hip action? Do you remember how he was fanning himself after nearly every word? I know you heard how he drags the word 'Hey.' Right?"

"What about it?"

"So, you didn't catch how he slowly looked you up and down?" he asks. "Right before saying his name slowly, Zan Quan. He was undressing you the whole time."

"I wasn't looking, that hard!"

"Man, you better watch yourself," whispers Franklin. "People get caught up every day. If you can't tell when a man is hitting on you, then you're in deep doo-doo. In this day and age, some men dress as women and sometimes it is very difficult to tell the difference."

"It sounds like you are speaking from experience."

"Don't play with me Brody," he whispers. "I'm just trying to put you on some game. I don't want to see you become a victim. Cause if that's the case then you might as well go back where you came from. That may be too much for me to stomach right now."

"You need to relax Franklin. Remember, I have traveled this beautiful world. But one thing remains the same no matter where you are in this world, people will look at you and label you based on their fears and prejudices. People fear what they don't understand. Instead of trying to gain knowledge of the situation, most rather be hateful. Just like what you just did with Zan Quan. But since your questioning my manhood, let me explain to you how I see things. You see, he observed us while we were still bickering. He made his own judgements in the process. He constantly threw out subtle hints, only to see which one of us would bite the bait. You nearly got hooked, while I just sat back and ignored them. The more you act like a school age kid, the more he will show out. Now, didn't we come here for a reason or are you too caught up to remember? That reminds me, how did you become a State Detective? I might have to keep an eye on you."

"Okay Brody," he replies, while repeatedly shaking his head up and down. "It isn't nothing for me to put down this gun and badge. We can go around the corner and handle this."

"Oh, you're not hiding behind your gun and badge? Well we don't have to go around the corner. You can pick a square, Franklin. Like I said before, there isn't nothing but air and opportunity out here. Just know if you jump stupid you might not remember how you landed."

"Should I take a seat?" Asks Zan Quan. "Or maybe go get some popcorn and my girls to watch the show? I haven't seen a good cat fight in a while and I do enjoy a good show. Just make sure it isn't quick. Quickies aren't always good."

"Sorry, pardon our rude behavior," replies Franklin.

"Well if you ladies are finish; can I get you two to sign-in on the visitor's log?" Asks Zan Quan.

A short plump man who wears his glasses on the bridge of his nose, appears while I am signing the visitors log book. His suit and shoes looks expensive. He walks up to Franklin and shakes his hands, while calling him Detective. He is clearly happy to see Franklin. They talk another minute before Franklin turns toward me.

"I'll meet you here in about one hour," he says.

"Wait a minute, Franklin. I thought you were accompanying me to talk to my pops."

"Yeah, I was," he replies. "Unfortunately, another matter has come to my attention. I'm sure you can accomplish your task without me. Unless you need me to hold your hands."

"No, I'm good."

"Already," he says. "When you are ready, Zan Quan will lead you to your destination."

"Detective, I told you that you can call me Quan," interrupts Zan Quan. "And you don't need to worry your pretty little head either, because you are in good hands."

Franklin looks at Zan Quan with a menacing look, before walking away with the guy with expensive shoes.

Who is also looking at Zan Quan with an even more frightening look. For a moment, it seems as if the guy with expensive shoes was going to tell Zan Quan something, but Franklin grabs him by his arm and leads him down a hallway. Zan Quan curls his lips then snaps his neck in objection. He rolls his eyes so hard, I thought one of them got stuck.

"Anyway," says Zan Quan sourly. "Who did you come to see?"

"I'm here to see Malcolm James."

"And what is your relationship to Malcolm James?" he asks.

"He's my father."

"I can tell too," he replies. "You resemble him a lot, but there is something about your eyes. But anyway, follow me."

Zan Quan leads the way down a spacious hallway which is decorated with numerous art pieces. A soft melody plays over the intercom giving the environment a calming feel. We turn down a dead-end hall, which has doors on both sides of the narrow hall. Zan Quan stops at the last door on the left and points inside.

"We will wait for my colleagues to bring Mr. James into this room for you," he says.

79

"That will not work for me. I need to talk with him somewhere I can breathe fresh air. Do you all have a garden available or somewhere else that is open to air."

"Well I thought you might have wanted some privacy," he replies.

"Well stop assuming."

Zan Quan's' expression changes but he quickly closes the door. Without speaking another word, he starts power walking down the previous hallway. He doesn't look back to see if he is leaving me behind and I don't walk any faster. Looking at the way the other guy addressed Franklin, it seems that he has been here numerous times. I better heed his words and keep a close eye on Zan Quan. He's already acting thirsty and now he's sour. I finally reach the hall where Zan Quan made a left turn to find him standing at a door, twirling his imaginary hair while obnoxiously chewing a piece of gum.

CHAPTER 6 – MALCOLM JAMES

From the general direction that I walked in, I assume that this garden is in the middle of the facility. I look up to see a blue sky filled with plush white clouds. I notice that no other floor has access to this area, but glass windows do allow each floor a view of the garden. I sit underneath a Gazebo which is away from the door that I entered through. A group of people lay on the ground looking up at the sky. A few more groups are scattered throughout the garden. Some are reading books. While blank expressions decorate the faces of others, as they stare off into their thoughts. The doorway on the opposite side of the garden swings open. Through the door steps my pops, his name is Malcom James. He grew up in a good situation. He was blessed to have both parents in this household and a strong support system all around. They were a successful family that love to give back to the community. He was a kid that was fortunate enough to have more than the other kids that he knew. Despite the proper upbringing, education, and attention that every kid needs and requires, Malcolm still chose to travel down the wrong paths. On many occasions, he took advantage of his parents' popularity and status in the community to get out of trouble. He was headed to the wrong place on the right street, until he met my momma. Her name at that time was Gloria De'LaReaux, but everyone calls her Glow. She helped him get saved for the first time, which helped him to change his life completely around. They got married and had two kids,

Bridgette and myself. There are no bad memories from my childhood, that I can remember or that I paid attention to, before my pop's epic failure. In my eyes, he was always helping my momma out around the house, while keeping a constant watch over the two of us. We thought he had psychic powers by the way he would stop us in our tracks. He would call us out before we got a chance to get into something that we shouldn't have been in. He was the kind of dad that every kid wished for and our family was happy. By the time, I returned home from the hospital; home was no more. I would occasionally see him whenever he stopped by the Big House for something to eat or to borrow some money from Paw-Paw. He was always in a hurry. I can't believe someone slowed him down enough to get him into Rehab.

I watch as he strolls through the garden. He makes eyes at the ladies and nods his head at the guys. He thinks he's the original smooth operator. I remember him being a tall, strong man. Even after Bridgette's kidnapping, when he rarely came around. From a distance, it looked like he stayed healthy. In his current state however, I would not let him go outside if there was a small chance of a mild wind gust. A strong wind gust would most likely, fling him a few states away. As he walks closer, I see him squinting his eyes; trying to gain recognition of who I am. He walks a few feet closer and stops. A faint smile begins to grow on his face as he starts to move again. When he is only a few feet away from me, he stops in his tracks.

"You're just the person I wanted to see," he yells. "I've been thinking about you a lot lately. You're on top of my list of people who I need to make amends with.

Actually, you're the first person I've seen since I've made the list. It has been quite a long time since I've seen you, son. There are some things that I would like to discus with you. Come sit with me at that table over there. That gazebo really freaks me out. Strange things happen around here when the sun goes down and that gazebo gets plenty of the action, if you know what I mean."

The last time I saw this man was the day I graduated from high school. My graduation present from him was a six-pack of beer and one of the beers was missing. I watched this man give up on his family and his life. I watched a broken man stumble through life, failing to learn from any mistake he made. He didn't teach me anything that was useful, except for tips on how to drink without getting a hangover. But, I did learn a lot from him by watching his failures and learning how to be more, from them. I vowed to be a better man than he ever was. He leads me to a wooden table that sits in the middle of the garden. Before I can sit down, I notice three names are engraved into the wood. They are surrounded by a heart. The drawing reads: Gloria, Bridgette, and Brody.

"What? Am I supposed to be impressed by your destruction of these people property? When you had all three of us, you still didn't do right by us. So, what are we now? Are we ghosts of your failures or are we your regrets?"

"Pump your brakes son, I am still your father," he replies. "Now, whether I deserve that title is another discussion for another time. So please don't let my failure as a father cause you to lose your integrity. This facility has helped me in ways that I would have never allowed in the past, but for it to work I need to talk to others that I have hurt in the past. Will you allow us to take our first steps to healing our broken relationship?"

"Sure, why not," I reply while taking a seat on the bench connected to the table. I've learned to forgive others. If I hold onto grudges, I will never reach my full potential. Thoughts of the past and of what could have been, begin to invade my concentration. Anger begins to rise as thoughts of reality over take all other thoughts. To control my rage, I find myself picking with a piece of splintered table. Darn it, now I'm destroying these people's property too.

"Thank you for this opportunity son," he says. "I have been in here taking it one step at a time. You are the first person outside of the staff here that I have been able to talk with. I can't put my problems on anyone or any one incident that has happened thus far. Rather, I can blame all my problems on the choices that I decided to make. I chose to drink alcohol heavily. My alcoholism led me to choose to experiment with other drugs. My drug abuse led me to places where no human should ever desire to stumble across. Now all my choices have led me here. I'm a shell of the man that I once was and I'm nowhere near my true potential. Don't get me wrong son, I'm not looking for a pity party or anything else like that. I know that I cannot make the things of the past right, but I can start the healing process for the future. Brody, I would like to apologize to you for not being a good father, I would like to apologize for abandoning you, and I would like to apologize for being a selfish man. I am sorry son and grateful at the same time. I am grateful to you for freeing me."

"How did I free you."

"For half a year while my little girl was missing, I was being held and awaiting trial for her disappearance and attempted vehicular manslaughter for your accident." He continues. "I nearly lost my mind in there but I did lose all hope. The District Attorney was convinced that I was at fault and nothing was convincing the judge nor the jury otherwise. I had completely given up and was prepared to work out a plea agreement, then a miracle happened. You awoke. You saved my life that day, without even knowing. You told the detectives that you didn't hear my car before your accident. You told them that you could hear my car a mile away because of the hole in the muffler. It was a good thing that I held off on fixing that muffler because that hole saved my butt. You helped me keep my freedom and I haven't done anything to repay you. Thank you, son! Somehow I will find a way to repay you."

"I'm not the only one you need to repay. You have good parents. Parents who did any and everything for you, including raising me. You need to find a way to repay them. Like you said, your still my father. That didn't end when I graduated from high school nor did it end when I turned twenty-one. You dropped the ball but I'll be living my life when you get out of here. Maybe you can start repaying me then."

"You're right. They are good parents and they are also on my list," he replies. "Before, I once believed that the world was out to get me, my parents included. I wasn't appreciative towards the many blessings that I overlooked each day. I was blind to the fact that many people struggle every day and most of their struggles are not self-inflected. I would convince myself that my life was just a show and everyone that I encountered was part of the act. I would show up to places only to show out. I figured that no one ever wants to see a boring show. I was truly lost son. I didn't have the power to help myself and I figured that no one else did. When I was at one of my low points in life, I awoke to find myself in jail, again. Because I was well known, I was only kept in a holding cell. Inside of the cell with me was a man who was arrested for burning down his home. But after three hundred and twenty-six days of involuntary confinement he was being released. After new discoveries in his case, proved that the fire was started from the initial wiring of his house being inadequate. The poor installation of his homes wiring led to the death of his wife, mother, father, four children, and nine grandchildren. For over four months, everyone who knew him blamed him for the death of everyone whom he loved. He mourned his grave loses during the darkest hours of the night, while sitting alone inside of a cold jail cell. But still he stood before me inside of that jail cell an unbroken man, with his faith emitting from his body. He whom had lost his entire family, home, and all his possessions endured through all his pain and suffering. His eyes told the tale of his lose but he confidently stood welcoming his next test. If this man could continue to move forward even with his momentous loses, without turning to drugs and alcohol, then what was my excuse. He opened me to being able to accept assistance when the family did their intervention. Brody, I now believe that there is more to this life than my own selfish needs and desires. I cannot tell you what to do but I advise you to find a way to find true happiness within yourself. Once you do, don't let the world control your life. Find a way to live your life to the fullest. Enjoy the things that bring you happiness and don't fall for the traps that the people with power has put into place. We are not on this earth to work all our lives for greedy corporations. I know that we could never get lost time back. But in the future, can I try to be a part of your life?"

"Well we will have to take that one step at a time, also. But I am happy to see that you have made the correct changes in your life. It looks like you may be on a good path. I am currently living at The Big House so give me a call whenever you would like to talk. It's good seeing you."

"Brody, you have to get out of that house," he shouts. "Those people spoiled me rotten. I'm not making an excuse for my actions but a man needs a place he can stretch his legs. You need to be able to walk around naked if you choose to. Hold on, I'll be right back."

Quickly he exits through the same doors that he entered the garden through. The result of this conversation should have been me knocking him out cold for all that he has done and for all that he didn't do. Since the accident, I've been mentally training to be stronger and smarter than him. So, on this day, I could avenge both my mother and sister. Instead, I find myself listening and obeying like a good child. I guess when I finally got my opportunity, I couldn't go against my core values. I won't let the past destroy the person that I have evolved into. However, Franklin will be mad, I didn't get a chance to talk to him about the camera. The words "Heads Up" takes me from my thoughts. I look upwards just in time to see keys flying towards me. I move slightly to the right to remove my face from the keys path and reach out slightly in front of me to catch them. A few keys dig into my hand but because I continue the keys path a few feet before stopping them, they didn't have enough force to break my skin.

"I tried to live in that house on numerous occasions," he says. "But I couldn't spend a full night in there, not without you all. The gas and water are still on and currently the lights are turned off but there is a generator connected in the backyard. There still should be a few days of fuel in the garage. Now Brody, she needs a little work but with a little sweat you can have her back in top condition. The house is paid for and your grandpa has been keeping up with the property taxes, which I need to pay him back for. All in all, the house is in good shape and now it's all yours; unless your mother comes back to reclaim it."

"Speaking of my momma, where is she now? When I left, she was in a hospital in Houston. No one has mentioned a word of her to me since I've been back. Is she still there?"

"No, fortunately she is not. After an incident happened at that hospital, Lady De'LaReaux moved her to a hospital that she recommend. Your mother is now a resident at St. Joseph's Ivory Tower, located in St. Joseph, Louisiana. You need to contact your grandmother if you want to see your mother. She can also shed light on what happened in Houston that caused her to move your mother to South Louisiana. If I could leave this place, we could have taken a road trip to visit her but that shouldn't stop you.

I just remembered something Brody, when you go inside the garage for fuel you will find a car underneath a blue tarp. The keys for that car is also on that set of keys. I won that car at a private, high-stakes Texas hold'em poker game. On my final hand, I went all-in. I got my first ever Royal Flush to win that car. The car is in great condition. I only drove it from that poker game. It's been parked under the garage since then. Now in the kitchen, look through the rolodex next to the phone. You will find your grandmothers telephone number. I know I don't have any right to tell you what to do, but I really think you should call your grandmother soon. She has been constantly on my mind, lately. Maybe if you see your mother, it can help to bring her back to us."

"Hopefully it will. I often wonder if I still remember the way that she looks. It's been a very long time since I last talked with her. I really miss that."

"I hate that you have been dealt a lousy hand son," he says. "Remember that the game isn't over until you run out of plays and always stay a few plays ahead of your opponent. Now, I think my time is up son, but I want you to think about everything we've discuss. Once I get out of here I will let my action do the talking. Well, I'm on a tight schedule and if you miss a step in here, two more steps will grow in its place. I love you and I hope to see you soon. Maybe next time that darn cat will allow you to speak."

He disappears through one door and Zan Quan reappears through the other. While I walk towards the door, I can tell that Zan Quan is still sour from our earlier encounter but I won't give him the satisfaction of having the slightest amount of my attention. As I follow Zan Quan back to the front of the build, thoughts begin to cross my mind, which fills my mouth with a bitter taste. What if? What if Bridgette had never been kidnapped? What if it was me instead? What if my momma never lost her mind? What if my Pop's never had a gambling or drinking problem? If I had a fifth of liquor for every "if" that crossed my mind, I'd be in here along with my Pop's.

"Hey man, I don't have all day to wait for you," yells Franklin. "Get in the car Brody. I've been waiting out here for ten minutes. What took you so long? Did your dad tell you where your camera was? Did he sell the house? Because the community has flourished in the past years and that location has a very good property value."

"Are you done, Franklin? I do have the keys. He told me that I could live in the house instead of living at the Big House."

"What about the camera?" He asks.

"We will have to just see if it's still there when we get there. Now, what are you waiting for? Let's get to moving! Oh, my bad, I'll wait until you let your girlfriend know that we are leaving. You may be a rooster-fruit also."

"Furiously Franklin replies, "You're testing my nerves, Brody. If you keep pushing me I will knock your head from your shoulders."

"Who's scared of the police? I'm not scared of the police, Franklin. Besides you all in law enforcement has been getting away with some distasteful stuff, anyway. I got my eyes on you. You'll killing innocent people and now you threatening to behead me. You all supposed to be protecting and serving, not threatening and killing. But I guess if you look like me, you better protect yourself."

"Shut-up and buckle your seatbelt," he replies. "Like me, there are some good officers out here. Not all of us are bad. It's just that the good ones may be scared to talk because of our brotherhood."

"Don't you all preach, 'If you see something, say something?'"

"That's right," he agrees.

"But officers constantly see their fellow officers commit murder and they don't say anything. Now tell me why would the community that's targeted by you all help you all with anything?"

"We all need to help each other to make this world a better place," he says.

"Say what you want Franklin but you'll brotherhood looks more like a legal terrorist ring. If you turn a blind eye when a cop does something bad, then you're no better than he is."

"That's exactly why I work alone," he replies. "I don't have time to install morals into grown people. Some people are not fit to be law enforcement but they still get the job. But because that person has a badge he gets away with all types of horrors. But like I said, there are good law enforcement. We just have to weed out the bad."

"Whatever!"

Surprisingly, the road leading from First Step Rehabilitation Center to the Highway is as smooth as a bald tire. I expected a neck jerking ride back to the highway but the return is short and sweet. Once on the highway, I look back to see a sign that reads: Visitors Entrance Ahead. Further down the road, we past the rough road we originally traveled to get to First Step Rehabilitation Center.

"So, you're a frequent visitor here, huh Franklin?"

"Yes, why do you ask?" he asks.

"Well, how come you didn't know about the visitor's entrance? You don't know that but it seems that you know Zan Quan quite well."

"Visibly irritated Franklin replies, "It's not like that Brody, the state works hand and hand with this rehabilitation center. There is an entire floor that is designated to the state. It allows the state to place people there. People who need extra attention, in an effort to help them kick their habit. Zan Quan is actually a good guy. Now, I don't know what got into him this time but normally he isn't the type that pushes himself onto people. Every time I've seen him, he was very professional."

"Well this time his behavior was very thirsty."

"The thirst is real in that one," adds Franklin.

"To real."

CHAPTER 7 – HOME

"How much longer until we get there? It looks like a storm is on the horizon."

"What are you a meteorologist now?" Asks Franklin. "You seriously don't remember this area? Look at that store on our right. The name has changed but that is the same store you once frequented. I told you that this area has been a focal point for city wide improvement. When our community came together and stopped people from bringing harmful things into it; the city finally took notice. The city now believes that there shouldn't be any place in town where any citizen wouldn't want to live. That thinking has led to city wide growth, which in turn has led to more businesses moving into the city."

Franklin makes a right turn onto a street beside the supermarket. The name of the supermarket has changed but the street name is the same. Once upon a time, Garvin Street was well known throughout the county because of the Jungle. The Jungle was the place to visit if you were looking for something illegal to purchase, from drugs to firearms. Now, none of these illegal products are manufactured in the Jungle but for some reason they seem to find their way in. The trees that once concealed any activity inside of this area are now removed. In the place of the trees are rows upon rows of houses, lining both sides of the street. The once feared Jungle is now no more than a subdivision. My heart begins to race as we drive closer to the area where Bridgette was kidnapped. We round the ill-fated curve but instead of a drop that leads up to a hill, there is a bridge with a river flowing beneath it. Apparently, the creek was made into a river and named in Bridgette's memory. The abandon houses are gone. They are now replaced by new riverside homes. The creepy Jungle which has haunted my nightmares for many years, has now been transformed into a luxurious neighborhood where everyone is welcomed to live.

"Your home now Brody," says Franklin. "I don't know what condition the house is in but it looks pretty good from my viewpoint. Do you need me to do anything before I leave?"

"Since your offering, there is a generator around back. Pop's was using it for electricity. I need you to crank it up for me. There should be fuel in the garage. Also, there should be a car in there underneath a blue tarp. Here are the keys. Can you check it out for me, also? I just need to know if it's in working condition."

Impatiently, Franklin disappears around the side of the house. The house that I remembered growing up in was yellow. Someone has painted it white and has added sky blue trimming. This house shows evidence of repairs being made. No longer is there a hole at the corner of the house just below the roof. The porch is finally completed and the steps has been replaced. Just knowing how my Pop's has been living, I bet he was fixing this place up to put it on the open market. For a reason unknown to me, this house now seems uninviting. I never returned here, not once after the accident. It feels as if this place is no longer my home. The memories here are no longer happy ones. Now they are nightmares of what life once was and will never return to. I walk towards the front door and instantly I begin to grow angry. If I am to sleep here, my wrath might demolish this entire house. Nothing good can come from me living in the past. He couldn't live here, what makes him think that I can? It's time I move on as well.

The trail that Franklin took around the house leads through the initial garage, which is positioned besides the house. Now, a newly built garage is located behind the house. The second garage cannot be seen from the front of the house nor can it be seen from the road. You wouldn't know that it's there unless you've been informed of its existence. A blue tarp laying on the ground is the only sign of Franklin. The generator isn't running, so he must have been distracted. A large wasp nest lay destroyed on the ground beside the garage door. As I walk past the tarp, the sound of metal bumping against metal can be heard coming from the garage. I see the lower half of Franklin's body sticking out from under the hood. He's concentrating so hard, that he doesn't notice my presence. I approach quietly, each step landing softly like a big cat on the haunt, getting ready to pounce on its prey.

"WATCH OUT, WASPS!"

I stand to the side to watch as a loud thud comes from beneath the hood. Franklin appears and he sprints out of the garage at full speed. He ducks and swings wildly into the air, to escape the invisible wasps. He disappears out of view as he run through the first garage. He reappears on the opposite side of the house. He is visibly winded but he I must admit, he was moving lightning quick.

"What are you running from, huh Franklin?"

Suddenly, Franklin stops and looks in my direction. Angrily he stomps in my direction while breathing heavily.

If I wasn't your cousin I'd beat you with this ratchet," he says heatedly. "Did you get the camera?"

"That's what I came to talk about."

"Well spit it out," he replies.

"I can't go in there, Franklin. If you want that camera you will have to go get it yourself. You should find it next to the bed. It's most likely inside of a backpack which should be between the bed and the nightstand."

"Not only do you play too much but you're also a chicken," he says.

"I don't have a scary bone in my body. I just choose not to go in there."

"I will go," he replies. "But not until I get this baby running."

"What are you doing under there? I'll be surprised if this old piece of junk still runs."

"Silence thy tongue," replies Franklin in a medieval voice. "Thee speaketh what thee doest not knoweth. Thee foul the air with thy ignorance. Thee shouldst respect this legend."

"What has you all excited ol' wasp runner?"

"I can't play with you all night," he replies. "I have things to do."

"Like what? Jousting? Are would you like to duel Sir Franklin?"

"Just start the car," he says. "I'll leave after you crank it up."

Let's see if this car will start. Surprisingly, the inside of the car still has that new car smell, which is shocking considering the old model of the car. The memory foam seat absorbs the pressure of my hand, as I lower myself onto it. As soon as I turn the key fully, it feels as if the car comes to life. It growls. The kind of growl that makes you look to see what kind of vehicle is approaching or if you're an automobile enthusiast, you know exactly what car it is.

"I guess it's in good condition, huh Franklin?"

"In good condition? In good condition?" he repeats. "No way Jose. It's in better than good condition. This baby is in mint condition. Uncle Malcolm got lucky with this one. I know he hasn't been good to you but this car is a great; baby, baby please take me back present."

"Stop dancing around like your Michael Jackson; fool you're not BAD. Go ahead and MOONWALK into something in this junky garage. You'll be looking at THE MAN IN THE MIRROR, with a face that looks like someone BEAT IT."

"♫ You know I'm bad, I'm bad come on, you know it. And the whole world has to, answer right now. Just tell you once again, Who's Bad. ♫" sings Franklin.

"Your singing, that's what's bad."

"Brody, you just don't understand," he says. "This is a 1970 Chevrolet Chevelle SS 454 LS6 convertible. With fat dorsal stripes, power front discs, F41 suspension, a domed hood, and a 450-horsepower engine. This baby can go from zero to sixty miles per hour in six seconds flat. You see this car right here, this car right here; it's like the superstar of muscle cars."

"Okay Superstar, but didn't we come here for something that's more important than a dumb vehicle?"

"HEY! I told you once before. You better put some respect on it," he shouts. "There is no need to be disrespectful. How about I run in the house and get the camera, then we can go for a spin."

"Sounds like a plan, just hurry up. Also grab the rolodex from the kitchen on your way out. It should be close to the phone."

"It's not on your face right now but once you get to know this car, you will fall in love with it. Just get more acquainted with your car until I get back," he says.

"There are more important things to life than a car, that will depreciate as soon as you drive it."

"Your right," he agrees. "You can just leave it here and walk everywhere you need to go."

"No need for that, I have a car now. Anyway, don't you have stuff you need to be retrieving?"

Franklin runs from the garage the same way he ran from the imaginary wasp. He's deceptively fast for his size. Now he wants me to get to know this car better but I know all about this car. It is the same car that Bridgette wanted for her sixteenth birthday, 1970 Chevrolet Chevelle. She talked non-stop about this particular car. She talked about how it was the beginning of "fast". I remember when my momma and pops asked her to choose an alternative, just in case they couldn't find the one she wanted. She told them that she would wait until they can find one. Bridgette was picky about what she wanted. She didn't ask for much but she always knew exactly what she wanted. Out of all the cars in the world, why did he have to give this one to me. Life really isn't fair. As I make my way to the front of the house, I notice Franklin sitting on the porch steps. He sits there with his hands positioned against his ears, while his head points downward.

"Sorry I took so long, I was caught up for a moment. If you are ready, we can go take this baby for a spin now."

Franklin doesn't say a word. He just sits there with his head dangling down. A strong honk of the horn still isn't enough to bring him back from his daydream. The smell of rain carried by the wind grows stronger as the wind picks up speed pushing dark clouds slowly in our direction. I keep the car running while I cautiously approach Franklin. If he is up to something, I will be ready for him but still with me standing beside him, Franklin doesn't move. I have never seen Franklin like this. Just a few minutes ago, he had enough energy to power the entire state of Texas.

"What's wrong with you, Franklin? I thought you was excited to take a spin."

"It was hard Brody. It was really hard," he says somberly. "I felt helpless and scared the whole time. What made it worst was the fact that the grown-ups weren't telling the kids much of nothing. All I gathered was that you were fighting for your life in an I.C.U. unit. I didn't even know what I.C.U. meant at the time. I overheard your mom telling Big Mama and Paw-Paw that Bridgette was missing also. Aunt Glo stated that she was waiting for you all to return from the store, when an overwhelming sense of pain ran down from her head along her spinal cord. She then checked the time and noticed that you all had been gone for nearly an hour and a half. She said she sensed that something was wrong. So, she began running down the street on the same route that you all would have taken. When she arrived at the top of the old hill, she was out of breath. She saw you lying motionless beside the old creek and Bridgette was nowhere to be found. A large search party was formed to find her. I remember being out of school for nearly a month. The entire community searched day and night for Bridgette. We searched every square inch of the county and still we found nothing. All the known child predators in the area, were questioned and their homes were searched. The Detectives on the case did determine that you were hit intentionally, due to no evasive tire marks left after the accident. They determined that the driver did not try to avoid you or decrease their car speed. Every day we would search for Bridgette, then we would visit you at the hospital. Before going home, we would have a prayer for both of you. After a month, the searches were called off and people began to point fingers. Things grew worse at that point. Without any evidence or suspects, the lead Detective named Uncle Malcolm their prime suspect. Their theory was that Bridgette must have known her kidnapper, due to no signs of struggle. They took Uncle Malcolm into custody and one week later you were moved to a hospital in Houston because you needed special medical attention. After that, Aunt Glo lost her mind and I can't blame her either. Everyone that she loved was taken away from her in a matter of one months' time. A few years back, I got the chance to read her report, it states that she began chanting in a broken creole language and she would constantly look for a Gris-Gris. She was diagnosed with catatonic depression. It was rough for everyone with the added stress of Uncle

Malcolm's awaiting trial. His was on trial for the kidnapping and attempted murder of his own children. For a while it looked as if he would lose his case but you awoke right in time. By awaking from your coma, you helped the family breath for the first time in six months."

Once again Franklin grows silent. I sit beside him and join him in staring off into the distance. We could have sat there all night but my concentration broke when water began hitting my head. A light drizzle has begun. I didn't even notice when the sky turned dark. I stand up and proceed towards the front door of the house.

"Where are you going?" Asks Franklin.

"I'm go get the things that we need."

"There is no need," he replies. "I found the camera and here is the rolodex. I also found some undeveloped film in your backpack. If you don't mind, I will get them developed along with the pictures from the party."

"That's fine. But looking at this weather, I will have to give you a raincheck on taking that spin we talked about."

"It's Okay Brody," he says. I have a lot of work to do. Besides, I'll just come borrow it when I need an undercover vehicle."

"The hell you will."

"Don't be like that Brody," he replies. "Here man, you can't be on the road without having a cell phone on you. If you haven't noticed, there aren't any phone booths anymore. This is my spare phone, you can use it as long as you need or until you get your own. I've set the GPS so you can get to the Big House with trouble."

"Thanks Franklin, be safe."

"I always am," he responds as he enters his vehicle.

I follow close behind him as we drive away from my childhood home. The down pour of rain makes it nearly impossible to see. Thankfully, everyone is driving safely below the speed limit with their hazard lights flashing. Except for Franklin who speeds away like it is a sunny day. An occasional truck or 18-wheeler comes speeding by without a care for other motorists or the current road hazards. I decide to pull over into a small gas station to wait out the storm. There is no time like the present to handle business. I reach into the passenger seat and grab the rolodex. The very first card is for Lady Catherine De'LaReaux, my grandmother. I only met her a handful of times because she lives in New Orleans. I looked at the 504 number. Should I call? No, I shouldn't bother her but she may have answers. I better call but I've never been big on telephone conversations and I really don't know much about her. With the card in my left hand and the phone in my right hand, I'm caught in a mental battle of to call or not to call. Something is telling me that I need to call her, especially since she is the only one who can tell me what's going on with my mother right now.

Anxiety starts to build as I dial her number. The phone rings and on the second ring I hear a flat but luring voice.

"I've been waiting for you to call me Ti Garcon (*baby boy*)," she says. "It took you long enough to call your Granme (*Grand Mother*). You've been home for two days now Ti Garcon and you never called. I want you to visit your Manman (*mother*) on tomorrow. Now, tomorrow morning at 9 am, I will meet you at St. Joseph's Ivory Tower. I will text you the address. Don't be late! Mwen renmen ou, Ti Garcon (*I love you, baby boy*). Now relax your nerves. We can catch up tomorrow. Da time grows near and I must prepare for my journey. I suggest dat you do da same."

I hear the click of the phone and just like that she is gone. Just as I put the phone down, the rain eases up. It slacks just enough for me to continue my journey. I start to think about the phone conversation that we just had or should I say the conversation that my Granme just had with me. I really didn't get to say one word. How did she know it was me calling? How did she know I had been home for two days? How did she know I was coming home? I guess I'll have to wait until tomorrow to get my answers.

Big Mama and Paw-Paw sits in the living room conversing as I enter the house. Each time I see them, they have that same look in their eyes. It's the look that you get from people who genuinely love you. It's a warmth you feel in their gaze.

"Is Franklin coming in?" Asks Big Mama?

"No ma'am. I went visit my pops, today and he gave me car. That's how I got back home. Franklin had some work to get to. He left from the old house. Since I have wheels now, I plan on going to visit my momma tomorrow. I talked to Granme and I'll be heading that way in the morning. Do either of you know how long it will take to get to St. Joseph's Ivory Tower from here?"

"I'm sure glad that you went to visit Malcom today," says Paw-Paw. "I saw that car he had covered up in that garage and it's a work of beauty."

"Anytime you want to take it for a ride Paw-Paw, you just let me know."

"Don't tell him nothing like that Brody. Manc is a speed demon and he will be in the wind faster than gas. We went to St. Joseph's Ivory Tower a few months ago. First, we met with Lady De'LaReaux in Lafayette for lunch. I know she's your grandmother but you watch yourself around those people. There is something strange about them. But anyway, it took us about three and a half hours to make it to Lafayette and another hour from there to make it to St. Joseph. He had my butt chewing on that passenger seat the entire time he was driving. I took so many chomps out of it, I'm shocked that there's any cushion left."

Paw-Paw doesn't reply to her remarks nor does he make any facial expression. He once told me in order to be happy in this world, you need someone to take the journey through life with you. Once you find that someone, remember that she is always right. A happy wife means a happy life. But he also explained that she had to be the right women. You can buy a woman anything in the world but you'll never be happy if she isn't right for you. Big Mama begins watching television and Paw-Paw's gaze makes it my way. He gives me a slight wink then he returns to watching his television show.

"Brody it's close to election time so be careful on the highway and please remember to always drive the speed limit," she says. "Law enforcement tends to strictly enforce the rules around this time of the year. It seems that they look for any situation or anyone to make an example of. Please don't give them a reason to stop you. With all that's happening, everyone is on the edge right now. But if someone does stop you, please call Franklin immediately.

"Franklin doesn't like use talking about this but a few years back I read an article stating that white supremacy groups have infiltrated law enforcement on the local and state level," says Paw-Paw."

"That's nothing new," adds Big Mama. "It's part of this countries legacy. Look at how one of the most notorious terrorist organization in world history, the Klu Klux Klan, is not label a terrorist organization. When I was growing up the KKK was led by police chiefs and sheriffs. That's why officers who kill unarmed black people will always walk free because they are doing what they were hired for."

"It's sad but it's true," says Paw-Paw.

"The laws of this land aren't for every citizen of this land," says Big Mama. "So please drive safely. Now, there are leftovers in the fridge if you're hungry. Also, would you like for me to make breakfast for you in the morning before you leave?"

"Thanks for the advice Big Mama. I'll remember to drive carefully. Don't worry about getting up to cook breakfast, I'll just grab something on the road."

CHAPTER 8 – ST. JOSEPH IVORY TOWER

Hardly anyone is on the road at four hundred hours. Still, I follow the posted speed limits. There is no need to get myself in any unwanted situation, especially traveling by myself and going thought small country towns. Drinking a cup of coffee, forces me to take a pit stop. Thankfully I made it to Beaumont without incident. It's time to relieve myself plus the break is much needed because I slept awful last night. I tossed and turned, never finding that comfortable position that would ensure a good night's rest. When I finally feel to sleep, the nightmares started again. Upon returning for the restroom, I stretch one last time before getting into the car. I'm glad that I am getting onto I-10 East because I've noticed increased school bus activity. Kids will start going to their bus stop soon and the buses will create early morning traffic. I'd rather not get caught in school traffic.

After three and a half hours of travel, a south turn onto Highway 90 is well needed. The sun rose an hour ago and it has been shining directly into my face. Some shades would have been clutch but unfortunately, I have none. My turn leads me directly into morning traffic. I didn't plan this trip to well. I sit bumper to bumper, catching every traffic light on the Evangeline thruway. I sit and wonder, why isn't there a loop that goes around the city of Lafayette? There is one in every other major city on Interstate 10, between Houston and New Orleans?

111

I guess it would only be for the cities use, since I-10 flows smoothly here, unlike everywhere else. Traffic eases just outside of the city limit when I exit Broussard. For the remainder of my drive, both sides of the highway consist of sugar cane fields. I follow a sugar cane truck into Saint Joseph. My nose is immediately attacked by an offensive smell. I notice the smell originates from the massive sugarcane mill that the truck turns into. I don't understand how something so sweet can come from a place that smells so horrendous but the smell diminishes the further I travel away from the sugar mill. Thankfully I bought a pack of chewing gum from the store in Beaumont because that smell left a foul taste in my mouth. Past the sugar mill, the community of Saint Joseph seems to be a quiet community. Even though the children are at school, I don't see anyone loitering around. I make a right turn onto Ivory Road which brings me to a bridge. The old bridge carries me over the Bayou Tech where humongous Live Oak trees flank the road. The Live Oaks reach limitlessly into the sky. The limbs of the trees intertwine high above the road. An exquisite display of Spanish moss drapes from the intertwining live oaks. The display makes it nearly impossible to see the sky. The Spanish moss compliments the Live Oak trees, giving them an ancient mystique. Not only is this sight astonishingly beautiful but it also possesses a spine chilling aura which makes the road appear endless. Every so often, the sun breaks through the trees; only to steal my focus and temporarily blind me. For a mile or so, I'm captivated by the beauty of nature. I escape from nature's hypnosis when a huge mansion appears on the horizon. As I approach the gates, I notice that St. Josephs Ivory Tower is a collection of massive mansions. A sign hangs from a call box stating, "Press button if guard is not available." Seeing no guard around, I press the button.

A light spoken voice comes through the speak box saying, "How can I help?"

"I am here to visit my mother. She is a patient of yours."

"Do you have an appointment sir?" Asks the voice.

"I'm honestly not sure. My Grandma, Lady De'LaReaux, instructed me to meet her here."

"Oh, Lady De'LaReaux," says the voice. "You must be Brody? I'll open the gate for you. Once you enter, go straight at the fork then turn into the first parking lot. Park on any row between the orange cones. Follow the path to the Atrium and I'll be waiting for you at the service desk."

The gate opens and I follow the path to the fork in the road. A sign that states, Maximum Security points to the left. Another sign points to the right stating front office. The sun barely peeks out of the now partly cloudy sky but the cool breeze helps to accelerate my walk to the Atrium. A short, plump red hair woman with rosy cheeks greets me as I enter the Atrium.

"We have been expecting you Mr. James."

She must've noticed the puzzled look on my face because she goes into a long apology about offending me and my grandmother. I just can't keep up with her because I am still trying to figure out why she was expecting me.

"I'm sorry Sir. I was expecting the grandson of Lady De'LaReaux," she says.

"Yes, I am Brody James. But may I ask why were you expecting me?"

"Well, Lady De'LaReaux called me about five days ago. It was an hour before my shift was over," she replies. "She asked me to add you to the visitation list for today. She also instructed me to get you acquainted to the facility before her arrival. So, let's get you signed in on this clip board. Please attach this security badge to your collar. You will wear it always during your visit. I also need you to sign this waiver. It states that we are not liable for any damages to you or your property while you are here at our facility but rest assure Mr. James, I've been here for 5 years and the staff has never lost control of any patient."

"Well Ma'am, I'll sign this waiver but know and understand that if I'm under attack, I will defend myself."

"That will not be necessary Mr. James," she replies. "A doctor and an Orderly will escort you the entire time you are in the facility. Here is your security badge. Now, I need you to have a seat and I'll go retrieve your mother's primary physician."

I watch as the red-haired woman disappears behind the security doors. I began to rock back and forth while thinking about someone striking me unprovoked. I continue to stare at the door that the red-haired woman exits through. While awaiting her arrival, I am suddenly startled when someone places their hand on my shoulder.

"Calm yourself, Ti Garcon," a voice says.

Slowly, I turn my head to the right to see a hand with black fingernail polish. On the ring finger, there is a large silver ring with a black stone in the middle. There is writing below the stone in a language that I don't understand. I look up to see an inviting smile outlined by black lipstick. Her eyes are intense, yet soft. They tell a tale of wisdom and knowing. Her long silvery dreadlocks flow neatly down her back. Her skin seems to be flawless, not being damaged by time nor nature. She stands there as pretty as the rising sun and as wise as an owl.

"Are you not happy to see your Granme," she asks?

She removes her hand from my shoulder then takes a step backwards. She lifts both of her arms and says, "Now, Come Ti Garcon and give dis ol lady, a great big hug."

Quickly, I rise to my feet, nearly tripping over in the process. Granme catches my face between her hands and softly kiss me beneath both eyes. I tightly embrace her, nearly getting my hands trapped in her multi-layered gown.

"Oh! It is so good to see you Ti Garcon," she says. "Dis is such a beautiful day for a reunion."

"Granme, a question has been bothering me. How did you know that I was coming home? The receptionist told me that you called on Friday to add me to today's list. Plus, Paw-Paw told me you instructed him when and where to pick me up from the airport"

"Da winds changed for you Ti Garcon," she replies. "I've been keeping close tabs on you since you were born. I gave you your first Gris-Gris on da day you graduated from high school."

"What's a Gris-Gris, Granme?"

"Stop interrupting Ti Garcon," she says. "Have a little patience. Your Gris-Gris was a talisman dat I made special for you. Unlike traditional Gris-Gris, yours was only a neckless and a pendant, instead of a pouch. When they are done right, a Gris-Gris will protect da wearer from harm. You used your Gris-Gris somewhere in the mother land. It protected you from harm dat day. After dat it was inevitable dat you would return home. Da spirits never lie Ti Garcon."

"What spirits and what do you mean it protected me from harm?"

"Now dat is enough of your questions," she says. "Dat brain of yours cannot begin to understand all dat is and all dat will be. My Gloria still haven't accepted her faith. One day when you are ready, I will try to explain your south Louisiana and African heritage. But for now, stop asking so many questions. Let your Granme enjoy

116

you. It's been so long since I last saw you and you've grown to be such a handsome man. You're strong too, I can tell both mentally and physically. You will need to be, Ti Garcon. If you don't want to end up in a place like this."

"It must run in our bloodline because you are beautiful Granme."

"Yes, it does Ti Garcon," she replies. "Black does not crack."

The security doors swing open and out walk the red-haired woman, a guy in black scrubs, and a clean cut, medium build doctor. The doctor stands average height. He wears eye glasses, along with green scrubs, and a white lab coat.

"Dat is Dr. Delasbour," says Granme. "He has been taking exceptional care of my Gloria."

"Good Morning Mr. James," says Dr. Delasbour. "And Lady De'LaReaux, it's always a pleasure to be in your company. I hope that your travels were pleasant."

"Thank You Dr. Delasbour," says Granme. "My travel was pleasurable."

"Now Mr. James, the receptionist here states that you have safety concerns," says Dr. Delasbour. "You have no need to worry. The patients inside of this building are nonviolent offenders. Some are here, so others will not harm them; unlike the patients in Maximum Security. My ordeal Gilbo and I will personal accompany you. Also, we have trained staff members stationed throughout the facility. There will be a quick response to any situation if someone is having an unpleasant day. You are in good hands Mr. James. Do you have any questions or concerns?

"No, Doc. You have covered my only concern."

"Well you all can follow me," he says.

Dr. Delasbour swipes his security badge which causes the double doors to open. The initial hallway we enter is short and dimly lit. Four doors align the hallway on each side. I notice the doors on the left side of the hall are offices. The first two doors on the right connects to the same room. Through the window of the door, various people can be seen sitting, talking, and eating. Vending machines align the walls. Tables and chairs are stationed in the middle of the room. The next two doors are both restrooms. Beyond the last door, we make a right turn which lead to another set of double doors. Dr. Delasbour swipes his security badge, which allows use to gain access to the next area. Inside the next room patients roam freely but under supervision. The furniture inside of this room is very elegant. Every bit of decoration from wall painting to potted plants are lavish. We take a few steps into this open area and suddenly a man in a wheel chair yells "charge." He wheels himself directly into the side of Dr. Delasbour leg. The impact is tremendous. The doctor falls over the wheelchair, his legs fly into the air before he falls onto the floor. Dr. Delasbour pushes the wheelchair away from his legs before clutching at his knee. He mumbles something underneath his breath that is inaudible. He then looks the man in the wheelchair in the face for a moment before Gilbo helps him to his feet. Dr. Delasbour begins to ask, "Why did you," but is interrupted by the man in the wheelchair repeating, "I didn't do nothing, I didn't do nothing." Dr. Delasbour continues his attempt to get his words out but the more he speaks the louder the man in the wheelchair gets. The doctor tries his best to compose himself but his disappointment is clearly visible on his face.

"Attention," barks Dr. Delasbour. "Sergeant Broussard, you are to report to your barracks. Now!"

His voice is so stern that I find myself straightening up my back and poking out my chest. I catch myself when my hand begins to rise for a salute. Sergeant Broussard looks around the room for a moment with a puzzled expression. He then closes his eyes, leans to the right, and falls soundly to sleep. Dr. Delasbour attempts to wake Sergeant Broussard without any success. Even though Dr. Delasbour and Sergeant Broussard creates a scene, no one else in the room seems to notice or even care. Many patients carry a blank expression on their face, while the rest are either playing with their clothing or talking to themselves. An uneasiness starts to make the hair on my arms rise. This place is neither cozy nor is it warm. Unlike First Step Rehabilitation Center, this

119

is not a place that one would visit frequently or voluntarily.

"Do you mind if we take a brief detour?" Asks Dr. Delasbour. "I need to escort Sergeant Broussard to his room. It will not take us much longer but we will take a detour through the isolation ward."

"Will we have to wear special equipment to detour through the isolation ward?"

"Not at all Mr. James. All the patients who reside on the isolation ward are not permitted to leave their rooms. That is where Sergeant Broussard here will be spending the next few days," replies Dr. Delasbour.

"Well lead the way."

Dr. Delasbour wheels Sergeant Broussard through the open room towards a hallway. The doctor is now walking with a noticeable limp but he tries to hide it by using the wheelchair as a walker. Looking at this long walk, it will only be matter of time before the doctor will need a wheelchair of his own. On this hallway, the facility grounds can be seen through a few windows. I am surprised to see people walking, exercising, and playing sports.

"Excuse me Dr. Delasbour. Are those people patients or employees?"

The doctor stops and with assistance from Gilbo, he gazes out of the window.

"Oh yes, they are indeed patients," he replies. "Here at St. Josephs Ivory Tower we try to motivate our patients to exercise daily. We encourage our patients to help us, help keep them fit. Out there are only a few of the daily activities we use to promote healthy living. Let's continue on and you will see some of the other activities that our patients participate in."

If I was stuck here, I wouldn't want to be inside of this eerie building either. Seeing those people outside only has intensified the jailhouse feeling of this place. Even though they are playing and walking freely, guards continue to monitor their every move. Not to mention, the perimeter of the grounds is fenced by barbed wire fencing. This place is exactly like a jailhouse but with a twist. The more we walk through the facility the more blank expressions we encounter on the faces of the patients. Even the staff have unhappy looks on their faces, similar to looks of dread. I don't know how the staff finds the strength to come here and work. The aura of this place feels of impending doom. I get a sense that most of the people here, will be here for the remainder of their lives.

I peek my head through a door because the sound that is coming from the room is familiar. Inside, people are seated throughout the room for a game of bingo. Unfortunately, no one in the entire room seems to have energy. They have no interest in the game. In a few minutes, everyone in there will be sleeping. A sign on the hallway reads isolation ahead and library to the left. I peek inside the library. The lights are dim and all is quiet. A little lady with silver curls look up with crystal blue eyes. She immediately closes her book and begins to stare at me. She then lifts her tiny fists in the air and shakes them threateningly, while snarling madly. I guess some people take offense to being disturbed while they read.

To enter the isolation ward Dr. Delasbour once again swipes his badge but this time he also must enter a security code. The doors open slowly and different sounds engulf my ears. The sounds of people banging on things and screaming are the loudest. With my head on a swivel I attempt to observe each occupant behind each of the closed doors. The doors have a long narrow glass window, which seems to allow the staff a viewpoint of the patient without having to enter their rooms. The rooms are padded but the patients are not in strait-jackets or any other type of restraint. They are free to roam their rooms. We follow the Doctor halfway down the hallway where he stops everyone to place Sergeant Broussard into his newly assigned room. Across the hall, I peek into another room. The sickening sight inside of the room causes me to haunch. As I gag and dry-heave, the others walk over to see what caused my sudden condition. Everyone quickly turns back, appalled at the sight.

The patient inside of this particular room is very alert, unlike the patients inside of the previous rooms that I have peek into. This patient stands with his legs spread shoulder width. He's hunched over, starring through the window on his door. His green eyes are intensely looking at everyone that pass in front of his door, while he slowly and deliberately masturbates.

No one says a word as another orderly rush over.

"Is everything Okay?" He asks. "What's wrong? Did something happen?"

Suddenly Sergeant Broussard comes to life. He whips his head around towards the Orderly direction.

He says, "He's chocking the chicken, he's bashing the bishop, he's massaging the helmet, he's shining the knob, he's adjusting the antenna, he's gripping the pencil, he's charming the cobra, he's draining the dragon, he's doing handiwork, he's firing the loooove rifle."

Another orderly rush over to Dr. Delasbour and hands him a needle. The doctor quickly gives Sergeant Broussard a shot. The effects of the medicine work rather quickly as Sergeant Broussard begins to fall back to sleep. As they roll him into his room, his final words echo throughout the hallway, "he's wanking it, wanking it, wanking it, wanking it."

"Sorry about that," says Dr. Delasbour. "We can't control how the patients express their free will. We have delivered Sergeant Broussard to his room. Shall we keep moving?"

With a bitter taste in my mouth, I follow closely behind Granme. To prevent myself from peeking into another room, I begin counting the squares on the floor as we walk. At square twelve, we pause for a moment before exiting the isolation ward. At the fourteenth square, we make a left turn. Then we make a right turn at square twenty-two. Finally, at square thirty-four everyone's feet stop moving. They all turn in my direction.

"Mr. James, I will let you enter the room first," says Dr. Delasbour. "Lady De'LaReaux and I have some matters to discuss."

Hesitantly my eyes slowly turn upwards. What will I find on the other side of this window? I promise that I have learned my lesson from the last window I peeked into. Cautiously, I turn to glance into this room. To my surprise, unlike the previous rooms, this room does not have padded walls. Instead, a light blue color engulfs the walls. It gives this room a homely feel. This room's occupant sits staring out of the lone window but the high-backed rocking chair sits motionless. Outside of the window, bars obstruct the view. I haven't seen her in years, ten years so I'm told. Slowly, I reach down for the doorknob. An unexpected surge of static electricity zaps me. This place does not like me. I rub my hand on my pant leg. Cautiously this time, using my pointer finger I tap the doorknob. I embrace for another jolt. Not feeling any electric shock, I over aggressively burst through the door.

"I'm sorry for my sudden intrusion. That was both reckless and embarrassing."

There is no response. She doesn't move a muscle nor does she have any kind of reaction to my sudden intrusion. The wall here are full of pictures. They are pictures of myself, mom and pops. I notice not a single picture has Bridgette in it. A mound of greeting cards and letters remain untouched on a table, close to the rocking chair. Another chair is positioned on the other side of the table, creating a small sitting area. I navigate through the room to position myself directly in front of the rocking chair. With the window to my back, I am now the new focal point. Instead, her gaze stays fixed in the same position. She does not shift her gaze towards me. Her stare feels empty. She wasn't looking outside of the window, rather she is somewhere else altogether.

"Hi mom! It sure is good to see you again. This is your baby boy Brody. Well I'm neither a baby nor a little boy anymore. You will like the man that I have become, I think. That's a story for another time but I like your room. It's much better than the one you had in Houston. I didn't like that room, it felt like an old hospital room. Anyway, I love you, mom! I love you with all my heart. I've missed you so much. I like what you've done with your hair. I know how much you like your hair done right. At the other place, it was always matted and tangled. I didn't like that either, it used to make me furious. Now I'm happy because your hair is soft, natural, and beautiful. I can tell they take good care of you here but I can take care of you also. I miss you so much. We need you. No, I need you to come back to me. When you do come back to me, I want to take you around the world. I want to show you some of the natural beauties of this world, not the ones that are made by man but the ones that were created by nature. I want you to be happy again and traveling will help you to hit the reset button. I don't know what it will take but I must do something to help get you through this. I know we can't change the past but Franklin, the twins, and I are attempting to right the wrong that continues to plague our family."

A knock shifts my attention towards the door. Dr. Delasbour stands in the window tapping on his wrist watch. I nod my head and raise my thumb in acknowledgement.

"Well mom, I have to go but I promise that I will be back to visit you soon."

Instantly a sense of depression spreads from my chest outwards. Helplessly the only thing I can do is give her a kiss. I hope that it reaches her somehow. Holding her left hand in my right hand, I kiss her twice on both cheeks. Something moves in my peripheral. Before I can turn to see what moved, something soft lands on top of my right hand. I try moving but to my surprise I'm completely frozen in place. I struggle to free myself but still I cannot move. Attempt after attempt I fail. Ok, one more try, with all my might this time. Yes, I think I can move. Where am I? What's happening now? My vision! No! Suddenly, everything goes from blurry to black. This is just great, I can finally move but now I can't see a thing. From far up above a small light appears, it looks similar to a star on a clear night. Either I'm tripping or my mind is playing tricks on me but it looks like that light just grew bigger. Maybe I can get to the light. I hope I don't trip on something because the light seems so far away and I can't see the ground beneath my feet. At least I can feel that the ground is here. Suddenly the light intensifies and I'm blinded by the piercing light that engulfs everything. I close my eyes and cover them with my hands, using them to shade my eyes from the light, I peek ever so cautiously. To my relief, the light stops being offensive instead, the light shifts into the shape of a square. I must be tripping again because it looks like that square is moving. No, I'm not tripping, it's moving fast and its coming my way. If I move to the right it shouldn't hit me. That can't be right. Did that square just change course? No, I'm tripping, I'll just move over to the left a couple times. That should do it. No! I'm not tripping it is adjusting course. This collision is inevitable. I have no other chose but to shield my face. This will hurt a lot but nothing happens. I wait a second longer and still nothing happens. Cautiously I drop my hands. To my surprise a picture hovers before me. It's a picture of Bridgette. I remember she took that picture at school when she was in the sixth grade. Mom had that picture on an end table in our living room. Suddenly, the picture vanishes but at fast as that one disappears, another picture reappears. I miss looking at Bridgette's face. I miss following her around everywhere. Most older sisters see their younger brothers as a nuisance but not Bridgette. She loved having me around. I liked making her smile because her smile possessed an uncanny ability to put a smile on anyone's face, even if they weren't in the mood to smile. Something about her gave her a glow. A glow that I now see. In a blink of an eye, the picture vanishes. No other picture appears in the place of the last. Once again, I'm left in darkness. I find myself back in the middle of nothingness. In all directions, my eyes cannot see anything, not my hands nor my nose. How in the world will I get out of here?

"Brody! Brody!" a voice says.

"Is someone there? I can't see a thing."

Slowly, light appears from what seems to be a door opening. A shadowy figure stands in the doorway.

"Come quickly," the shadowy figure says.

I don't know why but I feel like I should listen to that person. I step towards the door but with my first step, the floor lights up beneath my foot. Inside of this square is the letter 'M'. What is this? Again, my name is called clearly through the door, but louder this time. I step forward again and this time the letter 'H' appears. I lift my foot that's standing on the first square and instantly the letter 'M' disappears. A loud click comes from the direction of the door. What was that? It sounded like a lock. I watch intently but nothing happens. Another click comes from the door but this time the light begins to decrease. More and more the light decreases. From through the door the shadowy figure says "Run! Its closing. You will be trapped in there forever. You don't have to tell me twice, well a fifth time. I sprint towards the light but I notice with each step a new letter appears.

128

The letters; R, P, E, O, L, U, E, G and E. This will be close. I hope I make it. I better make it. Head first I dive through the door. Unexpectedly, the light grows extremely bright. I try to close my eyes without success. It feels as if my eye lids are being forced open. The light reduces to a single stream shining solely in my right eye, then it moves to the next eye. It grows smaller as it moves back and forth.

"Oh, Thank the heavens. He's back with us," says Dr. Delasbour. "Mr. James, Mr. James, would you like a drink of water."

"No, I'm fine Doc."

"It's a good thing this chair was here to break your fall," he replies. "You don't seem to have a concussion, but you did give us quite a scare. Have this ever happened to you before?

Before I can answer that question, a pain begins radiating from underneath my arm. I look down in search of what is causing this sudden pain. Granme!? Ouch! She hasn't pinched me this hard since I was a kid. I look up at her and magically the pain vanishes.

"Has this happened before?" repeats Dr. Delasbour.

"Yes, every single night Doc. Every time I fall asleep? Sometimes twice a day depending on if I take a nap. My traumatic experience earlier must have fatigued me."

"It seems like your fine Mr. James. Well at least you have your sense of humor," says Dr. Delasbour. "But I do advise you to get a C.A.T. scan. As soon as possible."

There is no way that I can tell this doctor what I just experienced, not without looking like a psychic patient. I haven't traveled from Africa to Texas to Louisiana just to be locked up in the same institute as my mom.

"Are you fine Ti Garcon?" Asks Granme.

"I'm fine. I just need some fresh air."

"Well look at the time," says Gramne. "Dr. Delasbour would you be a dear and walk us out?"

"Yes Ma'am," he replies. "It'll be my pleasure Lady De'LaReaux."

Flanked by Dr. Delasbour and Granme, we walk through the Ivory Tower back to the Atrium. The entire walk back to the atrium they both pay close attention to my every movement. It felt like I didn't have any room for error. The thought of having to stay in this dreadful place is frightening enough. The warm light that the security doors let through once Dr. Delasbour swiped his badge is a welcomed relief. That walk felt like it took an eternity.

"Thank you Dr. Delasbour. I will call you soon to schedule another visit," says Granme. She leads me by force out of the Atrium into Saint Joseph's Ivory Towers parking lot.

"What did you see?" she asks. "I know a trance when I see one and dat definitely was a trance you were in. Now, tell me what you saw!"

"It was dark Granme and then extremely bright. I saw pictures of Bridgette, letters on the floor, and a door. There was a person standing in the door. That person helped me to escape by telling me to run before the door closed. I would've been trapped."

"I see," says Granme. "You experienced two different extremes."

"What does that mean? I don't understand anything that is happening."

"Well my Gloria has had dis effect on people for quite some time," she replies. "It hasn't happened again since she has been here at da Ivory Tower."

"So, this has happened before?"

"It started while your mother was in an institute in Houston," continues Granme. "A crocked doctor opened a small institute and promised us dat he knew how to help my Gloria. Once she was admitted he started giving her an experimental drug without permission from da family. We only found out because one of his staff didn't agree with his methods. She decided to tell us before someone was seriously injured. On many different occasions during dat time, Gloria put several people into a trance like state. It was never da doctors, da nurses, nor da other patients, it would always be someone dat was visiting her. I didn't know until Malcolm's parents brought it to my attention. So, we decided to move her here away from da city and dat wretched place."

"What happened to that doctor?"

"Dat is still a mystery," says Granme coldly. "His institute has since been closed."

"Do you know what it was he was giving her?"

"Not exactly but it really doesn't matter," replies Granme. "You see da woman of da De'LaReaux family are special. Your mother, your sister, and myself, all were born with a veil over our face but dat is a common occurrence for woman of our bloodline. It was only a matter of time before your mothers' abilities would surface. I think that drug only speed up the process. You see we come from a great line of woman who possess enormous spiritual energy. Some were referred to as psychics, while others were referred to as witches. In New Orleans, we are considered High Priestess. So, don't be too concerned with what just happened to you."

"What are you talking about, Granme? Have you been watching too much television?"

"I don't own one, Ti Garcon," she replies. "Just listen boy."

"Yes ma'am."

"You also were born with a veil covering your face," she continues. "Now that has never happened in our family before. Da males of our bloodline have never been affected by this gift. Throughout your life, until you left ten years ago, we closely monitored you to see if you would develop any abilities but you never did. I still don't know what it means for you just yet, but my Gloria trances have been proven to be truly significant. You will need to think it over and figure out what it means."

"Will she get better Granme?"

"All in due time," she replies. "Gloria is in a critical phase in her life. Since she was born, she has been running away from her heritage. So right now, she is stuck in limbo battling between who she is and who she wants to be. Once she accepts her true self she will be able to walk out of dat building."

"What happens if she never accepts herself?"

"Then we will be visiting her here or in a place just like dis one for a very long time," she says. "But her condition is not uncommon. When I was only five years old, my gifts came to me and nearly drove me insane. You see, I can see things dat most people believe is not real. I also can see past events and things that haven't happened yet. My abilities work on everyone but you Ti Garcon. I only see you, not your past nor your future.

133

Nothing is set in stone for you. I believe dat a special destiny awaits you. So, I will need you to tell me whenever something out of the ordinary happens to you."

"There is one thing Granme."

"What is it, ti garcon?" she asks.

When I came home, I thought that I was only away for a year. I soon found out that I had been gone for ten years but I can't remember anything within that period."

"Oh, dat is nothing, Ti Garcon," she replies. "When your Gris-Gris activated, it triggered one of its side effects, which is temporary memory loss. First your long-term memory will return to you and then your short-term memory will return. Da timeframe in which it will return depends on rest, stress, and meditation. Give it a little more time."

"How much time? Will you help me?"

"I say your memory will be fully restored in a few days," she says. "Well you be safe and tell Big Mama I say 'Hi'. I must be back in New Orleans for four, so time is of the essence. Here, take dis and keep it close to you always. Never open it or sneak a peek inside of it, I don't know where you get that noisiness from but please stop peeking in things. Dis will give you protection, just like the last one. Don't try to say anything, just think about all you have learned today. Oh, by the way; nice car. Mwen renmen ou, Ti Garcon."

A gentle breeze blows as she drives away. I stand there, left to ponder these new revelations. Well that explains why my mom was always in my face and why she never wanted to visit Louisiana. But what did Granme mean by a veil covering my face when I was born? What can't I remember from these missing years? Well it won't just pop into my head right now, so I better get far away from this beautifully, spooky place. Whatever comes with my memories and this veil stuff, I guess I'll just have to deal with it when it arises. As for now, back to east Texas. All this thinking has made me hungry, I guess I will stop in Lafayette on my way back so I can dine on some of their world class foods. My stomach is starting to growl at me. I better stop thinking about those pepper jack cheese stuffed boudin balls.

CHAPTER 9 – I'M NOT ARGUING

An assorted aroma from breakfast being prepared lingers into my room. My stomach reacts waking me from a sound sleep. Everyone around here wakes up before the sunrise. It has been that way as far back as I can remember. Besides, time waits for no one. That's one of Sting-Ray's favorite sayings. Sting-Ray is a man who is full of quotes. He's stern with a touch of unexpected humor. Slowly, I open my eyes. I find myself still tired from my turn around trip to South Louisiana. Laying on my back, I stretch my limbs. I don't have any plans for the day. I think I will just sleep in. Slowly, I close my eye lids. I move around to find that perfect spot. There it is, now this will be some good sleep. The night stand vibrates. Come on, I haven't set any alarms. I grab the phone and notice three missed calls from Franklin; plus, four text messages. The messages read:

"When you awake, meet me in Lufkin at the office."

"The photos have been developed."

"Are you up yet."

"I'm leaving now, don't forget breakfast."

Some rest would have been nice on today but knowing Franklin, he'll be busting down the door if I try to get any. Today will be boring looking through photos but I would do anything for Bridgette. I text: I'm up. I will head your way shortly. I stumble downstairs and as usual Big Mama's spread is a bountiful feast. I always wondered why she cooked so much food but it never fails; somehow all of it disappears every day.

"Good morning my boy," says Paw-Paw. "Come sit with this old man before I go on my morning walk."

"You're not old Paw-Paw. Maybe by age but you are in better condition than most men your age and much younger."

"I would not be healthy, if I didn't learn how to eat your Big Mama's cooking," he replies. "I remember when you were small, you would try to eat up everything, then you would go back for seconds. I thought you would grow big as a house. Well, you have grown big but not wide."

"That's true Paw-Paw but I am more like you now. I also learned how to eat. Now I eat to live life, instead of living life to eat food. I found out that I was using food to give me brief happiness. The first year I was gone, the scholars taught me that I didn't know who I was and I didn't even like who I thought I was. Before they taught me anything, I first had to discover myself. Once my self-discovery was over I didn't eat as much anymore. I was no longer in denial."

"I'm proud of you my boy. You have been taught well," he says. "The hardest thing for most people is to evaluate themselves. Would you like some coffee and a bagel?"

"What's up with this bagel Paw-paw?"

Paw-Paw looks over his shoulder then replies, "Your Big Mama makes me try different things. She says I need to at least try things once, just to know whether I truly like it or not. I think she got tired of me saying that I don't eat foods that I have never tried."

"That's interesting because I now eat some foods that I hated when I was younger."

"We all evolve in some way or another my boy," he replies. "For example, like what you all are doing by going after that kidnapper. Personally, I think that crazy fool has been busy kidnapping many people. I watch the news, read the newspaper, and surf the internet and there are too many people turning up missing."

"And that's just what we hear about."

"Yeah, your right my boy," he says. "People don't like to talk about their misfortunes like back in the day. I think they get ashamed and afraid. Plus, no one wants to do anything about it. The Politicians talk a good game during election times but after that's over we don't see any results during their entire term. We need more young people like you all to stand up for what is right and to fight for the many injustices that plagues the common folk."

"Good Morning Brody. I see he is talking your head off already," says Big Mama jokingly. "I hear about it all the time, but I do agree with what he says most of the time. I just don't like talking about political issues. It's a fact that the two topics that can get you killed are religion and politics."

"That is true my boy," Paw-Paw adds.

"But on to more important matters," says Big Mama in a serious tone. "I know you all will try to do your best but I need you all to keep each other safe above all else. Remember when you swim in dangerous waters, the true predators strike unexpectedly. Now, I know that you all are head strong."

"More like stubborn," adds Paw-Paw. "And they get it from you."

"Hush you ol fool," replies Big Mama. "Anyway, all I am trying to say is, watch each other's backs."

"Yes ma'am, we will be careful. This is some pretty good coffee."

"Yes, my boy! I got a modern coffee machine for Father's Day," replies Paw-Paw. "I've been upgraded to making gourmet coffee now. I was buying the popular brands at first but now I experiment with different beans and creamers. Who knows what I like better than me?"

"That would be me," says Big Mama.

"Well I can't argue with that," laughs Paw-Paw. "The coffee we are drinking now, is the very first one I ever created. I made it this morning just for you to taste."

"Enough with all of that, Manc. You are procrastinating," says Big Mama. "It is time for our morning walk. Oh Brody! In that bag on the counter is enough breakfast for you four. Franklin told me that you all would be starting early this morning. He came by last night. He tried to wake you up but a massive earthquake wouldn't have awakened you. You were tired, baby. Well we are off. Make sure you lock up."

"Be safe on your walk."

"Don't worry my boy," says Paw-Paw. "I have three hundred and fifty-seven reasons why no one will bother us."

Well there isn't no reason for me to procrastinate. Quickly I grab the food and lock the Big House. I sip on my cup of coffee as I travel to Franklin's office. As soon as Franklin's office becomes visible, so does Franklin. I notice him standing in his parking lot looking towards the main road. He starts waving his arms like crazy when he spots me. I bet he started his career as a traffic cop. He waves his hands until I park where he is pointing. Before I can turn off the engine, Franklin opens the car door.

"Man, I heard you coming," says Franklin. "You must have been at least two blocks away. I came by the big house last night so we could get a jump on the photos but you were sleeping like a baby. I started to put some cayenne pepper on your lips like we did you when we were younger. You're lucky Big Mama stopped me in the kitchen."

I clinch my teeth just thinking about how horrible it is to be awoken in that manner.

"Oh yeah, Franklin. Well I'm glad you didn't because there isn't anyone around that would have stopped my war path."

"Yeah, yeah, yeah," repeats Franklin. "You're lucky I grew up while you were gone. I'm not into childish pranks anymore. Anyway, how was your first trip on the highway in this baby?"

"Man, she ran like a thoroughbred, one who's primed and ready for a derby. During one stretch I was the fastest car on the road. If anyone would pass me by, they would soon find themselves in my rear-view mirror, in less than four seconds. But I wasn't breaking any speed limits Detective. I was driving within the posted speed limits, even when they didn't make any sense."

"Whatever Brody," he replies. "What's in the bag? I know Big Mama sent breakfast, so pass it here. I haven't eaten since I left the big house yesterday evening. I've been waiting for this all morning. Did Paw-Paw send any coffee? Man, he makes the best coffee. I tell him all the time that we should open him his own coffee shop. I told him to name it 'Pot of Black Gold'. He made me into a believer. I didn't even drink coffee before he stared making his own."

"Too bad for you. He sure didn't send any coffee. Fortunately for me, I had the chance to sit down and relax to a cup of his delicious coffee. You should've been there, I finished the rest of it just before I got here."

"That's sad," he replies. "You didn't even think about your boy."

"Awe, Franklin don't be sour. You should have asked him to send you some. You did ask for the food, right?"

"Already, you're right," he agrees. Let's hurry up and get inside. The twins should be here shortly. We need to eat breakfast before their hungry butts arrive and eat up everything. Food isn't safe before those girls get their fill."

"Those are some strong words behind their backs, Franklin! I bet you aren't man enough to say that again when they get here. You know, I would love to stand by to see the outcome of that match. Oh, I will have to record that. You're sure to go viral. I think I will inform them when they get here."

"I can't let you do that," says Franklin. "I'm going to have to arrest you for police endangerment."

"Your job keeps you in danger Detective. Oh, I forgot; all your good days are behind you now but you are good at pushing paper and pen. Keep up the good work."

"Stop playing," he says. "Those girls truly know how to hold a grudge. I can't afford to watch every step I take. Simple tasks like walking through a door would get very dangerous."

"Stop being a drama queen. That is not manly."

"I am serious Mr. Manly," he replies. "One Saturday at the Big House, we were all joking and relaxing. I may have had a little too much to drink. Man, I went in on Saundra. I had jokes for days. We all left that night and I thought everything was good. The following Saturday we were back on the front porch at the Big House. One second I was standing and joking. The next I was going through the railings. She sent me slamming into the ground. I looked up to see Saundra breathing heavily. She still was looking down at me with a scowl on her face. It felt like I had been hit by an all-pro linebacker. I bruised six ribs and nearly broke my right leg. I started to file assault charges on her."

"Well if you talk any louder, I won't have to tell them anything. All they will have to do is rewind the security footage and listen to the recording. I'm sure you have a top-notch security system."

Looking at Franklin run through the office avoiding obstacles, makes me feel sorry for anyone that is being chased by him. That would be more frightening than going on a safari and the jeep you're riding in breaks down, then your guide tells you that you all must walk back to the main building. Knowing that you just past a pack of lions and hyenas. That big man has moves.

Breathing heavily Franklin says, "Man Brody you're a life saver."

"Looks like you need to skip breakfast a few times Franklin."

"This is nothing," replies Franklin. "I already ran five miles this morning. I still can run another five if I need to. Don't let this smooth look fool you, I'm a beast. You're looking at one of Texas Elite."

"Well, go put the tape back Mr. Elite."

"How about you go to the table and take the food out," he replies. "I told you that I'm hungry. Now let's eat some of this good food."

After breakfast, we get straight to it. For nearly an hour Franklin and I look through photo after photo. We search for someone who seems out of place. Halfway through I switch to reading through the background checks. That job is much simpler for me. All that is required is to separate the people with criminal records from people without a record. I forgot the girls were going to join us, when their truck pulls into the parking lot. They break my concentration with their loud voices, they seem to be arguing over something. If I didn't personally know them, I would be rushing outdoors to try to stop the impending fight or to record it. People don't stop altercations anymore, they just stand there and record. I've never seen those girls fight each other before. I bet things got interesting in their house when they were growing up. The door swings open and Saundra walks through first. Her face is serious as she shakes her head from side to side with Shondra following close behind her. She is also serious. The walls of the office shakes as she slams the door.

"Tell this girl it is not good to forget your responsibilities," shouts Saundra. "It's never good to burn bridges."

"Well tell this girl that we also can't renege on promises either," responds Shondra.

"Hold on a second ladies. We don't have the slightest idea of what you are arguing about. If you want our opinion you will need to inform us on what's going on, then we can come to some sort of a solution."

"Okay Brody, then hear me out first," says Saundra. "Not long ago, I received a phone call from the District Attorney office in Houston and they have a delicate case that needs our help. Now take in mind that we have done small jobs for them before but nothing of this magnitude. We can't disappoint the people who support us."

"Okay Saundra, we heard your point of view. Now let's hear Shondra's side of the argument."

"I am not arguing," replies Shondra. "I'm just stating the facts. When we all were kids, we made a pact and I don't go back on my word for anyone. Besides that, I promised Franklin yesterday that we would help on the photos. Remember this is our case also. For us to be successful, everyone needs to participate completely. It's okay with me if we don't collect any cases until this case is closed. Besides, Franklin was the first one to throw us a bone anyway. He is the main person who supports us."

"I think we should all just work on this case," says Franklin. "We now have an eye witness and maybe some new evidence. The photos are developed. Plus, I have some hilarious photos of Brody trying to take a selfie with a camera. Way before selfies became cool. Just let someone else take care of that case. I promise, I will personally make sure that you to have more than enough cases to work on."

"That just will not work for me Franklin," interrupts Saundra. "The District Attorney's office did not reach out to anyone else except for us. They want someone they can trust to be professional and discrete. They need this wrapped up within twenty-four hours or less. Things would become a nightmare for us and the city of Houston if we backed out now. It will become impossible to get work anywhere, no matter who we know."

"Listen everyone, I must agree with Saundra. There is no way I can stand by and let all that you have worked for be thrown away. I can't let you disappoint a friend in need. We are a team of four, there is no reason why we can't split into two teams when the need arises. I can go with Saundra and you two can go through the new evidence. We need everyone's head to be clear and we can't afford to have anyone upset with us either. We don't know who we will need assistance from. I think I am fully capable of filling in for Shondra if there aren't any objections."

"Whatever," replies Shondra. "But these are some big shoes to fill."

"You weren't any help anyway," says Franklin. "Go make yourself useful and don't take all day."

"Come on Brody," says Saundra. "Let's get our gear. Time always moves forward and our window is shrinking by the second."

CHAPTER 10 – BIG WAYNE

"Thank you, Brody!" says Saundra.

"For what?"

"Thank you for backing me in there," she says. "Neither Shondra nor I, was smart enough to check with the other before obligating each other's services. Typically, we work as a cohesive unit."

"It was nothing Saundra. Before you two arrived, Franklin and I decided to get a jump start on things. As I look through those photos, I realized that I didn't know most of the people in the pictures, besides family. Before he suggested I read the background checks, Franklin had to explain to me how I should know the person on each photo I showed him. So, you really saved me today.

"Don't thank me just yet," she warns. "This guy who we are after is a true maniac. He is the kind of person who would try to mess up this nice car of yours. We should have taken my truck instead."

"Stop worrying so much. Let's concentrate on the mission at hand."

"Well don't blame me if your car gets messed up," she replies.

"Tell me about this suspect that you are so scared of. After you tell me where we are going?"

"Take Highway 69," she replies. "We are headed to Tyler, Texas. Our suspect name is Avery Wayne Simon. He is a Caucasian male. He goes by the name of Big Wayne. Our suspect is seven foot tall. He weights around two hundred and ninety pounds. He served in the United States army for two full tour of duties. He is a veteran of the Iraq War but he was dishonorably discharged at the beginning of his third tour. After being discharged, he utilized his connections and began trafficking drugs. Within six months, Big Wayne became one of the largest drug kingpins in the United States. He has one tattoo on his right arm that says Big Wayne."

"Kingpins normally don't go down. How was he captured?"

"His entire origination was taken down by our very own Detective Franklin James," she says. "Franklin went deep undercover for three years so he could infiltrate Big Wayne's organization. He became Big Wayne's right-hand man. Before the bust, we all thought that Franklin had turned to a life of crime. He didn't come around during that time nor could anyone get in contact with him. His office even told his parents that they could not share any details. They told them not to contact Franklin if they valued his life. We value his life but that wasn't good enough. With sheer persistence and great investigation skills, we gathered enough information to pinpoint Franklin's location. We tailed him one day but he noticed he was being tailed. We nearly got into a shootout with him but luckily, he was alone. That was a dark day, but the same night his field office called to spill the beans. We stayed away after that, everyone just prayed and waited. One Sunday evening there was breaking news, that news was that Big Wayne's organization had been taken down. There was no mention of Franklin but there was a lot of casualties on both sides. That left everyone scared and confused. We thought the worst, until Franklin walked into the Big House later that same day. You could have sworn that someone had just hit the lottery. Everyone was happy and Big Mama insisted that he 'spill the beans'. Franklin told us that for three years he had been deep undercover inside of Big Wayne's Crime Family. He entered as a bodyguard but was quickly promoted when he consistently proved that he was an asset. He gained Big Wayne's complete trust one day when he saved Big Wayne's life. Another crime family got real close to ending Big Wayne's life that day. They would have succeeded because Big Wayne was set-up by a close friend. Luckily for him, Franklin prevented that assassination and earned an untouchable status within his organization. Unfortunately, that started a deadly turf war for the city of Houston. A war which lasted nearly two years. Eventually, Franklin took down Big Wayne and his entire family. Not one surviving member is now part of society. With the evidence that Franklin acquired, none of them will ever get out of prison. Unfortunately for us, last night while Big Wayne was being transferred for his upcoming trial, he escaped.

When the guards were found, Big Wayne was nowhere around."

"Do you think Big Wayne knows that Franklin took him down? Could he now be after Franklin?"

"No, that would be hard to believe," she replies. "Big Wayne believes that Franklin is deceased. Franklin's character was killed during Big Wayne's arrest."

"Well what makes you certain that he is going to Tyler? If I was to escape, I would head across the border. Right now, I would be halfway drunk on Salty Dog's and Tequila shots."

"Me too," she agrees. "Once Franklin told me that Big Wayne took him to Tyler to meet his family. Big Wayne grew up in a wealthy household in South Tyler. He was a decent kid growing up. He played sports, he went to church, and he stayed out of trouble. He married his high school sweetheart right after graduation since they were expecting their first child. After high school, he decided to join the United States Army to provide for his family and to protect the country. He successfully built both a family and a career. With four children total, Big Wayne became the model father, citizen, husband, and soldier. That all changed the day his oldest daughter was in a bad car accident that nearly took her life. The result of her numerous surgeries left Big Wayne's family drained both financially and mentally. The only reason he re-enlisted for the third time was because he needed the money badly. To make extra money he began signing up for special missions. On his fourth mission, he was sent to South America. Their mission was to eliminate a notorious drug lord, who was responsible to forty-five percent of all drug trafficking into the United States. At a critical point during the mission Big Wayne was ordered to kill the drug lord's wife and children. Big Wayne told Franklin that at that moment the only thing he could think about was his wife and children. He could not obey those orders. Instead, he escorted them through the war zone and to safety. Another soldier saw what Big Wayne did and reported his actions to their superiors. Eventually after a lengthy investigation, Big Wayne was dishonorably discharged. After a year of struggling to find a job, one day Big Wayne was abducted while taking his morning jog. It turns out that the same drug lord who Big Wayne was sent to South America to execute now wanted to thank Big Wayne for saving the lives of his wife and children. The drug lord explained to Big Wayne that his wife is bi-lingual. She overheard his superior's give a direct order to execute them. The drug lord offered Big Wayne two options. The first option was five million dollars. The second option was to become his partner and control half of his empire, which included complete control of all operations within the United States. Even though five million dollars is a lot of money, Big Wayne choose the second option. He made one hundred and twenty-five million dollars in his first month of operation. Because of his new-found wealth and power Big Wayne's daughter made a full recovery. Big Wayne would take Franklin to Tyler to deliver large sums of money to his family. Franklin said that Big Wayne loved them more than life itself. So that's why we are going to Tyler. There is no way that Big Wayne will leave his family behind. Franklin said, no matter how many women would throw themselves onto Big Wayne he would not cheat on his wife. He truly loves that woman. Love like that is rare in this day in time."

"This Big Wayne actually sounds like a good person. Isn't he the type of man that every woman fantasizes about? I'm talking about a man who is a protector, who makes a lot of money, and who is faithful to his wife. Now how many categories did that check off on your list? Huh?"

"I have to admit," she replies. "Quite a few and all major categories too. I find that most men don't know what they want. They can't think pass what they want right now. For a man to be that committed is an extreme turn on. Unfortunately for them, most of those committed fools find themselves in relationships with the wrong woman, while the men that I date fear a strong woman. I'm talking about a woman who knows exactly what she wants. A woman who doesn't have time for nonsense and childish games. A woman who handles business. Now I'm not one of those women who says, I don't need a man because lord knows I do. He just has to be able to be enough for me."

"It might help if you tone it down just a little, you're bossy."

"What woman isn't," she shouts. "If you're weak, you're beat. I wasn't raised to do whatever a man orders me to. Some girls are raised that way but not me. I was raised to think freely and to get whatever I want. On my own! If I want or need anything, I will not ask anyone for it nor will I expect it to be handed to me. I will go buy it on my own. But you're right Brody, I wouldn't mind having my very own Big Wayne. Minus the life of crime of course. Wanting a bad boy is foolish for any woman. Women who think like that put their men in a corner. They find themselves forced to live that life especially since there aren't many opportunities out there for him. I want someone to grow old with. I want that special love. When he walks into the room and looks at me, in his mind I'm the only woman who matters."

"Good luck finding that. Your special someone is out there but you have to be patient, open-minded, and not so judgmental. Never change yourself or try to change someone else. When the time is right, you shouldn't have too much of a problem."

"I have my eyes open but I'm not looking," she says. "Pull into the next gas station. Let's prepare ourselves for a long stake out. We must make sure we check all our gear and use the restroom. We don't have far to go and this might be the last toilet we see all day. This could also become a long day. Do we have everything Brody?"

A nod of approval satisfies her curiosity. I believe we have everything. I grabbed everything she told me to grab. How am I supposed to know? I've never worked with her before. I'm still in awe that I'm on a mission with Saundra and we are hunting a giant. Even though our target is seven-foot-tall, Saundra still has this look of determination and confidence. The only thing that seems to matter to her is the success of this mission.

"Saundra, do you think Franklin knows that Big Wayne has escaped?"

"He surely does not. If he did, he would be after Big Wayne instead of us," she replies. "He would have felt obligated. Big Wayne was a stressful period in his life. I didn't want him to relive it all over again. If I would have declined this mission, it would have been all over the morning news. Franklin seeing that would have derailed our current plans. Any more questions?"

"No ma'am please continue."

"As for our plan, we will have to adapt to whatever is presented to us. First thing we will do is drive past Big Wayne's house. We will try to identify the suspect. If we can't identify him, we will question neighbors to see if anyone has seen him. We will keep in constant contact with these headsets. If we separate for any reason we can still talk to each other. You have not seen Big Wayne before so don't move until I have confirmed his identity."

"How may seven foot guys are you expecting to be there? I'm sure he will stand out."

Disregarding my statement Saundra continues, "If you can confirm that it is him, just inform me first before you move in. I will not be like those bounty hunters that have harmed innocent people because they identified the wrong person. You will only move on my cue. Big

Wayne is known to be violent and I'd expect him to be extremely territorial with his family around. We have to make sure that no innocent bystanders are harmed in the process."

"What's our evacuation plan?"

"Once we have Big Wayne we will transport him to my office. That's where the Assistant District Attorney will meet us. She will transport him back to Houston," she replies.

"I don't like that plan. There are too many moving parts to it. Plus, it will put Big Wayne too close to Franklin. I suggest that we take him all the way to Houston, that way we know he made it to his destination."

"Well I didn't want to burden you any further than I already have," she says. "It was very kind of you to accompany me in the first place. Thank You Brody."

"Don't sweat it but where are we headed now? I also need to look at that map of the area. I want to get familiar with the roads, just in case we need to make a quick escape."

"Well while you are studying that map, I will touch bases with Houston to see if I need to inform Tyler Police Department of our actions," she says.

I might need to find a way to calm Saundra. She has told me that Big Wayne can be a violent man but still she is willing to rush right in, without making any workable plan. Rushing in with our emotions is a sure way to a quick defeat. No matter what situation arises, it is my job to protect her; even if she doesn't think she needs protection. Visibly disappointed by her conversation, Saundra throws her phone to the floor board.

"Well Brody," she says dryly. "It looks like we are on our own. Houston cannot provide backup because they have their own people searching for him in different places. Tyler Police Department has been informed but we are out of their jurisdiction. What makes things worse is that local sheriff and state troops are tied up with some big festivities. It will take hours before we get any back up."

"Do you normally call local enforcement for back-up?"

"No," she replies. "We call local law enforcement to notify them that we are working in their area. I don't know if we need back-up but it would be nice to know that someone is a phone call way."

"That's exactly why you were called Saundra. Their situation fits your private status. Even if you're a little more than an inch high, Ms. Private Eye."

"Don't get it twisted," she replies. "I wasn't looking for any help. I'm just making sure I am not stepping on anyone's feet."

"That's right, you must C.Y.O.B. in all situations."

158

"What's that?" she asks.

"Cover your own butt."

"Already," she agrees. "Now we have to find a way to locate Big Wayne and convince him that going back to Houston is his only option."

"I was thinking, maybe Big Wayne has accepted his faith. You told me how much he loves his wife and children. Maybe he just wants to see them one last time, as a free man. Plenty of people don't allow their children to see them behind bars, especially if they won't ever get out."

"I hope you are right," she replies. "That would make things much easier for us."

"It sure would. If that is the situation, what will you do if he is willing to cooperate but only if you allow him to see his children? You know, school won't be out for a while."

"If that is the case, then I will allow him to do so. I will just call and inform Houston of the situation," she says.

"Good, but what if?"

"That's enough Brody," she interrupts. "We need to get going. There are millions of 'what if' scenarios we can come up with. It is best that we easily adapt to whatever situation we are presented with. Now are you comfortable with that?"

"I'm just making sure you have more than just a plan 'A' or 'B'."

"Well let's go," she commands. "And I will not say it again."

"Yes a ma'am. I'mma take Ms. Saundra where ever she wanna go. I's a hopping on to it. Just point ol' Brody in the right direction."

"Stop it," she laughs. "You're killing me."

We leave the gas station still joking and laughing. Saundra has a good sense of humor but when it's time for business she gets serious. It is good to see a woman shatter the stereotypes that has been put on her. Whoever came up with the idea that women were inferior to men must also be responsible for slave trade and mass genocide. A left turn from Highway 155 takes us onto a private road. We travel for another two miles looking at professionally maintained landscaping. I reduce my speed to prevent alerting the residents of our arrival. With insistence from Saundra, I pull over off the road onto the grass.

"What's the plan?"

"I'm not sure," says Saundra. "Questioning neighbors has gone out the window since no one lives within five miles of this compound. We need to get a good look at how their security is set up. Let's get close to the gate without alerting security. Then we both can survey the property by walking around the fence in opposite directions. We will meet in the rear of the property to discuss what we saw. Use your headset if anything goes wrong. We don't want to go in until we have determined that Big Wayne is here. Once we have identified him, then we will approach the best way possible."

"Already, we should see things more clearly once we make that turn up ahead."

The turn opens to reveal a sixteen-foot-high stone fence. The fence runs along in both directions for at least a mile. One-foot-high spiked tipped iron rods rise from the top of the fence. Two huge wooden doors lay on the road in ruins. It looks as if someone uninvited drove through them in a hurry. One door is destroyed, except for pieces of wood that hang from the hinges. A larger portion of the other door hangs to its top hinge on the other side. Two security cameras at the gate are blown to pieces and the call box is also destroyed.

"Scratch that plan Brody," she says. "Let's get in there."

I hate when all plans go out of the window but we don't have any other choices. I press the brakes while giving the engine a large amount of gas. I release the brakes when smoke begins to rise from the tires. The force of our instant acceleration forces Saundra back into her seat. We clear the gate's debris without any damage to the tires or the car. This is not the ideal place to get a flat tire, if that place does exist.

"It looks like Big Wayne's family is living large."

"Yes, they are," agrees Saundra. "This place is nice. Look over there! That must be the truck that knocked down the gate."

"Looks like the gate destroyed its engine in return. Whoever it is made a straight line to that house. There is a trail leading through the grass."

"Let's hurry to that house," she says in earnest. "I have a bad feeling about this."

For the first time since we left, I now sense nervousness radiating from Saundra. She even has a wide-eyed look. Upon arriving at the Mansion, we notice that the front doors have also been destroyed. As planned, Saundra takes the lead. She jumps out of the car before I can take it out of gear. Quickly, she maneuvers to the far side of the door. She then motions for me to position myself opposite of her. Before we can proceed any further, a gunshot rings out from inside of the house. Without hesitation Saundra rushes through the door. I hurry behind her, covering the rear. Signs of a struggle are evident throughout the house. Carefully we move through broken glass and drywall, following a path of destruction. We pause for a moment at the staircase to listen for movement. A vase standing on top of a pedestal is still in one piece, implying to me that the struggle did not lead upstairs. Cautiously we walk briskly through a dining room and into the kitchen area. A faint sound becomes audible once we enter a hallway beyond the kitchen area. Slowly, we proceed toward a lone door at the end of this narrow hallway. The noise grows louder as we inch closer to the door. Saundra puts her hand in the air and she makes a fist. Slowly, Saundra opens the door without making a sound. With her gun drawn before her she proceeds to enter the room. A body greets us as we enter the room. The victim is resting in a pool of his own blood. A knife, screwdriver, and hammer lay on the floor not far from the victim. They all are stained with blood. I guess he died from multiple stab wounds to the chest and abdominal region. Suddenly, we hear the noise again, this time it is much clearer. We maneuver around the body and Saundra peeks around the wall. Without giving any further direction, she calmly walks out into the opening. I'm shocked to see the source of the noise we have been hearing. The source is this enormous man. He is kneeling on the ground and he's crying uncontrollably. We circle around the bed to get a clear view of Big Wayne. Saundra points towards Big Wayne. I'm unable to see what she is pointing at. I maneuver around her for a clear view. Laying at Big Wayne knees, is a woman. She is also lying in a pool of her own blood. I think that woman is his wife and she seems to be a victim of a gunshot wound to the face. The gun lays on the floor a few feet behind Big Wayne. Quickly, I kick it underneath the bed, while Saundra positions herself to apprehend the suspect.

"Big Wayne, I am Private Investigator Saundra James. I am here on behalf of Houston's District Attorney office. I am tasked with returning you to their custody. Please, come with us quietly," she says.

Saundra motions for me to stay where I stand. Patiently, we wait for a response from Big Wayne but he ignores Saundra and continues to kneel before his wife's body. He continues crying but he begins shaking violently. After a moment, the shaking stops. Big Wayne starts to hit himself with open hands to the head. Repeatedly he hits himself with extreme force. The impact of those blows would give a normal man a concussion or knock him out completely but he seems unfazed.

"Do you see what you made me do?" Asks Big Wayne. "Y'all ruined my life! All your lies and deceit has destroyed my family. She told me! She told me! She told me what y'all said. Y'all told her those lies. All lies. Y'all said that she would never see me again, but here I am. Live in living color. Y'all told her to move on with her life. To Move Past Me! Past Me! There is no past me! We made vows; that you convinced her to break! Do you remember our vows hunny? For better or for worse. We went through hell with Kelly's operations but she is now better. Do you remember, through richer or poor? We were dirt poor. We came from poverty. We were raised on welfare and food stamps. Your family was living in a rundown trailer but I took you from all of that. I joined the U.S. Army so we can have a better life. I fought war after war. Wars we shouldn't have been fighting. And for what? The government paid me pennies. But I endured and now look at all I've acquired.

164

You know me woman! You know me better than anyone. You know me. I was supposed to be your soulmate. Your Soulmate! THERE IS NO PAST ME! We took vows. To love and to cherish each other. Until death do us part. NOW death has done us part! NOW! You may move past me."

"Calm down Big Wayne," says Saundra.

Big Wayne stands up, still looking down at his dead wife. He turns around. He starts breathing heavier and visibly grows redder by the second. He points towards the wall.

"She had that fool living in my house." says Big Wayne. "Like he owns the place. How as a man, can you live comfortably in someone else's home? Knowing that another man made all this possible. I paid for all of this, with cold hard cash. Actually, blood money, money that some great people died for. I sacrificed so much so my family would never know hard times again."

Big Wayne turns towards our direction with his gazed fixed on Saundra. Calmly and coldly he says, "But look how I was repaid. This is all your fault and now death will become you."

With one step, Saundra finds herself within Big Wayne's reach. With one quick swing, he knocks the gun from Saundra's hand. With the back swing, he knocks Saundra off her feet. She flies across the room and lands on top of the bed. She falls to the floor between the bed and the wall. Big Wayne's attention now turns towards me. His eyes are red as fire, with a steady stream of tears still flowing down from them. He charges, swinging an overhead right. He's fast, his blow nearly lands on top of my head. A slight spin ending with a backwards lean, helps to take me out of the path of the punch. Instead, his blow crashes into the top of a dresser. His fist reappears through the second drawer as he throws pieces of the dresser and drawer everywhere. Quickly, I retreat into the hallway to avoid the flying debris. Big Wayne follows closely, throwing fist after fist each with deadly force. Blocking these punches isn't enough because each punch still causes pain upon impact. I must do something else, I don't know if I can take this trauma. Big Wayne takes a breath, then unleashes his next flurry of punches. Successfully, I dodge the first punch but Big Wayne readjusts. He grabs me by both shoulders and attempts to pull me closer to him. I struggle to get free. Suddenly, I feel a rush of adrenaline pumping through my veins, which triggers fight or flight. Simultaneously, I punch Big Wayne underneath his arms, in both armpits. He releases his grip and drops me to the floor. I deliver a straight kick to his chest which puts distance between us.

"I will kill you first or should I say third," snarls Big Wayne. "After you, I will go back to kill that girl. Then I will get rid of everyone else that is responsible for these lies."

I back up until I find myself in the kitchen area. This man is huge. I have nothing but respect for Mike Tyson for fighting all those giants in the ring. Big Wayne enters the kitchen area with a face glowing of confidence.

"I will smash you!" he growls.

He reaches on the kitchen counter and hurls an item towards me. I escape into the dining room as a toaster oven smashes into the wall. Suddenly, I'm forced to jump onto the dining room table to narrowly escape a crock pot, which rushes past my head. Then I roll to the floor as a microwave oven bounces off the table and smashes into a china cabinet. From underneath the table, I watch as Big Wayne slowly approaches. Suddenly, the entire table starts to rise.

"You can't hide from me, no one can hide from me. No one is safe," he screams.

His words trigger a memory. The sky is pitch black and the only visible lights are the torches held by five men. I stand in the middle of a circle made from rocks. There are people gathered around staring at me and someone else; rather it is two someone's. They are also standing in the circle but it looks like they are on the same side. They are big and the looks on their faces are serious. No one else stands in the ring but on the outside of the circle stands Sting-Ray.

"Come here," he says. "Always remember, there are no rules to street fighting. Remember your training and be confident in what you've been taught. Look for your opponent's weakness and exploit them. If there aren't any weaknesses, then you create one. You can defeat them if you stay focused. Now kick their butts so we can get out of here."

Dishes fall to the floor as the table continues to rise. What was that vision? It felt real. Suddenly, the table flips backwards revealing Big Wayne. I'm astonished at how big this man is. He has muscles everywhere, it might be hard to find an opening. Oh, I remember, one fact stands true for all; the fact that no one can take damage to their knees. Big Wayne steps forward with his right leg. I place a kick to his knee. The pain from hyperextending his knee causes Big Wayne to yell. He stumbles backward a few steps. He might just be big enough to shake off a knee shot, but he won't shake this off. I run forward a few steps and punt Big Wayne in the groan. The impact of the punt leaves me momentarily suspended in air. Shockingly, Big Wayne still has the strength to push me back into the debris before dropping to one knee. He is visibly in pain, I better use this time wisely. Quickly, I roll out of the debris and scurry into the living room to give myself breathing room. This room seems to be the most spacious room of the house. If I have any chance of stopping his rampage, I need space to freely move around. Not being familiar with this layout of furniture might make that easier said than done.

Like a demolition ball, Big Wayne erupts through the wall that separates the rooms. He tackles me, knocking me over a sofa causing us to fall onto the cold stone floor. That impact hurt but I don't have time to be in pain. I roll backward before rising to my feet. Simultaneously, Big Wayne also rises and like a machine, he begins swinging again. Something is different this time. He doesn't show any signs of slowing down but his movements seem slightly slower. I can see every punch and anticipate its trajectory. He squints his left eye before he throws a punch. He isn't ambidextrous because his left is also weaker than his right. He has military training so he tries to cover up all his weaknesses but they still exist. Easily, I allow a wild right hook to sail pass my face. I counter with a kick to his inner thigh followed by an elbow uppercut. He grimaces but the blows do not have the effect they were intended to have. Quickly, Big Wayne counters me by reversing his swing. The power of his back swing sends me flying. I crash into a statue. Pieces of the broken statue crumble beneath my feet as I stand to confront Big Wayne once again. I attack Big Wayne with a hard kick to the ribs which causes him to wince. I deliver the same kick to the opposite side. Instead of wincing, he grabs my leg after impact. Caught with one leg in the air, he easily lifts me from the ground. He releases his grasp and gravity sends me down into his embrace. Like an anaconda, his arms constrict around my body. He squeezes tightly causing nearly every breath within me to escape. Tighter and tighter he squeezes his massive arms, with the intent to snatch my life away. With all the strength left within me, I push then claw at Big Wayne's face with my left hand. He adjusts his arms slightly and squeezes tighter. His adjustment allows me to free my right arm. Repeatedly, I swing my right elbow down onto the side of his head. Finally, he releases his grasp after the fifth elbow opens a gash. I fall to the floor landing on hands and knees while Big Wayne stumbles towards the sofa. I spring back into action, attacking the dazed big man. First, a left uppercut finds its mark, followed by a right uppercut which lands flush beneath Big Wayne's chin. The big man stumbles backward grabbing onto a coffee table to regain his footing. I run full speed and jump into the air knees first. My right knee lands to his head. The impact of the blow sends Big Wayne flying into and knocking over the oversized recliner. Is Big Wayne down for good? I hope so. Cautiously, I move closer to investigate whether he is down for the count. I pause because the recliner moves slightly to the left. Slowly, he rises to his feet. Blood pours down into his face from the side of his forehead. He wipes his face and looks at his hand. He licks his blood. A sadistic smile appears on his face as his stares at me behind ice cold eyes. I spit out a mouth full of blood that has gathered. I smile back.

"I haven't had this much fun in a while," says Big Wayne. "There was only one other man that could stand toe-to-toe with me. He was my right-hand man. He was a good man. I would offer you a job but unfortunately for you, that was my favorite recliner. I will kill you! Then I will use your bones to rebuild that recliner. You can now die knowing that you will be more useful after your death."

"Come on Big man, I'm ready for you."

We stare at each other intensely. It feels like high noon in the Wild West and the duel starts when someone moves a finger. His murderous intent is now flush on his face. He moves his massive neck around causing multiple cracking sounds. His left eye twitches and here he comes. Big Wayne lets out a thunderous howl. He begins to shake violently and white foam spills from his mouth. His eye rolls behind his head and he collapses to the floor.

"One hundred thousand watts will stop you," shouts Saundra. "Don't you ever put your hands on me again or any woman! You must have lost your darn mind."

"Saundra, are you alright?"

"I'm good Brody," she replies. "Fool made me hit my head but you're the one that fought that monster. Are you alright? You look like you been through a war."

"I'm good also but I'll probably be sore tomorrow."

"Man, y'all made a mess in here," she says. "Let's look through this mess and find something to bind him with. I'll make the call to Houston, also."

With a telephone cord, I tie-up Big Wayne. It Seems like Saundra's call is taking her longer than she expected but the hard work is done for now. During that fight, I felt something strange happen to me. I became more alert. It felt as if my awareness was improving. His punches didn't stop hurting but I was able to anticipate his movement. I wonder, does this have something to do with me regaining my memory? Granme said it would be a few days but she didn't know exactly. It doesn't feel like I remember anything new but I really can't think with these bruises forming all over my body.

"Hey Brody," interrupts Saundra. "First part of the plan is complete. I just got off the phone with Houston and they are informed of Big Wayne's actions. We are to leave immediately. They will take further action."

"Well help me get this dude in the trunk."

"Do you want to put him in the backseat," asks Shondra?

"Do you want to die today? If he can get free, things would become tragic."

"This whole situation is tragic if you ask me," she replies.

CHAPTER 11 – WELCOME TO HOUSTON

Our trip to Houston via Interstate 45, passes quickly. Three hours and thirty-five minutes usually isn't considered quick but the peace of the highway, along with the ibuprofen Saundra gave me seems to have calmed my nerves. I needed to be medicated more than I knew because I never found that peace inside of this vehicle. Every now and then I would hear Big Wayne pounding the inside of the trunk. When the pounding subsided, he would cry for at least thirty minutes straight. I feel kind of sorry for the guy, but that's life. If you play the game, you must play the dominos you pull. Life is full of trials and tribulations and If you choose the wrong path, then you become another Big Wayne. Yes, life can be hard at times but you must constantly progress. You should learn from each situation that arises and learn from the past. Once you've learned from your tests, then you won' be presented with that test again. Neither will you struggle or doubt yourself if a similar situation arises. My nerves have been tested since we left Big Wayne's house but Big Wayne is nothing compared to Saundra. I have never personally witnessed someone talk continuously on a phone before, that's until now. I witness Saundra talk for three hours straight. How much do you really have to say to the Assistant District Attorney of Houston? They talk non-stop. At first it was all business. After that was handled, they turned into two gossip girls. Saundra still would have the nerve to take time away from her busy conversation just to tell me how to drive. She's still talking and it doesn't look like she will stop until we get to downtown Houston. Up until now the only thing I have done in the city of Houston is fly to and from the airport. Houston is one of the largest cities in the United States and one of the top party destinations in the world. I can't believe I haven't had the pleasure to explore this city. Growing up in the country you only see this on the television. Country folk say things like "if you go to the city, don't let city folk fast talk you." Some are scared to come to the city because they think they will be hustled. That might have been how it was in the past but now everyone is trying to hustle you. The hustle game has changed so much that some are even hustling people without meeting them in person. Technology has changed the world and has made the hustle game expand. I'm country but I'm not one to fear what will or won't happen.

A diverse collection of people walk around everywhere. Some are in a hurry, some are minding their own business, while others are sitting around people watching. Some people watchers are just curious people. With one glance, they can take in a group of people and tell you exactly what they had on. While some people watchers are dangerous people who watch with bad intentions, sometimes stalking a person to learn their every habit. They even follow them on social media, making numerous accounts with fake profiles. Thinking about fake profiles. Unfortunately, I've been cat-fished before. It was right after my high school graduation. Sting-Ray was pressuring me to travel with him but I was hesitant. I didn't want to leave my family nor the safe confines of this country. I decided that I wouldn't go with Sting-Ray. So, I stopped visiting his cabin. With my free time, I started getting online. I met a lady online and we hit it off. We shared pictures and eventually our phone numbers. We talked day and night constantly. We developed a strong connection. I was falling so hard that I would look at her picture while talking to her. We agreed that we should take our relationship further. It was time that we met. I remember borrowing Paw-Paw's truck that day. I drove down to Beaumont to meet my mystery woman who I had completely fallen for. I was nervous but excited at the same time. So much so, that I showed up two hours earlier than we discussed. I went to the address she gave me. When the lady answered the door, she told me that no one named that lived there. I was baffled. I knew I had the right name and the right address. I walked back to the truck. I heard their door reopen. I looked up to see a young lady running out the door asking me to come back. Her voice sounded familiar but I didn't recognize her face. Curious, I walked back to the house. I figure that she might be able to point me in the right direction. When I walked up to the lady, she tried to kiss me. I nearly broke an ankle running from her. Come to find out. This chick had me falling for her alter ego, the person she wanted to be. She looked nothing like that picture. Then she had the nerve, to think that I should get over it. She thought that I still should be with her; talking about she accidentally posted her sisters picture. So, I asked her where her sister was because I came there for her. That too was a lie. She later admitted to being an only child. She really thought that her game was still strong enough to get her what she wanted. I thought that my brutal honesty would teach her a valuable lesson but I was wrong. She was still at it with her fake tears flowing. She started saying, "I can't live without you." I told her that this entire situation was her fault. She had her opportunity but chose to play games. She should have had more confidence in herself. I left and as soon I as arrived home, I erased my online presence. Shortly after that I left with Sting-Ray. A broken heart tends to help one make drastic changes.

"Brody, Brody," shouts Saundra. "You need to pay attention. Where's your mind at? Your light is green. Now listen because you need to make a right turn in two blocks. Then you will turn into a parking garage which will be on your right also."

The buildings of downtown Houston tower high into the sky. There are even new construction sites seeming to rival them all. Driving up to the roof of this twenty-floor high parking garage, I notice the beams hang low. In fact, it looks as if the beam will rip off the car roof, especially on the turns. Who would put hanging beams there? Now that's questionable construction. We turn to proceed to the next level and I duck my head to see if we will make it pass the beam. Saundra realizes what I am doing and bursts with laughter. In my defense, it does look like the cement beams will rip the roof off. I bet her truck could not make it in this garage with those huge mud grip tires. Also, I've never been in this type of parking garage before, I guess that's just something you get used to.

Five parked, heavy tented, unmarked vehicles wait on top of the garage. Two helicopters circle high in the sky. They seem to be keeping their distance but staying close enough to keep visual contact. A guy exits from each vehicle but they don't approach. A lady emerges from the middle vehicle. She stands just above average height. She is in top physically condition, which is made evident by how toned her body is. She beams with confidence and swagger as she stands with her head held high. She begins walking towards us and the guys follow her lead. Saundra exits the car and briskly walks towards the lady. She instructs me to wait for her at the trunk. I exit my car and while closing the door, I notice two of the guys walking towards me. They wear identical dark shades and tight jackets.

"Hey Brody," shouts Saundra. "Come meet Houston's Assistant District Attorney. Those two will retrieve Big Wayne."

I walk towards Saundra and through the two guys. While passing they both puff their chest out. Saundra stands between the cars with a huge smile on her face.

"Brody, it is my pleasure to introduce you to Houston's future District Attorney. Meet Assistant District Attorney Daphne Turner," she says.

"The pleasure is all mine Ms. Turner."

"You can call me Daphne," she replies.

"Well it's a pleasure to meet you Daphne.

Daphne turns around to whisper to Saundra. Either my ears are very sharp or she just doesn't know how to whisper because I can clearly hear every word she says.

"Where did you find this chivalrous hunk of a man," whispers Daphne. "Is he yours?"

"Girl no," Saundra replies. "Girl that's my cousin. He has been overseas and he just returned home."

"Well hook your girl up," whispers Daphne.

"We'll talk about it later," says Saundra. "I got you girl. Look! I think your guys are ready to take Big Wayne into custody."

"Hey guys, you may need more help with him. Why don't you call over your other teammates to help with this guy? He is bigger than your average man."

The shorter guy of the two replies, "For what? I'm enough by myself. My partner is just insurance."

"Well, he was tied up when we put him in the trunk but he has been moving around a lot. It's safe to assume that he is free."

"We're good," says the taller guy.

"Well, let me know when you're in position and ready. I'll come open the trunk."

"We were born ready," replies the shorter guy. "As a matter of fact, we are trained professional. We do not need help from a civilian. You can give us the keys. We got this! Move back!"

I hand them the keys and move out of their way. Confidently the shorter guy unlocks the trunk. He immediately tosses me back my keys. I grab them from the air and place them into my pocket. Before they can hit the bottom, the trunk swings open. Big Wayne arises from the trunk enraged. He plants his massive feet into the chest of the taller guy and the face of the shorter. The impact of the blow sends them tumbling down to the pavement. They roll backwards a few feet before coming to a stop. They moan as they grab at the new road rash on their faces. My instincts and reaction time is on point. I move in but my reaction isn't good enough. Before, I can reach him, Daphne appears. She pulls two guns on Big Wayne. One pointing at his temple and the other firmly pointing in his groin.

"Give me a reason to make your family jewels a permanent part of this trunk," says Daphne. Her gaze is so intense that it would make a wild bear change its mind.

"Just go ahead," says Big Wayne. "My life is over anyway."

"Get your butts off the pavement," screams Daphne. "You can lick your wounds later. Get this idiot out of here and read him his rights. You have the nerves to say that you're more than enough. You will have more than enough training and workouts added to your daily routine. Embarrassing yourselves and making me look bad. GET HIM OUT OF HERE! NOW!"

The more she speaks, the more enraged she grows. Her team is in a state of shock and panic as they retrieve Big Wayne and places him into a car. Quickly, they drive away. My phone begins ringing in my pocket as Saundra tries calming Daphne.

"Excuses me ladies, I have to take this."

"Go ahead," replies Saundra.

"Hello"

"Hey Brody, how is your case going?" Asks Franklin. "I hope you are done because I think Shondra and I may have found a clue."

"We just wrapped up. We are currently in Houston. It shouldn't take us to long to get back. What clue did you find?"

"We had been looking through the photos and background checks since you left," he says. "We couldn't find anything new and it was starting to agitate me. So, we decided to take a lunch break to clear our heads. After lunch Shondra decides that we should only focus on the photos. Later she notices a guy in a few of the pictures who only lingered far in the back. Fortunately for us, you were pretty determined to take a picture of every person at the party."

"I sure was. I remember that I wanted to make Bridgette a scrapbook. I wanted her to have those memories forever."

"OH," interrupts Franklin. "I see you're a natural little crafty home maker. Do you know how to sew, as well? I have some socks with holes in them. I'd really appreciate if you sewed them for me."

"Weren't you telling me something, Franklin? Focus man, it's hot on top of this roof."

"I'm serious man. Those are my good socks," he says. "Okay, on the serious tip. On one of those pictures, you managed to get a side profile of this guy. We checked through the background checks but his face could not be found. I think the system I used only pulls the background checks for full profiles. So, I sent it to one of my friends in the crime lab. I remember that he is always talking about a new program that can build a 3D model profile from an incomplete profile. After I talked to him, we had the results back within two hours."

Suddenly, the phone goes silent. I eagerly wait for Franklin to tell me the results. A minute passes but still nothing. I look at the phone but it says that the call is still in progress. "Hello. Hello" but still no response.

"Franklin, check your phone. I can't hear anything and I don't know how to work this phone."

"My bad Brody, my face must have muted the call," says Franklin. "I was wondering why you was so quiet. What's the last thing you heard?"

"You were just about to tell me the results."

"His name is William Baldwin II but unfortunately, he is deceased. I couldn't get information on his history but we did discover that his parents are still alive. Shondra gave them a call."

The call goes silent again. I check to see if it was me this time. All is fine on my side. "Franklin. Franklin! Check your phone again. Your fat face must have pressed mute again." Another minute goes by and still nothing from Franklin. Suddenly, laughter erupts through the phone.

"I'm just playing with you Brody," laughs Franklin. "But anyway, we have set up a meeting with his parents on tomorrow. They live in Houston. You and Saundra should stay there for the night. We will come meet you in the morning."

"You play to much Detective. I told you it's hot up here. The sun plus this hot pavement will have me a few shades darker. Just call me when you'll make it."

"Okay, later," he replies.

I turn around to see Saundra and Daphne staring at me, both with an inquisitive expression.

182

"Who was that Brody?" Asks Saundra.

"That was Franklin, he said they have a new lead for our other case and that we should spend the night here in Houston. They will be coming here in the morning."

"Well that's perfect," shouts Daphne. "You guys can crash at my house tonight. We can go out and celebrate today's success."

"I'm sorry Daphne but I don't want to inconvenience you. We can get a room somewhere for the night."

"I insist, Brody," she replies. "You guys saved my butt today. You will not be a burden. I live alone in a very big house. I have enough space for you, Saundra, and ten other people.

"Girl it would be our pleasure to spend the evening with you," says Saundra. "Brody's just an old country man at heart. They never want to burden anyone. He's such a gentleman."

"Girl I though gentlemen were extinct," replies Daphne. "There is nothing gentle about any man I know."

"I can't play with you Daphne," says Saundra. "We need to go before I faint. It is too darn hot out here."

For the first time today, my drive is peaceful. Saundra riding with Daphne was a true blessing. We arrive at a gated community where they stop at a call box for a moment. The gate opens and I follow Daphne's car through the security gate. About halfway through, the gate starts to close on me. The rear end of my car is hit by the gate as I pass through. If this car was a dog, right now he would be running with his tail tucked between his legs. I can't believe that gate hit me. I thought I had it. When the sign says one car at a time, they actually mean it here. Every house in this community is massive. By the look of the neighborhood, you can tell some very well-off people live within this community. We pull into the driveway of a single-story house. Both garage doors rise and Daphne drives into one of the garages. Saundra signals me to drive into the other one. We exit the vehicles and Daphne welcomes us to her home. Daphne's house is very elegant. It's a modern style home with a few classic touches. Walking into her home I can tell she is a cultured person. Her strong patriotism is on full display with flags hanging from her vaulted ceilings. Her red, white, and blue flag, her Texas state flag and her red, black, and green flags hang proudly.

"Brody, you can sleep in the first room to the left," says Daphne. "Make yourself at home. Saundra and I will be leaving for a while, we have some legal matters to handle."

"Do y'all need my help with anything?"

"No, I think you have done enough for us today," she replies. "You should relax your body for a while. Here is some medicine. We will be back in a few hours, then we will party all night long."

"Thanks Daphne, I believe I will lay down for a little while."

I close the door and lay onto the bed. Instantly the comfort of the bed put my stress to easy. I close my eyes but moisture in the air makes me stir.

"Stop playing Saundra, I just closed my eyes. I thought y'all had things to do?"

I open my eyes but It's not Saundra. I feel around and I'm no longer laying on a bed. I find myself lying on the cold ground, surrounded by thick fog. "How did I get here? What's going on?" I stand up and attempt to focus my eyes but still I see nothing but fog. I can clearly see everything from my waist up but I can't see anything else. Oh-oh, not this again. Granme must have been wrong about my mom causing that vision I had, unless there is a lingering affect. Well, I know I must walk on the glowing letters until I reach the door. I must make it through before it closes but there wasn't any fog last time. I guess it's better than being in darkness. I reach forward into the unknown but I feel only air. I open my mouth to call out into the fog but no sound comes forth. The fogs movement resembles slow movement of clouds. I pick up my foot and to my surprises, I can move. I move forward into the immeasurably thick fog. I stumble a bit as the ground begins a rocky incline. The size of the rocks beneath my feet grow and the incline gets steeper. Blindly, I climb a rocky sloop. I attempt to stop my climb

185

but my body continues to move on its own. My hand reaches for what seems to be the top of a cliff and I pull myself up onto it. Rocks crumble below my feet; caught by the force of gravity, I start to fall backwards. Wildly, I swing my arms trying to catch my balance but still I continue to fall. Suddenly, a gloved hand appears through the fog and grabs my arm. The force of the pull from the gloved hand helps me regain my balancing, preventing me from falling. A sense of relief overtakes me as I find myself back on solid ground but the hand vanishes back into the fog. I try to call out again but still no sound comes forth. I quicken my pace. The ground here feels more level than before. I begin to run in hopes that I run into the person who just saved me but I notice that the quicker I move the more the fog grows thicker. The fog forces me to come to a complete stop, as it inches up my body, towards my face. I no longer can see anything from my chest down and it's continuing to inch higher. It seems to stop just below my nose. I raise a hand to eye level and only parts of four fingers are visible. I watch intently and inhale deeply as the fog covers my nose and takes away my vision. No longer able to hold my breath, I release it and inhale deeply. Amazingly, I breathe in cool, clean air. I place my hands in front of my face until I nearly touch my eyeball. I can see the tip of my fingers. Well I'm not blind and it feels like the ground is still here. I take another step forward through the fog. Nothing happens. I take another step and another step. Suddenly, the fog starts to decrease until for the first time, I can see my feet. Plush green grass covers the ground. The fog ahead of me starts to part and a shadow emerges. I move forward towards the figure but the same gloved hand, which saved me from falling, emerge through the fog.

This time its palm faces my direction. Does he want a high five or something else? The fog thins slightly to reveal the figure of the person connected to the gloved hand. The shadowy figures head begins to move towards me. The fog begins to dissipate. I move to see the man connected to the hand but suddenly everything turns bright.

CHAPTER 12 – I'LL DRINK TO THAT

I awake from the dream; perspiring profusely. "What was that? Who was that? Why are these sheets so wet?" I throw the sheets from my body. I sit up to contemplate what I just dreamt but a knock at the door breaks my concentration. The door opens, even though I didn't respond to the knock and Saundra enters the room.

"Get up Brody," she says. "Ugh, your sweeting. What have you been doing in here, working out? Get yourself cleaned up and meet us in the living room. It's time to celebrate."

"Okay, I'll be there in a few minutes."

"Don't take too long," she says. "We let you rest long enough."

Saundra turns around and exits the room. I hear her singing a joyous melody as she walks away. My body feels tight and soar, as I stand to stretch. I walk into the bathroom and splashes water onto my face. Somehow, I need to clear my head. I hope these ladies can help me clear my mind tonight. I'll take a quick shower, being clean tends to lift one's spirits.

I walk into the living room to see Saundra and Daphne standing by the fireplace. The ladies look stunning from head to toe. It looks like they did a little more than handle some legal matters. Their hair, fingernails, and toenails

189

all seem to have been retouched. They talk and laugh unaware of my presence.

"Excuse me ladies. Looking at you two makes me feel a bit underdressed. Are you sure you ladies want me accompanying you, looking like this?"

"Don't be silly Brody," says Daphne. "You can wear anything and still look handsome."

"Thanks Daphne. Well excuse me again ladies, I forgot my keys."

"Don't worry about driving Brody. We will go in my car," replies Daphne."

Relieved by not having to drive more today, I sit in the backseat to enjoy just riding for a chance. Since I've been home, I have traveled many miles. I've put more miles on my car than most people will put on theirs in three months. I like to drive but I'm starting to think its overrated. Daphne drives up to a club and parks at the entrance. Here, the valets wear uniforms that match the color scheme of the club. I thought all valets wore those same red uniforms but these valets are the sharpest I've ever seen. Their uniforms look more like tailor made suits. On top of that, the energy from the club's atmosphere is electric and that's from the people who are parking lot pimping.

"Now I really feel underdressed."

"Oh Brody, you're good," says Daphne. "You have one of those faces, where you can pull it off. Unless you're just slumming it. Otherwise you're good."

"Girl that's what you call good genes," says Saundra. "He woke up like that. He woke up like that."

"Amen to that," shouts Daphne."

"Now come on Brody," says Saundra. "Let's enjoy this night."

Saundra grabs a hold of my right arm with both hands. Daphne does the same to the left. With two beautiful women on my arms I now feel dressed for the occasion. We enter the club and it seems to be packed to capacity. Surprisingly, navigating from one end of the club, to the other is quite simple. We follow a thin path through the crowd that leads towards the back. I walk behind the ladies as we squeeze in between people. Someone must have groped Saundra because she punches a guy in the chest. He retreats into the crowd. We walk towards the back of the club where a V.I.P. section is reserved for us. Before reaching our destination, a woman jumps out of the crowd in front of me. She has on a short mini skirt with a short top. She is very attractive and well put together. She starts dancing. She turns around and shakes her butt, pressing it against my groin. She begins to twerk. She drops it low and picks it back up. A foul smell rises as she continues to dance. As she continues to dance I side-steps her and continue to follow the girls.

"I saw that woman dancing on you Brody," says Saundra. "She was HOT. Why didn't you mingle a little?"

"Saundra," shouts Daphne.

"What?" she replies. I'm just saying."

"Listen ladies. If you would have smelt the smell that rose when she did; you would understand why I ran from her."

"Awe, poor baby," replies Daphne. "She should have washed her stank behind before leaving the house."

"Somebody will take her home tonight but it won't be me. They better make her wash up first.

"You can't wash away a disease," says Saundra. "But anyway, this place is really nice."

"It sure is," replies Daphne. "Girl, this is actually my first time here. I've been wanting to come here but I never get a chance to get out anymore. If I'm not working; what am I saying? I'm always working. I don't get a chance to enjoy myself outside of work."

"No work tonight girl," says Saundra. "You are going to enjoy this night. You need to let loose. Look at this, we have two bottles. It's so on right now. Let's take a shot. It's sure to loosen you up and you too Brody."

I watch as Saundra pours three shots to the rim of the glass. Neither Daphne and Saundra spill their drink, they take their shots like true pro's. They might drink me under the table tonight; I don't think I drink often. I guess I'll be considered what some might call a light weight. Well, down the hatch. The drink is smooth without any after taste. I bet it's one of those sneaky drinks. The kind that if you mix it with the right juice, one would forget that you are drinking an alcoholic beverage. That's until it hits you all at one time. Then you find yourself sitting down, holding your head.

"Alright everyone," shouts Saundra! "Time for round two! Now, let's toast to our successful return of Big Wayne!"

"I'll toast to that," replies Daphne.

"Me too. That's one fellow I don't care to run into again."

"When I'm finished with him, you never will," says Daphne.

"Girl that's my song," says Saundra.

Saundra stands and begins dancing in one spot. She then grabs Daphne by her arm and forces her to her feet. She drags Daphne down to the dance floor. The atmosphere inside of this club is more intense and electrifying than it was on the outside of the club. The jazz music being played begins to morph the whole world into music. Everything outside of this smooth melody, just don't seem to matter. The only thing that matters is just grooving to the music and enjoying every moment. This feeling is intoxicating. I'm drifting away on a seemly endless ride, only to be brought back to reality with the changing of the song. This is my first time inside of a club. I haven't even been inside of a hole in the wall joint. Listening to certain people, one would think that someone will start shooting at any moment, but everyone seems to be enjoying themselves. Not two seconds after the ladies return from dancing, Saundra starts pouring our third shot. I better watch these ladies, someone must drive us back safely tonight.

"Here you go Brody," says Saundra with a huge smile on her face.

"No thank you. I think I will pass on this round. I am a light weight when it comes to drinking. It might be best if I space my drinking out."

"Come on Brody," says Daphne. "We all are light weights. Our bodies weren't designed to drink this stuff. You can be just a social drinker like me. Just one more shot. Please? You went toe to toe with Big Wayne and lived to tell the tale. You deserve another one."

In unison, the ladies begin chanting Brody, Brody, Brody. Daphne must be just as country as Saundra because they keep getting louder and louder by the second.

"Quiet down you two. I'll take this one but you must promise me that you will chill for a while. Besides we just got here. Let's enjoy ourselves for a moment, before we don't remember the rest of our night."

In unison, the ladies tilt their glass and say, "I'll drink to that." Then they down their shots.

"So, Brody, can you tell me a little about yourself?" Asks Daphne.

"There's not too much to tell."

"Don't be like that," says Saundra. "You've been gone for ten years. You must have tons of stories to tell."

"What I mean is, a few months ago I got into an accident which is responsible for me losing a portion of my memory. Until I talked to Paw-Paw, I had no idea that I've been gone for ten years. So, there are things about me that I don't know at this moment. I was told that all should return to me within a week or so."

"Awe Brody," says Daphne. "I'm sorry to hear that."

"I didn't know either," adds Saundra.

"I didn't know until I saw my Granme, yesterday. I didn't have the time to tell anyone because we were after Big Wayne but enough about me. We are supposed to be having fun. Why don't you tell me a little about yourself Daphne?"

"I though you wanted to have fun?" She asks. "There is nothing fun about my story. Let's just celebrate the fact that with hard work and dedication, I managed to crawl out from my past and build a brighter future for myself. Without any help from anyone but I didn't forget where I came from. Too often our people reach success only to turn their back on the rest of us. I use my upbringing as fuel to motivate my fire. Now I use my success to uplift and rebuild our communities."

"You have done an excellent job Daphne. Being Assistant District Attorney in the city of Houston is not something you can just pass off as minor. No matter what's in our past, we determine the course of our future."

"Well said Brody," says Daphne in a soft tone. Almost as low as a whisper. "Let's toast to leaving the past behind us and building towards an exciting future."

As I gaze into Daphne's eyes, my body begins to move on its own. My fingers open before closing with a firm grip. I close my eyes and open my mouth. A sense of coolness engulfs my mouth. I can't believe this, I'm now four shots in.

"You look absolutely radiant tonight Daphne. Would you like to dance," asks a really confident guy?

I look up to see him standing at the entrance to our section. He is starring at Daphne like she is meat on a hook.

"No Elliot," yells Daphne. "Not now! Not later! I don't want to dance with you. I've told you that before. Now leave before I call security."

"You don't mean that," he replies. "Just come dance and talk to me for a while. I'm pretty sure that I can change your mind."

Slowly with every word, Elliot start inching his way closer, while starring intensely at Daphne. He's not paying attention to us or even caring about who is sitting with Daphne. I rise from my seat and I turn to block his way.

"Move out the way," he says!

"I suggest you find another pretty lady to dance with, Friend! This one is not interested."

"Excuse me Buddy! What did you say? Do you know who I am, huh buddy?" He asks.

"No, I don't and I really don't care who you are. All I care about is you moving along."

"Like I was saying before you rudely interrupted," he says. "I am Elliot Richman. I am one of the richest men in the world. So, get out of my way before I make you."

His eyes burn with fire as he looks at me. An animalistic instinct of excitement mixed with rage begins to flow through my veins. Whatever chemical reaction is taking place inside of my body, I can now taste in my mouth. This guy is barking up the wrong tree and he's clearly at a height and weight disadvantage. Plus, he is two steps below me and I have the reach advantage.

"Like I said little dude, I suggest you take your little party somewhere else."

A smirk briefly crosses my face as his eyes attempt to erupt. Sandra and Daphne quickly step between me and Elliot before we come to blows. Daphne call for the security guards, as Saundra yells at Elliot to leave. The scene causes for a temporary break in the music as the DJ calls for security. Two huge security guards arrive to usher Elliot away. Not once do our eyes lose connection until he disappears from my view.

"Girl what was that about?" Asks Saundra. "Got my cousin ready to go Bruce Lee-Roy in this club. Clearly, he is suffering from little man syndrome. You know Brody would have smashed that fool. He has already gone toe to toe with Big Wayne today. Girl I must say, that little man had some balls. He didn't have an inch of back down in him neither. Sit down and relax your nerves Brody, he is long gone by now. Now, back to you Daphne. We're all ears."

"I met Elliot a few months ago when his father was in town looking for endorsements and donations," says Daphne. "Senator Richman and the District Attorney held a fundraiser to raise money. My job was to show Elliot a good time as a favor for the District Attorney. To be honest it was more to keep him out of his father's affairs. That night he was everything a woman could imagine her idea man to be. He was sweet and patient. He made me feel like I was the only girl in the room. He was such a gentleman. We exchanged numbers and said that we would keep in touch. They left for Washington D.C. the next morning but a week passed before we got a chance to talk again. I thought it was just a coincidence when we ran into each other on my jog in Hermann Park. He told me that he had moved to Houston for good. We exchanged numbers again because he said he lost his phone and we setup a second date. This date was totally opposite from our first meeting. He suggested that I pick him up since he didn't know his way around the city. That was my first red flag because every phone comes with a GPS. When I arrived at his place, he was nowhere near ready. He told me that he was tired and needed to rest a little while. I hesitated at first but decided that it was okay. I should have followed my first mind because that was the second red flag. He laid in his bed and I sat in a chair to watch television. He then told me to turn off the television and come lay beside him. I wasn't tired, so I told him to sleep and we could reschedule another time. So, I left. When I reached my car, there he stood. He was already dressed and waiting for me like I was late. Even though I had two red flags, we went ahead and kept our reservations. The final red flag came at the restaurant. He began to act extremely jealous and possessive. He started accusing me of flirting with the hostess and I don't even like girls, like that. Then he told me a sob story of how his ex-fiancé left him for another woman. He was so controlling that we had a heated argument about what I was going to eat. At that point, I threw twenty dollars on the table and told him to find his own way home. I thought that was the end of it but now he tends to appear everywhere I go."

"Have you reported him?" Asks Saundra.

"Yes, I have," replies Daphne. "I reported him to the District Attorney. He said that he would have a talk with Elliot's father."

"Well girl, don't leave home without your gun," says Saundra. "There have been too many cases of women being stalked and police doing nothing to prevent their eventual murders. That man has serious issues; I can see it in his eyes."

"I thought you was taking it easy on the drinks Brody," says Daphne.

"I think I just changed my mind, besides we're with the Assistant District Attorney."

"You're in safe hands," says Daphne. "Slightly impaired but still safe."

"Enough with the pity party" says Saundra.

"Yeah, we're here to celebrate," says Daphne. "Let's dance. Are you coming Saundra?"

"No girl," she replies. "You go ahead. I will sit here and wait for the food to come. I'm starving."

"Well do be a gentleman and escort me to the dance floor," says Daphne sheepishly.

Time sure fly's when you are having fun or if you're in a hurry. We dance for two songs and a line dance. We walk back to the section just in time to witness Saundra smashing everything in front of her. She doesn't even realize we have return until Daphne starts eating along with her.

"Slow down Saundra, before you choke."

"I'm good Brody," she says with a mouth full of food. "I don't know what it is about club food but man, it's always on point."

"It might have something to do with the atmosphere and alcohol," slurs Daphne.

With her glass raised in the air Saundra adds, "I'll drink to that."

Seeing the garage doors open nearly brings tears to my eyes. Dealing with these two women is a tougher task then fighting Big Wayne. The night has been highly entertaining but finally it is coming to a needed end. I don't know how I made it to Daphne's house without losing one of these wild girls. First, they both got so drunk that I needed help from security to get them out of the club and into the car. I though the worst was over because they both were sound asleep. Twenty minutes into my peaceful drive, Daphne awakes. I looked at her through the rear-view mirror and all I did was smile. She looked at me with a puzzled look. She then starts screaming for her life. Next, she proceeds to assault me. She grabs my seatbelt then punches me on the side of my head. It took everything I had not to collide with oncoming traffic. Seeing her opportunity to escape she tries to open the car door. Every time she unlocks her door, I relocked it. After a few rounds of that, her frustration reached its limit. So, she decides to get out through the window but when she lowers her window, a strong gust of wind rushes through the car and awakes Saundra. Daphne is half-way out of the window before Saundra grabs for the first thing she sees. With one pull she rips off Daphne panties. When she realized what she was holding, she throws the panties out of the window. With haste, I find a safe place to pullover and park. By the time, I get out of the car, Daphne is jumping on to me. She straddles me and says, "Oh Brody, you rescued me, I thought I was a goner. That man was trying to kidnap me. You're my hero." It takes me fifteen minutes to calm Daphne. In which, Saundra decides she will sleep in the backseat. At that point, I'm totally cool with keeping Daphne where I can keep a close eye on her. See falls fast to sleep as soon as I buckle her in. For the next fifteen minutes, all is peaceful. There is no traffic and traffic lights doesn't change often. Suddenly Daphne pops up from her sleep. She looks at the backseat, then she begins to yell again. This time very loudly into my ear. Her yelling nearly causes me to hit the guard rail.

"Stop the car," she yells. "We lost Saundra. She was in here and now she isn't. Someone has taken my friend. Did you leave her? You need to find her. Someone HELP!"

I look at Daphne and all I can do is shake my head. This is the effect of drinking too much. I attempt to calm her and ensure her that Saundra is sound asleep on the backseat but she isn't having it. She unbuckles her seatbelt, turns around in her seat and stare into the backseat. She then hits me on the shoulder and says, "No she isn't, look for yourself." I glance into the rearview mirror but I don't see Saundra either. I turn around to look into the backseat but still don't see her. So once again, I find a safe place to pullover. I get out of the car to check for Saundra. When I open the back door, the sight sent me to my knees and into laughter. I laughed so hard that my side started hurting. Trapped between the front seat and the backseat I see Saundra lying face down on the floor board, sleeping like a baby. Finally, it took over thirty minutes for me to get the gate code out of Daphne. She started talking about going get coffee. Nothing she said made sense.

The situation that I now face is getting these two ladies into the house. I'm glad they are still resting soundly because I can't have them running around like chickens with their heads cut off. They haven't even noticed that the car isn't moving anymore. I walk to the door and fumble with the keys until I find the right one. With two keys left out of ten, the door finally unlocks. Quickly, I input Daphne's security code. I'm glad she left this sticky note on the wall for us, I can't afford to let that alarm go off. I walk the halls to make sure they are clear of any potential trip hazards then I prop the door open. Now, I will start with Saundra, first because the room she is sleeping in is much closer. I open the backdoor to see Saundra halfway on the seat. She's still sleeping soundly which is evident by her drooling and snoring. Grabbing her underneath both arms, I use leg strength to pull her out of the car and onto her wobbly feet. Thankfully, she still doesn't wake up. I turn around and place her arms around my neck. Upon lifting her, Saundra begins to squeeze tightly. So, tight that for a moment it feels as if she would choke me out. I drop down to one knee to ease the pressure. It seems that no matter who you give a piggy back ride to, that person will choke you accidently. She's lucky I didn't drop her but somehow, through the tussling, I manage to get her secured. Sweat begins to travel from my head to the tip of my nose as we make our way to her destination. I stumble into the room, after tripping on a rug. We fall onto the bed. Saundra unwraps her arms and rolls over into a comfortable position. Exhausted I look up towards the ceiling. That's one down and one more to go. I sit up to gather myself, before proceeding back to the car. I reach into the passenger side to retrieve Daphne. I try to wake her but she is not responsive. First, I unbuckle her seatbelt. Next, I position both of her legs outside of the car. Her upper body leans backwards and her head nearly touches the driver's seat. This woman is very limber. I grab both her hands and with one motion, I stand her up and put her onto my shoulder. I kick the car door close as I straighten. I carry Daphne through the garage and into the house, closing and locking the doors behind me I proceed. Not three steps inside of the house I hear a loud eruption of gas pass from Daphne's buttock. I've never heard a woman fart so loudly. Most men would agree that they hardly hear their lady fart at all. I quicken my pace just in case she is smelling foul. Drinking normally leads to bubble guts and foul odors. I bet this is the only time one would hear a woman fart. They like to keep it beneath the sheets. I don't understand what women are tripping on, passing gas is natural. Ok, you don't pass gas while eating nor in a confined space but if we are chilling, then have at it. Like Big Mama says, "There's more room out than there is in." We enter the living room and I maneuver around the couch but accidentally run into a coffee table. Not only did I bang my shin good but my collision also causes Daphne to pass gas for the second time. That one sound like it hurt. Daphne better keep it together. If she has an accident, I will put her butt in the shower under cold water. Please let this girl keep it together, especially since she doesn't have any panties on. Finally, we arrive at Daphne's room. I lower her down onto her plush king size bed. It's decorated with drapes hanging down from all sides. She falls backwards and sinks into the plush covers but her eyes suddenly open. She springs back up. She looks up at me staring with a seductive look before falling back onto the bed.

"Come and get this, Big Daddy," she says. While spreading her legs into a full split.

"Daphne, we shouldn't. I mean we better not. I mean I can't."

"You're a grown man and I'm a willing woman," she replies. "So, don't be afraid. She only snaps, she doesn't bite."

"Your intoxicated."

"Just be quiet," she says.

Daphne closes her legs. She leans up and begins to unbuckle my pants. She then pulls them down to the floor along with my underwear.

"I see, I'm not the only one that believes we should get to know each other on a personal level," she says. "He has told me all I need to know. Now give him to me."

Everything in me from the waist down is telling me to lay it down; so, good, that she passes out on climax. But something else is strongly telling me not to, it's telling me that I shouldn't. I don't know why not but I'm getting a sense that I will regret this if I do. It feels more like a warning.

"I see your mind is racing," says Daphne. "Let me put your mind at ease. You know you want this!"

"Hold on Daphne."

"No," she replies. "I want you and I want you now. Besides, if you didn't want me then you would not still be standing here."

"Okay, Okay, but give me a moment to freshen up. It's been a long night and I've been sweating. Why don't you lay back and relax yourself? Close your eyes and imagine all the interesting things that you want to do to me."

"Okay, but make sure you hurry back," she says. "I love a clean man."

She reaches behind me and slaps me forcefully on the behind. Then grabs a hand full of my butt. Reluctantly, she releases her grip and returns to the bed. I pull up my pants up. I'm confused, was that supposed to be hot because I'm feeling kind of offended. I walk to the bathroom making sure to lock myself in. I turn on the faucet and stare into the mirror. I splash water onto my face. I don't understand. What is stopping me? This woman is gorgeous. She is self-made and a hard worker. She is not laying around waiting on a man nor anyone else to take care of her. So, what is my problem? I'm not intimidated by a powerful, independent and beautiful urban queen. She has the right curves in all the right places. What is stopping me? I need to figure this out. This would be the perfect time for me to regain my memories. Repeatedly, I hit the palm of my hands against my head. Come on. Come back to me. I need to remember. Whatever it is, it's definitely strong. Now, what will I do about Daphne? I can't hide in here all night. I must control the situation. I can't let her manipulate me. I'm the man. I must control the situation. Slowly, I crack open the door and brace myself just in case she jumps onto me. Instead of Daphne leaping through the air, I hear noises coming from the bed. I try to make it out of the bathroom without being heard. Those noises are unfamiliar to me. It's the same pattern over and over. Slowly, I creep towards the bed and the closer I get, the louder the noises becomes. The noises grow even louder, before beginning to falter, then they stop. I walk closer to bed and again, the noises start but this time even louder than before. I peak inside of the drapes and I see Daphne spread wide eagle in middle of the bed. She is knocked out cold and the source of all the noise is her snoring. I don't know whether I should be disappointed or relieved. I slowly crawl into her massive bed and I reposition her onto a pillow. Ever so slowly and gently I close her legs, cover her body and tuck her in.

CHAPTER 13 – ALPHA PAINT AND BODY

My phone vibrating inside of my pocket awakes me from a sound sleep. I sit up in a panic. Where am I? I don't recognize this room. Trying to focus my eyes I notice that I didn't make it too far, I must have collapsed on the couch. The vibrating in my pocket begins again. I retrieve the phone and notice an incoming call from Franklin.

"Hello, Hello, wake your butt up Brody," says Franklin. "We are only an hour away. I will text you the address to where we will meet. Brody, Brody are you even listening? Come on man, wake up."

"I'm up, I'm up. I heard you. Just text me the address. I will meet you there."

"I already have," he replies.

"Hey Mr. Officer, no texting and driving; you guys are not above the law. That's extremely dangerous. Plus, you're putting people's lives in danger. You know better than that. You have to lead by example."

"Just get up already," he says. "Shondra is on the phone with Saundra. So just concentrate on yourself."

"I got you man. We will meet you there."

"I hear you," he replies. "But the problem is that you're still laying down."

"Yup, I sure am and if you keep me on this phone, I will continue to do just that."

"Just be there Brody," he says. "Later. Don't keep us waiting"

I don't feel like moving. I'm soar and my head is pounding. Now Franklin said I have an hour before he gets here, that means that he just left. Plus, I am already in the city. I will lay down until the ladies start moving around.

"My body hurts all over. I don't know what happened to me last night. It feels like I was stuffed inside of a small box. Did we get into an accident or something?" Asks Saundra.

"No car accident but you girls were indeed a wreck."

"I wish I could remember because Daphne is still knocked out. She's all tucked in. It's so adorable. I couldn't wake her up at all," she says. "She must be having a good dream to because she has a stupid grin on her face."

"She might be in the bathroom dream."

"What's the bathroom dream?" Asks Saundra.

"It's a dream where going to the bathroom is your primary objective. Now it's hard to reach your goal because everyone you run across delays you. That can go on until you awake or until you make it to the bathroom. I've never personally made it to bathroom in that dream but I heard that if you do relieve yourself, you will actually wet your bed."

"Boy I know a dream that's worse than that," says Saundra. "It's called the I need to quit drinking dream. Now that's when you dream of making hot, passionate, drunken love all night long. Possibly the best sex of your life and when you wake up, you notice that there is a strange man lying in your bed or you're lying in his bed."

"That walk of shame wasn't happening on my watch. I made sure you ladies were safe and that you didn't do anything that you would have regret this morning."

"Awe you're so sweet," she replies. "You know I really enjoy having you around again. Oh, I have an awesome idea. Why don't you come and work with me and Shondra? With you on board, I'm sure Daphne will give us all the cases."

"I'm sure she would but I really can't commit to anything until I regain my full memories. Until then let's focus on our current mission. Who knows? I may already have a job. Besides, our bond goes beyond just being family. I will always be on your team, unless you lose your mind. Then I will be there to either stop you or help you, all because I love you."

"If I lost my mind, you would not be able to stop this," she says. "You better climb on and enjoy the ride. Boy let me stop clowning with you; I came in here to make sure you were up and getting dressed. I left Daphne a note on her mirror, so she will know where we are."

"Well let's get dress. We need to get there on time because my head is hurting and I don't think I can take unnecessary bickering from Franklin today."

The address Franklin sends me takes us to a set of Loft's near the Medical Center. It looks like Franklin and Shondra has beat us here. Franklin waves his hand to signal me to follow him through the security gate. I press the accelerator to follow closely behind him. I'll be a monkey's uncle before a security gate hits me again. I learn from my experiences, when the sign says one car at a time, it really means business. Signs that read "Towing Strictly Enforced" are posted everywhere in the parking lot. I park next to Franklin in one of the only four spaces marked for visitor parking.

"What's up Brody and Saundra," says Franklin. "Man have I missed you two."

"We were only gone for one day," replies Saundra. "What are you buttering up to us for? What kind of trouble are you walking us into?"

"It's nothing like that," replies Franklin. "I just miss y'all. I wanted to drive out here last night but Shondra couldn't."

"Who lives here?"

"Dr. William Baldwin and Dr. Elaine Baldwin lives here," replies Franklin. "We found their son William Baldwin II, in the background of one of the pictures. That's what has brought us here today. I will lead the investigation and you all will observe them and the surroundings. I want you to look at their reactions, mannerisms, attitudes, and emotional state. Look at pictures, mail, magazines and look around for anything out of the normal. Feel free to join the conversation at any time, but don't cut anyone off. We want them to speak freely but most of all, we have to be beyond professional."

Franklin leads the way to Loft number 301. He knocks rather hard on the door. I don't know why people in law enforcement knocks on people door so hard, its offensive. If you are looking for a sure way not to get invited into someone's home, knock like the police.

"Who is it?" Asks a woman from the other side of the door.

"I am Detective Franklin James and I am joined by three of my colleagues. We spoke yesterday on the phone," answers Franklin.

A slender woman in what seems like her prime, opens the door.

"Good Morning, I am Dr. Elaine Baldwin we have been expecting you Detective. Please come in," she says.

"My husband is in the other room but he will be joining us shortly. Please sit down. Would you all like any tea and muffins while you wait?"

"Yes ma'am," replies Franklin. "We would love some."

"It's nice to finally meet a state detective in person," says a slender man who suddenly appears through the same door that Dr. Elaine disappears through. "Hi, I am Dr. William Baldwin," he says. "For the past fifteen years, I have been trying to get a meeting with anyone from your office."

"That's truly unfortunate, I don't know why you didn't get a chance to talk to someone. I've only been a state detective for a short time now," replies Franklin. "But I believe that we should not give up on any case. Which is why I'm choosing to reopen this one involving your son."

"Well it's about time they hired someone like you Detective James," says Dr. William."

Dr. Elaine reenters the room with tea and muffins for everyone. She hands them out then sits beside her husband.

"My only requirement is that you use the coasters that I have provided, please and thank you," she says. "Now detective where would you like to start?"

"Let's start at the beginning. Why did you fill out a missing person's report after your son had been pronounced dead by the coroner office?" Asks Franklin.

Dr. William clears his throat. "My son William II is a genius.," he says. "William has scored in the top percentile in every aptitude test he ever took. He has an I.Q. above 140 and he loves cars. They told us that William was accidently killed while working on an unauthorized project but no matter if it was authorized or not, William could tear a car apart and rebuild it easily. The detectives that started this case was convinced, no foul play was involved but that don't give us any clarity."

Dr. William pauses and everyone keenly watches his every movement. Eagerly we await his next words but he says nothing. He blows on his tea then sips it, which in turn causes everyone to sip tea along with him.

"Are you comfortable talking about this?" Asks Franklin.

"We have been talking about this for fifteen years now," says Dr. Elaine. "It's now time for you Detectives to listen."

"Dr. William continues, "The body was burnt beyond recognition and we couldn't identify him."

"William was working on a BIG innovative project for this guy named Luke," adds Dr. Elaine. "William and Luke became inseparable once they started working on that project. I didn't care for Luke not one bit but William insured me that Luke was from a good family but after

215

the fire, we never saw nor heard anything from Luke again."

"I don't have anything in any of my files about a person named Luke," says Franklin. "Do you know his last name?"

"No," replies Dr. Elaine. "He never talked to us and William never talked about him. After meeting him the first time I told William that I didn't want him in our house."

"What was it that you didn't like about Luke on that encounter?" Asks Franklin.

"He was a spoiled brat who didn't have any manners or home training," says Dr. Elaine.

"Did you all tell the detectives about Luke?" Asks Franklin.

"Yes, we did but talking to them was like talking to a horse's behind," replies Dr. William. "At that time in our lives we were not complete with our residency. So, our words held very little weight."

"I see," says Franklin. "Did anyone else have any dealings with this Luke person?"

"I'm pretty sure the guys at the car shop had to know him," says Dr. Elaine. "That's the only place William and Luke would work on that project. It was located on Almeda Road last I checked. The name is Alpha Paint and Body."

"One last thing," adds Franklin. "Can you look at this photo? Can you identify whether the person that is circled is your son?"

Dr. Elaine and Dr. William takes the photo away from Franklin. They both stare very intensely while whispering to each other. Dr. Elaine walks into the kitchen before reappearing with a magnifying glass. They view the picture through the magnifying glass.

"Yes, that's our boy," says Dr. Elaine. "I can tell because of that scar he got on his first fishing trip with his father. Apparently, someone let him hook himself in the face. We couldn't get that child to go anywhere near water after that. He wouldn't eat fish neither."

"Where did you get this photo?" Asks Dr. William.

"This photo was taken one year after your son was pronounced dead," says Franklin. "On this photo, he was very much alive."

"Hallelujah! I knew it," shouts Dr. Elaine. "Please tell me that you will find my son and bring him home?"

"Well that is part of the plan," replies Franklin. "Here is my card. If you remember anything that you think will be helpful or if William contacts you, please don't hesitate to call. I commend you for staying strong and sticking to your faith. Despite what others said, you still believed and you fought for that belief. Lately it's been extremely easy for people to give up and follow the crowd but as soon as I receive any information on this case, I will contact you."

"Thank You Detective James," says Dr. William. "Here is my card, also. You can reach me at any time with either of those numbers. I hope to hear from you soon."

"Hopefully you will," replies Franklin. "Again, thank you for your assistance and hospitality. Please enjoy the remainder of your day."

Upon exiting the lofts, I notice that it is extremely bright today. The morning sun baths the parking lot with bright rays. The reflection of the sun off the concrete becomes nearly blinding upon exiting the lofts. I am impressed by the way Franklin took charge and controlled the situation up there. I remember him being a different person before I left home but life tends to mold and shape people into better versions of themselves. Evolution is inevitable if your determination is unwavering. I guess the hard part is getting family and friends that haven't been around you, to accept and appreciate your evolution.

"Snap out of it Brody and listen up," demands Franklin. "I need you three to follow this lead and go to Alpha Paint and Body. Find out whatever you can about this Luke person and ask about the fire that supposedly killed William II. We need anything that can lead us to his whereabouts."

"Why aren't you coming along?" Asks Shondra.

"With our newly found information, I will relocate my base of operations," says Franklin. "I need to contact my superiors to see how they want to play this out. Oh, by the way, my car is currently at home. Can I borrow your car Brody? I will be extremely careful. Plus, we can save time by splitting up."

"Sure, Franklin it's only a car; one that you can replace if anything does happen while you take command of it. Being such a big shot Detective and all, I'm sure you get paid handsomely."

"Speaking of getting paid," interrupts Saundra. "Franklin, when you make that phone call make sure you persuade whoever is on the other side that we need to be paid accordingly. We don't work for free and we are doing the ground work."

"I'm already on it," replies Franklin. "I will contact you all with the address to our new headquarters; please don't kick up too much dirt. From here on, we may be entering dangerous waters. The fact that no one cared to follow up on their story seems strange to me. Be careful!"

"You just make sure that we are taken care of," adds Shondra. "You don't want to open the book to this Texas Horror Story."

"I'm on it," says Franklin.

For the last forty-five minutes, I've been stuck listening to Saundra talking non-stop. She's been bringing Shondra up to speed with the whole Big Wayne situation, which leads her into the Daphne situation. Which then causes Saundra to call Daphne. Please still be sleeping or working. Nope, she isn't sleeping and she answers the phone. I'm not sure what Daphne remembers from last night but Saundra is growing excited by the second. It's a dead giveaway that they are talking about me, by the way she keeps looking back here with side eye. Her conversation sounds more like a text message. All I hear is, "Hey Girl. What? No! He did what? Baaaaahaaaaa! Girl, no you didn't! I'm dead. I can't believe you. I bet. Okay then, bye-bye."

"Brody, Brody, Brody," repeats Saundra. "Boy, we can't bring you nowhere. You just met that woman yesterday and now it sounds like my girl has fallen for you. Now tell us, what exactly did you do to that woman last night?"

"Are you sure you want those details?" Asks Shondra.

"On second thought, I don't want to know," says Saundra. "Whatever you did, you go boy! Well, she would like to exchange numbers with you and maybe go on an official date."

"I didn't do anything for her, that I didn't do for you. As for a date, I don't think we have time to play the dating game. Didn't you just ask Franklin to get us paid?"

"Well at least let me give her your number," Saundra demands. "You two can keep in contact when you do have time."

"This is actually Franklin's phone so that won't be a good idea either."

"What's wrong Brody?" Asks Saundra. "Are you scared of the kitty-cat? Are you a rooster-fruit?"

"You just might be worse than Franklin. But to answer your question, I'm not scared of the kitty-cat nor am I the rooster-fruit. I just don't think it's a good idea for me to get a relationship started in the middle of this crucial investigation. The last thing we need is Daphne on my mind, when I'm supposed to be watching your backs."

"Well, I will just tell her that after the investigation is complete we can set up a date," says Saundra.

"Enough of all that," interrupts Shondra. "Brody is right. It's time to focus. We are here."

Alpha Paint and Body sits off Almeda Road; down the street in the distance, the Beltway-8 is slightly visible. Despite the grounds and parking lot being clean, the building itself looks long past its glory days. Two cars sitting in the parking lot is the only sign that the place is still open. Shondra parks near the entrance to the building.

"We don't know what we will find in here so I will take the lead. Our story will be that we are investigating this Luke person. If the people here know anything about fifteen years ago, they will recognize that name."

"I'm cool with that," says Saundra.

"I've never worked with you," adds Shondra. "I don't see why you're taking the lead. From what I understand you barely escaped Big Wayne."

"It's just plan A, if circumstances change then one of you take the lead."

"He is structured and I trust him," says Saundra.

"I do trust her and her judgement," says Shondra. "So, if she thinks it's cool, I guess I'll go along.

A bell rings upon opening the doors to Alpha Paint and Body. Leading the ladies, I move slowly into the building; letting our eyes adjust to the change in lighting. The room is dimly lit because of a few lights that seem to be on the verge of expiring. A young man in his late teens or early twenties emerges from a door behind the counter. He looks in our direction but he ignores us and proceeds to dig underneath the counter. His hands reappear holding a clean cloth towel. He tosses his black hair backwards, then he slowly wipes away the oil and sweat from his face. He keeps his eyes on Shondra in the process.

"Hola, ¿en qué puedo servirle?" he says. *(Hello, how can I help you?)*

Shondra immediately asks, "Man do you speak any English?"

"Yo no hablo Inglés mi diosa de chocolate," he replies. ¿Quieres salir conmigo?" *(I don't speak English my chocolate goddess. Would you like to go out with me?)*

With a puzzled look on her face, Shondra looks towards Saundra.

"Don't look at me," says Saundra. "I don't speak Mexican either."

"Yo tampoco," interrupts the guy behind the counter. "Pero yo puedo presentarle mi cultura Latina, mi amor." *(Me neither. But I can introduce you to my Latin culture, my love.)*

Loudly, I clear my throat. "Basta, muchacho amante." *(That's enough, Lover Boy.)*

Simultaneously, Saundra and Shondra turns to look me square in the face, while the guy behind the counter stands there in a state of shock.

"I know you understand me because you answered appropriately to the ladies. Now, I have a few questions for you. We are looking for a man named Luke, who once frequented this place. Do you know anything about him?

Like a deer in head lights, he just stands there. He's staring as if he can't believe that one of us speaks Spanish. Frantically, he's eyes start darting around the room. With the palm of his hands he hits the bells, which is placed on the counter for customer use.

"Hold your horses, I'm coming," is heard coming from another room.

A guy emerges from the door and immediately takes the bell away from the younger guy. The youngster quickly scurries away through the door but not before receiving a swift kick to the behind. Without saying one word, the new guy looks me over once before his focus shifts to the ladies. He hesitates for a moment before leaning over the counter for a closer look.

"My eyes must be playing tricks on me," he says. "It can't be the James Twins. I follow you girls on everything. I even have this blog where we mainly talk about how you two should have your own T.V. show and stuff. We collect any footage that is taken when you are doing your thing. I love you girls. You always get your man."

"Thanks for taking notice," says Saundra.

"I have one question? What are you, Private Investigators or Bounty Hunters?" He asks."

"Don't try to put a label on us," replies Shondra.

"Yeah, we are free spirits," adds Saundra. "There is never a job to big or small that we can't handle."

"Wow! The James Twins. What brings you to our shop?" He asks. "My name is Hector. I want to be a bounty hunter or whatever you are.

"It's a pleasure to meet a fan," says Shondra.

"No, the pleasure is all mine," replies Hector. "I'm actually President of your fan club."

"Hey Hector, we are always looking to help someone achieve their dreams," says Saundra. "We know a lot of people in the bounty hunter and the private investigators communities. If you help us, we will do the same for you."

"I'll help you any way I can, but you have to take a few selfies with me," replies Hector. "Who is this guy? I never seen a dude with you before."

"That's how important this case is," says Saundra. "You are getting the pleasure to meet our Boss, Mr. B."

"It's an honor to meet you Mr. B.," replies Hector.

Hector reaches out his hand. Shondra smacks that hand and steps in-front of me.

"Sorry Hector, you can't touch Mr. B. He only talks to the person in-charge," says Shondra. "But since you have been such a great host, he might choose to talk to you."

"I can't believe you just touched me," says Hector. "I'm not washing this hand. The guys won't believe this."

"You also cannot mention this meeting in your blog. We will be watching!" threatens Saundra.

"It's cool I can keep a secret. What can I help you with?" Asks Hector.

"On August 24, 2001 at 9:00 a.m., a fire was reported on these grounds. A kid a few years out of grade school, named William Baldwin II, was killed in that fire. He was in association with a man named Luke."

"Sorry Mr. B, I will have to cut you off right there," interrupts Hector. "The only person around here that was around back then is Uncle Juan. Uncle Juan is a strange fellow but he was a mechanic back around the time you're talking about. He owns the place now. He is always preaching to us about what a sharp, trained mind can achieve."

"When are you expecting him to be back?"

"He never leaves this building," says Hector. "He hasn't left this place in over fourteen years."

"Is there any way that I can speak to your Uncle Juan?"

"Sure," says Hector. "Follow me."

We follow Hector behind the counter and through the door. We step into a huge car garage but the size of the shop may be magnified by their lack of customers. Three cars that are stripped completely down, display the only signs of actual work. As we walk across the shop I notice someone peeking through the blinds of what seems to be an office.

"Wait here while I make sure it's okay to enter," says Hector.

"Sorry Hector but Mr. B. waits for no one," replies Saundra. "Either we accompany you or we leave."

Hesitantly, Hector proceeds towards the office. Hector knocks on the door then stands back and waits. The rhythm of his knock indicates that he is using a code. Loud noises can be heard from the other side of the door, as eight deadbolts are unlocked. The door cracks open slightly.

"Follow closely behind me," says Hector.

Inside of the building the lights are completely off and dozens of candles are lit throughout the room. Shadows dance across the wall, growing larger as they move before disappearing into blackness. The room resembles a small one-bedroom apartment. The scent of candles fights to mask another smell that still lingers in the room. Hector's Uncle Juan sits in a recliner with his legs crossed, holding a cigar in his left hand and a drink in his right hand. He looks up with eyes harder than diamond and redder than fire.

"¡Tonto. ¿Por qué trajiste les aquí?" Asks Uncle Juan. *(You fool. Why did you bring them here?)*

Before Hector can answer, I step forward., placing myself between Hector and Uncle Juan. I stare into Uncle Juan's cold red eyes.

"Mi nombre es Sr. B. En mi presencia hablarme solo. *(My name is Mr. B. In my presence, you address only me.)*

"Calma mi amigo," replies Uncle Juan. "Un hombre en mi posición debe tener cuidado en todo momento. *(Calm down my friend, a man in my position must be careful at all times.)*

"No estoy aquí para ponerlo en peligro." *(I am not here to put you in any danger.)*

"Can we speak in English?" Asks Uncle Juan. "My Spanish is a little rusty."

"Sonido perfectamente bien antes de que me uní a la conversación." *(It sounds perfectly fine before I joined the conversation.)*

"You got me Mr. B." replies Uncle Juan. "But I'll be more comfortable and cooperative if we were to continue this conversation in English. I haven't left this building in fourteen years now. My nephews speak a little Spanish but not enough to keep me as fluent as I should be.

"Your nephew tells me that you worked as a mechanic here long before you became the owner."

"Si amigo," says Uncle Juan. "Back then we were the number one shop in Houston. I think we started the candy paint revolution, amongst other things. The city was hot and we were hot like screw music. Back then you couldn't ever find a parking spot out front. There were no walk-ins and appointments stayed booked for at least two months or more."

"Do you mind if I call you Juan?"

"That's fine amigo," replies Juan.

"I actually came here to talk with you about the events that transpired back in the year 2001."

Juan stares blankly at the ceiling before downing the rest of his drink. Juan's glass was more than half full. He wipes his mouth on his sleeve then stands up. With his head high in the air, Juan relights his cigar.

"Hector sacarlos de aquí, han sobrepasado su bienvenida," Juan nervously says. *(Hector get them out of here, they have overstayed their welcome.)*

"Juan, usted sabe que todavía hablar en Español." *(Juan, you know I still speak Spanish.)*

Juan looks up with eyes as innocent as a puppy. "I'm sorry Mr. B but thinking about that period gives me an uneasy feeling," he says. "That was my last year of freedom."

229

"I'm sorry Juan but we must talk about that time. What do you mean, your last year of freedom? Can you start with explaining to me the reason why you won't go outside?"

Juan franticly looks around. His expression grows more desperate as we wait for his response. "You're going to get me killed," he says somberly.

"I'm sorry Juan but you can't run from death, no one can. Once you're born into this world, there is only one certainty, and that's we will all die one day. The most important thing is how you live your life in-between. Have you grown wiser? Have you learned from your mistakes? How did you treat others? Did you teach the next generation anything? What I'm saying Juan is that you're not living life by hiding in this shop. Whoever is trying to kill you has already won the battle because you have given up. They don't have to worry about you. I'm sure that whoever is after you, is completely confident that you will die in your self-imposed prison."

Tentatively Juan replies, "If you can ensure my safety, we can go for a walk out back. I can use some fresh air."

I turn towards Saundra, Shondra, and Hector and nearly burst into laughter, seeing them jump out of their seats and stand at attention.

"You three go secure the facility and report back to me as soon as it is safe for Juan to take a walk."

"Yes Sir," they reply.

The three of them eagerly hurry out of the building.

"Is that better Juan? You should be able to breathe a little better now.

"Thank You Mr. B." replies Juan.

"Now, tell me why haven't you left this building in over fourteen years?"

"Can I offer you a drink?" Asks Juan anxiously. "I don't feel like drinking alone.

"Sure."

Juan pours me a shot of tequila and pours himself, half of a glass. He downs it as if it was a shot, then pours himself a full glass.

"Well, the first half of 2001 was business as usual," he says. "We were so popular that young aspiring mechanics would come to train under us. I already had a young mechanic that was hands down better than anyone else. At first, I was extremely tough on that kid but no matter what I said and did to him, he continued to work hard. Eventually, I took him on as my apprentice and I taught him everything I knew. He was positioning himself to start his own business. His name was William. Our cliental at that time consist of some wealthy folk, local rappers, and random people from Louisiana. This was the most exciting place to work in the city and it had been that way for twenty years. The owners were brothers Tommy and Shawn Bennett. I loved the Bennett's. They treated everyone with respect and in turn they were loved by all. In June of 2001, my apprentice started to spread his wings. He began working on new innovative projects. His ideas were different from anything I've seen before. William started gaining popularity throughout the city and people started requesting him personally to modernize their vehicle. You know it wasn't easy for us older folk to jump onto the technology wave but William made our transition easy. He knew about all the new technology that was currently out and he knew about pending future technology. He kept us ahead of our competition. The kid was awesome and he would have made an awesome inventor but he loved working on cars. His new-found fame attracted all types of people. Some were good and some were not. I tried my best to keep him away from Luke but I wasn't successful. In two months, everything went from peaceful to turbulent."

"How did things become turbulent?"

"On August 24, 2001, I pulled into the drive way to find a raging fire. I thought someone was burning the building down but instead, I found Williams project up in flames. After the fire was extinguished and the smoke cleared, we found out that William's body was found inside. After that incident, stranger things started to happen. One after another, employees of Alpha Paint and Body started turning up dead. The owner Shawn Bennett was killed two days later in a car accident. A carbon monoxide leak killed four other employees who car pooled together. After that Tommy Bennett wasn't the same. He came to me one day with the deed to this place. In a shocking turn of events, he signed his company over to me. I thought he was suffering from post-traumatic stress or something. Alpha Paint and Body was all mine but when we embraced he told me that we were not safe. He told me if anything happens to him, I need to disappear. He told me to sell the place and use the money to start a new life somewhere far away. That same night, Tommy Bennett was found dead at his own home. The police report states that he died of an accidental overdose but if you knew Tommy you knew that he and his brother were both straight-edge. They did not smoke, drink, take over the counter medication, nor did they take prescription drugs. So, I took Tommy's advice. I closed the shop and I decided to hide. But everywhere I went, it felt as if someone was always following me. I spent months looking over my shoulders and hiding in some horrible places. On one stormy night, I decided to come back to this shop. I snuck in through a broken back window and I haven't left since. I believe someone is out there to get me and I don't want to find out who it is or why.

A loud popping sound is heard from outside. Juan looks at me with curious eyes. For a split second, all is silent. Then a heavy stream of gunfire begins, which is much louder than the initial popping sound. As quickly as it started, it's over. Both Juan and I hurry to extinguish the candles that illuminate the room. I position myself close to the door to focus on the chatter that is coming from outside. Saundra burst through the door, along with Hector holding his left shoulder.

"There was a sniper on top of the water tower," says Saundra. "He was at least one hundred yards away but he shot Hector in his shoulder because Hector spotted him with his binoculars."

"I think the bullet went through cleanly," says Hector while grimacing in pain.

"I told you! You'd get me killed," says Juan frantically. "We need to get out of here."

"We have a window to escape," replies Saundra. "We forced the shooter to bail from the water tower and Shondra went to retrieve the truck."

"Let's get out of here. We need to get ahold of Franklin."

To put as much distance between ourselves and the shooter, we decide to go south on Almeda. Shondra exits onto the Beltway-8 and drives into the EZ-tag entrance. A camera takes a photo of the car and driver. If anyone is following us they will have to risk giving up his or her identity. It's a good thing that the Beltway-8 circles the city because Franklin is not answering his phone. Juan is in the backseat shaking and moaning. He has been hiding underneath his jacket since we left Alpha Paint and Body. He's convinced that today is the last day of his life. Honestly, I don't blame him for being scared. He has lived in fear for the past fourteen years. It would be miraculous for him to suddenly find his missing courage. My phone vibrates in my hand.

"Well it's about time you call back. We had a situation at Alpha Paint and Body."

"I heard about it just a few minutes ago," says Franklin. "I instantly knew that it was you all. Is everyone okay?"

"Yes, everyone's fine. Saundra and Shondra managed to drive off the shooter but a mechanic named Hector was shot. He said he'll be fine but I'm no medical professional and neither is he. He will need a second opinion."

"Where are you located now?" Asks Franklin.

"We are driving on the Beltway-8. We have a witness named Juan also. He knows valuable information about Luke and William II. Alpha Paint and Body has been his self-imposed prison, for the past fourteen years. I think our shooter was hired to make sure he never stepped out alive. His life is in danger and now we are responsible for it."

"This new information may speed things up," says Franklin. "I just received the approval and I will text you the location of our new headquarters."

"Thanks, Bye."

"Was that Franklin?" Asks Saundra.

"Yes, he is about to send me the address to where he wants us to meet."

"Okay, but I text Daphne also," she adds. "She is also sending us an address to meet."

"Why did you text Daphne?"

"Because Franklin wasn't answer and someone just shot at us," she replies. "It's too dangerous for us to stay on one path. So, I contacted Daphne."

"I'm cool with that, it's always good to have a 'what if' plan."

"Well which plan will we go with?" Asks Shondra. "People are driving too unsafe for us to stay in this traffic. They are cutting us off, then slamming on their brakes because they made the wrong move. That just sends my temper through the roof. They are lucky I am suppressing this urge to just start running them off the road."

"Please don't girl," says Saundra. "Houston has enough road rage incidents. Don't cause the next one."

"I'm just saying," adds Shondra. "Look! She is on her phone texting with her head down. What makes things worst is that we are in stop and go traffic. It's just too dangerous to stay in this traffic and I might become the danger."

"Girl, stop acting like momma," replies Saundra. "We came here to help the people not traumatize them."

"You know I'm a country girl," says Shondra. "I take being cut-off as a sign of disrespect and I was raised not to let no one disrespect me."

"Stop being a drama queen," says Saundra. "You can't use our upbringing to justify your behavior."

"Shondra please relax. You don't want to hit anyone. You're just frustrated about our current situation. I know this situation is extremely stressful but just think for a moment. I don't think the shooter is following us and when has Franklin ever left you hanging? Now, don't think back to childhood, I'm talking about since you started your own life's journey. Has Franklin ever let you down?"

"No, I guess not." she replies, "I just don't like it Brody, not one bit. We don't have control of anything. I feel like a pawn."

"Don't worry because in the game of chess, the least you would be, is a knight."

"You mean the least I'd be, is the Queen," replies Shondra.

"I just received an address from Daphne," interjects Saundra.

"Franklin just sent me his address also."

"Well, where are we going?" Ask Shondra.

"Simultaneously we reply, "San Felipe."

CHAPTER 14 – COMMAND CENTER

The address given to us by Franklin and Daphne leads to even more traffic. I am relieved when the building appears within sight because Shondra has reached her boiling point. Which puts us in the middle of the calm before the storm. Saundra is on high alert as she is now tasked with calming her. The building which is now our new headquarters is hidden in plain sight. It sits amongst shopping stores, cafes, banks, and other businesses. The mirror tent windows make it impossible to see inside of the building. Instead we can see the reflections of Old Glory and The Lone Star Flag flapping proudly in the wind. Besides the flag pole the only other decoration is a concrete slab with the buildings address on in. From this viewpoint, I don't see a way inside of the building.

"Parking on the street is not an option, there is nowhere to park," says Shondra. "Where do we go?"

"Past that building up ahead, then take a right onto the next street," replies Saundra. "Up ahead we should see a park on our right. Turn into the park, now drive towards that construction area over there."

"Girl have you lost your mind?" Asks Shondra. "There is nowhere to go."

"Just follow my directions," replies Saundra. "Now, onto that slab and drive between the restrooms. This should lead us to an underground parking garage."

239

"What, drive into the wall?" Asks Shondra.

"That's not a real wall," says Saundra.

"It better not be!" shouts Shondra.

We vanish into a dark tunnel. If we didn't have working headlights we wouldn't have lights at all. The downward drive does not take long as light from the hidden garage illuminates our exit. Waiting for us inside of this underground parking garage is Franklin, Daphne, and a few others that I haven't met.

"I'm so happy to see you guys," says Franklin. "I'm sorry for putting you all in danger. Now it's a strong possibility that you all are targets of this shooter. I will now be placing you all into protective custody."

"That will not work for me. I did not come this far just to tuck my tail and run in the face of danger."

"Unfortunately, you all are civilians," replies Franklin. "Neither the Government of the United States nor the State of Texas will allow for civilians to participate in harmful activities."

"Well that don't apply to us," adds Saundra. "We are licensed professionals and Mr. B here is leading our current investigation."

"We have rights and we are conscious to what they are," says Shondra.

"Either we can continue to team up or Saundra, Shondra, and I can do this on our own. Believe me, we will not stop."

"Well everyone, are you satisfied? I told you this group would not take it lying down," says Daphne.

"What do you suggest?" Asks Franklin.

"Don't worry," replies Daphne. "This is my city, we will work something out. Besides, I owe them a great deal. No! This city owes them a great deal."

"In that case, welcome to our joint operation," says Franklin. "The city of Houston, the State of Texas, the Federal Bureau of Investigation, the Central Intelligence Agency and you all; has now joined forces on this special operation."

"Texas State Detective Franklin James will lead the team," says Daphne. "The city of Houston will provide the necessary resources and manpower if available. The F.B.I. will cover forensics and the C.I.A. will provide technical support."

"What about us?" Asks Hector.

"Who is this guy and why is he here?" Asks Daphne.

"This is Hector, he was responsible for spotting our shooter but he also took one in the shoulder in the process. That fellow over there is Hector's brother; he doesn't talk much. This gentleman here is their uncle, his name is Juan. Right now, he is our key witness. He worked in the past with both Luke and William. He may have knowledge that can help in our investigation."

"Mr. Juan, my name is Detective Franklin James. It's a pleasure to meet you," says Franklin. "We need to ask you some questions, after which we will place you and your nephews into protective custody."

"Sure," replies Juan. "But only if Mr. B is there, I'm more comfortable with him around."

"Listen up everyone," announces Franklin. "From this point forward we are on strict lock-down. No one knows of this operation, except for a few leaders of each organization. We want to keep it that way. DO NOT! I repeat. DO NOT tell anyone where we are. This tower will be our new headquarters and because of our new findings, we were granted permission to fully reopen this cold case. This operation was given assistance from the F.B.I. because we are dealing with a potential serial killer. They have been pursuing several cases which resemble serial killing. The C.I.A. has been tracking our friend that you met earlier. The shooter on the water tower is an international assassin who they have been pursuing for some time. Each organization has key knowledge on different subject matters which can help us in our case. Because we are operating on speculation, we weren't granted a full team but we were given one member representing each organization. With you all aboard, this team looks full to me. Now let's get out of this dusty garage. This way please!"

The elevator seems to be the only way to get into the tower from the garage. We board the massive elevator, everyone has room to board without incident. According to the elevator panel this tower has twenty floors. We stop on the second floor where the doors slide open. Franklin is the first to step into the hallway.

"Welcome to the Command Center," he says excitedly. "This building has been recently renovated to act as the command center for all agencies operating throughout the southern half of the United States. We have been granted the pleasure of being the first team to operate from this Command Center. Everyone please have a seat. It's a little messy but that will soon change. Hector, would you please follow the nurse. She will take care of your wound."

"I NEED A DOCTOR, NOT A NURSE!" shouts Hector.

"Is that so?" Asks Franklin.

"YES!" shouts Hector. "I'VE BEEN SHOT! Have you ever been shot?"

"Yes, I have," replies Franklin. "More than once. One time I had to dig the bullet out myself and stitch the wound. I wish I had a nurse to help me but you want doctor. In most cases, you rarely see your doctor. Once a day for sure, maybe twice if you're really sick. You will be taken care of though, twenty-four hours a day. Seven days a week. By no one else but your nurse."

"No disrespect. I don't mean to be rude," says Hector. "But I've never been shot and it really hurts."

"Well, your choices are either to go with her or to stay in here with us," says Franklin. "I'm pretty sure there are a few PhD's in the room. So, if you want a doctor, your choice is one of us."

Hector can be heard apologizing to the nurse as they exit down a hallway with his brother trailing close behind them. Franklin takes Juan into one of the adjacent rooms. Franklin then reappears and stands before everyone with a sharp, stern expression on his face. He stares into the face of everyone in the room, making sure to establish eye contact before proceeding to the next person.

"Look at everyone in this room," says Franklin. "These seven people are now your new teammates. No matter what agency you belong to, this is now your new family. The three newest members to this family is Assistant District Attorney Daphne Turner, C.I.A. Analyst Douglas Jackson, and F.B.I. Agent Max Jones. These three will operate mainly from the Command Center. Unfortunately, because of how the day has started, we will not ask anyone to do anything further. Brody, Saundra, and Shondra will share the fourteenth-floor apartment. You all deserve to rest for the remainder of the day. We will finish setting up the Command Center. This place is totally secure, so rest well. Oh, I almost forgot. Can one of you call back home and make sure Big Mama don't put out an Amber alert for the four of us? You all are free to go up to your apartment."

"Excuse me Douglas. Can I talk to you for a moment?"

"Sure," he replies. "It's Brody, right?"

"Yes, with so much happening I can't really explain everything to you but I have these scrambled letters that I don't understand. When you have time to spare, can you use your analytical skills to examine them? I'm not in any rush. Actually, I really don't know where to start or who to go to."

"Sure Brody, no problem," he replies. "I don't mind helping. What are they?"

"The letters are M, H, R, P, E, O, L, U, E, G, and E."

"Okay, When I have the time I will work on it," says Douglas.

"Thanks"

"We're waiting on you Brody," says Shondra.

Don't be rude, I was getting acquainted with our new teammate.

Daphne and Franklin accompanies us on the elevator. The fourteenth-floor apartment Franklin put us in has an open floor plan which makes it huge. The decoration is minimal but there is an overall sense of warmth and security enveloping the entire place.

"Girl will you be staying with us?" Asks Saundra.

"No," replies Daphne. "I just wanted to make sure you all are okay. Today, I have other obligations to the city."

"Can we tag along?" Asks Saundra.

"Sorry," replies Daphne. "We are not certain whether the shooter saw your faces. For right now we ask that you all just relax and lay low."

"Well when you come back, bring us something good to eat," adds Shondra.

"The refrigerator and pantries are stocked," says Franklin. "You have everything you need. You can cook or just contact me and all your needs will be met."

"Not all my needs," says Shondra.

"Girl Bye," says Daphne.

As soon as the elevator door closes, the twins run off. I let them choose their room first, I'm still left with plenty of options. Plus, I'm not that picky, this apartment is cozy. I could sleep on the floor in front of the fire place. There's a weight room with its own spa and a game room with its own bar. Unfortunately, I'm too tired to get into anything else. I still haven't shaken off yesterday. I need a bed and this room will do. I collapse into an extremely comfortable bed; laying here surrounded by comfort, helps me clear all thoughts.

I open my eyes to see, the day is clear and the sun shines brightly. I find myself walking behind a man dressed in camouflage from head to boot. Even his hat is camouflaged. He is carrying a backpack that seems to be quite full. He stands a little taller than me. We walk along a rocky ground. The area appears unpopulated and there's nothing around except for trees and overgrown grass. We pass through a small forest to reveal an ominous mountain looming in the background. The camouflage man hacks at the grass to clear a path. We reach the foot of the mountain and begin our climb. He goes first, he chooses which boulders to climb over and establishing foot and hand holes when none are available. A huge boulder blocks our path but impressively he climbs it, then he scales the wall behind it with ease. Standing atop of the cliff with his back to the sun he looks down and shouts, "Are you coming?" His voice is strangely familiar but the light from the sun blinds me. My temporary blindness prevents me from getting a view of his face. I follow his lead and find myself scaling the boulder and wall as effortlessly as he did. Once on top of the cliff I turn to see a breathtaking sight. A river with water as blue as the sky can be seen surrounded by lush green trees. Birds fly high in the air and many other animal sounds can be heard down below. The air is clean and despite the sun being out, a cool breeze blows. I turn to proceed but slips on loose rocks. I struggle to regain my balance without luck. Before gravity forces me off the cliff and down to the rocky ground, the camouflage man pulls me to safety.

"YOU MUST NEVER LOSE FOCUS!" He yells.

With both hands on my knees I find myself gasping for air. I notice that I also wear the same camouflage that he wears. While rising to straighten, I realize that I am also carrying a backpack. My backpack feels heavier than his backpack looks. I speed up to catch the camouflage man but stumbles over an exposed root. I gather myself before continuing to move on but lose sight of him. I round a huge tree to see the camouflage man standing there with his palm out. Five men stand in front of him holding AK-47's. I stop but I am spotted by one of the men. The camouflage man turns and mouths, "Run Rouge, it's a trap. Don't let them get the device." I turn and sprint back down the mountain. I run and duck as bullets zip past my ears. I reach the cliff where I nearly fell earlier. Without hesitation, I jump off the cliff. I land on top of the large boulder and I roll from it roughly, forcefully hitting the ground. Bullets ricocheting off the boulder and the voices of my pursuers rush me to my feet. I run through the overgrown grass towards the river I saw earlier. I stop and hide my backpack underneath a tree with large roots sticking out from the ground. To erase my trail, I double back making sure my pursuers spot me. We run through the bush until I spot the river. They shot again causing me to jump into the river. I swim to the other side but find myself staring down a waterfall. My pursuers emerge from the river. I find myself trapped between them and the waterfall.

"Where is the device?" They ask.

I look at them trying to find an opening but there is none to find.

"Just shoot him," a guy with a scar beneath his left eye says. "We can torture Sting-Ray until he tells us where the device is. There is no way he would have entrusted it to this scared peace of trash."

Without hesitation, the other guy smiles and shoots. His first shot misses completely, which causes him to look at his gun curiously. It appears as if the bullet changed its course in midair, as if it ricocheted off something.

"How did you miss him?" Asks the guy with the scar.

"I don't know but I won't miss again," he replies.

He shoots again, this time emptying his clip. It appears as if the first bullet that arrives, explodes before hitting me. The explosion sends me flying, causing me to fall over the waterfall. I crash into the water and instantly, feel the force of the current pull me down the river.

My eyes open and immediately, I claw at my chest. I gasp for air but realize that I'm not underwater. I set up in the bed.

"What was that? When was that? Can this be my memories? Sting-Ray!"

My head begins to throb as if I was being hit repetitively by a hammer. The throbbing increases causes the pain to grow stronger. I attempt to stand but a rush of dizziness causes me to crumble back onto the bed. Even though I'm in pain, there is one question on my mind. "What happened to Sting-Ray?"

CHAPTER 15 – OPERATION VANISHING ACT

"Brody! Brody! Wake up! Brody! Brody! Wake Up!" says a desperate voice.

My eyes open and I notice Shondra is on her knees beside the bed. It looks as if she wants to tell me something because she has a bewildered look on her face. She looks like she is extremely mad about something. She looks down and I follow her gaze. I notice that I am holding her hand in a firm grasp, effectively restraining her. Quickly, I let go of her hand. I sit up and immediately, I must dodge a flurry of punches. I successfully roll out of bed and onto my feet.

Infuriated Shondra says, "Boy, you are lucky that I don't like to be awoken either. Otherwise, you would have to fight me every time you see me. Now, get out of my way. I should've punched a hole through your face, bending my hand back like somebody trying to do something to you. Boy you're lucky that you're my cousin. Move!

She pushes me, then exits the room. I hear her fussing and complaining as she walks down the hall.

"Sorry, Shondra!"

I turn to see that the room looks like a tornado stopped by last night. Quickly, I scrounge about to find something

251

to wear. I put on clothing and hurry to the elevator. What time is it? I must have slept for nearly eighteen hours but I feel rested and rejuvenated. I hear a group of people talking before the elevator doors open. Cautiously, I step out the elevator and the building goes quiet. Everyone turns to look at me except for Shondra. She sits there looking off in the other direction while she rubs her wrist. Without saying a word, I walk to the table Shondra is sitting at and I sit right beside her. She moves over a little to create space between us. I move closer to her, erasing the space she created. We continue moving along the bench until she runs out of room. She stops and looks at me.

"I am so sorry Shondra. I don't know what got into me. I think I had a rough night but I'm not making an excuse. I'm terribly sorry; I hope I didn't hurt you.

"No, you didn't," she replies. "I'm alright. Just don't ever do it again. I don't know what got into you either but you scared me. Are you okay? Saundra just told us about you losing your memories. Does this incident have something to do with that?"

"I think it does somehow. I only recently found out that part of my memory was missing. I was told that my memories would return to me eventually. I think that eventually may have taken place last night. Unfortunately, you awoke me from it."

"Well I knew you didn't mean me any harm," she replies. "I can't believe how you have grown. You finally got me back after all those years. I remember putting cayenne pepper on your lips while you were sleeping when we were kids. I think it was your first sleep over and you fell asleep first. Boy you awoke like a Tasmanian devil after licking your lips. We couldn't stop your rampage but it was funny. You got so mad you decided that you would walk home in the middle of the night. The only way to stop you was by waking my parents. You're much stronger now. I tried to make you let go but that made things worse. I can't believe you took me to my knees before you awoke. I couldn't even react to your movement."

"Again, I'm sorry Shondra. Now, I remember that I have been trained by various experts throughout the continents of Africa and Asia."

"It hurts too," she says. "But the nurse looked at it. It's not broken nor is it sprained. I would say no harm, no foul, but you owe me and I collect on all debts. I don't know what I want but when I figure it out, I will let you know. I might get you to train me in some of that stuff. That could be handy.

"Are you two good?" Asks Franklin.

"Just peachy," replies Shondra.

"Well come, we are about to begin this morning's briefing," says Franklin.

There are visible changes to the Command Center from yesterday. This place looks totally different. The books are unpacked, computers are stationed, there is a functioning Bistro, a projector screen is mounted to the wall, and a projector hangs from the ceiling. The room is shaped in sort of a semi-circle. Franklin now stands front and center preparing himself for the briefing. He turns on the projector and starts what seems to be a slideshow.

"Good Morning Team and welcome to Operation Vanishing Act," he announces. "As of 1600 hours on yesterday, a picture of the shooter was sent to every news station and posted online to various media outlets. Thanks to Hector and Douglas, we sketched an accurate picture of the shooter. We also put a wanted poster of him in this morning's newspaper. The poster holds a ten thousand-dollar reward. He is wanted for yesterday's shooting at Alpha Paint and Body. Both local and state police are patrolling the roads in search for him. Airport officials are on strict security alert. So as of now, the shooter is out of our hands. We will only chase one ghost at a time. Our target is this man, William Baldwin II. William is wanted for faking his own death on August 24, 2001. We know this information because a photo was taken of him one year later. By this man."

The room bursts into laughter. The next slide is a slide of me, from high school my senior year. I had on a wig and I was dressed in Seventies clothing. Homecoming Week dress up day was one of the best days of the school year. Big Mama didn't like my costume but she had to get over it because I was on a mission. I didn't tell anyone of my plans but everything went perfect. The highlight of my day came when the cafeteria served cake. I remember walking around smearing cake into kids face. I targeted the most popular kids first. My actions caused everyone to start throwing their food. The ensuing food fight was hilarious. Teachers were trying to stop it but found themselves the new targets. That's when the food fight became epic, because the teachers retaliated. I took the blame for everything but I didn't mind being suspended, it was worth it.

"It's our very own Brody James," continues Franklin. "Sorry, Brody I had to get you. I found that picture on some film I found at the Big House."

"I remember that day," says Saundra.

"That was the best school day ever," adds Shondra.

"The next photo was taken on September 13, 2002. On this photo, William has been identified in the background and later it was confirmed by his parents. Unfortunately, the next day on September 14, 2002, Bridgette James was kidnapped. Brody James was also hospitalized for nearly a year. To our knowledge, eight more girls have disappeared the same way. Each time the kidnapper leaves neither evidence nor witnesses. We believe William Baldwin II has been kidnapping girls between the age of thirteen and sixteen. He has been praying on young girls throughout the state of Texas. With the help from a C.I.A. age enhancing program, we can get an age enhanced picture of William. Currently he is now 35 years old but with plastic surgery he can look like anyone. I know it's a long shot but we must start somewhere. As we speak Douglas is running the enhanced picture through his facial recognition software. This software allows us to compare his enhanced picture against every person's mug shot, both living and dead, who has been arrested in the state of Texas since the year 2000. Most criminals hide in plain sight. With the city of Houston being the home to at least two million people, we think he is still somewhere close to home. Because the different agencies don't allow their software to be seen or ran by agents of other agencies, we will split into two teams. Team Bird-Eye will consist of Myself, Saundra, and Douglas. Using the C.I.A.'s software we will look through the mugshots. We will also run the picture of our shooter through the facial recognition program. Hopefully the city's traffic cameras can help us pinpoint the location of William Baldwin II and the shooter. Team Interrogation will consist of Brody, Shondra, and Max. Your job is to talk to Juan and gather all the information that he knows about William Baldwin II. We need to know everything that he knows. Due to other obligations, Daphne will not join us today. She has been responsible for getting the information about the shooter out and she has done a wonderful job. Any questions?"

"I have a question. With us not having anything to do today and being so close to the Galleria Mall, can Shondra and I leave around lunch to do a little shopping?" Asks Saundra.

"AB-SO-LUTE-LY NOT!" yells Franklin. "No one! I repeat! No one, can leave this Command Center. Especially you two. Not until we have a firm grasp on our shooter situation. With ten thousand dollars one phone call away, our shooter won't be able to look outside of a window without someone calling on him.   We shouldn't have to be locked up long."

"Well with so many eyes looking for him, we should be safe going shopping," replies Shondra. "Don't you guys want a nice, hot home cooked meal?"

"And what type of food are you buying from the mall?" Asks Franklin. "Like I said, no one is to leave no matter what. If there aren't any further questions, this meeting is adjourned."

I walk over to the bistro area and prepare myself some coffee. I grab a bagel, also. I really don't like being confined in one place. I don't like my freedom taken away from me either but being on lockdown might be the best thing for me right now, especially not knowing if there's any other side effects from my memory lost. What happened yesterday was scary. I really don't want to hurt anyone here anymore either. If I can isolate myself from everyone else that might be best but unlike yesterday, I feel great. I feel stronger and more confident; I feel more everything. If I would have known what I do now, my fight with Big Wayne would have had a definite conclusion. I now remember my training in the various Martial Arts of Africa. I spent my second year away from home training in five different styles of martial arts throughout the continent of Africa. In West Africa, I learned Dambe. Dambe is a Western African boxing style of fighting. This style was a test of bravery. My test of strength came when I learned the West African wrestling style named Lutte. In southern Angola, I performed my rite of passage and learned Engolo. Engolo is a leg-based fighting style, which is believed to be the origin of Brazilian martial arts. In South Africa, I learned the bare fist boxing style called Musangwe. Sting-Ray seems to have a strong connection to the Venda people in the Chifude Valley where it is taught. In the Ancient city of Kemet, I learned Tahtib. Tahtib is an ancient stick fighting martial art that was once used by Ancient Egyptian soldiers. I wasn't trained to lose nor have a draw. My third year gone I was finally accepted by the Grand Master. The Great Sung Lee Fu in the mystic mountains of Asia, believed in being the best possible version of yourself. Sung Lee Fu taught me to polish my crafts. A tie would have meant twenty hours of training for thirty days. After which mind, body, senses, and spirit all would be put to test. After completing nearly three years of training in the mountains I continued my training under Sting-Ray. Sting-Ray took pride in testing my limits but somehow, I failed you Sting-Ray. I lost you and the device. Now I am half-way around the world with no way to know if you are safe.

"BRODY! BRODY!" yells Shondra. "Are you catching this elevator? Team Bird-Eye will be working on this floor. We will be on the fourth floor."

"Sure, I'll be right there. Where's Juan?"

"He's already on the fourth floor," says Max. "We moved Juan, Hector, and the kid last night. That's most likely going to be their home until we complete this investigation."

"I don't think Juan will mind one bit. This is a much-needed upgrade from where he spent his last decade."

We take a short elevator ride to the fourth floor, where Juan and Hector are waiting. Hector's shoulder is wrapped in bandage and he grimaces when he moves.

"What's behind your back, Hector?"

"Oh, Oh, this. It's nothing," says Hector. "Just a vase. You can never be to safe Mr. B. It's for just in-case everyone downstairs were taken out. We must protect ourselves. I even sent my brother to cover the stairway."

"And how is that going?" Asks Max.

"It's going smoothly," replies Hector. "He covered the entire shift last night and didn't need any relief."

"It looks like he has the best job on the floor," says Max.

With a puzzled expression on his face Hector asks, "Why do you say that?"

"Because this building does not have any stairway," replies Max.

"What do you mean?" Asks Hector.

"When this building was built. It was designed to only house the best of the best. In other words, if something happened and you're trapped on this floor you must use your skills to escape," answers Max.

"You put us in a death trap," replies Hector.

"No, you'll be fine," says Max. "There's an escape system. It's similar to the system airplanes use. All you do is pull an emergency cord, then the window blows out and a giant slide travels down to the ground. A couple floors higher and you would have to use a parachute."

"But that cord does not work," says Hector. "I pulled on it last night and nothing happened."

"That's because there wasn't an emergency last night. In case of an emergency the elevator will not work. We briefed you about all of that, when you came up here."

"He was too busy claiming a room," says Juan.

"Oh, I see," says Hector. "Well excuse me. I have a foot that needs to kick someone in the behind."

"That kid is smart," says Shondra. "He played you like a sucker."

"Hey, I had better things on my mind okay," says Hector sourly. "You must have forgotten that I took a bullet in the shoulder for you yesterday."

"No, it wasn't for me," replies Shondra. "We told you not to spy in the open but you wanted to prove yourself. You took that bullet for your pride. Now go on, we have business to conduct that doesn't involve you."

"Hey Uncle Juan, I'll be down the hall if you need me," says Hector.

"For what exactly?" Asks Juan sarcastically. "You go make sure that no one tries to sneak up on us from the stairway."

Hector's face turns red, he stands there in thought before turning to rush down the hall. Juan leads Team Interrogation into a large room. He has covered all the windows in here with newspaper.

"Juan, what is the newspaper for?

"Sometimes if the right amount of light hits the window, the tent on the window will not prevent someone from seeing through it," he explains. "And I like being safe over being sorry.

"It's cool Juan. Have you met Max?"

"Yes, we met last night when he helped us move to this floor," he replies.

"Today we have the pleasure of working with Max. He will help us to gather information from you. This information may lead to you becoming a free man once again."

"Thanks Brody," says Max. "Mr. Juan, I will connect you up to this polygraph machine. After that Brody will ask you a serious of questions. We are connecting you to this polygraph because it is important that we get factual information the first time. It has been years since these events transpired. We want to make sure you remember the events correctly. All the questions are directly associated with our on-going investigation. Feel free to take a break at any time during this process. If you feel overwhelmed, tired, or just exhausted let us know immediately. It is very important that you only state facts. Emotions and opinions are subjective and we can't build a case around that. If you do talk about your emotions or opinions, please advise us beforehand. Do you have any questions before we begin?"

"No, I don't have any questions," replies Juan.

"Okay, I will begin with some easy questions to test that the machine is working correctly," says Max. "What is your name?"

"My name is Juan Felipe Gonzalez," replies Juan.

"Where were you born?" Asks Max.

"I was born on the outskirts of Monterrey, Mexico," says Juan.

"Are you hungry?" Asks Max.

"No, not at this moment," replies Juan.

"Okay, Brody I will leave the rest of the questions to you. I will monitor his answers and let you know when something isn't true," says Max.

"How are you feeling Señor Juan?"

"I'm kind of nervous and scared at the same time Mr. B.," answers Juan.

"And why is that Señor Juan?"

"I don't know," he replies. "I guess I never imagined that I would get to walk out of Alpha Paint and Body alive. I couldn't confirm that I was the next target but I was convinced that I was. After the place was burglarized and nearly destroyed, I was certain that I wouldn't live to see another day. But five years passed by and then ten years passed by. I was planning to walk outside of the doors when I reached the twenty-year mark.

"How long did you work for Alpha Paint and Body before your self-imprisonment?"

"I was there since the doors opened. The owners found me standing in front of a convenience store begging for work," says Juan. "At that time, I was an illegal immigrant looking for the American Dream. I couldn't speak any English but they choose me anyway. That was nearly forty years ago."

"How did you meet William Baldwin II?"

"Around the shop, we called him Willie," he says. "At first, he hated the name but he grew to like it. He lived in the Bellaire area so he started calling himself the 'New Prince of Bellaire.' That didn't catch on because he wasn't as cool as the one and only Fresh Prince.

Besides, the brothers shut that down quickly. I met Willie when he was just a junior in high school. He stole his parents' car one night and wrecked it. Luckily for him, they were out of town. He was in such a frantic state when I drove up to him in the tow truck. When Willie finally calmed down, he began demanding that the car be fixed by the morning. He kept saying that money was not an issue. So, I took him up on that offer. I told him that I would try my best but only under one stipulation. That stipulation was that he had to help me as much as he could. Meaning if I was up working, he would be also. Once I towed him back to the shop, I made the kid pay me upfront. I also explained to him that without another mechanic or someone that knew what he was doing, it would be nearly impossible to meet that deadline. I offered to call in some other mechanics but he didn't want to pay them all. Instead, he volunteered to help. I explained that this was hard work which requires focus. He would have to listen and be very attentive. That kid made me proud that night because he was a natural. He paid attention to the smallest details and I didn't have to repeat myself. not even once. He absorbed every bit of knowledge I shared that night. So much so, that when I stopped to take a bathroom break or to get something to eat, he never quit working. As a matter of fact, he started putting everything back together by himself. We did one heck of a job that night. When he left that morning, I didn't expect to ever see him again."

"When was the next time that you saw Willie?"

"The very same day," he says. "That kid came back to the shop after he got out of school. He offered to apprentice under me, for free. I talked to both Shawn and

264

Tommy about hiring him on part-time and they both agreed. We all agreed that no one should work for free. After that he worked with us for three years, up until his unfortunate death."

"For a kid to be that smart and choose to be a mechanic, had to be kind of a letdown. How did his parents take the news?"

"They didn't like it at all," says Juan. "They came to the shop one day but Willie handled it outside in the parking lot. They never came to the shop again. That kid was good at manipulating people. Eventually his parents came around and were planning to invest in Willie opening his own shop in Bellaire."

"How was Willie's relationship with you and the rest of Alpha's crew?"

"Everyone loved Willie," he says. "He stayed to himself but man did his work speak loudly. Business tripled because of him and he helped reduce our turn-around time. He started taking on special projects and Alpha started getting rewarded with big money projects. After that we started having high-end customers."

"Willie was working on one of those special projects when he was supposedly killed in the fire. Tell me more about that project."

"That project was supposed to take Alpha to the next level. It came about when a guy named Luke came to the shop. He wanted a car built for an upcoming movie that he was working on. We didn't hesitate to take on the job. This job was going to give us national recognition and open the door for us to work with movie stars and other celebrities. The base model car for the project was a year 2000 Ford Excursion. Luke wanted to remodel the entire inside with working mechanical parts. He wanted the inside to be soundproof and the outside bulletproof. All the seats except for the driver's seat were to be replaced with fully reclining seats. A track system was to be installed onto the floor, so the seats could move freely using a remote. The things that he asked for were beyond our work scope but we took the job anyway. Luckily, we had Willie. Shawn and Tommy introduced Willie to Luke. Together they built plans and worked out the specifications for the project. After that, the two of them were inseparable. They mainly worked on that project alone. We knew that our top mechanic, which was now Willie, was working on the most important project. Everyone else was free to deal with other customers and the shop's daily activities. All was working out good."

"How are you feeling Juan? Do you need to take a break?"

"No, I'm fine for now," replies Juan. "I'm not in any rush Mr. B. It's not like we can go anywhere."

"Well let's continue. How was Willie and Luke's relationship?"

"Those boys were inseparable. True brothers from another mother," jokes Juan. "They worked together, they ate together and they even played together. I never saw those two get into one argument. I assume they were around the same age but Luke never shared any personal information with us."

"Did Willie's attitude or behavior change after he met Luke?"

"He still was the same spoiled brat but I did notice that he was growing as a man," replies Juan.

"What do you mean by growing as a man?"

"He basically put down his childish things and started doing things that men do," says Juan. "Before Luke, Willie would bring his video game system to work with him every day. He would rush to go play his game on breaks, at lunch, and during down time. After Luke, he stopped bringing his game to work. Before Luke, he would clown and joke around all day long. After Luke, he was zero tolerance. Before Luke, he never mentioned girls nor did I ever see him talking to one. After Luke, let's just say he became in frequent need of companionship."

"Excuse me Mr. B," interrupts Shondra. "I hate to interrupt you but you are needed down stairs in the Command Center. Franklin says that only you are required to come."

"Okay! Looking at the time, lets break for lunch. We will convene in one hour."

CHAPTER 16 – WILD BOYS

From the elevator, this view of this part of the city is breathtaking. I didn't realize how busy Houston is. Just passing through on my way to and from the airport, I didn't get to see Houston like this. One day, I hope I get enough time to see the sights but with this investigation and now remembering that Sting-Ray has been ambushed, I don't think I will have much free time. The elevator doors open and Franklin stands there waiting with two cups in his hand.

"Man, Brody I really needed to take a break," he says.

"Where's the rest of Team Bird-Eye?"

"I left them looking at the monitors," he replies. "I was happy when my phone rung. Assistant District Attorney Daphne Turner gave me call, she saved my day."

"What's going on now?"

"Let's speak somewhere more privately," he whispers. "No one is working in any of the offices down this way. Let's talk inside of this one."

"What's so important that you need privacy? I've worked on a few teams and the number one rule is trust."

"I know how the game goes, Brody," he says. "I just don't want Saundra nor Shondra to know what we are talking about. Not until Daphne gets here later.

"Spill the beans already. You didn't call me down here to beat around the bush."

"Here man drink your coffee," he says. "Okay you know that we are currently on lockdown until we flush our shooter out. With support from the local news stations and the newspapers, I had a feeling that we would have to deal with the shooter today. Well, I was wrong. According to Daphne, the shooter was slick enough not only to leave the city but he was able to leave the country. Our sketch picture of the shooter was circulated to various agencies around the globe. Daphne received information about our shooter from one of those agencies. The shooter's name is Marcus Ramsey. He is ex-military but he now works independently as a hitman for hire. This guy will work for anyone who can afford his price tag. Somehow, he managed to fly into Paris, France last night where cameras caught him exiting a private jet. It is safe to say that the shooter is no longer a concern of ours. Daphne is currently trying to get information on who owns that jet which flew him out of the country. She is also investigating which airport that jet flew out from."

"That's good news for everyone involved, why the secrecy?"

"I know," he replies. "If I say anything right now, the twins are sure to go on a shopping spree. That would be cool under normal circumstances but there is no time to waste. As of right now, I am sitting in hot water. We have uncovered new information in a cold case that has some people in my department uneasy. Normally I have support from everyone, but this time the only support I received was from the Deputy Director of the Texas Department of Public Safety (DPS), Criminal Investigation Division. Since I work with both the Special Investigations Program and the Drug Program, I get space to work, if I produce results. This time I'm on the end of a very short leash. I added you all to the Texas DPS Criminal Investigation Division list of active civilian support personnel. Time might arise when you have to take the lead, so be prepared."

"I'm ready to do whatever you need. When are we to expect Daphne?"

"Why are you looking for Daphne?" Asks Franklin. "You need to worry about that chick that called me earlier, looking for you."

"Now you want to play. Why would anyone call me on your phone? I'm going back upstairs."

"I'm for real!" he exclaims.

"What's her name?"

"I don't know her name," he replies. "All I know, is that she has a very polite but sweet voice. I told her that you were extremely busy working on a case. She asked me for your number but I told her I would check with you first. So, is it cool to give her the number?"

"You don't even know her name but it's your phone so do as you wish. I don't have any idea who she could be. I've been too busy to show interest in any lady and the one who showed interest in me, would not call you to get at me."

"I guess we will have to find out when she calls back," he replies. "Saundra told us about your memory lost. I suggest you remember who this woman is before she calls back. It sure is good to know that you're not a rooster-fruit but don't get me wrong, whatever your preference is I will support you. I even know an area of town where you will fit in."

"I don't have time to be clowning with you. Just let me know when you have shared the number. I'm heading back up."

"Hold on one second," he shouts. "How is the interrogation going?"

"Now you're concerned about the investigation. It's going smoothly, Juan is long winded so I don't have to pull the information out of him. I think he is just happy to be away from Alpha Paint and Body."

"Have he given you anything useful yet?" He asks.

"Everything is useful, Franklin. You know that. It's a process; I'm walking him through the time that he worked with William but once I'm done, we can analyze the information before proceeding."

"Well don't take all day," he says.

"By the way, how's team Bird-Eye doing?

"We need more updated information," he says. "I think we are going nowhere and fast. Thankfully, my team doesn't have any quit in them. If there is anything to find, they will find it."

"I have confidence in you Franklin. Don't let the stress of the situation get to you. Whatever decisions you make; we will back you completely. Now, I must get back to my team. Lunch break is just about complete."

"Okay, well come back down as soon as you wrap things up," he says as the elevator door closes.

The halls are clear as I exit the elevator. I find my team laughing and having a good time while enjoying their break. Juan is reconnected to the polygraph and waiting to continue our interrogation.

"What did Franklin want?" Asks Shondra.

"He is bored. He's tired of staring at the monitors. What y'all been up to?"

"Oh nothing," replies Shondra with a mischievous look on her face. "I was just playing with Juan. I was questioning him about what he likes in a woman and how do I compare to his standards."

"I have been alone for fourteen years. I haven't felt the touch nor the companionship from a woman," says Juan. "You can become my new standard of what my woman should be but only if you can live up to those golden standards."

"Juan, are you trying to come for me?" Asks Shondra.

"He sure did and it sounds like he gave you exactly what you were looking for."

"I'm serious too," adds Juan.

"Enough with all that. You two can continue your conversation when we are complete. Franklin said that he doesn't want us to take all day, so let's get back to it.

"Let's do this," says Juan.

"Okay Juan, what exactly did you mean by Willie needed frequent companionship?"

"Let's just say that Willie finally tasted a cookie for the ultimate cookie tree and it changed his life forever," he replies. "Every day after work, William would go to a strip club with Luke and he eventually started dating one of the dancers. I think her name was Star. That girl broke him down. I never saw a man cry as much as he did."

"So, did this Luke person start him going to Strip Clubs?"

"Yup," he replies.

"Excuse me," interrupts Max. "That is not correct."

"No, actually that was me," corrects Juan with a smirk on his face.

"Juan! I'm shocked," says Shondra,

"Like I said earlier," continues Juan. "Willie and I became great friends and I wanted to do something about my friend being a square. So, I took him to gentlemen's club but after the first visit, I could tell he was caught like a fish on a treble hook. His eyes would light up each time we visit one; I was so happy for him. He was graduating high school but he was still a virgin. Let's just say that he walked in as a virgin and he walked out a new man. After that he became a regular. I couldn't stop the kid."

"That's not correct," says Max.

"I meant I never tried to stop the kid," corrects Juan. "I don't think I would have been able to because of the games that Star played with poor Willie. He was too naïve and she was too experienced. I regret introducing him to that life. He would have at least been spared that broken heart. That really damaged him mentally."

"Don't blame yourself Juan. Every individual is responsible for his or her own actions. Even when blindly lead, that person still makes his or her own decisions."

"Yeah, you're right," he says. "Still, I often wonder if I wouldn't have introduced him to the strip clubs, would he still have been easily persuaded to hit the streets with Luke."

"Did Willie begin to sell drugs because of Luke?"

"No Mr. B," he replies. "Willie stayed away from drugs. He smoked a little marijuana every now and then but he never used or sold drugs. I'm talking about the other streets, where the ladies of the night stroll. He graduated from making it rain to tricking. For him, every night was Halloween and he was out for the treats. I was shocked that he would do such a thing, especially after his horrible relationship with Star. He talked as if he would never deal with another woman again. He was angry at women and was developing a woman hating attitude. I thought he had eyes for Luke."

"How often did Willie take to the streets?"

"Was you not listening?" Asks Juan. "I said, he went every night. That's Monday through Sunday or Sunday thru Saturday, however you like it. I couldn't understand how he had the stamina to go every night but he did. Youth should not be taken for granted Mr. B."

"Did you ever take to the streets with Willie?"

"He convinced me to hang out with him a few times," he replies.

"That is not true," objects Max.

"Let me think for a second," says Juan.

"Take your time."

"By a few times I meant, for two weeks straight, except for Sundays," he corrects. "I couldn't believe the number of ladies that would be walking the streets. They were hustling hard to sell the one thing, that should be held on to the tightest. I mean you have a choice out there Mr. B. In a two weeks' time frame, I got a little personal with just about every race that calls this diverse city home."

"Juan, I'm shocked!" says Shondra.

"Don't be pretty lady," replies Juan. "Those two weeks were my last pleasurable moments for a long time."

"I guess you was stocking up for that long winter," says Shondra.

"If I would have known that drought was coming, I would have gone hard with Willie for the entire three months," replies Juan.

"When did Willie kick his habit?"

"He didn't," replies Juan. "He kicked the bucket or so we thought."

"That supposedly happened the morning of August 24, 2001. Tell me what you remember about that morning?"

"I didn't expect anyone to be at the shop that morning," he says. "Normally I arrived first and I would unlock the gates and the building. There was a huge wooden privacy fence that I would unlock last, that's where Willie projects took place. That morning I saw the blaze maybe two miles away. I arrived at the same time police officers and fire fighters arrived. I assisted by unlocking the gates but I wasn't allowed to get close to the fire. Once the fire was completely out, Willie's body was found completely burnt inside of his project. They had to use his dental records to identify the body."

"That's just about what we also know about that day. What we don't know is anything about the project William was working on. You said if he needed any help he would call on you. Earlier, you also gave me a brief description of the work that Luke wanted done inside of the 2000 Ford Excursion. I know a little about cars and I can't wrap my head around what would have caused that car to catch fire. Were there any special flammable liquids beyond oil and gas present?"

"That had been puzzling me also because I helped Willie put the final touches on the project. There were no flammables beyond gas in the tank and oil in the engine. Luke had been out of town for two days but once we finished, Willie called Luke to tell him the good news. A truck was scheduled for a morning pickup and the entire shop went out that night to celebrate this enormous accomplishment. We partied but not too late because we all had to work the next day. Willie told me he was going to his normal spot to continue his party. That's why I couldn't understand why he was there that morning," he says.

"Where was Willie's normal spot?"

"Willie always frequented the same area," says Juan. "He has a craving for only thick women who don't play. Now, that was total opposite from his ex-girlfriend Star. She was the typical skinny model shaped girl, who played tons of games with Willie's mind. After her, he only wanted to deal with woman who were strong and straight-up. Back then his desired women were located on the Southwest side of town. My amigo would almost lose his mind when he saw a thick woman. He would probably act like a caged gorilla if he saw you mi diosa. Corramos lejos juntos, mi amor. Voy a hacer la mujer más feliz del mundo. *(Let us run away together, my love. I will make you the happiest woman in the world.)*"

"I'm sure that was sweet Juan but I don't understand anything that you're saying," replies Shondra."

"That will be enough, you did a great job Juan. Everyone, great job! Let's gather our equipment and head down to meet the others. Juan enjoy yourself. You gave us great information. We will do our best to get you back into the world, as quickly as possible."

"Don't rush amigo," replies Juan. "This place is wonderful. It is way better than where I was and where I will be going to. Hey Mr. B. can I speak to you in private?"

"Sure, let's step out into the hall.

Juan assists Max with removing the polygraph equipment, then he scurries into the hallway away from everyone else.

"What's on your mind?"

"Mr. B. I like you," he says. "I have faith that you will do what you say. I need you to talk to those in charge and get me paid for my assistance. Hopefully this information will lead to an arrest because I need money, I have nothing."

"I give you my word, I will make sure you are taken care of."

"Gracias Mr. B.," he replies. "Once this is all over, I will have to start my life over. I will start by finding all of my family members that are still alive."

"Your nephews can help you with that search."

"No Mr. B.," he objects. "We are family but we are not related. Those kids found me hiding out in the shop. We struck a deal and I allowed their father to open the business back up but only if my existence was kept secret. I don't know where my blood family is."

"I will talk to C.I.A. analyst Douglas Jackson and ask him to assist you with your search. Once you are away from this place, I want you to live as happily as possible."

"Gracias amigo," replies Juan. "You're a good man."

"De nada, Juan."

"Excuse me, Brody are you ready?" Asks Shondra.

"Yes, let's head down and meet with Team Bird-Eye."

"Bye Juan, see you later," says Shondra.

"I most definitely will be waiting on you," he replies.

"I didn't mean it like that Juan. Get your mind out of the gutter," she says.

"Adios mi amor," says Juan.

He blows kisses at Shondra until the elevator door closes.

The elevators reopen and we find Franklin, Saundra, and Douglas chatting in the bistro area. They all look happy to see us but they attempt to hide their smiles behind their coffee mugs.

"Please tell us that you all have something," begs Franklin. "We will take anything. Anything to keep us out of that room and away from those monitors. Another day like today and I might lose my mind."

"I can't do it either," adds Saundra. "You'll will have to make a trade or something. I can't do it."

"Relax everyone. Juan gave us some useful information, but we are looking for a diamond in the middle of a snow-covered field. William Baldwin II is a very smart man. He faked his own death and he got away with it for fifteen years. By now, he is comfortable with his new life and I'm sure he has many safe guards in place to ensure that he will not be captured. But he is only a man and most man suffer from the same weakness."

"What's his weakness?" Asks Saundra.

"His weakness is women or should I say the powers that women possess."

"He must have run into one of those snappers," says Franklin.

"Excuse You!" says Shondra. "We have virgin ears."

"Whether it's a snapper or not, our friend William is addicted. Three months prior to his death William bought prostitutes every night. An addiction as strong as his, must be satisfied."

"Yup you're right I have the same addiction," says Franklin. "Not prostitutes though. I'm talking about...."

"Continue and I will punch you in your face," interrupts Shondra.

"Never mind," says Franklin. "Just continue."

"I propose that we conduct an undercover operation. We know that he once favored the women of the southwest area. We also know he like his women thick and feisty."

"We match that description," says Saundra. "Don't we girl."

"We sure do," replies Shondra.

"Don't even think about it," says Franklin. "I am not putting you in that type of danger."

"Whether you like it or not, we are part of this team Detective," yells Shondra. "I volunteer to go undercover."

"And I'm going with her," adds Saundra.

"I will go undercover to protect them, as their pimp. Two new ladies on the scene will get hazed and harassed all night if they are not properly represented. They can mingle amongst the ladies to gather anything they can. Unless you want to go undercover with a wig on."

"Oh, we can help you cross dress," adds Saundra. "It could be your coming out party."

"What's the word he like to use?" Asks Shondra. "Oh, I remember. Boy you will be a huge rooster-fruit."

"Ha, Ha, Ha, very funny," says Franklin.

"Excuse me I may be of assistance," says Douglas. "I have a collection of gadgets that I've created to be unnoticeable. They can help us with audio and video while they are in the field. I can also upload the facial recognition software to those cameras. It would help us to identify all threats."

"With that, we will have a great chance to help clean up the streets of Houston," adds Max. "I know we are after William but it would be great if we could get other bad people off the streets in the process. If William has used plastic surgery, we will need fingerprints and D.N.A. to identify him. We can set up a sting operation and arrest everyone that comes to pick up any girl in our radius."

"Okay, get on those cameras Douglas," says Franklin. "I'll go along with this plan but you girls are not allowed to enter any vehicles. Just stay focused on getting a clear view of everyone's face. Also, alert us when someone fits William Baldwin II description."

"If we are really going to do this, we need to go shopping," says Saundra.

"That's right girl. Our faces are recognizable," adds Shondra. "Hector knew exactly who we were when he saw us at Alpha Paint and Body. We will need to wear disguises."

"Daphne will be here shortly," says Franklin. "Once she gets here I will update her on our current plan."

"I'm updated," says Daphne.

"When did you get here?" Asks Franklin.

"I've been here long enough to hear the mission," replies Daphne. "I like the plan and I agree with the twins."

"What's the plan for going out safely?" Asks Saundra.

"You haven't told them," says Daphne.

"Told us what?" Asks both Saundra and Shondra.

"As of now, our shooter is no longer a threat to us. He was last seen exiting a plane in Paris, France. Your lockdown has been lifted," says Daphne.

"That's great news," says Shondra. "Franklin, why didn't you tell us this."

"I was going to but I was waiting for everyone to assemble before doing so," replies Franklin. "Daphne just beat me to telling you."

"If we are all on the same page, you three should get going. Make sure you pick out something that's right for me also. You two can't out shine your pimp."

"Don't worry Brody," says Daphne. "I got you."

"Don't take too long," shouts Franklin. "And bring back something good to eat."

CHAPTER 17 – DADDY B EEZY

Usually I try not to smile but being as sharply dressed as I am, I just can't help myself. All day long the ladies have been busy making sure we all fit the part. Of course, I was the easiest to dress. The twins on the other hand, has made it an all-day affair. While they have been doing hair and makeup, I've been studying up on my pimping. I started out by looking at the Legendary Rudy Ray Moore as Dolemite. Next, I watched The Mack. Finally, I finished my studies off with Black Dynamite. I got so caught up in those films that I forgot about the twins, the mission, and everything else. For hours, I've laid back on the bed and watched television. I've been so busy lately with these missions, that I never found time for myself. No matter what you do in life, if you don't find time for yourself then you aren't living. People mostly spend all of their time at work or spend it on the wrong people. People that won't spend their time on them in return. It's funny how all these pimps showered their ladies with time and attention and in return their ladies spent time doing anything for them. But if this is what an entire generation grew up idolizing, it no wonder people can't find a faithful partner. They all grew up wanting to be pimps. Now with the women working hard and the men out of the home, the new generations are misled.

"It's time Brody. Sorry, I meant. Are you ready Daddy?" Asks Shondra.

"Be easy Sugarcane, see you're moving too fast. Your job is to make sure I don't get thirsty but I'm looking at a desert in this glass. Now get on your job before you make me get on mine."

"Look who's sounding the part," says Daphne.

"Hush Daffodil! Now wipe that drool from your mouth. If I had a little more time, I would make you scream, 'Oh daddy be easy,' all through this house."

"Attention everyone," announces Daphne. "I need you all to exit the building."

"Girl stop playing," says Saundra. "You don't have time for that."

"Listen up everyone! Please gather around for a moment," announces Franklin. "From this point forward Brody, Saundra, and Shondra does not exist. Until this mission is complete their names are now Daddy B. Ezee, Sugarcane, and Bombstik. What's the status on the cameras and microphones?"

"Cameras and microphones are a go and the program is also functional. I've put it on standby," replies Douglas.

"Daffodil, oh I'm sorry. I meant Daphne. What's the status on H.P.D.?" Asks Franklin.

"Ha, Ha, funny Franklin. I see you got jokes," replies Daphne. "My team is on standby, along with a few tow trucks."

"Daphne, Douglas, and I will monitor your progress closely. We will be able to talk to you individually through your ear pieces. If anything looks suspicious bring it to our attention immediately. It's important that you don't bring attention to yourselves. The people that you will be walking amongst may feel threatened by your sudden appearance on their turf. Max will be your chauffeur and he will stay in the shadows and assist when needed. Please be safe."

"Be easy Franklin, Daddy got this. Just make sure you don't eat too many donuts tonight. Let's go ladies."

Outside the night air is unexpectedly cool, as a nice breeze blows in from the gulf. It has definitely helped to remove the heat of this night. The outfits the ladies wear would cause a father to lose his religion. On second thought, looking at some of the outfits the other ladies have on tonight, makes them look classy. Franklin spared no expense renting us a luxury vehicle for Max to chauffeur us in. I thought he don't want us to bring attention to ourselves. Right now, I couldn't imagine stepping out of anything less. Max chauffeurs us around a few blocks until he reaches a trashy looking motel. He drives into a parking lot and parks in a place where he can have clear view of the streets. He opens the door. First, Bombstik exits the car followed by Sugarcane. Next, the ladies assist me from the vehicle. To think that some people says chivalry is dead. While Max is closing the door, I notice a slim sharply dressed man running towards our direction, waving his hands frantically.

"You can't park there," he yells.

"What was that?"

"Man are you deaf or dumb?" He Asks. "I said......."

Before he can complete his next sentence, using the back side of my hand; I smack him. I connect just as he gets within my range. I hit him soundly, harder than I intended. With all the fluid that escapes his mouth, I now see how they coined the phrase about somebody slapping the taste from one's mouth.

Franklin yells "NOOOO" through my earpiece, while Max and the twins' jaws drop.

"I know it can't be proper etiquette for you to run up on another pimp like that. You had to be expecting some sort of retaliation. Now straighten yourself up and try again. This time address me with some respect."

Snatching Max's handkerchief from his coat pocket, the sharply dressed man wipes his mouth. He looks towards me with evil intent. If looks can kill, I think I would be a ghost.

"The last person that touched me like that, never awoke to see another day," he says. "I am the wrong man to mess with. I am RainBo! I run the Southwest Side of this town. You just made a big mistake fellow. What's the name of the man who don't love life?"

"My name is Daddy B. Ezee and it's nice to meet you."

RainBo repeats, "Daddy Be Easy."

"Okay, Okay. Since you asked, I will be easy; but you ran up on me too fast RainBo. That was a natural reflex you received. I didn't mean you any harm. I was only protecting myself. Now what can I help you with?"

RainBo looks at me with a confused expression on his face. I can tell that his thoughts are racing.

"I do not allow anyone to park in these parking spots," he says.

"My bad, it's my first time here., now where is your southern hospitality? Daddy's home! Now make some elbow room for me."

RainBo turns around and signals a group of girls, who are standing near the motel.

"I will only say this one more time Daddy B. Ezee," he says.

"I am being easy. This is a nice place you have here. I just wanted to visit the infamous RainBo."

"How many do you have in your flock?" He asks. "Forget that. It's time for you to leave or you will be a permanent fixture here."

291

"Calm down RainBo. I only brought the two you see standing before you."

RainBo looks at Sugarcane and Bombstik with a salty expression. Then he turns to me as says, "What kind of name is Daddy B Eeeeee…..."

RainBo's eyes widen as his words drag. He howls and begins jumping in place. I look down to see Bombstik clutching a handful of his family jewels.

"Finish that statement and you will lose your marbles," she says. "Now, was you saying something?"

Frantically, RainBo shakes his head from side to side. Gesturing the response "no."

"I could have sworn that you were saying something," says Bombstik.

"He was saying how awesome Daddy B. Ezee's name is," adds Sugarcane. "Right, RainBo?"

"Yes, yes, it's an awesome name," he replies.

"Be easy babies. Let the man breath."

"Do you want me to be easy daddy?" Asks Bombstik sheepishly.

"I'm not too sure, it really won't benefit me. I guess it all depends on our friend here and his southern hospitality."

"Well, RainBo?" Asks Sugarcane.

"Yes, yes, yes, yes," he says.

"Then, what's his name?" Asks Bombstik.

"Daddy B. Ezee," he replies.

"You heard the man, Bombstik. Be easy baby. Now that wasn't so hard, was it RainBo?"

"That wasn't the only thing that wasn't hard," replies Bombstik.

"That's enough Bombstik! Treat this pimp with the respect he deserves. RainBo, I came here in peace. I only brought two women from my flock of thirty as a sign of respect. This is not a hostile takeover nor am I trying to stop you from getting yours. I only came here because I was told from a great source that if I was ever in the Houston area, you were the man to see."

"Who told you that?" Asks RainBo.

"I was told that while in California at the Professional Pimping Associations quarterly meeting."

Quickly, RainBo turns around and signals the ladies at the entrance again. This time the four men who were trying to sneak upon us, instantly stops and retreats.

"Were you actually at the P.P.A?" He asks. "Did they really mention my name?"

"I'm a member of the board and Yes, your name was mentioned. I figure you had to be doing something right down here but if they were wrong about you, please forgive my intrusion. I can inform the board at the next quarterly meeting."

"There is no need for that Daddy B. Ezee," he replies. "Welcome to Rainbow Run. Whether it's rain, sleet, snow, or sunshine, RainBo has exactly what's on your mind. Let your fantasies run wild, you can get dirty or have a lavish style. Yes, I am the man that you are looking for. Please forgive me for running upon you. I'm truly sorry. I didn't mean any offense. I'm strict because I get special clients that want to be discreet but they tend to break rules. Some people think they are special, like they aren't buying the same product that everyone else is. That causes me to throw my weight around."

"That's really dangerous. Anyone else with my set of skills would have taken you out but pimping is pimping and scary money don't make any money. This product sells itself but if you sprinkle in a little magic, you can have all the wealth."

"Daddy B. Ezee you sound like the Mack, who trained me," he replies.

"If you want to be the best, you should only study the best. Then keep your ladies clean because you'll be standing atop the rest."

"Already," says RainBo. "Well make yourself at home."

"Okay, but how do you operate. We don't want to run your customers away nor do we want to make things hard for you."

"First thing first, I need you to get your driver to park in garage number three," he says. "My clients are creatures of habit and this parking lot is routinely empty. They only park behind the last building, away from the eyes of the public. Your girls can mingle with my girls on the street but there is a good chance you will not make any money. My flock is the best in town."

"That's fine with me. We have no plans to take one cent out of your pocket. My girls will only observe how the tricks behave in this city."

"Are you pimping your driver also?" He asks.

"No, he is also my bodyguard."

"If you change your mind, please let me know. I can set him up in his own private room," he replies.

"Why inside of a room?"

"Many clients of mine like to hide their dirty secrets," he says. "I have clients who would prefer to keep their sexual preference private. They hide their secrets, whether it's from their wives or their bosses but they choose to live a double life. I tried once to let my flock of men walk the street, like the women but everyone was arrested that night. It seems that people don't want to see men selling themselves on the street, unless they are dressed in drag."

"Did you start using this motel as your base of operation after that?"

"I actually own this place," he replies. "I bought it for cheap because it was a known crack house. I cleaned it up, along with the rest of the neighborhood. Now, this is a place where judges, oilfield executives, city officials, and police officers frequently visit. Between us, I am nearly untouchable due to the amount of dirt I have on people in high places."

"I see the P.P.A. choose well to keep their eyes on you."

"Everyone has their eyes on RainBo," he replies. "After every rain, with the right amount of light, there will be a rainbow. I just don't hang around with the clouds but you can find me pimping the leprechauns while collecting my pots of gold."

"Sound like you have this game on lock."

"You know how it goes," he says. "The game constantly changes. To be successful, you must adapt to those changes. I've seen everything in these Houston streets. People come to this city with country mind frames and find themselves victims."

"Watch yourself RainBo, I'm also from the country."

"Yeah but you're different," he replies. "Some of these kids are hitting theses streets before they have a chance to see what life is about. They are too young and naive. They have no dreams nor any goals. All they want is money. They are growing up without any guidance. Especially if they come from a small country area, it's like they are sheltered so much that they believe anything."

"Do I hear a conscious coming from you? You do know that we make our money off the weak and naive?"

"Yeah, but also from the smart and strong," he replies.

Two women with practically nothing on, comes up to RainBo. One is a thick yellow bone, wearing a G-string with a bikini top. The other one is chocolate tone and she's built as if someone chiseled her from stone. She has on white see-through lingerie, but only the top, her bottom is completely bare. They stand tall in their high heels as they whisper in his ears.

"Excuse me," he says. "I need to handle a few things. If you need me, I will be in the motel lobby. You should come chill with me. I can see everything that happens out here from in there."

"The night is young, we will see how things go."

"Well if you change your mind, I will let you sample some of my candy," he says. "You can have them both if you like. It's on me tonight."

"Unfortunately for you ladies, I don't have a sweet tooth tonight."

"I really suggest you take me up on this offer," he says. "Just look at them. Twirl for him. You are missing out."

"Ladies! Twirl for them."

On command both Bombstik and Sugarcane walks up to RainBo and the ladies. They stride as if they just hit the runway. They twirl right in front of them, flipping their hair in those lady's face before walking back.

"Did you look at that? Like I said, I'm good."

RainBo turns around and hurries across the parking lot and vanishes inside of the motel.

"Are you out of your mind," shouts Franklin. "You nearly blew this entire operation."

"Hush you ol' fool, I got this. You just sit back and do your job. Now, don't shout in my ears again."

"You're crazy Daddy B. Ezee," says Sugarcane. "I thought we was going to have to call in backup."

"Be easy Sugarcane, no matter who is in my presence, I am the one and only Alpha male. Now take to the streets before you find yourself on sale."

"Don't say nothing girl," whispers Bombstik. "Because we will have to jump his crazy butt. Come on let's just walk over there."

"He doesn't know who he is talking to," she replies. "Talking about putting me on sale. He must have lost his mind."

"Did you say something?"

"No, Daddy B. Ezee," says Bombstik. "See you soon."

"Be easy babies."

CHAPTER 18 – LIFELINES

The humidity outside forces me to take RainBo up on his offer. Besides from a few of his loyal clients, the night has been slow but entertaining. Before, I choose to go inside I made a few checks. Franklin and Douglas are fully functional, they are recording everything while eating donuts. Max is keeping to the shadows, he's watching for any suspicious behavior. The twins have finally gotten over being mad with me. Since then, they are doing a great job of getting a clear video of everyone that has stopped so far. I don't see how they move so well in those heels. Their feet must hurt. I told all the ladies that if they were to fall in those heels while trying to run to those cars, then I will get RainBo's videos and post them online. It's sure to go viral. One lady told me that she ran track in high school. She says that she was the fastest girl in the state at one time. Her confidence in her ability to run fast in heels caused her to challenge one of the other ladies to a race. They took off like bees were chasing them. I must admit, she is as fast as she was bragging but I think she should have her eyes checked though. She must be blind because she didn't even attempt to avoid that pothole in the street. Everyone knows to be mindful of the city's streets but she stepped right into it. She fell forward and slid across the pavement. Her fall would have been worse if she would have hit her head but somehow, she prevented it. It still looked painful. I thought she was hurt but she stood up, wiped herself off, and walked into the motel as if nothing happened. When she returned, she revealed a street rash that traveled from her breasts to her knees. With no thought of leaving to seek medical attention, she jumped into the very next car that pulled up. Bombstik and Sugarcane mixed with the ladies so well, they began telling them all their business. A lady named T-Bone is convinced that her and the twins look identical, she believes they should be triplets. I must admit she is pretty in the face and thick in the waist. T-Bone described one of her clients as being an extra clingy man. She informed the twins that he visits her every night and if she is not available he will not choose anyone else to replace her. I instructed the twins to stick close to her. If the twins fit the description of what William likes in a woman, then she most definitely fit that description as well. The motel lobby smells of a mixture between corn chips and mildew. As I walk in RainBo is busy keeping an eye on his collage of camera monitors. One positive about this motel is that the air condition works.

"Hey RainBo! Man, it's colder than an Eskimo's deep freezer in here."

"I like to keep it that way," he replies. "Cold air kills some germs and bacteria."

"To each his own my brother but why are you so concerned with bacteria?"

"You're now in the Dirty South," he says. "Things get really dirty around here; So, I keep my flock as clean as possible. Look at this screen and watch her, observe how she gets out of that car and goes straight into that building. In there, she will remove all germs and bacteria that's

302

present on her skin before coming back out to the streets. Before she showers, she will undress in a room that is a few degrees colder than this one. In there she will send her clothing down the laundry chute, where they will be cleaned and sanitized. Any germs or bacteria present on her skin should be killed by the cold air. The shower is to eliminate any germs that wasn't killed."

"So, you have a decontamination chamber?"

"Not exactly," he replies. "It's more like a decontamination station but I nearly have the chamber completely built. I'm still waiting for a few key parts to arrive from oversea. Until then if one germ is killed, I am happy."

"Are you a clean freak or something?"

"Call it what you want but I have to stay on top of things. Health care can get expensive and my girls do not like going to the County Clinics. They tell me that men and women stare and try to holla. Now they are up there sick and still trying to make a move," he says.

"The thirst is definitely real."

"It sure is," he replies. "That's why my pockets stay fat. But if one in my flock gets sick and it goes uncontrolled, it will spread throughout the whole team. Medical expenses alone would close me for good. That's why I take these precautions."

"It's better to be safe than sorry."

"In deed," he says, as he makes his way across the room to a bar area.

RainBo's desk is full of screens. Thirty-six in total. From this spot, he has eyes everywhere. No one can sneak up on him without being spotted first.

"It's impressive how you can see everything from here."

"That's the main reason why I have so much blackmail material," he says. "I never know when I might need it because trouble is easy to find."

"Sometimes it comes to find you."

"Indeed," he replies. "If you're going to be hanging around this town, I might be able to help you out one day. That's if you find yourself in trouble because it goes down in H-Town. There's so much money here, that a sticky situation can appear out of thin air."

"You would do that for me?"

"Sure would," he replies.

"But you don't know me like that."

"True, but your good people, I can tell. Life throws different circumstances at us and you never know who you will see again," he says. "I'd rather not be on your bad side but if anyone opposes you in my city, just call on me and I'll deliver you a lifeline."

"You can give it to me now."

"I wouldn't keep things of that value anywhere near my place of business. I would be placing a bullseye on my own back. You have to be smart if you wish to hold leverage on someone and that would be totally opposite," he says.

"Well thank you for the lifeline. Hopefully, I'll never have to use it."

"Would you like a drink?" Asks RainBo.

"Sure, what do you have?"

"I only drink cognac, like most of my people," he says, while walking across the lobby with two drinks in his hand. "Did you know that Hennessey is mostly consumed by people of color."

"Yeah, everyone knows that."

"Well, did you also know that Hennessey does nothing for the communities of the people that consume it?" He asks.

"Well RainBo, the truth is that no one does anything for our communities, except profit from them. Are you currently an activist?"

"No," he replies. "I just don't understand why people don't support the people that support them."

"Well, you and our people need to broaden your horizons. You're depriving yourselves from experiencing other things that this world offers. You all need to get out that box you've put yourselves in because of our lack of knowledge of our history. We need to stop adopting different things into our culture, like Hennessey and menthol cigarettes."

"Well, the only drink you're drinking tonight, is this special reserve cognac that I've been saving for a special occasion," he says. "I'm about to take you back to your roots. Have a seat and enjoy yourself. Let's toast to tonight being a long night."

There is something wrong with the way RainBo is looking at me but people normally start acting funny when drinking. This special reserve is smooth but I taste something strange in it. Wow, this has gone straight to my head. I better get up before I can't stand. What's happening to me? My eyes grow heavy and they close.

I reopen my eyes and I find myself sitting on a cot. My hands are taped but they feel bruised. I'm not wearing any shoes and the ground feels cold. Sting-Ray appears through the opening of the tent and he sits beside me.

I told you nothing will be easy," says Sting-Ray. "You had your opportunity to stay home but you wanted this."

"Yeah, but they are hitting me harder than everyone else. You know they say Africans don't like African Americans."

"That is a lie that was created to keep the black people of the world separated. Africa is the most valuable continent on the planet. Everyone wants this continent and its resources but they hate the people who live here. Look at how they have taken control of Egypt. If you keep believing everything that they say, then you will always be a puppet," says Sting-Ray. I better never hear you say anything like that again. We have been here in Africa for over a year now and everyone has treated you with respect and kindness."

"I know but they are still hitting me harder than everyone else."

"You have a lot to learn, kid," he says. "I have instructed them to be rougher on you. You are taller than these villagers and you have the potential to be stronger. You thought it was going to be easy since we spent a year studying history and making you more knowledgeable of the real world. Well, that all has ended and things will get much worse than this. We don't know when a spot will open for you. You might be on this continent for two more years. If so, everywhere we go I will educate the locals on how you feel."

"Don't be like that Sting-Ray, I don't feel like that. I will focus and I won't complain anymore. No matter what you want me to do, I will do it."

"I'm glad you feel that way," he replies. "Now it's time to increase your poison immunity."

"MY WHAT?"

"Your poison immunity," he repeats. "Some of the deadliest animals in the world live on this continent. If you are going to reside here until we are allowed into the mountains, then you need immunity. Plus, if you're going to be my disciple then you never know when someone will try to poison you."

"Aww man."

"Here drink this," says Sting-Ray. "We will slowly build up your immunity to fatal doses."

"To what poison?"

"All of them, even to fatal man-made drugs," he says. "By the time, we leave this continent your immune system should be better than mine."

"Ok, I trust you. Don't let me die."

"You're in safe hands kid, just lay down," he instructs. "This will be rough, both mentally and physically but I will keep a close eye on you. Remember, you are strong and this will make you stronger. Now, close your eyes."

I open my eyes unable to control them. I place my head in my hands and rub my face.

"Wake up, Daddy B. Ezee. WAKE UP!" Yells someone through my ear piece. "That a boy, shake it off."

"What just happened?"

"We think RainBo slipped something into your drink; it was probably Rohypnol. He then tried to exit the building through the rear exit but he decided to turn around because Max was out there. He is headed back your way now," says Franklin. "Don't blow your cover. If he moves on you again, take him out without disturbing things outside."

"RainBo roofied me?"

"Yeah, now he is headed back your way," replies Franklin.

"Hey Daddy B. Ezee, you're awoke," shouts RainBo with a startled look on his face. "Man, I though you would be sleeping for a while, you were snoring loud."

"Were you going somewhere?"

"No!" he replies. "That's just my laundry. Are you okay? Your eyes are doing something funny."

"It must have been that drink you gave me."

"Nah, it wasn't the drink," he replies. "You were tired my friend. Look, you didn't even finish the whole drink. You dropped your glass."

"Whatever RainBo. I'm going outside before things get heated in here. How's it going out there?"

"Like clockwork baby," he says, as he pretends not to be watching my every move. "We tend to get really busy once the clubs close. You might want to stay seated until you regain control."

"Stop with all this foolishness, I know exactly what you did. I can still taste it in my mouth but I'm choosing to give you a pass, only because I slapped you earlier. But do trust me when I say, 'If you try anything else you will need a lifeline."

I leave RainBo standing there trembling with his mouth open. It's a good thing Sting-Ray took the time to increase my tolerance to all types of poisons and chemicals. I stumble out of the motel and onto the sidewalk. The street is now congested. It resembles a Mardi Gras parade but no one is throwing any candy nor any beads. Well they are slanging candy but no one is throwing beads. Women walk fast on both sides of the street as they move from car to car. They are lifting their clothing to show a preview of their goods. Well some are, others are just raising a leg. I notice the back-door special is a popular buy tonight. The cars that are holding up traffic seem to be waiting for a chance to drive into the motels parking lot.

"Take it easy," says Franklin. "Your balance is still off. I'm glad you're back with us sleeping beauty. While you've been sleeping, we have made twenty-five arrests and counting."

"Did we catch our man, yet?"

"We won't know until everyone is processed but our chances are getting slim by the minute. This traffic jam is not helping," he says.

"I'm on it."

"Roger that," replies Franklin. "I'm glad you're okay. Keep your senses sharp because this is around the time."

"Around the time for what?"

"It's time for the freaks to come out," he says. "You know! The freaks come out at night. Franklin out."

Max appears from around the building holding a cup. He walks toward me with his hand extended.

"Here drink this," he says. "It should neutralize the effects of the roofie RainBo gave you. Man, you should still be sleeping for at least another four hours. None of our top agents can shake the effect as quickly as you have. How did you do it?"

"With special training but the way my head is hurting I think he doubled the dosage. The effects of one dose would have only taken me down for a few minutes. The way I've had to fight it, tells me that he over did it. My tolerance levels are above normal, I've been trained to withstand many drugs, chemicals and poisons."

"Indeed, they are," replies Max. "You would make a great F.B.I. agent. What do you want to do with this cluster? RainBo was too busy trying to escape, so things quickly got out of control."

"Let's redirect everyone that wants to turn into the motels into the parking lot next door. We need to keep the traffic on this street rolling."

"Some of RainBo's girls were talking about making them leave," says Max. "I wasn't sure if that was the right plan of action so I had them wait around."

"Did you record their faces?"

"Yes, I got everyone on the street," he replies. "Also, I got the faces of everyone who entered one of the motel rooms. Douglas should be running them through his software.

"Come in, Daddy B. Ezee," says a female voice. "This is Daffodil. You can release them all. With the success that we are having tonight, I was granted more officers and we just opened a few more check points. Now, no matter what direction they leave in, I have people in place to take them into custody."

Suddenly, I hear my name being yelled. It's coming from a group of girls on the other side of the street. Sugarcane and Bombstik emerges from the crowd waving their hands. Car horns and loud whistling is heard as they walk between cars to cross the street.

"Hey Daddy B. Ezee," says Sugarcane. "Come with us."

"What's going on?"

"We, we aren't quite sure but we think T-Bone may be in trouble," says Bombstik.

"What happened?"

"We don't know but she has been gone for well over forty-five minutes now," says Sugarcane."

"She might be having trouble getting the job done this time."

"Not her," replies Sugarcane.

"Oh no, not her," adds Bombstik. "That girl is always back in ten minutes or less."

"Are you sure?"

"Yes, we are sure," reply the twins. "We have a feeling that she is in trouble."

"Okay, I was just talking to Daphne right before you called my name. Let's see if I can get a hold of her. Come in Daphne."

"Yes, go ahead," she says.

"Have you arrested any of the ladies tonight?"

"Yes, we have but we have been bringing them back in unmarked cars," she replies.

"Can you check to see if a Ms. T-Bone is in custody?"

"Stop playing," says Daphne. "What's her real name?"

"That's all we got. That's all she goes by."

"For you, anything Daddy B. Ezee," she replies. "I will get someone on it right now. Let me know if Daffodil can help you with anything else. Daffodil out."

"While Daphne works on that, I will get with RainBo. You two keep looking for T-Bone. If I find out anything I will let you know."

Standing before me with identical puppy dog stares are the twins. The sadness in their eyes suggest that we need to find their friend. They are the only ones that know she may be missing. No one out here is concerned with the next person; their only concern is making that money. With so much going on, T-Bone could be anywhere. No matter how many cameras RainBo has, it still doesn't help him keep track of his flock's whereabouts. I hope the twins aren't being hasty. After assisting Max with the traffic, RainBo walks toward the motel. His eyes are scanning and observing everything that's happening along the street. A smile briefly decorates his face as he spectates.

"How's it going Daddy B. Ezee?" He asks, while keeping a safe distance. "Are we good?"

"Actually, we are a little concerned about one of your girls."

"Who? What did she do? Where she at?" He asks. "I knew sooner or later someone would make me show out."

"It's not like that, we think T-Bone might be in trouble. She's been gone for nearly one hour now."

RainBo stares intently at each woman on the street. He frowns as he continues to scan the crowd.

"Come with me," he says. "Every one of my girls wears a phone watch. The watches are water proof so they are trained to never remove them. I can pin point her location using an app on my pad."

RainBo taps his foot on the floor while he waits for his app to load. His nerves cause him to chew on his finger nails.

"This can't be right," he says.

"What can't be right?"

"She is currently traveling north on Highway 59," he replies. "Now she is headed south on Highway 288."

"Is that normal for her to be so far away?"

"No, not at all," says RainBo. "My girls never leave a two-block radius.

"Could someone be after her?"

"Who knows," he replies. "A woman as fine as T-Bone has many stalkers; the only difference is that her stalkers can pay to lay with her."

"Could she be trying to escape you?"

"No, no, no," he repeats. "I love her. I mean, she loves being with me. She'll do anything for me. Out of all these women, she is my number one lady. She keeps all these ladies in line. I even paid for her surgeries. When I met her, she was over four hundred pounds. She had secluded herself away for everyone while eating her life way. I helped her gain confidence. Plus, I paid good money so she could get the attention she required. She would never leave me."

"Can I borrow your pad? It is the only way I can track her."

"You can take this pad," he replies. "As long as you bring both back to me in one piece. Would you like me to watch over your girls while you are gone?"

"No, they are coming with me. Be easy RainBo, I will get her back."

Max, Sugarcane, and Bombstik waits for me as I exit the motel lobby.

"Did you find her?" Asks Bombstik.

"Yes, you girls were right. She is in a car heading out of the city but with this pad, we will be able to track her. Max get the car, we're going after them."

"Come in Daphne, this is Daddy B. Ezee."

"Yes, go ahead Big Daddy," she replies.

"I need you to let us through a check point. A car got through with one of the ladies onboard and we are going after them."

"Stay on the main road, I will have you waved through," she says.

"Come in Brody!" says a rough voice.

"Who's using real names?"

"Sorry, this is Douglas. We will lose communication with your team once you leave our two-mile radius," he says. "Do not discard of your earpieces, we will be able to track you using them."

"Brody, this is Franklin. Once you get there, I need you all to only do surveillance," he says. "I need to get the necessary warrants before we can go in, wait until backup arrives."

"Make sure you don't take too long."

We follow RainBo's tracking app to a suburban neighborhood south of Pearland. The neighborhood is still under construction. I received a call from Franklin a while ago to inform us that H.P.D. would no longer be of any assistance because we have crossed county lines.

Franklin is now trying to get Texas State troopers to back us up. Even though the neighborhood is under construction, every house that's built is occupied. The house that we are interested in, sits in the middle of a circle, on a dead-end street. Surveillance of the house from the perimeter is impossible without drawing suspicion to ourselves. There is also neighborhood watch signs posted and the two neighboring houses sit too close to our target.

"What's the plan?" Asks Shondra.

"We don't have any police support but I have a feeling that we shouldn't wait. There hasn't been any movement within the house since we arrived, we should make a frontal attack. Do anyone know how to pick locks?"

"I can pick any lock on any door," says Max.

"We don't have any time to lose," replies Saundra. "T-Bone is in trouble."

We separate into two groups. Max and Shondra proceeds to the right side of the street, while Saundra and I flank to the left. Sticking to the shadows we round the circle, being careful not to trigger any security alarms. We reach our target house and surprisingly, no dogs bark nor do we alert any nosy neighbors. Max unscrews the front porch light before attempting to pick the lock. On high alert, we survey our surroundings. Quickly, without raising an alarm Max successfully unlocks the door and cautiously we enter. We stand in the living room motionless; letting our eyes adjust to the darkness. We listen for any sound or movement from within but we hear noise coming from above and below us. On the drive while in pursuit for T-Bone we all agree to use non-lethal force because too many people are being murdered and we refuse to add to those statistics. We replaced our bullets with rubber ones but unfortunately, Max only had enough rubber bullets for two clips. So, we agree to give the guns to the girls for their protection. Max and I can use our hands for our protection. The twins are also serious about sticking together. They say that in the movies, everyone is killed except for one lucky fool and only because they separated and went off in different directions. For the sake of not arguing we all proceed upstairs. The stairs make little noise as we approach the top of them. Max look through a mirror to see if anyone is in the hallway. The hallway is empty and dark. Slowly, I proceed to the first room with Max flanking the door. The twins wait and watch the stairway, along with the other doors as we check the first room. The first room is empty, only boxes and newspaper litter the floor. We proceed to the next room and again, this room is also empty. The bathroom door lay open and with a quick sweep, we confirm that it is also empty. The last door seems to be of some importance because of the two pad locks on the door. Max reaches into his pocket and pulls out a black tool pouch and begins wrestling with the lock. With a click, the first padlock opens but the sound made by the padlock is heard by the twins on the stairway.

"Keep it down, you guys," whispers Saundra.

319

"Did anyone hear it? Is anyone coming?"

Shondra replies by shaking her head "no". She places a finger on her lips.

"Here we go," whispers Max. "Prepare yourself."

The lock slides through the inner working of the locking mechanism, securing itself in the unlock position. The door is unlocked and Max cracks it slightly. Swiftly, I move to the corner of the room. No light shines in this room, forcing my eyes to struggle to focus against the darkness. Suddenly, two figures emerge in the darkness. They are sitting in the middle of the room, side by side. Max and I slowly walk towards the figures. Two girls sit in matching rocking chairs, with duct tape binding their ankles and wrists to the chair. Duct tape also covers their mouths. They notice us, which causes their breathing begins to intensify.

"Don't panic, we are here to help you. Is the people who did this to you still in the house? Blink once for yes and twice for no."

The girls breathing continue to race but one of them blinks once.

"Okay good. How many people are currently in this house?"

Again, she blinks only once.

"Thank you. Don't make any noise until we come back. You are safe in here until we catch this person."

Both girls nod their approval. Max and I slowly exit the room and close the door behind us. We make our way back to the stairs where the twins are posted.

"That took a while. What's in that room?" Asks Shondra.

"Two girls are in there, taped to chairs. I told them that we will come back once we finish searching the house."

"Let's let them free now. They must be scared and hungry," says Saundra.

"No, they are safe for now. We don't know who else is in this house, remember it was your idea to stick together. Let's stick to the plan, we can come back for them later."

Quietly we descend the stairs. We search the remainder of the house but we find the house to be empty. Inside of the garage we find a black Ford Excursion. We continue to search the house, when Max hears the faint sound of music playing. We scurry around house trying to locate the source of the sound. Unable to find the source we grow frustrated. Shondra disappears up the stairway, Max sits in a chair and Saundra follows behind her sister. Slowly, I walk back through the house. I stop next to a wall and kneel on the floor. I place my ear on the floor and the sound grows louder.

"I think there is a basement."

Max and I scurry around the house with our attention fixed on finding a way into the basement. Still we find nothing. I stop and stare into a wall mirror. I don't know why but for some reason, something draws me to it. I hear the twins whispering as they appear on the stairs. Shondra walks across the room with a smile on her face.

"One of the girls told me that somewhere on side of that mirror is a trigger that leads down into the basement. She said that they were down there until this morning," says Shondra. They overheard their kidnapper saying something about having a big night tonight. He only moved them upstairs a few hours ago."

"Good work Shondra. Let's see where it's located."

"Look at this funny spot Brody," she says excitedly. "I think it's a button."

"Get ready everyone, we don't know what to expect."

"Now Brody?" Asks Shondra.

"Yes, Now."

The mirror slides over to expose a door hiding behind it. Immediately, Max unlocks the door as soon as the knob is visible. As we walk through the doors threshold, a stairway is detected. The sound we were hearing becomes louder, as rock music engulfs the stairway. We inch closer to the basement with our presence being masked by the music playing. Suddenly, the music turns off.

"I didn't think you would ever awaken," a whiny voice says. "I get excited when I'm near you because there's nothing like a prime T-Bone. I miss you so dearly when I cannot she you. The thought of not seeing you drives me insane. Unfortunately for us, I will not be able to see you for a while but I can't accept that. I won't accept that! So, I've decided that I would bring you along with me. Now, I know I didn't ask you for your permission but I figure that I'll just pay you for any money you would lose. I know I give you around one thousand dollars every week because your mine and only mine. I figure since you are mine, then you won't miss out on anything. But things changed as I sit there at Rainbow Run trying to decide whether to bring you with me. I saw you climb into car after car and you didn't even let the two ladies that stood with you get any action. I knew at that point that you're just like all the rest. I thought long and hard about living without you and I determined, that wasn't an option. That left me wondering what to do with you. You are a liar and you're impure. To sit beside me on my throne you must be pure. I decided, you must repent before we can truly be one. This process will be painful but once it is completed, you will faithfully and happily take me as your one and only. Just like you promised. I've created a fun game which should lighten the mood. Look, I call it the Wheel of Misfortune. Now let's spin the wheel to see how we will begin this process. I'm so excited. Aren't you?"

We hear the wheel begin to spin. It starts fast but it suddenly stops.

"Let's get in there Brody," whispers Saundra.

"Just another minute. Max isn't done scanning the room for anyone else."

"Awe," says the whiny voice. "I agree with the wheel. You will be a born-again virgin. We should rewrite your sexual history. You're a tainted T-Bone but when I'm done, you will once again be a prime T-Bone. Now, I will not be giving you any pain relief medicine. I need you to embrace the change you will go through, it will make you a better person. It will make you cherish our most valuable possession. Now this process may cause you to pass out a few times but I'll make sure that you survive. I will be here for you throughout the process and I will also be there throughout the healing process. Our bond will grow with each waking second. When, I insert this hibachi into your vagina, you will experience marvelous pain. Pain which will cleanse your body of all impurities. This will make you pure for me and only me."

Max passes his mirror to me and I see T-Bone strapped to a chair. A chair which one would find in a gynecologist office. Her eyes express the terror that she is experiencing. They also grow redder by the second, due to the equipment that is holding them open. A rubber ball is forced into her mouth, preventing her from speaking or calling out for help. She doesn't notice our presence because her eyes are glued intently to the red-hot hibachi that's approaching her vagina. Her kidnapper sits on a stool positioned between her open legs. He starts salivating, as he focuses on his task.

"Now everyone."

Together we charge into the room, positioning ourselves in a semi-circle.

"Don't move another inch you twisted freak!" shouts Shondra.

T-Bone's kidnapper spins around on his stool. The look on his face changes from pure happiness to instant rage when he sees our faces. With the red-hot hibachi in hand, he swings wildly at Max. Max avoids the blow by retreating a few steps. The kidnapper uses that opportunity to stand.

"I don't forget faces," he yells. "You are those two ladies that were standing with my T-Bone in front of Rainbow Run. Once I get rid of these two worthless trolls, I will save you also. I will have my very own set of triplets."

Bang, Bang, Bang, Bang! Two shots each from both Saundra and Shondra causes the red-hot hibachi to fall from the kidnapper hand. He stumbles a few steps, before falling to one knee. Breathing heavily, he grabs at his chest. He realizes that he is neither shot nor is he bleeding. He rises to his feet.

"You can't stop me," he roars.

Desperately he scans the room for a weapon. His eyes stop on the hibachi that he once held. He steps forward towards the hibachi but the deafening sound of the girls firing their weapon again forces me to cover my ears. I watch as fire explode from the barrel of both guns leaving a faint trail of smoke. The kidnapper falls backwards, he flips over the cart holding his medical supplies. The smell of smoke and gunpowder engulfs the small space. Both Saundra and Shondra drop their weapons to the ground and runs to T-Bone. While they remove her from her restraints, Max quickly places handcuffs onto the kidnapper. Free of her restraints, T-Bone struggles to her feet; she embraces the twins. In harmony, they cry uncontrollable. We escort Saundra, Shondra, and T-Bone to the car before going back in to retrieve the girls who are still tied up upstairs. Both girls are fourteen years of age, one Black and one Latina. The last thing they remember was walking to school, for their last day before summer break. They didn't know each other nor did they attend the same school but now they will be forever connected. It feels like a huge weight is removed from my shoulders, as Franklin arrives with the state police and ambulances. Looking at their faces I can tell the team is fatigued but we wait and watch as the ambulances drives away with the two girls and T-bone.

CHAPTER 19 – CONDOTTIERI'S DAUGHTER

"Wake up sleepy head, we have work to do," says a seductive voice.

I open my eyes to see Daphne looking at me face to face.

"You finally awoke," she says.

"What are you doing here?"

"Franklin needs you downstairs but you looked so adorable," she says.

"How long has you been in here?"

"Oh, I would say about twenty minutes," she replies. "I just wanted to get in bed and cuddle with you. So, I did just that."

"Didn't Shondra tell you what happened to her when she tried to wake me?"

"Yes, that's why I have you pinned down," she says. "I knew the risks."

"Get off me and get out of here, Daphne."

"Don't be like that Brody. I really wanted to congratulate you for the awesome job you did last night.

Boy you're on a roll," she says. "I also want to offer you a job. Just think about it, I know you have other things on your mind. Like going to pee. Go relieve yourself, then we need to meet everyone in the bistro. We have a lot of work to do. Well, what are you waiting for?"

"For you to leave the room."

"There is no need to hide," she says. "I know your friend is up."

"Bye Daphne."

"Bye Brody," she replies. "And hurry up."

Daphne exits the room but closes the door extremely slow. Man, that woman is a handful. I am not use to a strong, confident, and aggressive woman but I guess I can't hate on her for trying. Two missed calls from a private number causes my phone to vibrate. Neither caller left a voicemail nor a text message. It's probably someone else trying to congratulate us for last night. My body aches all over, I could have used a few more hours of sleep.

"Brody! I'm waiting for you. Now hurry up," says Daphne from the other side of the door. "The twins and I are waiting for you."

"Okay, I'll be out in a minute."

The entire team, except for Franklin, eagerly awaits my arrival. We board the elevator to see what Franklin has for us today. The thunderous sound of clapping welcomes us as the elevator doors open and Franklin is the first to greet us. The Command Center seems to be at max capacity. Most of the faces that are smiling and clapping are unknown to me. I didn't think this many people knew of this location. We watch as Franklin and Daphne walks over to a podium.

"Last night our joint task force made an impressive eighty-three arrests," Franklin announces. "We caught two fugitives who were on the America's Most Wanted list, one escaped convict, two suspected terrorists, and thirty-three other people with outstanding warrants. The rest of our arrests are ordinary working people. Some of whom will have a lot of explaining to do, especially to their significant other. Others probably will have to resign from their jobs once their bosses read today's newspaper. Somehow all the names were leaked to the newspaper. Also, the two girls who were rescued by our undercover team, has been reunited with their families. Their kidnapper has been treated for his injures and he will arrive here, for interrogation. His name is Alfred Mitchell and he has been threatening to sue the city for police brutality and illegal search warrant. It's a good thing our undercover team took him down because as civilians they are protected under the Good Samaritan laws."

"He will be prosecuted to the fullest extent of the Law," adds Daphne.

"We also made a surprise finding," says Franklin. "The SUV that was found inside of the garage, has unique devices installed within; both are similar to the one that William II was supposedly burned in. Once we get a chance to question our suspect, we will know whether the two cases are tied together."

"You know you will have to offer him something," adds Saundra. "He will not talk for free."

"I believe he will take any deal that we put on the table," says Daphne. "He kidnapped three people that we know of. Actually, he doesn't deserve any kind of deal. People like him deserve to be locked away. If he has any information that will assist you with your case, then he will take anything that will keep him out of the prisons population. Most men don't like guys that hurt little girls or women. He won't last a month in any prison population."

"Did anyone contact Mr. and Mrs. Baldwin? They might know Alfred or they can tell us whether he was around William. We still don't have anything on the Luke person."

"Good idea," agrees Franklin. "I will get someone on it after we take some time off to enjoy this wonderful feast. This feast has been provided to us by the City of Houston, on behalf of the Mayor, the Chief of Police and the District Attorney. The city of Houston would like to thank you all for helping to keep its streets safe. Congratulations!! Now please, please enjoy yourselves. You all deserve it."

"Hey Brody, if you're interested in joining the F.B.I. let me know. With this on your resume, you are sure to be accepted. Plus, I can also put in a good word for you," says F.B.I. agent Max Jones.

"Brody is too smart for the F.B.I.," says C.I.A. Analyst Douglas Jackson. "You should join the C.I.A., we could use someone as rare as you."

Daphne interrupts, "Let the man breathe; he hasn't even eaten yet. You can talk to him after that."

"Here Brody, take my card, just think about it," says Max.

"Take mine too," says Douglas. "Also, when you have time, I need to talk to you. I have a few results from our word scramble."

"That's enough guys. Now if you will excuse us." says Daphne as she pulls me away from those two."

"What do you have up your sleeves Daphne?"

"Oh nothing," she replies. "I just know that you are hungry and tired. I heard your stomach growling."

"I may need to file a restraining order against you."

"Would you like to go by my office to get one?" She asks.

"Daphne, sit your thirsty butt down and let that man eat!" yells Shondra.

"Come sit over here Brody," says Saundra. "Here, I fixed you a plate."

"Daphne was supposed to rescue you but it looks like she has other plans," says Shondra.

"I don't see any ring on his finger," says Daphne. "Don't fault me for being a woman who knows what she wants and who is not afraid to go after it."

"You do know that I am sitting, here right?"

"Well I'm going to just be straight forward," says Daphne. "Brody, would you like to go out with me?"

I guess I will not have time to enjoy myself nor this nice plate of food that's sitting here. All three ladies look keenly into my face, awaiting my response. It feels like I was set-up from the start. If I had a checklist, then Daphne most definitely would meet all the criteria. She is smart, brave, courageous and a beautiful woman. She also has a nice body. Let's compare, if ten is Beyoncé and one is someone's wrinkled one-hundred-year old grandmother, then I would give Daphne a nine.

"Excuse me," interrupts Franklin.

"Go away Franklin this is important," replies Saundra.

"Well it will have to wait," he says. "Brody, you have an important phone call."

"Who is it?"

"I don't know," replies Franklin. "She wouldn't tell me. All she said was that you gave her my number to contact you. She also confirmed that by telling me something that only you and I knew."

"Excuse me ladies, I need to take this call."

"The phone is in my office," says Franklin. "It's the last door down that hallway. Take as much time as you need."

I can feel the ladies staring daggers into my back as I walk towards the hallway. Franklin could not have picked a worse time to come get me. He doesn't know it but he just walked into a hornet's nest. I open the door to Franklin's office and resting on top of his desk, lays his open phone. The caller is still patiently waiting. Who could this person be?

"Hello, this is Brody James speaking."

A soft seductive voice, on the verge of flirtatious replies, "Hi Brody James. It's funny to hear you say that. This is the first time I have ever heard you call yourself Brody James. It's been a long time since I last saw you and it is about time that we meet for our annual meeting."

"Who is this?"

"Oh, you don't know me when you're in the states?" She asks. "Well the next time I see you I will make sure you never forget me again."

"Don't make threats, I have a slight memory problem. My memories have improved but I'm still foggy in some areas."

"Like the area of love," she replies. "This is Sandy. Have you forgotten me?"

Oh! Sandy! How could I have forgotten her.

"No, No, I haven't forgotten you. I remember you Sandy. We spent two years together at Sung Lee Fu's palace."

"That's Master Sung Lee Fu to you," says Sandy. "I thought I beat that into you?"

"Don't brag, you know when I arrived in the mountains Sung Lee Fu demanded that I do not touch his daughter. I thought you were his daughter, so for four months I didn't fight you back. I couldn't touch his daughter, I thought it was a test. But that's the past."

"I know," she replies. "You never were a quitter. You're hard-headed but you will strive to be the best. You're also teachable and that's why I love you."

"That's how I gained all of your respect. No matter what I was hit with, I took it. I endured and got stronger."

"Enough of the old stuff," says Sandy. "We can reminisce face to face. I miss you Brody, even though you can't remember the times we spent together. I will have to help you remember."

"I remember a little, like the two years we spent together were the best two years of my life. I could have stayed at Sung Lee Fu's with you for the rest of my life but your dad had other plans for you."

"It is heart breaking how little you remember," replies Sandy. "Yes, my dad had plans for me. He's grooming me to lead you all. Besides, I had already been at Master Sung Lee Fu's palace for a year and a half before you arrived there. It was time for me to start my journey. After you left the mountains we reconnected again when Sting-Ray brought you to Vincere Miles. Remember my father is the Condottieri and Sting-Ray is his right-hand man? Just like when I become Condottieri, you will be my right hand. Speaking of right-hand, is Sting-Ray with you?"

"Unfortunately, that's where things get foggy. I've been having these dreams that we were double crossed in Africa on our last mission. We foiled a terrorist plot in West Africa and retrieved the device they wanted to detonate. When we arrived at the rendezvous point, things didn't go as planned. I lost my memories after being shot and falling from a waterfall. I think they got Sting-Ray."

"You know if anything has happened to Sting-Ray my father would have assembled an army to go retrieve him," she says. "You may not remember but I do. You always have dreams about different things. Sometimes they are wild adventures and other times they are love stories. But to ease your mind, let's just say this ambush did happen. So, after you fell, you followed your instincts and returned home?"

"Yes, but I haven't seen or heard anything from Sting-Ray since."

"I knew something was wrong with you because you haven't contacted me. If anyone would know Sting-Rays whereabouts, my father will," says Sandy. "I will call him as soon as we hang up. I am also scheduled to meet up with him in New Orleans."

"When is your meeting with Condottieri Hawk?"

"In one month," she replies. "I will find out about Sting-Ray. After that we can meet up and I will help you remember what you hold dear to your heart."

"Ok, so I have one month to finish this mission."

"Yes, or a little longer. You know you can't show up until my father is gone," she replies.

"Yes, I remember that much."

"I know it's not professional but may I ask what mission are you on?" She asks.

"It's a personal mission. Franklin reopened my sisters kidnapping. I think we are on the right track so far."

"Awe, Brody. I wish I was there to help you through this," she says. "I know how much your sister meant to you and how you wished to avenge her kidnapping. Please trust your training and know that you are well equipped to take on any situation. Trust your instincts and you will be fine."

"Thank you, Sandy. I needed that."

"I've been calling Franklins phone for days now," she says. "So, I know how busy you are but find the time to save this number to your phone and text me. I will update you about Sting-Ray after I talk with my father. So, please don't worry about Sting-Ray. You know how loved he is by all; I'm sure he is fine. Please concentrate on your current mission. I will let you go now but think about me because I think of you constantly. Until we meet again, Au Revoir Rogue."

"Au Revoir Deathstalker."

Now things make sense and I am happy that I didn't do anything with Daphne. Sandy would have killed us both. She would have killed me, then revived me; just to do it all over again. Her wrath would have been catastrophic. Sting-Ray always says that if you're not certain, follow that nagging thought. I hope she's right about Sting-Ray. I know Condottieri Hawk would torch the earth to find him. He's a fierce man but we don't see eye to eye. I asked Sting-Ray who would win a battle between them two and he said Condottieri Hawk would because he has an army. I'm sure it's just a dream like Sandy said and it could also be a lingering affect from the trace Mom put me in. Plus, with the veil stuff who knows what's going on. Anyway, I will do like she said; I will concentrate on this mission. Upon exiting Franklin's office, I notice the building is much quieter than before. Small groups of people are still sparsely gathered but the majority of the people are now gone. I can tell that the twins were talking about me because their mouths stop moving upon my arrival.

"Where is Franklin and Daphne?"

"Franklin went down to the garage to walk the Mayor out and Daphne left," replies Shondra.

"What are you worried about Daphne for?" Asks Saundra. "Franklin told us who you were on the phone with."

"What did he tell you?"

"He said that you were on the phone with your girlfriend," says Shondra. "He said she has been trying to get in contact with you for days now."

"Poor Daphne left on the verge of tears when she heard that," adds Saundra.

"You didn't do anything wrong Brody," says Shondra. "She's just a water-head. You won't catch me crying over a man that is not mine."

"Or any man at all," adds Saundra.

"I told that girl that a man will show you when he is interested in you," says Shondra. "He will make you feel like no other woman matters to him. If he is chasing after everyone he see, then he is nothing more than a dog chasing tail."

"Where's Daphne now?"

"She has been gone for about fifteen minutes now," replies Saundra.

"Let Franklin know that I'll be right back. I can't leave her like that."

"Alright Captain Save 'em," replies Shondra. "But how do you think your girlfriend will react to you chasing after another woman?"

"I know I'd be furious," adds Saundra. "I would either dump your or I would hurt you."

"I probably would hurt you," replies Shondra. "Then dump you."

"I must meet this woman," says Saundra. "I need to see if she is strong enough to tame a James man."

"I know she's strong enough to make him turn down a woman," adds Shondra. "A woman who delivered it to him on a platter, too."

"I'm out of here, just tell Franklin to call me."

"Hold on man! Where are you going, Mr. Cake Baker?" Asks Franklin. "You can't go anywhere. It's time, Alfred Mitchell just arrived."

CHAPTER 20 – ALFRED MITCHELL

Everyone watches Alfred Mitchell through the window of the interrogation room. The observation room becomes crowded because everyone wants to see Franklin interrogate him. Alfred sits quietly with his head down. He rocks back and forth in his chair. His shackles don't allow him to move his hands above the table.

"Brody, would you like the honor of accompanying me?" Asks Franklin.

"If no one objects, it would be my pleasure."

No one disapproves of me accompanying Franklin as long as they get a chance to watch. The temperature in the interrogation room seems to be much colder than the temperature in the observation room. As I enter the room, the hairs on my skin rise and goosebumps form on my arm. Alfred sits in a chair at the only table which faces the two-way mirror. Another chair is stationed at the table and a barstool sits in the corner close to the mirror but out of camera view. I sit on the barstool while Franklin walks behind Alfred Mitchell. He circles the table twice.

"I once tracked down a man who just like you, loved to prey on little girls," says Franklin. "He was a man full of pride and he loved to dominate the fairer sex. He thought that all women should be submissive and obedient. He did not last two weeks in the penitentiary.

341

You see, most inmates will band together to help rid this world of pedophiles like you. If I wanted to, I could just lock you up right now. I have everything I need to put you on that two-week countdown but I can't shake this feeling that there is more. Do you feel that?"

"I sure do; the force is strong."

"Exactly my point," replies Franklin. "I want to know what you know, Alfred. You remember my colleague, that's sitting in the corner right. His team took you down and they told me some disturbing facts of what you wanted to do to that woman. Right now, I have another team thoroughly searching your home. What will they find Alfred? If there is anything you would like to share with me, now is the time. We can give you some time to think things over. Just remember that we have you on three counts of kidnapping. On each charge, you are looking at 20 years to life. Also, remember that Texas does carry the death penalty. Plus, you have the pleasure to be in the county that leads the state in executions."

"Can I have a smoke and some coffee?" Asks Alfred"

"I'll see what I can do," says Franklin. "If you're willing to cooperate, I may just return with what you are asking for."

"I'll cooperate," replies Alfred. "Cooperation builds the nation. Up, Up, Up!"

Franklin looks at me with a confused expression. A knock on the door stops Alfred from repeating the word "up". Franklin motions for me to get the door. Quickly, I walk from the barstool, upon opening the door and I'm handed a pack of cigars and a cup of coffee. I close the door, hand the items to Franklin, and then walk back to the barstool.

Alfred is visibly nervous. He constantly moves his thumb up and down while keeping his eyes fixed on Franklins' every move but Franklin stands confident as he stares back at Alfred. Franklin lifts the cup of coffee to his nose and smells the aroma.

"Not bad," he says. "It has nothing on the coffee that my Paw-Paw brews but its good enough for you. Here try it for yourself."

Franklin places the coffee on the table in front of Alfred. Alfred struggles to reach the coffee; his shackles prevents him from doing so. Disappointed by not being able to reach it, he decides to do as Franklin did. He lowers his head and smells the aroma also.

"It would be better if I could reach it," says Alfred.

"Well tell me why you kidnapped the lady named T-Bone from Rainbow Run?" Asks Franklin.

"She's going to be my wife," replies Alfred. "I didn't force her to get into my car. I didn't force her to get into my chair. I just needed to purify her so we could start our family. That was infection and disease control. I refuse to catch anything. I'm clean, clean, clean."

"And did the two girls, who were found upstairs at your house; just kidnap and tie themselves up also?" Asks Franklin.

"They are my daughters; I mean our daughters," replies Alfred. "I hope they are safe. I didn't want them to see their mothers' operation. No, No, No!"

"Yes, they are safe," says Franklin. "Safely at home with their real families."

"I'm their real family!" yells Alfred. "Those people didn't love them like I do. If they did they would not have let them wonder the streets unsupervised. Those girls walk the streets at all times of the day and night. If the so-called parents really love them, then they would not let boys sleep at their houses. If they loved them, it would not have taken them a week to notice that they were missing. I would have known instantly. That's what you call love. They are happy with me because I take care of them better than anyone else. Now, I'm not saying another word until my family is back together."

"Let's give Alfred time to think and gather himself," says Franklin.

Upon exiting the interrogation room, three men approach Franklin. One of the men wears blue scrubs and a white lab coat. The other two comfortably wears suits and ties.

"I've observed all I need to," says the Doctor. "This man is clearly suffering from a case of Psychosis. I've seen this plenty of times. This man lives in an alternate reality. He believes everything that he is saying. His delusions are typical for a patient that suffers from Psychosis. To make an official diagnosis, I will have to perform a psychiatric evaluation as soon as possible. How soon can you have this man delivered to my facility?"

"Let's hold up on that Doctor."

"Who is this man?" Asks the Doctor.

"Don't get offended Doctor," says Franklin. "He is the man that arrested Mr. Alfred Mitchell. He witnessed the horrors that Alfred tried to commit."

"Are you some sort of medical expert?" Asks the Doctor.

"No, I am not a medical expert but we have more questions for that man."

"This man is a security threat. He is mentally unstable and he needs to be treated NOW!" yells the Doctor.

"Aren't we all unstable? The behavior that you are displaying right now is very unstable. So, you're telling us that he is dangerous but you want us to let you take him to a less secured location, for you to get into his mind. That is the only dangerous situation that is present."

"Thank you for your opinion good doctor but we no longer will be needing your services," says Franklin. "I think we will get a second opinion. Can you gentlemen please escort the doctor back to his facility?"

"This is preposterous!" shouts the Doctor. "I will file a report against you."

"Feel free to do so," replies Franklin.

"Excuse me Detective James. Here are the reports that you requested," says a slightly overweight uniformed police officer.

"Brody, I need you to contact Daphne," says Franklin. "I need to know what the District Attorney wants to do with Alfred. I will go through these files to see if any of our suspects match William Baldwin II profile. I also need to find a new doctor; someone with some darn sense. Hey officer, I need you to go into the interrogation room and loosen Alfred's restraints. He need to be able to reach his mouth with his cup of coffee. Brody, meet me back here when you are done. I will be inside of the observation room."

"Roger that Detective James."

Franklin smiles and walks into the observation room. I find Saundra standing in the bistro, snacking on a bag of chips.

"You want some Brody?" She asks.

"No, I'm good but I do need to know if you have spoken to Daphne?"

"Not since she left earlier. I've called her a few times but she isn't answering," she replies. "With all that is going on, I'm sure that she is really busy. But my girl will call me back once she sees my missed calls."

"When you talk to her, please tell her that Franklin would like to take the next steps with Alfred Mitchell. I don't think any deals are going to be made because he is attempting to plead insanity. We also need a Psychiatrist."

"Brody, you know Daphne really likes you," says Saundra. "I've never seen her act this way around any man before. She is normally always professional. She is good with keeping her emotions in check but for some reason, that all goes out the window when you're around. Now, I don't know whether you have a girlfriend or not but Daphne is definitely a catch. Besides, dating is just that. You date someone until that person proves she is the right fit for you or until someone better comes along. People put too much importance on dating. More importance than actual marriage. I know y'all James men loves to try to wife a broke, can't spell, don't work, too many children having, ratchet woman; but please don't follow in those footsteps. I just want to see you happy."

"That definitely can't and will not happen. To be honest, I don't know our relationship status because my memories are returning a little. I can say that what I feel since I've talked to her is something special. I know that she is my best friend. I remember that she helped me grow into this man that stands before you. She helped me to get out of my stubborn ways. She helped me to see the world, without blinders on. For all that I am and I will continue to be eternally be grateful to her. But enough talk about girlfriends, lets focus on the mission. Do you remember the mission?"

"Yes, I remember the mission," replies Saundra. "I would never forget about Bridgette. But…."

"No buts Saundra. My love life is complicated enough, I can't hook up with Daphne."

"Okay, I will pass the word to Shondra but I still don't think that will stop Daphne," she replies.

"Why not?"

"Because you are so charmingly handsome," she says.

"I'm going back to meet Franklin. Don't forget to relay that message to Daphne. Franklin wants to get this guy processed."

"Brody!" yells Shondra. "Franklin is looking for you and you better hurry up. He is waiting for you in front of the observation room."

"Where have you been Brody?" Asks Franklin. "Let's get back in there. Hurry, hurry, put a pep in your step."

"Don't rush me, I was doing what you asked of me."

Without any further delay, Franklin swings the door open. He storms into the interrogation room like a man possessed. Quickly, I hurry into the room to take my place. Franklin opens his files. He removes some papers from it and slams them onto the table. He knocks over Alfred's coffee in the process but Alfred doesn't flinch nor does he bat an eyelid. Instead, he calmly looks up at Franklin.

"Why is it that you don't have fingerprints Mr. Mitchell?" Asks Franklin.

"I…. I…. I was celebrating the fourth of July with my daughters. During our celebration, I forgot that I lit the next round of fireworks. Black-cats explode rather quickly. They exploded in my hands causing the deformity that you see now," says Alfred.

"There's nothing wrong with your hands," replies Franklin. "You're just missing your fingerprints."

"You won't track me! No, No, No! You won't track me!" repeats Alfred.

An intense stare down ensues between Franklin and Alfred, which lasts a whole minute. Without saying a word, Franklin exits the interrogation room. Alfred smirks briefly as Franklin storms out. Joyfully Alfred taps on the table, creating a rhythm. He hums until he notices, I'm still in the room. Alfred looks up, turns his head in my direction and says, "You won't track me! No, No, No! You won't track me! No, No, No!"

I exit the interrogation room and I find Franklin in the bistro. He is talking to that same Doctor from before. I overhear him saying his name is Doctor Ford. Doctor Ford continues to plea for the custody of Alfred.

"I am one of the top Psychiatrist in the country," he says.

"We know all about you Doctor Ford," replies Franklin. "I knew your face looked familiar but I couldn't pinpoint where I knew from. Not until you said your name. Years ago, you treated my Aunt Gloria James."

"And how is she doing now?" Asks Dr. Ford. "Is she enjoying life better now?"

"She's currently a resident at Saint Joseph's Ivory Tower in South Louisiana," says Franklin.

Doctor Ford inhales deeply causing his eyes to widen. "Impossible," he says. "I keep track of all my patients."

"But you gave up on this patient," says Franklin. "Do you remember a female patient, named Gloria James? She went into a catatonic state after her daughter was kidnapped. You couldn't help her, so you gave her an experimental drug without consulting her family. Now tell me, how are you still practicing?"

Uncontrollable rage swells up within me. Time seems to have stood still as I dash towards Doctor Ford. Franklin turns to block my path just as the doctor is within

350

arm's reach. Doctor Ford uses that opportunity to run to the elevator.

"Brody this is not the time nor is it the place for this," whispers Franklin. "He will get what's coming to him. Let's focus on the task at hand."

"So, he's the reason Granme took my mom to Louisiana?"

"Yes, Doctor Ford is a piece of work," replies Franklin. "I really need you to forget about him right now, let's focus Brody. Did you get the D.A.'s response? What about the new Psychiatrist?"

"No, Daphne is currently unreachable but Saundra will continue attempting to contact her. I'm not your secretary. Plus, I've been in there with you."

"Man! I really don't want him to get off on an insanity plea," says Franklin. "I need Daphne to convince the D.A. to let him stand trial. I want him to get the maximum penalty for his offenses. People in power need to stop being easy on guys like him. There shouldn't be any gray areas when it comes to right and wrong. We know there isn't any gray area when the accused is one of us."

"Do I hear a police officer, stating that the justice system is broken? Well officer what do you plan to do about it?"

"Personally, I believe that we must continue being good factors in our community," says Franklin. "We can only remove the wicked people by standing together. That's why I like to leave a positive impression on people. So, when they talk or think about me, it's in a positive light. Unfortunately, some people are just naturally evil. No matter how good your intentions are, there will always be those who oppose the good that you are doing. Oh, and put some respect on my title, I'm Detective not officer."

"Excuse me Detective James," interrupts an officer. "Mr. and Mrs. Baldwin has arrived."

"Thank You officer," replies Franklin. "Can you please escort them to the observation room? We will meet them there."

We wait on the hallway for the Baldwin's to arrive. Franklin paces along the hallway. He looks stressed but we don't have to wait long.

"Detective James, it's a pleasure to meet you again," says Dr. William. "Have you found our boy?"

"Good afternoon Dr. Baldwin," says Franklin. "Unfortunately, we did not find your son but we need your help. We need your assistance to help identify a suspect who may lead us to your son."

"That's good news. Really good news," replies Dr. William. "We will do whatever is needed to help you find our son."

"Good," says Franklin. "Let's go into this room."

I open the door to the observation room. Franklin, Dr. William Baldwin, and Dr. Elaine Baldwin enters the room. Two uniformed police officers are recording and monitoring Alfred's behavior due to his impending insanity plea.

"He cannot see you nor can he hear anything you say," says Franklin. "It's impossible for any sound or light to travel through our window. Our suspects name is Alfred Mitchell. He was arrested while we were in search of your son. In his possession was a car that may have been modified by your son. We would like for you to look at him. Maybe he is a friend, a relative, or just someone that William knew before he went missing."

Dr. Elaine turns and stares at Alfred through the window. Her eyes sharply scan every surface of Alfred. Dr. William looks down at his hand, which his wife is holding. They both stand there starring through the window in silence.

"So, do you know Alfred Mitchell?" Asks Franklin.

Both Dr. Elaine and Dr. William are startled by Franklin's question. Dr. William clears his throat. He turns to Franklin and says "NO". He then turns towards his wife. Dr. Elaine clears her throat.

"We have never met this man in our life," she says. "Now can we go? You've wasted enough of our time."

"Yes." Replies Franklin. "We did not intend to waste your time. Your help is greatly appreciated."

"Excuse me Dr. William Baldwin. We will need a sample of your D.N.A. to help with our investigation."

"And what do you need that for?" Asks Dr. William.

"When we find your son, we will need it to identify him. His D.N.A. should be a match to yours. Also, it will help to prevent this type of false alarm. It would save you time and we all know how precious time is. If not, then we will have to call you back up here for each suspect. So, look forward to eighty-two more phone calls. You may have to call-in until we finish this process."

"Why so many calls?" Asks Dr. William.

"I saw on the news this morning, that eighty-three people were arrested last night," says Dr. Elaine.

"We can also get a warrant for it," adds Franklin.

"That won't be necessary," says Dr. William. "I did say anything to help."

"Thank You Dr. William," says Franklin. "If you would now follow this officer. She will collect your sample. After which you are free to leave."

Franklin slaps my back causing the door to slam shut.

"Good thinking," he says. "Now all we need to do is get Alfred's sample first. I don't know why I didn't think of this myself, but you most definitely have saved us some time."

"Do you mind if I talk to Alfred after we get the sample?"

"Please feel free," he replies. "I'm done talking to him."

CHAPTER 21 – GENIUS

"Good evening Alfred, I am Detective James."

"You're not Detective James," replies Alfred. "He is. You're just his stool pigeon."

"I am indeed Detective James but sometimes I can play the role of stool pigeon. Isn't it kind of strange to be interrogated by two Detective James'?"

"No, not really," he says. "You may be kinfolk."

"Indeed, we are kinfolk. Can you bite down on this mouth piece for me?"

"Yes, sure," he says. "I told the other Detective James that I will cooperate anyway I can."

Eagerly Alfred takes the mouthpiece and bites down onto it. He looks it over once before returning it back to me. I pass it over to Franklin and he immediately exits the interrogation room. Happily, Alfred twirls his thumbs until Franklin reenters the room.

"Thank you, Alfred. You're actually helping us on a different case."

"What case is that?" He asks.

"A Dr. William Baldwin just left the building, along with his lovely wife Dr. Elaine Baldwin. We are currently looking for their son, William Baldwin II. Now, William II is what I now believe to be an idiotic pervert. You see, he faked his own death back on August 24, 2001. Now everyone thought he was smart, they even considered him to be a genius but the more I've learned of William II, I've concluded that he is an imbecile. The is guys extremely overrated."

"He must have been smart if he got away with faking his own death," interrupts Alfred. "That couldn't have been an easy task. That would require genius level smarts, don't you think?"

"I thought the same thing until we started our investigation. I must admit, he executed a well lead plan but a puppet is still only a puppet. He can only do as much as he is allowed. A true genius always leads. The only mistake that William II made was targeting my family. Since he kidnapped his first victim, he has become complacent. The only reason he has gotten away all these years, is because we had to grow up."

"What did he do to your family?" Asks Alfred.

"His first victim was my sister. He also hit me with his vehicle, nearly cost me my life but he didn't get the job done."

"What make you believe that you have him now?" Asks Alfred.

"You see William II is a creature of habit. No matter where he goes, he will always have to quench his thirst. Because of that, his so-called genius goes out of the window. A man who cannot control his habits does not deserve to call himself a genius. Everyone who does believe that he is a genius are all fools."

"I second that," adds Franklin.

"Do you know what D.N.A. is, Mr. Mitchell?"

"Yes, I do," says Alfred.

"Well we took a sample of Dr. William Baldwin's D.N.A. before he left. We will compare his D.N.A. to all eighty-three of the people we arrested last night. We will start with your D.N.A. first. Thank you for so generously giving it to us. It's only a matter of time before William II is discovered. I actually feel pity for the fool and I blame bad parenting."

"Why his parents?" Asks Franklin. "They seem like good people."

"I blame his parents because their obsession with his smarts lead to him being a person without morals. They wanted life to be better for him, like all parents should want for their children. The problem is, they never gave him true attention nor life instructions. Their obsession with his smarts lead to them stacking book after book in front of him, instead of spending time with him doing fun activities like other kids his age. He learned to manipulate them and before long he learned to manipulate other people. His parents never saw the bad person he was becoming because they kept calling him genius. People need to stop throwing the word genius around, they are dooming the person that they label. They knew what his I.Q. was but they never cared about his passions. They didn't know who their son was, they only knew who they wanted him to become. The pressure of the situation caused William's true self to be revealed. The weak-minded coward that laid, hidden just beneath his skin had finally emerged. He became delusional. He really believes that he is a genius. Poor fellow, he is naive plus he falls in love easily. I thought he would have learned his lesson from Star, but tender-meat fools never learn."

Alfred lunges forward as far as he can before his restraints stops his progress. His eyes are now red and watery. He stares fiercely into my eyes. Saliva fly from his mouth as his breathing becomes heavier. Franklin moves to subdue Alfred but I quickly gesture for him not to. Franklin stops as Alfred begins to talk.

"You don't know anything about me. I am a genius," replies Alfred. "I've never been weak minded. I will end you and your entire family. If I was driving that day you would have been killed on the spot. Don't talk about my parents because your parents abandoned you. Yes, I know all about it. You were left for dead. Forgotten by your own parents. They lost one child and voluntarily abandoned the other. I only see two weak minded individuals in here. It's genetically imbedded into your entire being. It's in your blood and your destined for failure."

"Finally! The weak-minded, perverted coward has emerged from hiding. I've been waiting on this day for a very long time, William Baldwin II."

Before I can make one step forward, Franklin appears before my vision. He impedes my path to William.

"Let's go get some fresh air. The stench from this sleazebag is polluting the air," says Franklin.

Franklin grabs me by one shoulder. He pulls me close and whispers, "Let's not be hasty in our actions. Let's make sure that it's him."

We exit the interrogation room and we are met in the hallway by Saundra and Shondra. They are smiling but their eyes are on the verge of tears. With arms open, they walk over to us. We all embrace. It's a huge relief to have accomplished the goal that we set off after. Shondra, Saundra, and Franklin's years of hard work has finally paid-off. I luckily stumbled into the right place at the right time. I'm kind of thankful that I lost my memories when I did.

"You have to tell me Brody," says Franklin. "How did you know?"

"I really can't explain it; It was a nagging feeling that I had. I just needed to talk to him to confirm my suspicions."

"Man, it had to have been more than just a feeling," replies Franklin.

"I am also very attentive. It was the little things that happened throughout the day, which alerted my suspicions."

"Did I miss something?" Asks Franklin.

"It depends whether you were looking or not. I am naturally a people watcher. Alfred and William shared similar taste in women. Alfred or should I say William, took pride in one upping you. Every time you expressed frustration he took it as a personal win. He showed his intelligence by trying to act psychotic, which he isn't. Even though he does have a few screws loose up there. He probably would have been released and on his way to a medical evaluation if it wasn't for you recognizing Dr. Ford. That gave us the time we needed. When Dr. Elaine Baldwin looked at Alfred, she started to squeeze her husband hand. Dr. William Baldwin had to look down at his hand because she was squeezing it so tightly. His fingertips were beginning to turn blue but still he did not make a sound nor did he try to free his hand. Instead, he turned his head to observe Alfred. That also gave me a feeling that alerted my suspicions. After that, everything agitated them. They were no longer the cooperate people from the condo. I then formed the plan to get a sample of Dr. William's D.N.A. I remembered how Juan described William and I thought that if Alfred was indeed William II; with the right motivation, he would show his true face."

"Good job," replies Franklin. "That's why I wanted you in there. That's the exact reason."

"Well, what's next?" Asks Shondra. "We got him. So, are we finish? Do you'll still need us?"

"Since we know that we have William Baldwin II in custody, we need to interrogate our new suspect," replies Franklin. "We need to find out what happened to Bridgette and the rest of the missing girls. Brody and I will go back into the interrogation room. I need you two to contact Daphne and get her up-to-date with our current status. Also, can one of you please find me a new Psychiatrist."

"I've been trying but she hasn't returned any of my calls," says Saundra.

"Well leave her a message," replies Franklin. "After you have located a Psychiatrist, I want y'all back in the Observation Room to watch Brody do his thing. He must have been trained in the art of interrogating."

"He's okay," says Shondra. "It sounds like you need to get your game up Franklin."

"No, don't be a hater," replies Franklin. "I give credit where it is earned. Brody has done a marvelous job. Let's not be those folks who hate on each other's accomplishments, secretly wishing that they do badly. Let's be the folks who uplift each other during these endless hard times. We will always lose if we fall for the divide and conquer strategy. Why do you think slavery lasted for nearly 250 years and the aftershocks still plague our communities today?"

"You're right Franklin," says Shondra. "But you know I am not a hater. I just state hard facts."

"More like alternative facts," adds Saundra.

"Whatever you say," replies Franklin. "You need to get out of denial and evolve from that slave mentality. You really need to learn how to shake your hater off. Now, we are headed back in."

Whether William knows we reentered the interrogation room or he just doesn't care, he continues to bang his head against the table. Franklin walks over to the table and pulls it out from under him. William sits there with his head hung down.

"We will not let you get out of this that easily," says Franklin.

"You may as well," replies William. "I am now a dead man. You weren't supposed to be looking for me. After all this time, I was supposed to be safe. After all this time, I was supposed to be free."

"Many criminals believe that they will never be caught. Few are intelligent enough to pull it off. Besides, its human nature to get complacent, especially when you become too comfortable."

"I am a genius," says William.

"Yes, you are. So much so that both of your parents are going to accompany you to prison. We will charge them with aiding and abetting a serial killer, a serial rapist, and a serial kidnapper."

"Leave them out of this," he shouts. "They didn't have anything to do with any of this."

"And who in their right mind, will believe anything from you. You lost all your credibility and now you have discredited your parents and they will lose their licenses to practice medicine. No jury on this planet will believe that your parents are innocent. Once the prosecutors are done with you; you will once again become one happy family. I have read up on your parent's actions since you were pronounced dead. I noticed that they have been gifted privileges also. Privileges they did not deserve. They both became prominent doctors in two of the most prestigious hospitals in Houston's Medical Center. That occurred within a year after they stopped pursuing their case. That's unbelievable since they had just completed their residency."

"Hold on a minute," says William. "We can work something out."

"Why in the world would I want to work any deal out with you? You have confessed on camera. You! The person who took my sister away from me. You! The person who hospitalized me for nearly a year. You! The person who destroyed my family. Why would I help you?"

"Let's get the facts straight," says William. "I did not hit you and I'm not the one responsible for kidnapping your sister either. It could have been any one of the hundreds of kidnappers or sex offenders that walk around freely."

"Franklin, please show him the picture."

Franklin walks over to William and places the picture in front of his face. William attempts to grab the picture but quickly Franklin removes it from his reach.

"How did you get this photo," Asks William. "Why am I in it? It must be altered."

"Oh, I've had that picture since I took it that very night. The night you decided that you would make Bridgette James your first victim. You remember that night? The night of September 13, 2002. A huge barn fire was burning that night, in honor of my sisters sixteenth birthday. I walked around capturing pictures of everyone in attendance. Except for one person who refuse to let me take a photo of him. I remember you even pushed me down once. Unfortunately for you, I don't take no for an answer. You presented a challenge to me; a challenge that I did not refuse. I managed to take your picture. You know it's ironic but your parents are the ones who are responsible for you being caught. Facial recognition could not recognize you because you are legally dead. We thought it was an accident but your parents confirmed that it was indeed you in that photo.

Boy, you had it all planned. You did some work to your face and had your fingerprints removed."

"I see a maximum-security prison in your near future," adds Franklin. "You may or may not be a genius but it really won't matter. They really like the smart ones where you're going. The only thing that matters there is what you did to get in. But look on the bright-side, you may be the smartest person in there."

We also found D.N.A. inside of your vehicle genius. Who knows how much trouble you will be in once the results are in? Unfortunately, the Justice System helps people like you. You all get a slap on the hand because you're privileged and because of that you have two options. Option one: you can let the course play itself out and see if that privilege helps you out this situation. Who knows, the judge may say you're stricken with affluenza. If you were in college, the Judge would've found a way not to punish you in fear that the punishment may ruin your college experience but you're not in college. Option two: you can help us retrieve those missing girls. You can help their families finally have peace. If you were manipulated like you referenced, this option may help you out. I would say option three is for you to call a lawyer but a dead man doesn't have any rights in this state."

"If I help you get those girls back, is it guaranteed that I can have a deal?" Asks William. "I'm a victim in this situation, also. I was forced to fake my own death; I had no choice in the matter. The person who is behind this also threatened to kill me and my family."

"Enough of your pity party," yells Franklin! "Tell me where the girls are."

"Not until I have a deal," replies William.

"Let's see. You kidnapped many teenage girls. In the eyes of some Judges you may still have been good but according to my list, some of those girls you kidnapped were Caucasian."

"You have done it now," says Franklin. "One thing that this nation has proven; is that if you mess with Becky, you're as good as dead."

"You also faked your death. Now that would not be too serious but you haven't paid taxes in years.

"You have dug yourself in a deep hole," says Franklin. "You just may get the most time from skipping on your taxes. Back in medieval times, it would have been 'off with your head.' You barely escaped the guillotine my friend."

"I will put it to you like this, if missing girls do not start magically reappearing, it will be impossible for you to have a deal. But I will play along with you. What do you want?"

"I want you to keep me and my family safe. I will tell you everything you want to know, if you promise that you will keep us safe," says William.

"You and your parents will be safe," replies Franklin. "You will live safely behind bars."

"I told you, they have nothing to do with this," shouts William. "They don't know anything."

"Like I said William, you will not get a deal nor will your parents; not until we get the girls back. If you're scared for your parent's life, then they may be in present danger. I'm sure your friends have noticed that you're not home. Instead of attempting to help your parents, you choose to play games. We can go pick them up, right now if you give us the location of the girls. You scratch my back and I scratch yours."

"They are on an abandon platform in the middle of the Gulf of Mexico," says William.

"What are the coordinates for that platform?" Asks Franklin.

William replies, "Uhm, it should be…"

"Don't tell me what it should be," shouts Franklin. "You better know what it is. If you really cherish your family like you claim. For their safety, its best for you to be accurate."

"Okay, okay," replies William. "The coordinates that I have are Walker Ridge 767. That is where you can find the girls but I have never been out there."

"We will see," says Franklin. "I'll have someone bring you a meal. Let's go Brody."

We exit the interrogation room and enter the observation room. Max, Douglas, Saundra, Shondra, and two uniform police officers gather inside of the room.

"What is Walker Ridge?" Asks Shondra.

"I don't know either," adds Franklin. "I will contact the coast guard and find out from them."

"No need to," replies F.B.I. Agent Max Jones. "Walker Ridge is a block in the Gulf of Mexico. The Gulf is broken down into blocks, like how the states are broken down into different counties or parishes in Louisiana. Oil Platforms, oil rigs, drill ships, and dive boats use the blocks names and the numbers that follows when they are to move onto a location. Walker Ridge is in deep water. I just hung up with the coast guard, the person I spoke to says that it's far out there. With help from my superior the coast guard has agreed to take action. A helicopter is being sent to retrieve us from here. Also, a team of Coast Guard cutters has been dispatched to that location. Only three of us can go and since it's in the Gulf of Mexico, the coast guard will take point. Detective Franklin James, Brody James, and myself will accompany them on this mission."

"That leaves Saundra, Shondra, and Douglas here to look after our prisoner," says Franklin. "I need you three to take care of the castle while we are gone. Everyone here is under your charge and no one can come or go without your permission. We will no longer allow for

370

visitors to come up from the first floor. When these two officers shift is over, you will lock up once their replacements arrive. Someone please bring William something to eat also."

"I'm not going in there with that pervert," replies Saundra.

"No need to worry ladies, I will be here to protect you," says C.I.A. Analysis Douglas Jones. "You're in safe hands. I also know how to lock down this Command Center."

"Thanks Douglas but I don't need protection from him," says Saundra. "If I get too close to him, I will choke the life from his body."

"Please don't do that," replies Franklin. "You, stay out of that room."

"Well do you want me to cancel the Psychiatrist?" Asks Shondra.

"No, we need that evaluation," says Franklin. "Who did you find?"

"Her name is Dr. Emory Sinclaire," replies Shondra.

"I've met Dr. Sinclaire," says Franklin. "Why didn't I think of her? She does work with the state. She was my Psychiatrist after I returned from being undercover. She is bold but at the same time she's reserved. She is straight to the point but also compassionate. She is very attentive. Sometimes it was as if she could read my mind. Great choice! We will leave his psych evaluation to you guys. Lock up after Dr. Sinclaire leaves."

CHAPTER 22 – WALKER RIDGE 767

When I first boarded the helicopter to leave Houston, I was excited. It's not like it was my first time on a helicopter but it is my first time on one of the Coast Guards Jayhawks. My adrenaline was pumping and I was ready for the mission but after sitting buckled down in one spot for an hour or so, I guess I passed out. Last, I remember was that all the lights went away once we flew past Galveston. I awoke when the helicopter suddenly dipped; I thought we were falling out of the sky. I don't like the feeling of not being in control, the feeling of not being able to do anything if we were to crash. A unique noise catches my attention. I look over to see Franklin passed out, he is snoring. Drool is running down his face. It's even dripping down onto his life vest. I stretch my legs and kick Franklin on the knee. I must have startled him because he nearly bangs his head on the ceiling of the helicopter. Three Jayhawks filled with Coast Guard Guardians, now fly in a v-shaped pattern towards Walker Ridge 767. The guardians who we are flying with are on high alert because the pilot relays the message that we are five minutes out from our destination. The Jayhawks descend from above the clouds. Instantly, I feel an extreme pain in my ears. Even though I am wearing both ear plugs and ear muffs, it feels like pressure is building in my ears. I inhale deeply and forcefully swallow air. Upon swallowing, my ears pop. Thankfully that relieves some of the pain. Again, I repeat the process. This time

I feel total relief after my ears pops again. I sat back happy that the pain is gone.

"Attention," says Commanding Officer Blackman. "The Cutters has reached the location. According to our records, this block should be empty but there is a massive semi-submersible platform on location. I have instructed the Cutters to stay a safe distance since there is no way to board the platform without being noticed. Prepare yourself! It won't be long until we arrive."

The moon shines brightly in the night sky. The lack of clouds magnifies the beautiful sight of the constellations up above. The Gulf of Mexico is totally black; if it weren't for the moons light, there would be no way to tell the difference between the night sky and the black Gulf. Four lights flashing on what seemed to be four corners of something large is the only indication that anything is located at Walker Ridge 767. Four large Coast Guard Cutters bobble up and down near the platform as white caps crash around them, in what seems like ten to twelve foot seas. They look like toy boats sitting on that water. Upon the first approach, the pilot discovers that the platform has three helipads. The Jayhawks circle the platform twice before going in. One by one, they attempt to land on the helipads but upon approach our pilot quickly maneuvers the plane towards our right away from the helipad. We hear something hitting the metal of the Jayhawk.

"We are under heavy gunfire," says the pilot.

"Guardians get into position," says Commanding Officer Blackman.

The night sky is now illuminated by gun fire as the Guardians maneuver away from danger. As commanded, the Guardians spring into action. One of the Guardians opens the helicopter door and returns gunfire, using a machine gun. Flashes of gunfire are visible as the Cutters return fire in the location the gunfire originates from. The Cutters fire on the platform from the water while the Jayhawks attack from the air. They strategically clear the platforms deck of any resistance. With the helipads now clear of gunfire, we circle around once again to attempt our landing. Simultaneously, all three Jayhawks land on the different helipads around the platform. I step out onto the helipad and notice that the platform is as large as a football field. We crouch low and move quickly to avoid the helicopters blades. An alarm sounding loudly throughout the platform can be heard once we move away from the Jayhawk. Our team comprising of Commanding Officer Blackman, two Guardians, F.B.I. Agent Max Jones, Detective Franklin James, and myself move to a safe location. At the base of the helipad, C.O. Blackman splits the group into two three-member teams. Franklin and I will accompany C.O. Blackman, while Max will accompany the two Guardians. Our team move to enter the building adjacent to the helipad. The other team travel down the remaining stairs to cover the outside. Quietly, we enter the building. All lights are off throughout the platform and only red emergency strobe lights flash. Thankfully the Coast Guard equipped us with night vision goggles. Cautiously, we move through the building. The first room we enter resembles an office. We move through the office into a narrow hallway. The doors that flank this hall are all open. We each check the offices until they are all clear. We enter a much larger room. Quickly, C.O. Blackman scans the surrounds. He proceeds through this area without incident but upon opening the next door, the butt of an assault rifle hits him in the face. He falls backwards into Franklin. Quickly, I spin away from the falling duo and kick the door. The assailant drops his assault rifle when the water tight door slams against his arm. He lets out a horrifying yelp as he clutches at his arm. I pull him into the room and swiftly deliver a knee to his stomach. C.O. Blackman knocks him out by cracking him on the head with the butt of his gun. Footsteps are heard retreating further into the building, then we hear another water tight door slam shut. Gun fire erupts from outside the building. From the sound of things, it seems as if there are a couple different gun battles transpiring throughout the platform.

"I think my nose is broken," says C.O. Blackman. "My eyes won't stop tearing up."

"Do you think you can go on," Asks Franklin.

"Yes," he replies. "But I need one of you to take the point. I can't trust my vision right now."

"No problem C.O. Blackman, I will take the lead.

I lead the team through the remainder of the building without encountering any additional threats. We exit the building to find the other team standing guard.

"C.O. Blackman we have reports that the assailants are retreating to the inside of the platform," says Guardian Roberts. "They rode down into the hull of the platform by using the west elevator. We attempted to pursue but the elevators are now offline."

"Are the decks below clear?" Asks C.O. Blackman.

"The other teams are clearing the decks now," replies Guardian Roberts.

We will proceed to the elevator," says C.O. Blackman. "We will attempt to override the controls. If that does not work, we will discover a new way to enter that hull."

Cautiously we run down four flights of stairs. I observe that the Guardians are an efficiently, cohesive team. We encounter no threats on our way down. Some of the assailants have surrendered, while some were not as fortunate.

"Platform secure C.O. Blackman," says Guardian Jenkins.

"Have we secured the hull?" Asks C.O. Blackman.

"No Sir!" replies Guardian Jenkins.

"Well don't be hasty son," says C.O. Blackman. "Has anyone found us access yet?"

"Over here sir," yells on Guardian.

"What do we have here?" Asks C.O. Blackman.

"Before joining this unit, my job was to do Hull inspections for deep-water platforms," says Guardian Watson. "On platforms that are not fortunate enough to have an elevator, we would descend through a hatch like this. I'm sure the tools to open this hatch is on this platform."

"Spread out and search this platform for tools," announces C.O. Blackman. "Bring back all that you find. Now hurry. Time is of the essence."

The Guardians quickly disappear as ordered. C.O. Blackman begins inspecting the hatch, that Guardian Watson points out.

"All it will take is some man power," says C.O. Blackman. "With the right tools, we'll have this baby open in a snap. After which, I will have three teams of four to repel down into the hull. You three will wait here with me. We will wait for the arrival of the elevator, after which we will storm the hull."

It doesn't take long for the Guardians to return. They bring back tools and other objects they believe can be used to open the hatch. Immediately, C.O. Blackman accesses the situation and with help from Guardian Watson, he chooses the tools for the job. He assigns a team to open the hatch. Instantly they begin unbolting the hatch with large hammers, wrenches and hammer wrenches. C.O. Blackman assigns the teams that will repel down into the hull. He also sends two pilots back to their Jayhawks to retrieve reinforcements from the Cutters. The Guardians work hastily but efficiently. After what seems like an eternity of sitting in the dark while listening to iron hit iron; one Guardian reports that they are ready to enter. The Guardians prepare a pulley system out of rope to repel down into the hull. They check and double check each other's harnesses to ensure that they are safe. One after another, twelve Guardians descend into the hull. Immediately, gunfire erupts. The sound of bullets ricocheting off steel rings out loudly on the deck. A Guardian reports that three Guardians are injured but the elevator is now in custody and on its way up.

The elevator arrives but only four can ride down at a time. C.O. Blackman, Franklin, Max, and myself ride down a surprisingly smooth elevator. At the bottom level, the elevator opens to reveal six Guardians trading fire at the intersection of a pathway. One Guardian greets us, while the other two tend to the wounded.

"Status report Guardian," says C.O. Blackman.

"Three wounded but none are critical," replies Guardian Roberts. "The assailants have retreated around that corridor. They are holding their position but it seems that their backed into a dead end."

"Cease Fire," shouts C.O. Blackman. "Stand guard until the rest of the Guardians arrive."

We wait patiently as Guardians slowly arrive, four at a time. Once C.O. Blackman is happy with his numbers, he shoots into the air once. In response, the assailants return fire. After a moment of gunfire things suddenly grow quiet.

Loudly C.O. Blackman announces, "I am Commanding Officer Titus Blackman of the United States Coast Guard. We currently have you outnumbered and out gunned. We have more reinforcements descending as we speak, with more on the way. I would rather there is no further bloodshed. I am giving you this opportunity to surrender peacefully. If you do surrender, you will not be harmed. You have exactly one minute to decide."

"Okay, we surrender," a voice says. "Please don't shoot, we are coming out with our guns held high above our heads."

One by one thirteen men emerge from around the corridor. Quickly, the Guardians takes them into custody.

"Where are the girls?" Asks C.O. Blackman. "Either you tell us or we will find them ourselves. If you don't cooperate, it will not be good for any of you. You have wasted enough of our time tonight."

The captives point in different directions. We scatter in the different directions in search for the missing girls. Located on the floor of the hull in the far corner I find something, inside of an oval shaped hole. It's a girl. She is tied, blindfolded, and gagged. She is dressed in all white but she lay motionless on the floor. She moves backwards when she notices my presence but she doesn't move too far due to the shackles and chains connected to her feet.

I call out loudly "Over Here".

Before Guardians can arrive to my location, I hear "Over Here", "Over Here", and Over Here". More and more Guardians begin to call out. We find fourteen girls in total. All of them are cold, scared, dehydrated and malnourished. They are scared and unable to walk properly. Anxiously, I grab a pair of bolt cutters from a Guardian. The girl screams through her gag, when I touch her shackles. I retrieve a knife from my pocket and I cut the strap to her gag. I remove it from her mouth and untie her blindfold. I notice her stress level eases tremendously once she sees that we are not any of her kidnappers. She waits patiently for me to remove her shackles. Once free, she throws her arms around my neck and refuses to turn me loose. I pick her up and carry her to the elevator. Franklin meets me at the elevator also carrying another victim. After securing the girls in the nearest Jayhawk, Franklin and I assist each Guardian with the rest of girls. I look each one over, examining their faces. The girls are scared as they board the Jayhawk but they are relieved. They have lived a nightmare that they will never forget but they will live to tell the tale. We watch as they fly off. They are finally safe. They are finally free. While we wait for a helicopter to return, Franklin and I decide to help C.O. Blackman search the platform. While searching for any clue of Bridgette's whereabouts, we find the control center

"Come over here," yells Franklin.

"What did you find something?"

"Man, I can't believe this," replies Franklin. "Apparently, this platform is being used as an auction site. Girls are being kidnaped and shipped to this location, where they are held until they are auctioned off to the highest bidder."

"It looks like these types of auctions are held twice a year," says C.O. Blackmon. "The next scheduled auction was to be held in three days."

"It looks like they canceled it when we arrived. Luckily they couldn't destroy everything."

"Yeah, but they destroyed enough," says C.O. Blackmon. "I was hoping to get names. I want everyone involved behind bars."

"Try to salvage the hard drive."

"We will salvage this entire platform," replies C.O. Blackmon. "I want to know who built it and who towed it out here. I will knock down enough doors until there aren't any more to knock down."

"C.O. Blackmon, The Jayhawks has arrived," says Guardian Roberts.

"Well gentleman, it has been a pleasure protecting our country with you," says C.O. Blackmon. "You all go on ahead, I will keep a team and continue to search for answers. My superiors will be here this morning to discuss further plans. Again, Thank You!"

"The pleasure was all ours," says Franklin. "We would have never found this platform without the help from the Guardians of the U.S. Coastguard. Thank You!"

CHAPTER 23 – SIGN OF A STRUGGLE

The Coast Guard Guardians are more than happy to fly us back into Houston. They inform us that they have been looking for that mysterious platform for over five years now. Each time they received a location, the platform would be gone when they arrived. The Guardians celebrate our night's work but exhaustion overwhelms me. Like these Guardians, I also have a passion to help others but this victory is bitter sweet. Franklin sits across from me with his head hidden in his hands. He looks up to wipe his face. The heartbreak, pain, and disappointment shows visibility on his face. He looks toward me with teary eyes. I know Franklin; I feel the same way. The sound of the Jayhawk flying through the sky prevents us from talking but no words are needed to rely our feelings. I don't know why but the flight into Houston seem shorter than the flight out. Even though I may have fallen asleep both times, the return trip still seems shorter. We exit the Jayhawk and hurry into the building where Saundra, Shondra, and Douglas are awaiting our arrival.

"How did it go?" Asks Shondra.

"Fourteen girls will be reunited with their families today," says Franklin. "There were more girls than I thought."

"These guys have been busy building a network but we may have disabled it tonight."

"Did you recognize the girls?" Asks Saundra.

"Yeah," replies Franklin. "Some of them were photos on the wall that I once stared at constantly."

"Was Bridgette there?" Asks Saundra.

"No, she wasn't but it's probably for the best.

"We found signs of human trafficking," says Franklin.

"The girls who were there, were kept in horrible condition. But I will not stop looking for her. I don't care if I have to comb the globe."

"Well you can start your search with that bum downstairs," says Shondra.

"William has been screaming to talk with one of you," adds Douglas.

"What does he want?" Asks Franklin.

"We don't know. He refuses to talk with any of us," replies Douglas. "He only wants to talk to you."

"After you left he was acting a fool," says Saundra. "The police officers were about to take actions but Dr. Emory Sinclaire arrived."

"How did her psych evaluation go?" Asks Franklin.

"At first William was not cooperating at all," says Shondra. "He was playing his role. He was working hard for an insanity plea but Dr. Emory Sinclaire was not having it. She started talking about safety concerns and how an immediate intervention will be required."

"It was clear that William had barked up the wrong tree," says Saundra. "His whole act started melting away."

"Before we knew it, William was answering her with 'Yes Ma'am and No Ma'am," says Shondra. "She made him remember his manners."

"After she was through with William, she had one-on-one assessments with each of his parents," says Saundra. "She left a detailed report on your desk. Along with her card."

"He was calm for a while after that", says Shondra.

Until Dr. Elaine Baldwin ran in there," adds Saundra. "She found her opportunity when the officers were taking a break."

"Man, that was an emotional scene," says Shondra. "Both Dr. William and Dr. Elaine was crying uncontrollable."

"We had to forcibly remove the Baldwin's from the interrogation room," says Saundra."

"Where are they now?" Asks Franklin.

"We set them up on the floor above Juan," says Douglas. "They are settled in now."

"Come on Brody," says Franklin. "There is no time to rest, William has a lot to answer for."

I'm forced to speed up my walk because Franklin is power walking to the interrogation room. The look in his eyes is intense. He has something up his sleeves and I better hurry before he does something he will regret. William is clearly nervous when we enter the interrogation room. His eyes grow large and eager once he spots us. Before he can say one word, Franklin slams his head into the table. Forcefully Franklin presses his head into the table. Two police officers open the door to enter the interrogation room. Quickly, I step in front of them blocking their path.

"Everything is under control officers. We will let you know if we need any assistance."

Reluctantly they exit the room. Franklin continues to press down on William's head. He leans forward using partial bodyweight to increase the pressure.

"Where is Bridgette, Carol, Amy, Stacie, and Elizabeth?" Asks Franklin in an ice-cold tone. "I knew of nine girls but there were fourteen. Plus, the three we found in your house. That's seventeen charges of kidnapping and human trafficking. It bothers me that only three of those girls were on my list. You have been busy, extremely busy. Where are the rest of the missing girls?"

"I don't know," yells William.

"You know something. You know everything," says Franklin.

"I have Thalassophobia," yells William.

"What is Thalassophobia?" Asks Franklin.

"It's an intense and sometimes uncontrollable fear of the oceans."

"How do you know that?" Asks Franklin.

"I've studied well. Knowledge is power."

"Thalassophobia, huh? What makes you so scared of the ocean?" Asks Franklin. "They say you're a genius so this could also be a plot of yours."

"No, it's true Detective," replies William. "When I was thirteen years old, my family went on a fishing excursion. We spent a few days out on the water. On the third day, they decided to go scuba diving. I wanted to go also and so my father let me. While in the water we saw all kinds of fish. I had a salt water aquarium at home, so I wanted to catch some fish for my aquarium. While I was in the process of catching some, I spotted a small octopus and I had to have it. Little did I know; its parent was close by. Things went quite fast after that. I found myself quickly wrapped up in its tentacles. I thought I was a goner as it squeezed me tightly. It felt like I was staring in its mouth for an eternity. Suddenly it let me go and vanished. I was helped back to the boat by my dad and uncles and I've never been in the ocean since."

"That sounds like your lying," says Franklin.

"I'm not," replies Williams. "It's the truth. Go speak to my parents if you don't believe me. They can confirm it."

"Well if you don't know where the girls are, who does?" Asks Franklin.

"I don't know," says William.

Franklin presses down even harder onto William's head. This time using his entire bodyweight. The pressure and pain causes William to yell loudly as his face and eyes turn dark red.

"You better say something William; before your head pops."

"Okay, okay," cries William. "Please stop. Please. We call him Luke, but his real name is Elliot Lucas Richman."

Franklin immediately stop pressing on William's head. He stumbles backwards a few steps as if he was hit by a wild right hook.

"Son of Senator Richman?" Asks Franklin.

"Yes, the one and only," replies William. "I thought my mind was playing tricks on me but looking at your expression, now I know I am right. I have seen you before Detective. I saw you at the Senators ranch."

"That's impossible," replies Franklin. "I've known Elliot since his father and I started working together."

"People wear masks when out in public," says William. "Their real selves are revealed when they are safely behind doors. The Elliot you know isn't the real Elliot. Elliot is no more. He is now Lucas. He has been for many years now. He knows how to act around people, but his true self lurks behind his smile. He is the most frightening, sadistic, cold-hearted person I know. Nothing is done without Lucas's approval. If anyone knows where the girls are, it's him. He knows where your Bridgette is. My job was to help with the abductions and to watch over them on land, until they were ready for transport by sea. Lucas would handle transporting them to that platform. That's all I know. What happens out there was never discussed with me."

"Franklin, I think Lucas is here in Houston. I had an altercation with him a few nights ago. The night before you arrived. Daphne took us to a club. Oh No, Daphne!"

"What's on your mind?" Asks Franklin.

"This Lucas person has a sick infatuation with Daphne."

"Yes, he does," adds William. "She is totally off limits. He talks about her all the time. She is his muse. Lucas wants her and Lucas always get what he wants."

Franklin dashes across the room. He catches William by the collar of his shirt and he lifts both him and the chair.

"Where is he?" Yells Franklin.

"I don't know," replies William. "I've been here all day and night."

"Leave him be Franklin. He has nothing left to give us. Let's go find this Lucas."

We exit the interrogation room and Franklin slams the door shut. Like normal the rest of the team meets us in the hallway.

"Has anyone contacted Daphne?" Asks Franklin.

"No one has seen or heard from Daphne since yesterday," replies Saundra.

"What's your plan Franklin?" Asks Shondra.

"I will contact the Chief of Police, The Mayor, and the District Attorney," says Franklin. "I will inform them of the possible abduction of Assistant District Attorney Daphne Turner. Senator Richman should also still be in town. If anyone knows where his son is, it will be him. I will get an A.P.B out for Elliot's arrest. While we are locating him, I will push for our warrants."

"Well get to moving," says Saundra. "You have a lot to do."

"Brody, wait. Where are you going?" Asks Franklin.

"I can't wait for the system, Franklin! Daphne is in danger. She is part of this team and we allowed her to get taken."

"I know," says Franklin. "That's why we will get the entire city involved."

"I will go check her house. That's the least I can do while sitting on my hands."

"Let me know how things are there," says Franklin. "I will contact you before we serve the warrant."

Without hesitation, I bolt for the elevator. Time is of the essence. With all the excitement and success of our mission, we still managed to mess things up. I feel responsible for Daphne's situation. I must find her. The elevator opens and quickly I board. I press the door close button as I enter. I notice Saundra and Shondra running towards the elevator. Shondra calls out to hold the door but instead I let it close. I arrive to the parking garage and it is empty and quiet. Quickly, I walk towards my parked car. I stop for a moment to admire how spotlessly clean it is. I don't see how Franklin had the time to get it detailed, but I surely appreciate him for returning it in the condition I gave it to him in. The engine growls loudly as the car starts. Having no time to spare I put the car in reverse. I look up into the rear-view mirror and immediately I'm forced to press on the brakes. Both Saundra and Shondra stands unflinching, behind the bumper of the car.

"What are you two doing? I nearly hit you."

"We know where you are going Brody," says Saundra. "And we are going with you."

"Yeah, Daphne is our friend," adds Shondra. "So, you aren't leaving until we are in that car with you."

"Well hurry up and get in."

"You go first Shondra," says Saundra. "He isn't going to pull off on us today."

"This backseat is small Brody," yells Shondra. "You need a big truck. You're a Texas man and Texas men drive big trucks."

"I'm good. It's only me. Now get in, already."

"Let's go Brody," says Saundra as she slams the car door shut. "We have no time to waste."

"Has anyone tried calling Daphne again?"

"Yeah but her phone goes straight to voicemail," says Saundra.

"Well call Douglas and ask him to track her mobile signal."

"He already tried," says Shondra. "It was when you and Franklin were off rescuing those girls. Douglas said that her phone was not giving off a signal."

"Do either of you know how we will get into this gate?"

"Yeah, I know the gate code," replies Saundra. "Just pull off to the side here."

Saundra exits the vehicle and walks over to the security box. After a few seconds, she walks back towards the car and the gate starts to open. As she closes the car door, the gate opens fully. Quickly, I drive into this gated community. The scenery makes me realize that I also remember the gate code and I also remember the route to Daphne's house. One block away from Daphne's house, I turn off the headlights. Fog lingers in patches blocking some of our visibility. The streets seem spooky; both quiet and empty. It is too early for morning traffic; it is more like that time of the morning when one rises from a sound sleep, just to go to the restroom. Then you check the time and become instantly happy to see that you still have at least one to two hours before your alarm goes off. The street light that shines onto Daphne's property, makes it visible enough to see a muddy tire trial on Daphne's lawn. Her garage door is open and her car is parked inside but lights are not on inside of her house. I park on the street to avoid destroying any possible evidence. Cautiously, we close the car doors without making too much noise. With only a flashlight in my possession, I lead the ladies up Daphne's driveway. The tire trail leads from the lawn to the driveway. Then a muddy tire trail leads from the driveway before disappearing into the street. At first glance, nothing seems out of place. Neither her car nor her house is visibly burglarized. We walk around Daphne's car and stop in our tracks. Around the front of her car I notice signs of a struggle. The drywall at the base of the wall has a hole in it. Daphne's keys hang from the door knob. One high heel shoe lay on the concrete a few feet from the door. There are also faint scratches in the drywall; which leads from the door, across the wall, and out of the garage. The sound of keys jingling catches my attention. I turn the light towards the door and I see Shondra and Saundra entering the house. I begin to follow them but I stop when my left foot steps onto something that makes a crunching sound. It sounds like I stepped onto something that was very expensive. I step backwards and shine my light towards the ground. Laying on the floor of the garage shattered into pieces, is Daphne's phone.

"The house is clear," says Shondra. "It doesn't even look like she made it inside."

"The reason why no one is able to contact or trace Daphne is because her phone is laying here in pieces."

"Oh no, she could be anywhere," says Saundra. Saundra disappears back inside of the house.

"I'll contact Franklin. They need a crew here to investigate this scene."

"Ok, I'll go back and check on Saundra," replies Shondra.

Franklin's phone goes straight to voicemail. As much as I hate to, I guess there is no other option but to leave a message.

"Franklin this is Brody. Our suspicions are confirmed. Assistant District Attorney Daphne Turner has been abducted. There are visible signs of a struggle at her home. Call me back when you get this message."

I'm sure Franklin is busy waking people up and trying to get warrants but someone must answer. We left Max to help the Coast Guard. He is busy getting the victims reconnected with their families. I'll call Douglas.

On the first ring, he answers the phone. "How can I help you, Brody?" He asks.

"How did you know it was me?"

"I programmed your number into my phone," says Douglas. "I like to know who I'm talking to. Plus, I only answer calls from numbers that are programmed into my phone. I remember a time when I could remember the phone number to everyone who I knew. Now with the advancement of technology, I probably only know a few of the numbers stored into my phone."

"I was looking for Detective James. Did you happen to see him around?"

"Not since earlier," replies Douglas. "He disappeared around the same time you did. Do you need help with anything?"

"Yes, can you get a hold of Detective James and tell him that Daphne has been abducted. He needs to dispatch a crime scene investigation team to her house. We need to find her as soon as possible."

"I might be able to help you with that," says Douglas. "Yesterday, Daphne left before I was able to get all of my equipment from her. With all the excitement since then, I forgot all about it. It didn't hit me until a few minutes ago. So, I've been preparing for your phone call."

"What are you talking about Douglas?"

"I bugged all of you," he says. "I've never worked with a team as inexperienced as you all. So, I bugged you all just in case."

"What do you mean by bugged?"

"I put tracking devices in something that belongs to everyone that is part of this team. Daphne's tracking device is inside of her locket."

"Are you able to track her?"

"Give me a second," he replies. "Just another tweak and Voilà. According to this information. Daphne is on the top floor of some condos in the Galleria Area. I'm sending the directions to your phone. Now, I'm hacking into their security system. I just sent you the passcode for their gate. Finally, let's peek into their camera system. The penthouse is guarded heavily. I count four armed guards on that level. There are also guards patrolling the grounds and guards stationed on the first floor."

"I never thought I would be thanking a man for bugging me but thanks. Douglas this is huge."

"No problem," he replies. "Our teammate is in trouble. I will meet you at the address I sent. I will be parked in parking garage A, on the fourth level. I will be in a white van that says E.I.U. Entertainment."

"Okay, I will go retrieve the girls and we will see you soon."

"See you soon," says Douglas.

"Who was that?" Asks Saundra.

"That was Douglas. I think he may have located Daphne."

"Well, these should help," she replies.

Saundra hands me a 9mm hand gun with two extra clips.

"These are Daphne's guns," says Shondra. "Let's use them to help get her back. The only thing is that the bullets are rubber,"

"That's no problem. I must warn you, Douglas has informed me that there are armed guards patrolling the grounds. But, if your aim is true, you should be able to stop someone with these."

"The second clip I gave you, has live rounds," Saundra adds.

"Let's go ladies, Douglas will meet us there.

CHAPTER 24 – TRUE PREDATOR

The information Douglas sends me is accurate. We don't have any trouble getting inside of the gate or getting inside of the condos parking garage. The white E.I.U. Entertainment van is parked as he instructed. I park my car beside the white van; in between it and the wall. Douglas exits the van and proceed towards the backdoors.

"Quickly, come inside," he says.

The inside of the van is full of computer screens and sound equipment. Douglas sits in the lone chair which sits in the middle of the u-shaped desk, the equipment is stationed on.

"Close the door," says Douglas. "Thank-you. Now since I've gained access to the security feed, I will guide you from here."

"How many guards are on duty?"

"Security here is thick," says Douglas. "We may need a diversion to reach the elevator. There is only one elevator that goes up to the penthouse and it's located on the first floor. Two guards are stationed on the hallway that leads there."

"What kind of diversion do you need?" Asks Saundra.

"A big one," replies Douglas.

"We can be the diversion," says Saundra.

"That leaves you Brody," says Douglas. "Once you get to the penthouse level, four guards will be waiting for you. That is a tall task. Are you up for it?"

"I am."

"Four on one is bad odds for anyone," says Douglas. "I've talked to Detective Franklin James, while waiting on you to arrive. I have informed him of the current situation and he will arrive with backup as soon as he can. We have the option to just wait for him."

"I'll be fine by myself."

"If you insist," says Douglas. "Here are a few items that may assist you. I'll be your eyes and ears but be careful."

"Will do."

Saundra and Shondra exits the van without any fear or doubt. I quicken my pace to catch up to them before they reach the stairs. Douglas checks the security footage before giving us the go ahead to enter the stairway. I crack the door and peek inside. The stairway is well lit and extremely quiet. The only noise that is heard is made by us. Cautiously we travel from the fourth floor down to the first. I stop at the doorway and with questioning eyes, I turn towards the twins. With a look of determination Saundra grabs the knob and leads her sister out onto the first floor. For one minute, I wait as planned. Eagerly I watch every second closely. One minute never seems long until you are forced to count every second.

Slowly, I crack the door. I listen for the twins but voices of excited men can be heard instead. One voice is asking for autographs, another is asking for phone numbers, and the loudest is asking for a date. Slowly, I make my way down the hall; cautiously, moving towards the lobby. I peek into the lobby for a quick second. The girls are holding the entire room's attention. I had no idea that they were this popular but I am glad that they are. I count fourteen guards total and they all are standing mesmerized by their charm. I proceed across the room towards the penthouse elevators. I move from one pillar to the next being cautious; just in case one of the guards decide to do their job. Without any incident, I enter the elevator destined for the penthouse. Before the doors can close, a loud deep voice screams out, "Hey, hold on one darn minute." I pause for a moment and positions myself for the impending altercation.

The voice continues, "You're married fool and if you don't want my sister to know how you act away from home, I suggest you get your hands off my woman."

The elevator doors close and begins its ascend towards the penthouse.

"Come in Brody," says Douglas. "The guards are aware that someone is in the elevator and headed up. They think it is one of their guys because I've looped the elevator camera with footage from earlier today. You will have a split second before they notice you. Make it count."

I examine the items that Douglas gave me before I exit the van. I notice that Douglas is very meticulous. Each item is perfectly labeled with a brief explanation of what each is. Without enough time to read each description, I choose the item labeled F84SG. It read "can cause temporary confusion" on its label. Standing on the left side of the elevator door, I wait in anticipation for its opening.

"Come in Douglas. Where are the guard's location?"

"They are gathered at their guard station and they are looking at the monitors," replies Douglas.

"What's on the monitors?"

"Either they are looking at the elevator camera or they are looking at the show the twins are performing in the lobby," he says.

"According to my position, what is the location of that guard station?"

"About 20 feet off to the right," he replies. Hey, that's a good choice Brody, just make sure you put on those goggles and ear plugs before using the F84SG."

As instructed, I insert the ear plugs and place the goggles over my eyes. The elevator stops and the doors open to the penthouse level. I activate the F84SG and roll it down the hallway towards the guard's station. The guards yell but everything goes silent. A sharp bright light signals me to proceed into the hallway. The light coming from the F84SG caused two guards to drop to their knees while holding their eyes. Two well-placed roundhouse kicks to the side of the head, helps to relieve their suffering. The guard that is still seated, regains his focus even though his eyes are bulging from his head. He sees my fist flying but still he cannot react to the incoming knockout punch. The momentum of the punch takes me over the desk and off onto the other side. On the monitor, I momentarily see a glimpse of Saundra and Shondra roughing up some guards. Saundra has one guard in a headlock while Shondra has another guard on the floor with her boots in his back. The last guard rises from the floor. He stumbles as he attempts to regain his composure. He pulls out a baton from behind his back. Suddenly he charges towards me. He's a big man, not as big as Big Wayne but he still has size. Unfortunately for him, he needed an additional moment to gather himself because his legs give out halfway through his charge. He stumbles forward but is unable to stop because of his momentum. He crashes head first into the guards table effectively knocking himself out. Quickly, I leap out of the way as desk slams against the wall. With modified handcuffs, which Douglas made from tie wraps, I hogtie each guard.

"Come in Douglas. Give me a status update for the twins. I saw them fighting."

"Stay on task Brody," says Douglas. "They are giving the guards a private training course in subduing a suspect. Those ladies play rough but they have their situation under control. Also, backup is on the way."

"Okay, well can you see what's going on inside of the penthouse?"

"I don't have access to the cameras inside of the penthouse," he replies. "The last thing I can do for you is to deactivate the security system. You're on your own after entering. On the guard's desk is the key to the penthouse. Good luck Brody and be careful."

With no other visible options but to walk straight into the unknown, I pick up the key. Being as silent as possible, I insert it into the key hole. With a click, the door unlocks. The noise of the deadbolt retracting, sounds like a car door being slammed shut. I open the door slightly; only wide enough for me to slip through. The penthouse is dimly lit but no movement is seen within. Cautiously, I crouch low to the floor. Moving only on fingertips and toes, I make my way towards the lone flickering light. The sight of Daphne being tied to a chair gives me mixed emotions. On one hand, I am happy that we found her, safe. While on the other hand, I'm mad that she's in this situation. Daphne is slumped over sitting by a lit fireplace, she sleeps uncomfortably in that chair. It seems as if she is in the middle of a battle between her and gravity. Gravity seems determined to force her down to the floor but it's denied of its victory due to her restraints. A loud yawn, followed by footsteps can be heard overhead. The footsteps trail to another room. A minute later the sound of a toilet flushing echoes through the penthouse. Next the sounds of scratching and feet dragging grows closer and closer. I position myself behind the chair that detains Daphne and I begin untying her from her restraints. The person who just awoke begins descending the stairs but stops halfway down.

"Good Morning My Love. Today is the last day of choices for you," the voice says. "I have patiently waited only because I love you and I don't want to see anything bad happen to you. I could have brought you to the rig but the guys out there would not have been able to keep their hands off you and I couldn't have that. The guys are good and loyal employees. If anyone of them would have harmed you, he'd be crab food. So, I did you a favor and I asked for nothing in return. Unfortunately, I know what your problem is Daphne. You want to go home but what you fail to realize is that, I am home for you. We will build a life together and you will finally get a chance to taste privilege. A privilege that you -couldn't imagine; not in your wildest dreams. My family is extremely wealthy and we have been wealthy for hundreds of years. I once told you that you were mine. What? Did you not believe me? Well, I meant every word of it. You should have checked the facts Daphne and the facts are that I always get what I want. So why? Tell me Daphne? Why? Why is it that you like to ruin things? You ruined the romantic night I planned for us and that's why you're in this situation. You did not have to be tied up. You're my queen, you will run the empire beside me. You should be euphoric to know that your children will someday inherit everything but you want to be restrained instead. So why? Why Daphne? Why won't you make things easier for both of us? You know what! Do you know what! You make me weak. I lose myself when I'm around you and I forget who I am. I am Elliot Lucas Richman and I always get what I want. I've dreamt of you all night long. I want you. I want you, bad! So, I'll just take what I want. Maybe then you'll see things my way. After which someone is getting killed for making that ruckus which helped to wake me."

Elliot walks down the remainder of the stairs but he stops and stands on the last step. Suddenly, he pulls his underwear down and he starts to play with himself while looking at Daphne with evil intent. What is it with people playing with themselves? I'm not watching this. From behind Daphne's chair, I point my gun at the oncoming man. I stand and step out from behind the chair which causes Elliot to stop in his tracks.

"Put your little meat up before I shoot it off."

"This must be a joke. Is someone pranking me? Who are you and how did you get in here?" He asks.

"Wow, Elliot or should I say Lucas! After all this time, that's all you have to say to me?"

"What are you talking about?" Asks Elliot. "I've never met you before. Get out of here! GUARDS!"

"Sorry, but they won't be coming to help you. They are tied up at the moment. Actually, no one can help you; you're all alone. DON'T take another step!"

"You have the nerve to draw your weapon in my house? MY HOUSE? I was going to let the police have you but you want to see the real me. That's fine but now, your mine!" Says Elliot. "Go ahead. Step out from behind that chair. Be a man and show yourself."

"You're not in charge little man. Daphne you're free. Get up. Get up now! Daphne!"

"It will not do you any good to move her. She drunk one of my infamous cocktails. She'll be like that for hours," he says.

"Brody, Brody, is that really you?" Asks Daphne. "I've had the worst nightmare."

Daphne struggles to keep her eyes open but falls back into a deep slumber.

"Don't worry Daphne. You just rest for now. This will all be over shortly."

The sound of metal scraping metal fills the room, as Elliot draws a sword from a statue. He turns towards me with a look of pure evil. He charges with his sword drawn out in front of him.

"Get away from my woman," he screams.

His shriek makes the hairs on my arms, legs, and back stand. A sense of urgency swells throughout my body as he approaches. Elliot swings his sword downward, slicing the air between me and Daphne. One foot to the right and he would have sliced Daphne. One foot to the left and he would have sliced me. I must get him away from her. I retreat a few feet and circle around a couch.

"Stay away from my woman," yells Elliot. "She is mine, not yours. If you want her, you will have to kill me for her."

"You talk really big for a small man. Now, put that sword down before I fill you with holes."

"Go ahead and shoot," he says. "Just make sure you don't miss."

Elliot walks around the chair that Daphne is still sitting in and places his sword on one of her shoulders.

"Don't look at me like that," he says. "She is safe. She's safer than you are. Now put that gun down and come meet your maker."

"I'll put the gun down if you put the sword down."

"No! You are not in control! I'm in control!" he yells.

"Who's in control? Elliot or Lucas?

He looks at me with a perplexed look on his face. He looks up at the ceiling then he smiles.

"You think you know me," he laughs. "Well I will let you in on a little secret. Elliot has been gone for a very long time now. You will die knowing that it was I, Lucas who has erased you from existence."

"Okay, Lucas! I am putting my gun down. Now step away from Daphne."

"Now, we will fight like the real men once fought," says Lucas. "We will duel to the death. Feel free to take any weapon off the wall."

I grab a pole from his wall. I wait as Elliot kick the furniture around the room creating an area for our duel.

"The rules are simple," he says. "Winner gets Daphne, while the Loser gets a funeral. You must really want to die today. Go ahead and choose a real weapon, that stick doesn't have chance."

Twice, I swing the pole wildly at Lucas. His footwork is good as he ducks both swings. We now have enough distance between us and Daphne. This pole has great range.

"If that's all you got, you're going to be a Shish Kabob today," he warns.

Lucas begins twirling his sword from side to side, making the figure eight. The speed of his swords grows as he moves in slowly. The way he holds his sword, I can tell that he was trained well. I take a deep breath to focus my mind. Where is his opening? Lucas tries to use his footwork to pin me into a corner. A faint smile crosses his lips as he closes the gap. He twirls his sword more. I try to move to the left but he widens his range with his sword. I try to move to the right but he does the same. His smile grows even more as he closes in. I thrust the tip of the pole forward towards Lucas hand which holds the sword. The pole passes by the sword and his hand, it hits Lucas's sternum squarely. He is shocked by the blow and he's momentarily frozen. He doesn't see the pole as I raise it above his head. The pole strikes Lucas on top of the head. I use the motion from my downward strike to circle Lucas. I sweep his leg from underneath him as I pass by. He falls forward but keeps his balance by grabbing onto the wall.

"You're not the only one who has a little training. Come little man, we've just begun."

Lucas is now on the verge of foaming from the mouth but he does not lose form nor does he lose focus. He grabs a second sword from the wall and without hesitation, he charges. One after another he swing the swords. His ruthless barrage forces me on the defensive as he hacks and slashes. I manage to block the swings with the pole but with each hack and slash, splinters from it fly across the room. He swings again but instead of blocking, I pivot and lunge at his left elbow. I flick the pole upwards causing it to slam into his elbow. The hyperextension of his arm causes the sword to fly from his hand. It sticks firmly into the ceiling. Eight well placed strikes send Lucas crashing to the floor. He bounces back up like a rabid dog. He lifts his sword high into the air and runs towards me like a charging rhino. I ready myself but Lucas changes course.

"If I can't have her, no one will," he says.

His fury blinds him and makes him a forgetful man. I reach behind my back and retrieve the second pistol. I take a deep breath, so my aim will be true and with no other viable option, I aim and squeeze the trigger.

An accurate shot to the right ankle sends Lucas spinning.

"Ahh, Ahh, I can't believe you shot me," he screams. "I think you broke my ankle. I will kill you! You're a cheater!"

"You left me no choice by going after Daphne."

Lucas begins limping towards me building speed as he gets closer. Again, he lifts the sword above his head. Lucas is enraged as he swings downward with the sword. I use the pole once again to block his oncoming slash. This time the blade gets caught into the wood of the pole. Lucas presses down with more force in hopes of splitting the pole. I throw myself backwards, landing on my back. Instantly, I place my feet at Lucas's hips and using his momentum, I monkey flip him into the air. Lucas goes crashing into an oversized vase, causing a domino effect. Five oversized vases crash into each other, making an expensive mess.

The dust from the vases makes it difficult to see Lucas's position. I walk to Daphne, who is still sound asleep. As I attempt to wake her, pieces of broken vase begin to move.

Now, I remember you," says Lucas. "She called you Brody, right? You, ahh. You were in the club with my woman. Ahh! I should have broken your face that night. I should have known you would be trouble."

The dust from the broken vases settles and light slowly brightens the room. I get a glimpse of Lucas crawling backwards. I pursue him with my weapon drawn.

"That a boy," says Lucas. I wanted to get a good look at that face in the light. There's something about you that's very familiar, almost personal. But it doesn't matter because at any moment this penthouse will be full of my men. What will you do then?"

"Who will help you Lucas? Are you talking about Alfred Mitchell or should I say William Baldwin II? Well, he will be of no service to you. He is currently in our custody. Oh, I almost forgot. Last night, we also shut down your rig. I think it's location was Walker Ridge 767. Your operation is completely over."

For the first time since I've known Lucas, he seems speechless. Growing redder by the second, he stands up. He dusts himself off, while trying to put pressure on his injured ankle.

"You and William have been a living nightmare to many families but that all stops now."

"Brody, Brody, Brody," repeats Lucas. "Brody James is your name. That's why you look so familiar to me. Now I get it, I thought it was Deja Vu in the club. I repeated your name over and over. Now I realize that I've done this dance many times before. It's funny but I once slept with your picture on my pillow. Of course, you were much younger. But every night for nearly an entire year, I dreamt of you. I was waiting for the moment that they would drop their guard and leave you all alone. For nearly an entire year, I waited. Every night someone slept in your hospital room. Your nurses were awful. I should have killed them all because they would not allow me access into your room. They prevented me from snatching your life away. Especially after people stopped sleeping there. You should have died on that cold street that day. I thought you were dead. I hit you going over seventy miles per hour. I remember laughing to William about how high you flew in the air. I really tried to run you over that day. I tried to spare you from your miserable life. William believes that you jumped right before impact but it really doesn't matter now. Right Brody? Do you know what else doesn't matter? Huh Brody? The name Bridgette James doesn't matter."

I've been trained to keep my composure no matter the situation. Sting-Ray put me through hours of intensive training. Daily, I was trained to be the best but training cannot compare to this moment. I feel blood rush through my veins at an increased rate. Pressure builds in my head. My first and only thought is to empty this entire clip into Lucas but that would be the easy way out for him. Instead I'll do this. I bend down and lift, the last remaining oversized vase. I hurl it towards Lucas and the vase explodes on contact. It shatters into what seems like a million pieces. Lucas crashes down into the floor with the rest of the debris. Again, dust from the broken vase engulfs the air but Lucas lay motionless in an expensive mound of broken vase. With Lucas sword, I cut away the restraints that hold Daphne. She slumps forward but I catch her before she falls to the floor.

"Daphne, Daphne."

She is not responsive. She must still be heavily sedated. I lift her up, cradling her with both arms. Carefully, I walk towards the door to exit the penthouse but the sound of moving debris stops me before I can reach the door.

"Don't take another step," says Lucas. Now turn around and slowly walk back this way.

With no other option, I must obey his command. But where did he get that gun from?

"Slowly, I said," repeats Lucas. "Now lay her on that couch. I must say, Thank You Brody. Thank you for demonstrating your strength. Thank you for pushing me to my limits. Thank you for waking me up but most of all, thank you for throwing me my gun. It was taped inside of the vase that you just broke. I thought it was in that pile of rubble. I didn't think I would be able to find it. Thankfully, you helped me with that problem. It was like a miracle; It fell perfectly into my hand. Honestly, I never thought I would ever get this moment again. Killing you has been number two on my to-do list for a very long time. You see I don't like to leave any loose ends and you James kids have been a pain in my back.

Before you die Brody James, do you want to know what's number one on my to-do list? Huh Brody?"

"Sure, enlighten me, Lucas."

"Number one on my to-do list is finding and torturing that foolish sister of yours," screams Lucas. "That's if she is still alive."

"What are you talking about?"

"Your sister was special to me," says Lucas. "She was my very first victim. I learned a lot from your sister, like how to properly tie someone up for instance. She nearly escaped the very first day. She even beat up William after she escaped from her ropes. She would have made it too, but she forgot I was there. She also taught me to choose younger girls. I learned that it was too much trouble taking a mature girl. She was strong. Very strong for a girl. We kept her hidden until she became too noisy. I had to move her. That girl had no quit in her. It was nearly impossible to get my hands on you and William was dying to get his revenge on Bridgette. That gave me the idea to use an offshore facility. With the right amount of cash and because I know the right people, I was able to get my facility."

"What happened to my sister?"

"You really should be concerned with yourself," says Lucas. "She is either really lucky or she sleeps with the fishes."

"What did you do to her?"

"While driving her out to the rig, a very bad storm caused me to get lost," he replies. "It might have been a hurricane, I'm not sure. Before the moment, I decided to sneak Bridgette out to the rig, I had never driven a boat. I saw it done a lot but I never thought I would have to do it myself. I was in the Yacht Club but I didn't pay attention to my lessons. I always thought that I would just hire someone to drive for me. The storm battered us for an entire night. When I awoke the next morning, Bridgette was gone. I searched the islands south of Cuba for two years after that. She was never found or seen again. So, it's safe to say she drowned. She probably was eaten by a big shark or an octopus. Well that's enough talking. Finally, goodbye Brody James. When you get to the other side, tell your sister I said Hi. Don't worry! You two will not be lonely. I will send your alcoholic father and psychotic mother to join you soon."

Without hesitation Lucas fires his gun. The gun makes a clicking sound but nothing happens. Lucas pulls the trigger once more. This time a loud explosion occurs. It is followed by a flash of fire and pile of smoke. Lucas screams uncontrollable. As Lucas's gun falls to the floor, particles of the oversized vase fall from the muzzle. Lucas holds his face as he screams in agony. I rush towards Lucas before he can regain his senses. I jump into the air. My boot lands flush on the side of Lucas's head. The strength of my kick causes him to spin twice before crashing into the debris that litter the floor. Quickly, I tie Lucas against the handrail.

Gently, I lift Daphne from the couch. I proceed to exit the penthouse. I open the door to see that the guards are now awaking. They beg to be released as I pass but I ignore them and continue to the elevator. The elevator doors open and out rush Franklin, Saundra, Shondra, and H.P.D.

"Freeze," says one officer. "Put the lady down and put your hands up."

"He is on our side," says Saundra.

"Are you okay?" Asks Franklin. "Where is Elliot?"

"Is she okay," Asks Saundra. "He better not have laid a finger on her. Poor Daphne.

"I hope he is dead," says Shondra. "Is he?"

"No, but he probably wishes that he was. He is inside of the penthouse."

I watch as Franklin, Saundra, and Shondra enter the penthouse. H.P.D releases the security guards from the restrains I placed on them, just to place handcuffs on them. The elevator doors open again and out comes an E.M.T.

"Excuse me sir," says the E.M.T. "We have a gurney on the elevator. I'll take care of her. We will get her to the hospital. Just place her on the gurney."

I refuse medical attention the entire ride down the elevator. I watch as the E.M.T.'s check Daphne's vitals and assess her status. The elevator doors open on the first floor and the E.M.T.'s quickly rush towards the exit. I notice Douglas waiting in the lobby. He starts walking towards me but he is stopped by police officers and media personnel. I hear them approach him with a barrage of questions. Sticking close to the gurney, I walk outside undisturbed. I watch as Daphne is loaded into the ambulance. As the ambulance drives away, the first light of morning peeks through the cloudy sky. The light illuminates the sky with shades of the colors, red, pink, blue, and orange. The colors intertwine as more light breaks through. Slowly, I exhale the cool air of the morning. While I enjoy the scenery, as the city of Houston awakes to turbulence.

"Excuse me Brody, I wanted to talk to you," says Douglas. "I never had the opportunity to give you the results of our word scramble."

"Did you unscramble them?"

"Yes," he replies. "But it makes no sense to me. Hopefully it makes sense to you. The letters M, H, R, P, E, O, L, U, E, G, and E unscramble to make three words. With those three words, I created two sentences. They basically say the same thing. Rogue help me or help me rogue. Does that make any sense to you?"

"Yes, it does. Thank you for all your assistance."

"No problem," he says. "It's the least I could do. You've been an excellent teammate. It has been a pleasure working with you.

"No, the pleasure is all mine. I don't know if we would have found Daphne without you.

I watch as Douglas walks away. Again, my head finds the sky. Help Me Rogue! Rogue help me! It must be a message from Sting-Ray but how did my mom deliver it? She has never met Sting-Ray before. I need to talk to Sandy. She told me not to worry but this is unsettling.

"Another thing Brody," interrupts Douglas. "I heard everything Elliot said and if you want help; I can help put your mind at ease. I will use my resources to check the islands south of Cuba. I know it's a long shot but she may have survived their boating trip. He did search for two years because he was unsure. I have your number Brody. I'll call you if I find a clue."

"Thanks Douglas. If I can do anything for you, just let me know."

"You already have," he replies. "Myself along with everyone else that has worked this case, will gain some sort of promotion and possibly a raise. Even the twins will benefit. This is the least I can do. It has been a pleasure working alongside you Brody James or should I say Agent Rogue."

A smile invades my face. I try to diminish it but it still grows larger. The thought that Bridgette may be alive after all this time has rocked my world. But even if she isn't out there, just knowing that we caught the people involved with her kidnapping is satisfying. They will no longer put families through the pain that we had to endure.

CHAPTER 25 – BREAKING NEWS

We now interrupt your normal scheduled programming with a special NEWS report out of Washington D.C. I am reporting out of the Richman Camp. Sources close to the Richman family has informed us that today Senator Richman, Republican from Texas; has officially dropped out of the race for our next U.S. President. He has also given up his seat in the Senate. This report now coincides with the reports that we have been getting out of Houston. Last week Ex-Senator Richman's son, Elliot Richman was arrested for kidnapping and human trafficking. Ex-Senator Richman has been the front-runner for this year's Presidential Election. Now it seems he may be out of politics for good. The Republican National Committee is now stuck with a huge task of finding their next candidate. That concludes our Breaking News report from Washington D.C. Now back to your regularly scheduled programming.

"Enough with the News, Big Mama," says Franklin. "We are here to celebrate."

"Franklin James! You better mind your manners or you will; how them kids say it these days? Oh, I remember. Or you will catch these hands," says Big Mama.

"No Big Mama, don't throw them hands on him," says Shondra.

"Y'all better ask your parents who I am," says Big Mama. "If you think you're bad, you're just a watered-down version of me."

"Not the kids Edna," says Paw-Paw. "They have done such a good job of cleaning up the streets."

"That's another thing I wanted to talk about," says Big Mama. "Why didn't the News or newspaper mention anything about Brody?"

"They didn't?" Asks Saundra.

"Nope, not one word," adds Paw-Paw.

"That's only because Brody doesn't have any licenses. He is lucky he is still a citizen," says Franklin. "He's lucky he hasn't been deported yet. I do get extremely nervous for you when I hear there's an immigration checkpoint."

"Don't listen to them Big Mama, I choose to not get any credit for the many arrests we had. It's better for me if everyone owes me a favor."

"Forget a favor," says Big Mama. "You should have bargained for some cold hard cash."

"Well my boy, what's next for you?" Asks Paw-Paw. "It looks like those three will be working in Houston. What will you do?"

"I have some loose ends I need to take care of before I can plant my roots."

"What do you have planned?" Asks Big Mama. "Because I have a lot of work that can use your hands around here and a lot of roots that need to be pulled."

"Brody has a girlfriend," says Saundra.

"Yeah, he's going to go meet her," says Shondra.

"Boy, I don't know how you got any work done," says Big Mama. "With snitches like these two loud mouth girls, I don't see how you all captured anyone."

"BaaaaHaaaa," laughs Franklin. "Big Mama just called you two snitches."

"Shut up Franklin," says Shondra.

"Oh, sit-down," says Big Mama. "You kids these days don't know how to joke anymore. You all are tender and always in your feelings. I don't know where you all get that from."

"Oh Edna, they been like that," says Paw-Paw. "Too late to change them now."

"Well back to you," says Big Mama. "Tell me about this girlfriend of yours. Where is she from and when can I meet her?"

"It won't be for a few more weeks but we are supposed to meet in New Orleans, after she meets with her father. I also want to visit my Granme, I have a few questions for her."

"Well whatever you decide to do, make sure you come back to us," says Big Mama. "Not ten years later."

"Get him Big Mama," says Franklin.

"You shut-up before I get you," she replies. "As a matter of fact, I need everyone to get out of my house. The food is outside anyway and you kids are really working my nervous."

"You know we aren't kids anymore," says Franklin. "We are grown now Big Mama."

"You think your grown," says Big Mama.

"Hold-up," says Shondra. "You called us four in here."

"Oh, I almost forgot," replies Big Mama. "You all did a wonderful job of saving those children, I need you all to know that. You protected each other and you made sure I didn't lose another one of you. Throughout this journey called life, we will lose people that we care for. During that time, we must stand strong enough to continue our journeys. Sometimes that journey leads to us healing other peoples' wounds, even when you still have a wound of your own. I know you all wanted to find Bridgette but we don't always get what we want. You have ensured that there won't be another victim like her. Every year there is an estimate of nearly half a million people that are reported missing. Most of those people are never seen or heard from again. Not only are children being abducted but grown-ups are being reported missing at an alarming rate. You put a major dent in that statistic for this year but stay vigilante because that type of people seems to appear out of nowhere. But enough with my talking. We prepared todays feast for you and we are so proud of you all. Now go out and enjoy yourselves."